Cracks in the Sidewalk
A Novel
Bette Lee Crosby

Cover Design:
Michael G. Visconte
Creative Director
FCEdge
Stuart, Florida

ISBN# 978-0-9838879-2-8

Bent Pine Publishing
Fourth Edition

Cracks in the Sidewalk

"To send a letter is a good way
to go somewhere
without moving anything
but your heart"

Phyllis Theroux

Claire McDermott

I'm an old woman now, but this dream I have has been with me all my life. Some people claim it's just wishful thinking. Whether or not that's true I can't say, but I do know these images have warmed the inside of my heart for more years than I can remember. When I close my eyes and drift into the dream, it's always the same. I see myself as part of the family that never was—imaginary sisters, brothers, aunts, uncles, cousins. We're crowded elbow to elbow around a dining room table, everybody talking at once and no one minding.

I created this family the year I turned nine. It was the same year I came to know the loneliness of being an only child. Luckily dreams have no limitations, so I was free to build my own world. For a lonely little girl that world meant a big family.

Sadly, that wasn't my life. I was an only child. My family was just Mama and Daddy, two loners who got married and had a single baby. I begged Mama for a baby sister or brother, but she'd squish her nose up like she smelled something bad and answer, "Claire, I don't know where you get these crazy notions. Certainly not from your father or me, we're practical people."

They were practical. Parents who believed children should be seen and not heard. As they discussed the news of the day, I sat at the dinner table, silent. That's when I began creating my imaginary family. In no time at all I could close my eyes and see every one of their faces. I knew all their secrets and what each of them would do in any given situation. First came my sister, Nora. After Nora came an overly protective brother, Paul. A lengthy succession of cousins, aunts, and uncles followed.

In time, Charlie happened along. He wasn't a member of my imaginary family. He was a flesh-and-blood person who loved me as I did him and agreed a dozen babies was just about the right number.

We were married in 1955, and one year later I gave birth to Elizabeth. She was barely three weeks old when I began to hemorrhage and woke up in the hospital with Doctor Kerrigan explaining how this was to be the only child I would ever have.

I know every mother claims her child is beautiful, but Elizabeth truly was. Lying there in her crib she looked like one of those paintings of golden-haired cherubs. Pink and dewy as a rosebud with the tiniest, most perfect fingers I'd ever seen. Many nights I slipped out of my bed to stand alongside her crib and watch the delicate whispers of breath rise and fall in her chest.

"It's not fair," I told Charlie, "that she should be an only child." I suggested adoption, but somehow Charlie could never wrap his arms around that suggestion.

"You never know," he'd answer. "Maybe Doctor Kerrigan is wrong. Let's not rush into something. Give it time. Wait and see."

So we waited, and God knows we tried, but we never did have another baby. In the end, Elizabeth had to travel the same road I'd gone down. Understanding how lonely that can be, I vowed to make it better for her.

No matter how much love a mama tries to give her child, they still need playmates. And my little girl had plenty. When she was so tiny she had to stand on a stool to reach the counter, we made cookies and invited over a bunch of neighborhood kids. After that it was Brownie Troop, then Girl Scout meetings, football parties, sleepovers, and almost anything else I could think of. Looking back I can honestly say Elizabeth's face never showed the loneliness I'd seen on my own.

She had more friends than a person could count. Elizabeth was full of laughter and kindness with eyes the color of a summer sky and a smile that made other people smile back. She was one of the most popular girls in Westfield High and could have dated any boy in town. But, wouldn't you know, she picked Jeffrey Caruthers—a lanky string bean with the personality of a footstool. He latched on to her like she was money in the bank and went everywhere she did.

Early in the morning, before we were fully awake, the telephone started ringing. It was usually Jeffrey calling to ask if he could walk her to school or take her to a movie. They'd spend an entire day together, then an hour after he brought her home the telephone would start ringing again. Some evenings we'd be fast asleep, and he'd wake us because he just had to say good night.

Jeffrey went way beyond being a pest, and it's regrettable that we didn't do anything to squelch it. But Elizabeth was barely sixteen at the time, so we figured he was little more than a passing fancy.

"Don't worry," I told Charlie. "The likelihood is she'll have dozens of boyfriends before she's ready to settle down."

Unfortunately, that didn't happen.

They continued dating all summer, throughout the fall, and right into winter—Elizabeth not the least bit interested in any other boy and Jeffrey attached to her like a Siamese twin. Four or five nights a week he'd have dinner at our house, and on the occasional night when he did stay home he'd telephone every few hours.

"Doesn't your family object to your not coming home for dinner?" I finally asked.

"Not at all," he answered. Then he and Elizabeth exchanged one of those lovesick puppy dog looks they'd begun to share. After a few years, Charlie and I realized that Jeffrey would probably become our son-in-law.

On Elizabeth's twentieth birthday they went out to dinner. She came home wearing the happiest smile I've ever seen and a two-karat diamond ring. That was that. They were engaged, and there was no looking back. Every time Elizabeth glanced at the ring she'd start talking about what a wonderful husband Jeffrey would be.

"Not just a wonderful husband," she'd sigh with happiness, "but, like Daddy, he'll be a wonderful father."

At the time I agreed, thinking only a man crazy in love would put such a sizeable diamond on his fiancée's finger. I didn't realize that's simply the way Jeffrey is—he's got an almost obsessive need to impress people with what he has or owns. Unfortunately, that ring earmarked our beautiful daughter as something belonging to him.

For someone with such an appetite for material possessions, it's hard to believe he could squander money the way he did. That's partly to blame for what happened. Money—or, I should say, his lack of it.

When Elizabeth married Jeffrey T. Caruthers, who by then answered only to JT, I trusted they'd live happily ever after. She was head-over-heels in love with him, and he seemed just as crazy about her. I've never seen anyone act more devoted than that boy. He was always wrapping his arm around Elizabeth's shoulder or twining his fingers through hers. And he'd tell anyone who'd listen how beautiful and smart she was. A man like that is simply not the sort you would have cause to doubt.

Charlie felt otherwise. He had misgivings about a lad who seldom looked a person square in the eye and labeled himself with initials.

"You can't do a thing about it," I told him. "Elizabeth loves that boy as much as he loves her."

Of course he grumbled and groused a bit, but I figured it had to do with him losing a daughter rather than Jeffrey's shortcomings. After Charlie learned to live with their relationship, he treated JT like a son.

Two nights before the wedding at their rehearsal dinner, Elizabeth beamed and announced, "JT and I are planning to have nine kids, right, JT?"

When he gave a nod of agreement, my heart almost exploded with happiness. Grandchildren!

"See, you were wrong about the boy," I whispered to Charlie. Suddenly I was on the verge of having the big family I'd always wanted.

I assumed they would start right away, but week after week went by with no further mention of babies. Then eighteen months after the wedding, on an ordinary Tuesday evening when they'd come for a meatloaf dinner, I noticed something different about Liz. She bubbled like a glass of champagne. After dinner she gave us the news that they were expecting their first child.

"Isn't it wonderful, Mom?" she said, rubbing little circles on her still-flat tummy.

I had dozens of questions. Was she feeling okay? Any morning sickness? When was the baby due? Were they hoping for a boy or girl?

"Boy or girl?" she said. "I'm hoping for twins!"

I expected a chuckle from Jeffrey, but he was busy watching an NBC newscaster tell about how some stock had gone up thirty-nine points in a single day.

"I knew I should have bought that," he grumbled. "See, Liz, I told you we ought to be putting our money where there's *growth* potential!"

"There's plenty of growth potential right here," she answered, still rubbing her tummy with those little circles.

After that Elizabeth and I went to the kitchen for some girl talk. "I've started knitting a sweater for the baby," she confided. "It's white with yellow edging. That way it'll be okay for a boy or girl, although I'm certain this baby's a boy."

It's been twenty-seven years, but I remember that evening as if it took place yesterday. We talked for hours about little things, such as how she'd decorate the nursery and what clothes a newborn baby might need. She was in the middle of writing a list when she stopped and looked up.

"You know, Mom," she said. "I've never wanted anything as much as I want this baby. I've got seven whole months to wait, but I'm already in love with him." She gave a sheepish grin. "I know you're going to think this is silly but I can even picture his face, along with the faces of all the brothers and sisters he's going to have."

I told her about my imaginary family and how I could picture each and every one of them right down to the freckles on their noses. After she'd laughed at how much alike we were, Elizabeth said, "I hope and pray I'll be a good mom—like you."

It's funny how hearing your child say something like that can cause a lump to rise in your throat. Elizabeth reached over and wiped a tear from my eye, and then we just sat there grinning at each other. In that moment I felt like my cup was full to overflowing, and it's stayed in my heart all these years.

David was born six months later. Two years after that Elizabeth gave birth to Kimberly, a beautiful little girl. I loved both of those babies as if they were my own and could barely wait to babysit.

"If you've got errands to do," I'd say, "I'll be happy to take the children."

"I know, Mom," Elizabeth would laugh. "Trust me, I know."

Back then when life seemed to be about as good as it could possibly get, I never imagined the sadness that would take over our lives.

Neither did Elizabeth.

1984

When Winter Wanes

In the early spring before the trees had begun to bud and snow flurries still came and went, Elizabeth Caruthers felt the movement of the baby she carried.

"It's probably gas," her mother said. "Two-and-a-half months is too soon, unless you've got the date wrong."

Elizabeth flipped through the pages of the calendar alongside the refrigerator. A calendar filled with reminders of birthdays, dinner parties, pediatrician appointments, and asterisks noting all the prior months when she'd been disappointed to find she was not yet pregnant.

She had never needed the calendar before, but in the last month Elizabeth had grown tired and forgetful. She attributed it to the headaches, a malady she hadn't suffered with David or Kimberly. Carrying them, she'd been in the best of health.

She scrunched the right side of her face into a half-frown. "I suppose it's possible I've gotten the dates mixed up," she murmured. "Maybe figured wrong." She turned to the sink, filled a tumbler with water, and chugged it.

"I'm obviously forgetting something," she mumbled, then refilled the glass and drank again.

Claire McDermott knew her daughter, and she sensed this pregnancy was different. Elizabeth was barely ten weeks, but she looked like a woman six or seven months along. And there was the faraway look in her eyes. The weariness that kept her in bed most mornings. The unenthusiastic shrug she gave in response to things that were previously cause for delight. The day before when Claire said, "Oh my gosh, look at how fast David put that puzzle together!" Elizabeth simply nodded.

Then in early March things changed even more. Elizabeth no longer noticed David's achievements or the way Kimberly fastened a crooked diaper on her baby doll. When Claire pointed them out, Elizabeth simply gave a weary sigh and mumbled, "Unh-huh."

Jeffrey also noticed the change. He began to pick at her for everything imaginable.

"Look at you," he'd say. "You're fatter than Aunt Sophie!" He found fault with Elizabeth's appearance, criticized her weight gain, claimed she did nothing to control the children, and insisted the house looked worse than a pigsty.

At times Elizabeth had to bite her tongue to keep from pointing out the true cause of his irritability—Caruthers Couture. A disastrous retail venture that failed to catch on. At one time Jeffrey had been the ideal husband, a man who adored his wife and covered her with compliments as lavishly as ladling hot fudge over ice cream. Now his words were resentful, harsh, and, at times, even cruel. They tore through Elizabeth and left her hiding inside herself.

When that happened, she'd try to remember better times. Times when he'd promised eternal love and placed the world at her feet. But how could she remember those things when she sometimes couldn't remember why she'd opened the refrigerator door? Last Tuesday, a morning when Jeffrey had been at his absolute worst, Elizabeth poured a puddle of coffee on the breakfast table because she'd forgotten the cup. On days like that she leaned on her mother.

The distance from one house to the other was less than two miles. Claire jumped from her bed as soon as the sun cleared the horizon, ran a brush through her hair, and drove the short distance. She had to be there in time to dress and feed David and Kimberly. Well, she didn't actually have to, she wanted to. Claire knew a woman had her grandchildren for only so many years. Then they grew too old and reached the age where a display of affection generated an indignant, "Geez, Grandma!"

"Good morning," Claire called out as she sailed through the kitchen door.

"What's good about it?" JT grumbled.

Most mornings he ignored Claire, which she preferred if he happened to be in one of his moods. She filled the pot and set the coffee to brew. "Have you had breakfast?"

"No time," he answered flatly, then tore through the house looking for an inventory report.

"Is this it?" Claire fished a stack of papers from beneath David's coloring book.

JT snatched the papers from her and stuffed them into his briefcase.

Caruthers Couture was in the downtown area of Westfield, a place where most merchants had thriving businesses. When Jeffrey cleaned out their savings account to purchase an expensive line of evening wear and designer clothing, he swore his store would make millions. It didn't. In fact, for two years it ran a deficit month after month.

"Is it my fault," he complained, "that the women of this town have no eye for fashion?"

Determined that his strategy would pay off, he sat behind the counter day after day and watched as the ladies of Westfield marched past his store in their wool slacks and parkas. After several months, he began chewing his fingernails down to the nub. In early March he told Charlie he'd been eyeing a high-end line of costume jewelry.

"I need something like that to bring new customers into the store," he said. "Thing is, I'm gonna have to borrow at least ten thousand to finance it."

"Another ten thousand?" Charlie grunted. "In addition to the twenty-five thousand you already got?"

"It takes money to make money," JT snapped.

"I don't know," Charlie said, shaking his head dubiously. "I'm gonna have to think it over." In the past two years, he'd given his son-in-law four sizeable loans, none of which Jeffrey had repaid. This, it seemed, was throwing good money after bad.

That evening Jeffrey brought Elizabeth a bouquet of pink roses and offered an apology for his sour disposition.

"Once your dad gives me this loan," he said, "I can get Caruthers Couture back on track, and things will be better for us. I promise."

They made love that night and then while they lay side by side in the dark, he suggested she ask Claire to talk to Charlie.

"Ask Mom?" Elizabeth said. "Why?"

"Because I need the money. Your dad will give me the loan if she tells him to."

The next morning when Claire arrived, the coffee was brewing and both children were already dressed. Elizabeth looked better than she had in days and smiled happily as JT breezed by with a quick kiss. "Don't forget," he whispered, then left.

Claire lifted an eyebrow. "What's up?"

Elizabeth poured some coffee and sat down at the table. "JT's planning to make some changes at the store," she said. "Changes to help the business."

"Like what?"

"He's gonna specialize in jewelry and more elegant evening wear. He thinks that stuff will attract customers with money to spend, and it's got a better profit margin."

Elizabeth spoke for a while longer, and then explained how JT needed additional financing.

"Mom, please tell Daddy he ought to help out," she said. "JT really needs the money, and he promised to pay Daddy back as soon as this new line gets going."

Claire didn't for one minute buy into the idea that the trouser-wearing ladies of Westfield would suddenly switch to party dresses, but despite these doubts she did insist Charlie give JT the money.

"Good or bad businessman," she argued, "it doesn't matter. He's our daughter's husband!"

So JT got the loan he wanted, and he filled an entire display case with evening bags, thinly-plated gold bangles, and sparkling rhinestones. When the new merchandise did nothing to improve business and sat there gathering dust, his moods grew blacker. In April he stopped talking about how the store would make millions and before long began saying it generally took years for a business to turn around. He finally settled into eating dinner alone, watching television, and trotting off to bed without a word to anyone.

Elizabeth, trying to cope with her explosive weight gain and burning thirst, paid little attention as she downed glass after glass of water. She felt ready to burst out of her skin. By mid-April she appeared to be on the verge of delivery.

Her forgetfulness seemed to get worse. In the second week of April, Elizabeth discovered three whole days missing from her memory. She woke on Thursday, believing it was Sunday, and insisted she had no recollection of having gone to the library on Tuesday or the dentist on Wednesday.

"Surely you remember, dear," Claire prompted. "Tuesday I made that delicious macaroni casserole for lunch, and Wednesday David skinned his knee on the front walkway. You remember that, don't you?"

"David skinned his knee? On our walkway? Where was I?"

"Sitting on the porch in the rocking chair. You put the Band-Aid on David's knee after I cleaned it, remember?"

Elizabeth's blue eyes filled with tears. "I'm afraid not," she said. "It must be because I've had this terrible headache."

Two weeks later Elizabeth went for her second prenatal check.

"Good grief," Doctor Watkins gasped. "You've gained forty pounds! That's way too much." He glanced at the scale a second time. "What have you been eating?"

"Some ice cream," she said. "Very little of anything else. With my stomach so bloated, the thought of sitting down to a meal nauseates me. I'm not the least bit hungry, but I'm thirsty all the time. I can drink a gallon of water and still be thirsty."

"Water? You're gaining weight on water?" Doctor Watkins asked incredulously. "No salty foods? Pretzels, maybe? Potato chips? Peanuts?"

Elizabeth shook her head.

Doctor Watkins grimaced. "These headaches you're having, did you experience that with either of your previous pregnancies?"

"Not at all," Elizabeth answered.

"What about the lack of energy? Thirst? Forgetfulness?"

She shook her head.

"Taking any supplements or medications I'm not aware of? Handling pesticides? Paints? Turpentine?"

Elizabeth shook her head again and again. When he'd run out of questions, Doctor Watkins scratched the name "Rebecca Sorenson" on a slip of paper and passed it across the desk. "This is an endocrinologist I'd like you to see."

"Endocrinologist?" Elizabeth repeated nervously. "Why?"

"There's something going on," he said. "It could be gestational diabetes. An endocrinologist can say for certain." Noticing the look of panic on her face, Doctor Watkins placed his hand atop hers.

"Don't worry," he said reassuringly. "It happens with some pregnancies but virtually never results in birth defects. The hormone helping your baby to grow can block your production of insulin. But once you've given birth, your body reverts back to its normal state. Then the gestational diabetes usually disappears."

"You're sure this condition won't be harmful to the baby?" Elizabeth asked.

Doctor Watkins shook his head, giving her hand a gentle pat.

That evening after tucking David and Kimberly into bed, Elizabeth sat on the sofa next to JT.

"I went to the doctor today," she began, waiting for him to ask the obvious. He focused on the words of a market analyst explaining why a recent issue had unprecedented gains.

"Well, if that don't beat all," JT grumbled. "Here I was gonna buy that stock and would've if I'd had the money."

Elizabeth snapped off the television.

He glared at her angrily. "I was watching that."

"I went to the doctor today."

"Okay, so?"

"Doctor Watkins thinks I might have gestational diabetes. He told me I have to see a specialist. An endocrinologist."

"Diabetes?" JT scoffed a sigh of intolerance. "No wonder, with all that ice cream you've been having. You should eat salads or something that doesn't make you gain weight. Yeah, I know, the pregnant piggy has a craving for ice cream," he muttered sarcastically. "Now I've got to pay for a specialist to tell you the exact same thing I've been saying all along."

Elizabeth felt her eyes welling. "How could you say such an awful thing? Don't you care about my feelings? Do you think I like being so overweight? Do you think—" She gave way to all that she'd held back and began sobbing.

"What about me?" JT said angrily. "You think I like having more bills than I can afford to pay? I bought this money pit for you! You're the one who wanted a big house and lot of babies! Now I'm the one who's stuck paying for it! I'm sick of it!"

He turned and stomped out of the room.

Almost two weeks passed before Elizabeth could actually bring herself to call Doctor Rebecca Sorenson, and then she did so only at the urging of her mother.

"Think of the baby!" Claire pleaded. "Think of yourself!"

Finally Elizabeth scheduled an appointment and nervously asked JT to go with her.

"Can't your mother do it?" he answered.

"No. I was gonna ask her to stay here and watch the kids. I thought you might want to—"

"Will you stop?" he said, rolling his eyes. "You always do that. You make it sound like I don't want to go with you. It isn't that I don't want to go, I can't. I've gotta open the store. Who else is gonna do it? All the responsibility is on my shoulders, but does that bother you? Nope, not one bit. It's never gonna end, is it?"

"I only thought—"

He grabbed the remote control and turned up the sound.

On the first Tuesday of May, a day so unseasonably warm that women switched to sandals and men pulled short-sleeved shirts from the back of their closet, Elizabeth rose early. She showered, washed her hair, and left it to hang loose across her shoulders. Then she dressed in the one maternity outfit that still fit. By ten o'clock she and Claire sat in Doctor Sorenson's waiting room, their fingers entwined.

This waiting room, with its line of light gray chairs pushed against a darker gray wall, had none of the usual baby magazines. No *Parenting.* No "What every mother needs to know" articles. Here, elderly people with brown spots freckling their hands read things such as *Living with Diabetes* and *Blood Pressure, the silent killer.* After waiting what felt like hours, a male nurse stepped from behind a closed door and called out, "Caruthers." They stood and followed him through the hallway into a small but somewhat brighter examination room.

Doctor Rebecca Sorenson was not what they expected. For starters, she was young enough to make Claire wonder how long she'd actually been practicing. She was the type of woman men turned to look at—tall, slender, dark eyes, and flame-red hair. She entered the room with a welcoming smile and a file folder.

"Well now," she said pleasantly, "let's talk about this problem you're having."

Elizabeth related the experiences of her first two pregnancies then told of her extreme thirst, rapid weight gain, forgetfulness, and recent feeling of depression.

"Any history of diabetes in your family?"

"None."

"Okay then, we start from square one."

By the time Elizabeth watched Rebecca Sorenson write orders for several tests that afternoon, she had begun to like her. Her smile, the casual ease with which she spoke. Under other circumstances, Elizabeth could envision them becoming friends. Going to parties together. Book clubs maybe. Sharing recipes.

"Do you have any children yourself?" she asked.

"Afraid not," the doctor answered laughingly. "I've yet to find my Mister Right."

"Children are a true blessing," Elizabeth said.

After spending hours at a nearby clinic, Elizabeth and her mother returned to Doctor Sorenson's office to learn the results of the tests.

Rebecca leafed through several pages of reports. "It looks like your obstetrician was correct. This is definitely not all baby weight. Something more is going on."

"What is it?" Elizabeth asked nervously.

The doctor shrugged sympathetically. "We don't know yet. The tests show certain abnormalities in your system, but the source of the problem isn't obvious. We know it's a neurological malfunction, but to pinpoint the origin we'd need a CT scan."

"Is that the next step?" Claire asked.

"Unfortunately no," Doctor Sorenson replied. "We can't do it while Elizabeth is pregnant. The scan involves radiation, and that's harmful to an unborn child."

She turned to Elizabeth. "Our best bet is to get you into the hospital. There, I can monitor you and control any complications that crop up. With a few more tests, maybe we'll get lucky and find out what's causing the problem."

"But I have kids at home, I need to—"

Claire eased her arm across Elizabeth's shoulder and squeezed. "Don't worry. It'll be okay."

Elizabeth looked at Doctor Sorenson and asked, "Will it? Is my baby really okay?"

"Right now, yes," Rebecca said, "and I intend to do everything possible to make sure it stays that way. You're the one I'm worried about."

JT had come to expect bad days. He'd settled into them the way one settles into riding an overcrowded bus. But this particular day was one of his worst. Before he left the house he and Elizabeth had another argument, and then Eleanor Morgan returned the opera coat she purchased last week claiming it was much too dressy.

"I can't imagine what I was thinking," she said as she collected her refund.

Not long after that, the sales representative from Lady Lorraine called to say his boss refused to ship any more merchandise until JT paid his outstanding invoices.

"You have three invoices that are over ninety days!" the rep growled. "You know our policy is ten days net!"

With his patience already worn thin, JT was unprepared for what greeted him at home.

"Where's Liz?" he asked Claire, who tried to coax Kimberly into eating some green peas.

"In the hospital," Claire answered, extending the pea-filled spoon toward Kimberly. "One little bite," she cajoled. "They're yummy, just try them."

"Hospital? What hospital?"

"Saint Barnabas," Claire answered absently. "But don't worry, she and the baby are both okay. The doctor just wants to keep an eye on her."

"What for? What's wrong?"

"They don't know yet. Doctor Sorenson said they need a CT scan to know for certain…" She turned toward JT, and in that instant Kimberly's hand shot out and sent the peas spiraling into the air.

"Shame on you doing that!" Claire scolded. She bent to retrieve the peas from the floor.

"When is this CT scan?" JT asked, ignoring the pea rolling past his shoe.

"She's not having it, at least not now. It's a radiation thing that's dangerous for the baby."

"So why is Liz staying in the hospital?"

"The doctor just wants to keep her under observation."

"I can't believe this!" JT said, slamming his fist against the wall. "How long is she gonna stay there? Until she has the baby? Until we don't have another nickel to our name? Until I'm totally bankrupt?!"

Claire tossed the handful of peas in the sink.

"Elizabeth is sick," she said, "really sick, and all you can think about is money? You should be ashamed!"

Jeffrey didn't jump down her throat this time. He stood there with his shoulders curling toward his chest and a hateful look in his eyes. "You're right," he mumbled resentfully; then he turned and walked out.

Claire expected he'd return in an hour or so, after he had time to collect himself, after he had time to reconsider the value of money when weighed against caring for someone you love. But he didn't come back. Claire finished feeding David and Kimberly, gave them their baths, and tucked them into bed. Still thinking he'd come through the door any minute, she waited until nine-thirty then called Charlie and suggested he fix himself some soup.

"There's no telling how long I'll be here," she said.

17

It was after eleven when she fell asleep on the sofa. When she woke the next morning, Jeffrey still had not returned.

Claire began to worry. She telephoned Charlie to ask if he'd heard anything from Jeffrey.

"Afraid not," he said. "But I doubt he'd call me."

Claire fed the children breakfast, read three stories, and dusted the living room furniture. When it was almost ten-thirty, she telephoned Maria Ramirez, a neighborhood babysitter, and asked for help. Claire got into her car and drove to Saint Barnabas Hospital. She walked into Elizabeth's room, wondering how to bring up Jeffrey—but there he stood, unshaven and still wearing yesterday's shirt.

"Hi," he said, looking sheepish.

"Hi," Claire answered, without showing her irritation. She crossed the room and planted a kiss on Elizabeth's forehead.

"Guess what, Mom?" Elizabeth said. "JT thinks I might get to go home today."

"Home?" Claire echoed. "Doctor Sorenson said that?"

"Well, actually, JT hasn't spoken to her yet, but I'm sure she'll agree. He says my color is good and I look well-rested."

Jeffrey wrapped his arm around Elizabeth in that same possessive way he did years ago and smiled.

Claire lowered herself into the chair alongside the bed and replied, "You're not going anywhere until Doctor Sorenson says so!"

"But, Mom," Elizabeth stammered. "JT said the kids need me at home, and we can't afford—"

Claire felt the muscles in her face grow hard.

"The kids are doing just fine," she said. "And as your husband, JT should concern himself with your well-being, not the cost of it!"

"He's worried about taking care of our whole family—"

"Well, JT won't have to reach into his pocket for a dime," Claire said in an icy voice. "We'll pay whatever your insurance doesn't cover." When a look of satisfaction slid onto his face, she added, "Providing he does not discuss money with you again while you're in the hospital."

"Mother McDermott," JT spat, "I think you've misunderstood my intention. I certainly didn't intend to upset either you or Liz. I simply thought I should mention—"

"Well," Claire said gruffly, "I suggest you don't *mention* it again!"

JT gave her a look of disdain, then said he had to get going since it was long past time for him to open the store.

Once he left, Elizabeth fell asleep and Claire studied her daughter. Elizabeth had never looked worse. Her fingers were puffed out like fat sausages, and her body was nearly twice its normal size. Her dry, crackled skin looked more yellow than pink. Claire knew Elizabeth was sick—sicker perhaps than anyone realized.

Claire McDermott

Many people believe the love shared by a man and woman is the most powerful on earth, and in some ways it probably is. On the day Charlie and I were married I thought I'd never know anything sweeter; but once I felt our baby at my breast I realized how big a heart truly is.

I'm only one person; Charlie too. But Elizabeth is the best of both of us. We loved her long before we saw the blue of her eyes and felt her tiny fingers locked onto ours, long before she looked up at us trusting we'd take care of her. When she was barely more than a flutter beneath my heart, I vowed that for as long as I had breath in my body I'd watch over her and keep her safe. Now she's lying in a hospital bed, and I can't do a thing to help her. I watch her suffer, and I suffer. Her pain is my pain.

It doesn't matter how old Elizabeth gets, she's still my baby. That's why I had to choke back my rage when I saw Jeffrey hovering over her. Okay, he's got financial troubles, but is he willing to sacrifice her health for a handful of dollars? The sorry truth is he's a man who thinks the measure of money is greater than anything else life has to offer.

Liz is a lot like me—just give her a house full of kids and she's happy. She loves babies. She'd have one every year if Jeffrey were willing, which he isn't. Personally, I think that's because he wants to keep her all to himself. He doesn't even like sharing her with their children. The minute he gets home from the store, he expects her to put the kids to bed and sit beside him while he watches whatever *he* wants on television. When she decided to breast-feed David and Kimberly, he was visibly annoyed. He'd grouch and grumble every time she nursed one of those babies. That didn't stop Elizabeth; she did it anyway.

I can still picture her creaking back and forth in that big rocking chair with a baby and a look of contentment settled on her face. Liz is a born mother, and she lives for her kids.

These days Jeffrey stays at the store hours after it's closed, and when he gets home he's like an angry bull. He snaps at anyone who crosses his path, especially Liz. I've tried talking to her about it, but she laughs it off. "You know JT," she says. "He's going through his usual pregnancy depression."

I believe it's more than that, but I won't say anything to her. She's got enough problems right now. All that weight she's gained and the way she can't remember to brush her own teeth, it worries me. It's not at all like Liz. She's one of the most together people you'll ever meet. I know how much she wants this baby, so I'm hoping she can carry it to term—but I don't know if that's possible.

Before they were married Jeffrey said they'd have nine kids, but the truth is he can barely deal with the two they have. He's none too good with money, and now I think he's worried about having another mouth to feed.

This financial dilemma is something he brought on himself. He bought that store from his Uncle Wally, who was a levelheaded man. When Wally Hawthorne had the store he sold clothes that the women in Westfield actually wanted to buy. But JT said the town was crying for a more upscale shop, so he tore down walls and expanded Wally's store until it was almost three times its original size. Then he brought in a bunch of fancy outfits no one wears. The construction wasn't half-finished before JT started borrowing money from Charlie. Now every time we see him, he's complaining about how he's nearly bankrupt.

In my opinion, any man with a family like Elizabeth and those beautiful babies is rich beyond compare. It's too bad Jeffrey can't see that.

In the Months that Followed

With Elizabeth in the hospital, JT grew more irritable than ever. Business was worse than last year. He moved a display of rhinestone necklaces to the front window, but the ladies of Westfield continued to stroll by. Two vendors stopped shipping merchandise and another said Jeffrey had until the end of the month, no longer.

The kids, missing their mother, grew whiny and difficult. Their toast was burnt, they couldn't find their socks, they wanted chocolate in their milk—until he put it in, then they didn't. Day after day the mailbox held nothing but bills, a number of the envelopes stamped "Final Notice!" And on top of everything else, he had to pay Maria Ramirez to watch the children while he was at the store. Every time he visited Elizabeth, which was happening less and less often, he filled her ears with a rundown of his problems.

"I don't know how much longer I can take this," he said.

"Mom is trying to help out," Elizabeth explained.

"Yeah, well, it's not enough. Your parents ought to be helping out financially. If your mother wasn't so wrapped up in you, she'd be watching the kids full-time."

"She's just worried that—" Suddenly Elizabeth couldn't remember what she wanted to say. That empty space had passed through her head again, a hole of nothingness with no doors or windows. She closed her eyes and slid into the pillow, her stomach a giant mound beneath the sheet.

"Great!" JT exclaimed, throwing his hands into the air. "I'm talking, and you decide to take a nap. I don't know why I even bother to come here!" He stomped out of the room and didn't return for five days.

Those empty spaces occupied Elizabeth's thoughts more and more. She began forgetting the day of the week, whether she'd eaten lunch, and the names of the nurses. Then there were the headaches. The terrible, terrible headaches that made her wish the empty space would return. She began to wonder what was worse, pain or oblivion.

Doctor Sorenson came almost every day and studied Elizabeth's chart with a worrisome scowl. "Not good," she'd mumble, "not good." Afterward she'd poke and prod Elizabeth's swollen body and ask questions. "Are the headaches worse? Are you having any vision problems? Can you twist your head side to side?"

Claire began spending longer and longer days at the hospital. She could think of nothing but Elizabeth and when she wasn't close enough to touch her, she worried about her. Determined not to pass along these fears, each day Claire came prancing into the sallow-colored room all sunshine and smiles.

"Oh my," she'd say, sounding lighthearted, "don't you look perky today!" It was a lie. Elizabeth's weariness was as visible as the nose on her face.

This day was no different. Claire arrived at the hospital, set pictures of the children on the windowsill, then began plumping pillows, straightening the blanket, and watering the plants. Eventually she settled alongside the bed and drifted into a stream of conversation to color the empty spaces in her daughter's mind.

"Imagine, it's already Tuesday," she said. "Why, this month of June is positively flying by."

Elizabeth listened but remained expressionless until the conversation turned to talk of David and Kimberly. Then she smiled and clung to every word.

Jeffrey slowly stopped bringing David and Kimberly to the hospital, but on the third Sunday of June, they were both there for Father's Day. Filled with laughter and sounds of happiness, the room became brighter, less yellow perhaps, and for that afternoon Elizabeth forgot the pain in her head. She even forgot about all the things she'd forgotten. Oblivious to the huge stomach between them, she hugged both children to her chest and covered them with kisses.

"Mommy," David said, his arms stretched wide, "I miss you this much!"

Not to be outdone, Kimberly repeated the gesture crying out, "Me too, me too."

For the one-hundredth time, she told them the story of Peter Pan and made them promise not to grow up until she got home from the hospital.

"We won't," they said. "Honest we won't."

Every visit with the children after that was hurried. The next time Jeffrey was barely through the door when he started saying he had things to do and had to get going.

"Please," Elizabeth begged, "just another ten minutes."

"Five," he said, then stared at the clock, shifting his weight.

The next visit was a repeat.

"What do you want from me?" he growled when she asked him to stay longer. "You think I should babysit you *and* the kids, is that it?"

"If you're busy, Mom will bring them," Elizabeth argued. "She'll pick them up on her way to the hospital. You won't have to pay Maria for babysitting, and I'll get to spend time with the kids."

"Get off my case," Jeffrey snapped. "I got problems enough trying to make a living."

The baby was due in late September, but in early August Elizabeth developed a strange weakness on her left side. On Monday her arm felt so heavy she could barely lift it to reach for her book. Two days later she tried to stand, but her left leg trembled then buckled.

"It's all this weight," she told the aide helping her.

But several nurses had also written "an increase in forgetfulness" on her chart.

"This is not something we can ignore," Doctor Sorenson warned. "I'm concerned this could be the onset of paralysis."

Elizabeth gasped. "Paralysis? Why? That has nothing to do with—"

"It could." Doctor Sorenson's scowl deepened. "We need the CT scan as quickly as possible."

"But you said—"

Doctor Sorenson shook her head. "I know what I said, but we can't afford to wait any longer. We're out of time. You'll have to have a cesarean."

Elizabeth's eyes filled with water. "It's too soon for Christian," she said, cradling her stomach.

With all the tests she'd known early on this baby was a boy, and she named him Christian. A name chosen because it signified strength and righteousness, both of which this baby would need. For almost three months now she'd talked to her son and called him by name. He was no longer a fetus or a baby, he was Christian, her third child, the one for whom she could give her life.

"Please don't," she pleaded. "Don't ask me to do this."

"I understand your concern," Doctor Sorenson said, "but the most recent ultrasound indicates the baby is fully developed. Twenty-nine weeks is early but not early enough to be considered high-risk. The probability is you'll deliver a healthy baby."

A look of gravity spread across the doctor's face. "You've got a serious neurological problem going on here, and we need a CT scan to know what's causing it. We have to pinpoint the source and do it quickly."

"Let's just wait another two weeks, I'm okay—"

"Elizabeth," Doctor Sorenson interrupted, "you are not okay. This situation is more serious than you seem to realize. They've

25

measured over five gallons of fluid expulsion in the past twenty-four hours, you're unable to use your left hand, and the memory lapses have become increasingly frequent. Those are *not* normal symptoms. Something is wrong, and I can't find it without a CT scan.

"I don't know how to make this any clearer—we are out of options. You can't wait any longer!"

"But—"

"No buts. Waiting endangers your life and the baby's. If something happens to you, there's no guarantee we can save the baby. If we take him now, he'll be a preemie but developed enough for survival."

Elizabeth tearfully agreed, and the cesarean was scheduled for the following day. Christian, the third child of Elizabeth and Jeffrey, would be born on Thursday, August ninth.

After the doctor left Elizabeth telephoned Jeffrey at the store. "Do you think you could come to the hospital tomorrow?"

"On a Thursday?" he groaned. "You know the store's open late. Thursdays I'm always open late."

"I know that, but—"

"I can't, I'm working twelve hours."

"Can't you get someone to mind the place for one day?"

"Yeah, sure," he said, annoyed, "and what am I supposed to pay them with, Cheerios? Forget it! Tomorrow's a late night, and there's no way I'm dragging my ass over to the hospital!"

"I thought you might want to be here for the birth of our son," she said icily.

"He's not due until September twenty-first," JT answered, "or is that something else you've forgotten?"

"I know exactly when he was supposed to be born, but Doctor Sorenson said I have to have a cesarean tomorrow."

"Oh."

"Do you think you could trouble yourself to be here?"

"I'll be there," JT said in a milder voice. "Is the baby okay?"

"Yes. They're taking him early because of me."

"You?" His voice registered concern. "What's wrong with you?"

For an instant he sounded like the old Jeffrey, like the man who slipped a two-karat diamond ring onto her finger and promised to cherish her forever. "Doctor Sorenson said she needs the CT scan right away. My symptoms are worse, and she wants to find out why."

"Oh. Okay. I'll be there."

Elizabeth hung up the telephone, leaned back, and closed her eyes thinking about Jeffrey's voice and that fleeting moment when he was still the man she married.

At eight o'clock the following morning, Claire and Charlie stood by Elizabeth's bedside. The minutes ticked by as the nurses readied Elizabeth for the operating room.

"Is Jeffrey here yet?" Elizabeth asked.

"Not yet," Claire answered.

"Would you call the house and ask if he's left?"

Charlie dialed the number. It rang seven times before Maria Ramirez answered.

"Is JT there?" he asked.

"No here," she said. "He gone long time."

"He left already?"

"Si, si. Long time."

Charlie replaced the receiver. "He's on his way."

They waited another fifteen minutes and still no word from Jeffrey.

"Call the store," Elizabeth said anxiously, "and see if he stopped there."

Charlie did. But a recording answered with the store hours.

"He's probably on his way, maybe stuck in traffic," Claire volunteered.

"That has to be it," Elizabeth reasoned. "He promised to be here."

The nurse pushed a gurney alongside the bed. "I'm gonna need you to slide over a bit," she said as she eased Elizabeth onto it.

"Could you wait five minutes?" Elizabeth asked. "My husband's already on his way."

The nurse gave a sympathetic smile. "Sorry. The operating room has a tight schedule, and you're on for nine o'clock."

Elizabeth gave a reluctant nod and settled onto the gurney. As she was wheeled from the room, she called back, "Tell Jeffrey I'm sorry."

Her parents watched the gurney disappear into the elevator, then Charlie turned to Claire and asked, "What is *she* sorry for?"

Claire shook her head in a remorseful way.

As Doctor Sorenson had predicted, Christian was born healthy. He weighed in at four pounds, five ounces, sizeable for a preemie.

The Sunday following the baby's birth JT came to the hospital with both kids, and they burst into the room like exploding popcorn. Kimberly, an excited three-year-old, demanded to see her new baby "brudder," and David tried to push ahead of her. They both ran to the bed and climbed in.

JT stood back for a long while then said, "I'm sorry. I had every intention of being here Thursday, but there were some problems at the store."

"What kind of problems?" Elizabeth asked.

"Just problems. Am I supposed to describe each and every one of them?"

"No, but I thought maybe you'd like to talk—"

"If I wanted to talk, I would," he said impatiently. "That's why I don't like coming here; you're always harping on me about something. I didn't get here on Thursday, and that's that. I said I'm sorry. What more do you want?"

"I don't *want* anything," she answered keeping her voice calm, even though the harshness of his words pressed against her chest. "I simply thought we could have a pleasant conversation."

"Oh, yeah, like that's possible. Try going through what I'm going through, and see if you feel like a pleasant conversation."

There was no use in pursuing the issue. When JT got in one of his moods, Elizabeth could only wait it out.

"I'm sorry you're having such a rough time," she said softly, then turned her attention to Kimberly who squirmed closer.

For a few moments JT stood there, a hard uncompromising look on his face, then without speaking another word he left. He was gone twenty minutes, and when he returned he said it was time to leave.

"No," Kimberly squealed. "I wanna see my baby brudder!"

"Me too," David added. "You said—"

"Okay," JT interrupted, "say goodbye to Mommy, and I'll take you to the nursery. That's where they keep the new babies."

"Okay," Kimberly said, scampering down from the bed. "Can I play with him?"

"Maybe when he comes home."

"Can he come home today?"

"Not today," JT said. He turned to David and told him to get a move on.

"I want to stay here with Mommy," the boy answered and leaned his head against his mother's shoulder.

Elizabeth wished she could wrap that one moment in cellophane and save it for a lifetime. David looked like his father but had her sensitivity. He was always ready to cuddle and lay his head on her heart. Kimberly was a three-year-old tornado whirling across the plateau of life, challenging everything. She would chatter in your ear until you were ready to scream *uncle* then give you a smile that melted your heart.

Christian. What would he be like, this child who had rocked the world with his entrance?

Elizabeth smiled at David. "Mommy will go with you," she told him. "Wait a minute, and I'll get the nurse to bring a wheelchair."

"That's gonna take too long," JT said. "I've gotta get home, I've got things to do."

"I'll ask her to hurry," Elizabeth replied. "Please?"

David, still sitting on the bed, curled closer to Elizabeth. "I wanna wait for Mommy."

"Me too," Kimberly echoed.

A short time later the fragmented family went to the nursery. JT pushed the wheelchair, David beside it and Kimberly scampering ahead. The pediatric nurse lifted Christian from his incubator and held him to the window. Although small, red-faced, and wrinkled, they all agreed he was the cutest baby there. When they returned to Elizabeth's room, the kids said goodbye. Just before leaving JT bent and kissed his wife's mouth, something he had not done in many months.

That day was one of Elizabeth's last good days. One she tried to hold in her memory during the months to come.

The following day Elizabeth was scheduled for a CT scan. Claire arrived at the hospital long before the breakfast cart came around.

"I thought you might appreciate some moral support," she said, sitting beside her daughter.

"Thanks, Mom."

Moments later a transport aide shuffled her off to Radiology.

Claire sat in the chair and waited. Minutes seemed like hours, hours like days. She checked her wristwatch. Liz had been gone less than twenty minutes. She clicked on the television and flipped through channel after channel. Soap operas with tragedies. People trying to win refrigerators by spinning a wheel. Frivolous endeavors for those with nothing better to do. Claire switched it off, stood, walked to the end of the hall and back again, checked her wristwatch. Twenty-five minutes.

Why so long, she wondered. Wasn't a CT scan like an X-ray, which took only minutes? Claire removed her watch and held it to her ear. *Tick, tick, tick.* It worked. She fastened the watch onto her wrist again.

Almost two hours later Elizabeth returned to the room, her skin flushed, glistening with beads of perspiration.

"Are you okay?" Claire asked, alarmed.

After a long moment Elizabeth answered, "I'm just very tired." She leaned back into the pillow and closed her eyes.

"Sleep," Claire replied, "it'll be good for you."

Long after the last visitors' gong sounded Claire remained by her daughter's bedside, listening for the fragile sound of air passing through Elizabeth's lungs. She stayed, trying to will the doctor to walk through the door with the results of the CT scan. She wanted to hear that Liz would be okay. That despite any treatment needed, Liz would, in time, return to her old self. When the sounds in the hospital corridor became the whispered hush of evening, Claire realized Doctor Sorenson wouldn't come.

The clock read almost nine when Claire arrived home. Charlie had abandoned hope of any supper long ago and sat at the kitchen table with a peanut butter and jelly sandwich.

"How's Elizabeth?" he asked before she was halfway through the door.

Claire gave a weary shrug. "Okay, I guess. Nothing new."

"Did they do the CT scan?"

She nodded. "This morning, but we haven't seen the doctor yet so I don't know what the results were."

"Oh." Charlie pushed back the half-eaten sandwich.

"I can fix you an omelet," Claire volunteered, "or a grilled cheese and tomato."

He shook his head. "I'm not all that hungry."

Claire watched as he slid the salt shaker first to the left side of the table and then to the right. After nearly thirty years of being married, Claire knew when Charlie was avoiding something that had to be said. He fidgeted with things—adjusted his belt buckle, shined his watch crystal, polished the fork lying in front of him, anything to keep his fingers moving so his mouth didn't have to.

After Charlie had moved the salt shaker a number of times, she asked if he had something to say.

"You're not gonna like this," he warned. "JT stopped by my office today looking for more money. He claims the store is on the verge of bankruptcy. He's four months behind on the rent and overextended with vendors."

"I hope you reminded him we're already taking care of Liz's hospital bill!"

"What good would that do?"

"It's *his* responsibility," Claire said bitterly. "Elizabeth is his wife! Instead of worrying about his miserable business, he should be thinking about her." The muscles in Claire's throat began to quiver. "He should care what happens to her, but he doesn't. He hardly ever comes to visit. He won't even let me bring the kids to see her. He won't—"

Charlie wrapped his arms around Claire as she began to sob. After a while he said, "Aren't you going to ask what my answer was?"

She held back the remainder of her tears and looked up at him.

"I said no. I told him we couldn't spare any more money."

"How'd he take it?"

"Not well. This was the worst I've seen him. He was like a crazy man." Charlie shook his head sorrowfully. "I feel bad for JT, with all the problems he's got, but I sure never thought he'd behave the way he did today."

"What'd he do?"

"Called me a son-of-a-bitch, punched the wall, knocked over a chair. He said if we're not willing to help out when he's down on his luck, he's through with us."

"What's that supposed to mean?"

"Probably nothing. I think he's just desperate right now. Once he calms down enough to think things through—"

The telephone rang and Charlie answered it. He listened for a minute then asked, "At Saint Barnabas?"

"Is that Doctor Sorenson?" Claire whispered.

He nodded. "Okay, I understand. Ten-thirty, right?" He replaced the receiver.

"Doctor Sorenson said she has the results," Charlie said, "but would prefer to discuss them with the entire family. She's already spoken to Jeffrey, and he's going to meet us at the hospital."

A washboard of wrinkles appeared on Claire's forehead.

"Don't worry," Charlie said. "I'm certain everything is all right."

Claire might have believed him, had she not noticed the way he picked at his belt buckle.

Saint Barnabas Hospital

Jeffrey planned to be on time for the meeting with Doctor Sorenson. After her phone call, he drove back to the store and taped a hand-lettered sign to the door. It read, "Caruthers Couture closed until noon."

But at 8:47 the next morning, a power surge sizzled through the downtown area of Westfield and triggered fourteen store alarms. The first call came from the security company minutes after Maria Ramirez walked through the door.

"Can you get that?" JT called from upstairs.

"A-llo," Maria said, wrestling herself from the arm of her coat. She listened for a half-minute then dropped the receiver and ran up the stairs.

"Policia! Policia!" she screamed. "The store, she's been robbed!"

"Robbed?" JT echoed. With his left shoe still untied, he flew down the stairs and jumped into the car. As he gunned the motor and roared out of the driveway, the tires kicked up a swirl of gravel that sprayed the mailbox.

Maria Ramirez charged only half what another babysitter would, but she sometimes listened with only one ear and was prone to hysteria, so she only caught one part of the recording that stated, "The alarm at Caruthers Couture has been triggered by an electrical overload. There has been no break-in. Please reset your alarm system as soon as possible."

Believing his store had been burglarized, JT rounded the corner at Elm Street without slowing and smashed into the rear fender of Ruth Kessler's Pontiac as she backed out of her driveway. Ruth, who prided herself on strict adherence to the proper way of doing things, insisted they call the police and fill out an accident report before any evidence was removed. She also insisted on taking photographs and documenting every spoken word, which was why at ten-thirty that morning Jeffrey Caruthers stood on the corner of Elm Street, instead of in his wife's hospital room.

At ten-thirty-seven, Doctor Sorenson entered Elizabeth's room with an armful of X-rays and a clipboard of notes. She placed them on the table and came toward Elizabeth. "How are you feeling? Any pain in that left arm? Dizziness? Headaches? Nausea?"

"I'm still having the headaches," Elizabeth answered. "Maybe I'm watching too much television."

Doctor Sorenson offered a sympathetic smile as she pressed her fingers to Elizabeth's wrist for a pulse count.

"I'm afraid that's to be expected," she said. "It's all part of this problem." She turned to Claire and Charles. "I'd like to review the results of our tests. Is Mister Caruthers here?"

"Not yet," Charlie said.

"A shame." Doctor Sorenson clipped a large X-ray to the wall-mounted viewer. "I know he's not much for visiting, but I'd hoped he would at least participate in this meeting." She glanced at her watch. "I suppose we should move ahead."

"He'll be here," Elizabeth said, looking toward the door. "Can't we wait five minutes?" she pleaded.

"Okay, five minutes."

Relief swept across Elizabeth's face. "He'll be here, I know he will."

But five minutes stretched into ten and then into twenty. Finally Doctor Sorenson said, "I'm sorry, but I really must get started."

Claire moved closer to Elizabeth and wrapped an arm around her daughter's shoulder. "Jeffrey's probably stuck in traffic," she said. "Morning traffic's the worst."

Claire called upon the lie often but had stopped believing it. The more likely scenario was that JT had blown off this promise, just as he'd blown off so many others. But Liz didn't need to hear the truth, especially not now.

"Elizabeth, I wish I had better news for you and your parents," Doctor Sorenson said, her voice solemn and strained.

Her left eye suddenly began twitching like a rapid heartbeat. "Sorry." She paused a moment, rubbed the back of her hand across her eye, then continued.

"Unfortunately, the CT scan shows a growth in the area of your brain behind the hypothalamus. It's the pressure from this growth that's causing your memory loss, the headaches, and the excessive weight gain.

"The hypothalamus, located here in the middle of the base of your brain" —she pointed to a section of the X-ray film—"is virtually the brain's control box. Think of it as command central. It sends messages to your body so that you know when to eat, when to drink, and a lot of other functions we consider normal.

"The growth, this dark area here"—she slid her fingertip ever so slightly to the left—"is pressing on the back side of your hypothalamus. Because of this pressure, your pituitary gland is malfunctioning."

The doctor rubbed her hand across her eye a second time, then continued. "A malfunction like this inhibits the release of certain hormones. They're the hormones that affect your thyroid and regulate your ability, or, in this case, inability, to lose weight. As a result your central nervous system, or what we'd consider your control panel, is being bombarded with a flood of mixed messages."

As they listened, Claire tightened her grip on Elizabeth's shoulder.

"Because of this particular growth's deep location," Doctor Sorenson continued, "it's inoperable. If it were located here on the pituitary gland"—she slid her fingertip a fraction of an inch to the right—"we could remove it surgically and follow up with radiation."

"If it's inoperable," Elizabeth asked anxiously, "then how *do* you treat it?"

Doctor Sorenson hesitated for a moment, again rubbed her hand across her eye, then spoke in a softer voice. "Unfortunately, there isn't any real treatment."

"Isn't any?" Elizabeth replied incredulously. "Isn't any?"

"Not given the position of the tumor." Suddenly the "growth" had progressed to a "tumor."

"What then?" Elizabeth asked, her eyes brimming with tears. "I stay this way? I keep getting worse? What?"

Without waiting for the answer to her question, Charlie said, "This has got to be a mistake! Liz is only twenty-eight years old. She's always been in good health. Did anyone check the X-rays? Did anyone make certain—"

"I wish it were a mistake, Mister McDermott, believe me I do. But unfortunately, the scan simply confirms what Elizabeth's symptoms have already indicated."

"How can something like this happen so fast? Up until a few months ago—"

"The probability is that it didn't happen quickly. Given its size, the tumor has probably been there for some time. Unfortunately, there was no reason to look for anything until Elizabeth began experiencing symptoms from the tumor pressing on the pituitary gland."

"Are you telling us there's nothing we can do?" Charles asked angrily. "Nothing? Given the technology of this day and age, I find that impossible to believe!"

"Medicine has come a long way," Doctor Sorenson replied, "but we've still got a long way to go. Elizabeth's tumor is inaccessible, that's the primary problem here. With a tremendous amount of luck, we might be able to reduce the size of it with radiation, but even that is iffy."

"Iffy is better than nothing," Charles said.

"That's yet to be determined. Before we decide on radiation therapy, Elizabeth needs to get a second opinion, preferably from Sloan Kettering or NYU."

"If a second doctor does suggest radiation," Elizabeth asked, "what then?"

"We try it and see. It might help, it might not. I can't promise anything. In a case like this, there is rarely an absolute cure. What we can hope is to put things in remission. Make this cancer something you can live with. If the therapy works, it will shrink the size of the tumor. Once the tumor is smaller, the pressure against the hypothalamus will be reduced."

"And then?"

"We wait and watch. Even if we're successful in shrinking the tumor, there's always the chance it will regenerate itself and start growing again when we stop the treatments.

"Also, radiation therapy has its own side effects," Doctor Sorenson warned. "Everyone responds to it differently. It's difficult to say how it will affect you, Elizabeth. You're young, and that's in your favor. You may tolerate the treatments quite well. But with your health compromised as it is, I can't promise that."

"I don't care," Elizabeth said. "If radiation is the only way I can get control of this thing then I'm willing to try." She wouldn't call it a tumor or cancer, it was simply a thing—an ugly thing that stood between her and a return to normalcy.

Doctor Sorenson smiled. "Well, before we proceed with anything, I want you to get a second opinion. That will tell us whether or not you're a candidate for radiation therapy."

"And if I am?"

"Then we start radiation treatments and monitor the tumor's response."

"How long before we know if it's working?"

"We could see improvement within two or three months. But we need to get some of this fluid out of you first and let your stomach heal from the cesarean. Even if we do get a favorable second opinion, you still have to regain your strength before we can start radiation treatments."

Elizabeth leaned back into her pillow and stared at the X-ray as Doctor Sorenson explained the medications she'd be taking.

"Am I going to die?" she suddenly asked.

The question sizzled through the air like a lightning bolt.

"Well," Doctor Sorenson said hesitantly, "the prognosis is never good when the tumor is as large and inaccessible as yours. But if, *if* you are a candidate for radiology, it's conceivable that we'll be able to shrink the tumor."

"Can I go home now?" Elizabeth asked.

"No reason why not," Doctor Sorenson answered. "Just realize you've got to take it easy, get lots of rest."

She handed Claire three prescriptions. "Have these filled as soon as possible. The Desmopressin will get rid of Elizabeth's thirst and help her reduce the fluid build-up. It replicates the hormone her pituitary gland is no longer producing."

Charlie prided himself in being pragmatic, a man capable of cutting through the emotional upheaval of a dilemma to focus on solutions. Claire would fly into a tizzy over some insignificant thing, but not him. He believed every problem had a solution and his job was to find it. As the doctor began slipping X-rays back into their envelopes, Charlie asked, "Is there anything we can do?"

"Families can always help," Doctor Sorenson said. "Radiation treatments, if we do proceed with them, can take both an emotional and physical toll on a person. Elizabeth will need a lot of love and understanding. And," she added with a touch of sarcasm, "you might mention that to her husband." She gathered her papers and left the room.

For a long while, no one said anything; the only sound came from a loudspeaker somewhere down the hall echoing out a call. The clock on the wall continued to move forward, minute after minute. Elizabeth looked at the clock and wondered how many of those precious minutes she had left.

She was so very tired—tired of the pain, of being poked and probed. Tired of the way this thing chipped away pieces of her mind and robbed her of yesterdays. Tired of struggling to move a finger or lift a hand. Elizabeth closed her eyes and saw three small faces looking up at her. Babies who needed a mother, children who would be left without someone to tell them stories, tuck them into bed at night, chase away demons, and offer a hand to hold.

She hesitated for a moment, looking at the future inside her eyelids. Then in a voice weighted with the challenge ahead, she said, "I *can* conquer this. I'll insist on the radiation. It'll work. It has to."

Moments later JT walked into the room.

"Don't get on me about not being on time," he said, shaking his head in disgust. "I've already had all I can take!" He gave the McDermotts a slight nod, then turned to Elizabeth. "I suppose the doctor's been here and gone, right?"

"Yes," she answered wearily.

Claire took Charlie's hand and said, "We'll step outside for a while and give you time to talk." Together they left the room and disappeared down the hall.

Elizabeth waited for Jeffrey to speak.

After a few moments of pacing, he said, "Sorry I'm late."

"What the doctor had to say was very important. You should have been here."

"What the hell do you want from me? I already said I'm sorry!"

"I wanted you to be here. It looks like—"

"Get off my ass!" he screamed. "I'm killing myself, and all I get from you is—"

"Don't take it out on me because you've got problems. You think I don't have—"

"I knew this was gonna happen! I busted my ass to get here, and you give me a shitload of grief for being late. But do you ask why I'm late? No! Cause you don't give a hairy-assed bean about my problems. All you care about is—"

"Okay," Elizabeth interrupted. "I'm sorry. What's the problem?"

"Not that I think you really give a shit, but I was in an accident. My car's got three, maybe four thousand worth of damage."

"Was anyone hurt?"

"Yeah, me! I'm up to my balls in debt now. How the hell am I supposed to pay for this? This shit's never-ending! It's one thing after another!"

"I know it's not—"

"You don't know the half of it!"

"Jeffrey, it's not that I—"

"Look, I feel for you, being sick and all. But don't compare your problems to mine. You don't have bill collectors banging at the door. You don't have kids bitching about this, that, and the other thing. You think my life's a picnic? Well, think again, because it sure as hell ain't!"

"I know it's been hard—"

"No, you don't! You've got no money worries, because Big Daddy takes care of you. But me, I'm dog-shit stuck to his shoes."

"That's not true."

"Oh really?"

"Yes, really. Daddy cares about you the way he would a son."

"Sure he does." JT gave a contemptuous sneer. "A son he's willing to toss to the wolves! You think I haven't told him how bad things are? My back's to the wall. I need a loan, or I'm gonna lose the store. Instead of helping out, he's paying for you to have a private room!"

"I'll talk to him," Elizabeth volunteered.

"You'd better, because I'm at the end of my rope." JT nervously paced alongside the bed. "If he doesn't come through soon, I don't know what I'm gonna do." His words rocked between anger and whine, then more anger, and now the pitiful sound of a trapped animal.

"I'm sure he will," Elizabeth said.

41

"I just can't handle everything myself," he moaned. "You've got to get out of here, Liz, and come home."

"I am. The doctor said tomorrow, maybe the day after."

JT stopped pacing and turned. "Great!"

"Yes, but there's more."

"More?" he said apprehensively.

Elizabeth took a deep breath and began slowly. "The scan they did showed a growth in the back of my brain—"

"A what?"

"A tumor," she continued, trying not to let her fear expose itself to him. "Doctor Sorenson said that's why I've gained so much weight and why I'm having trouble remembering things. This tumor's pressing on the part of my brain that—"

"So what happens now? They remove it?"

Elizabeth slowly shook her head. "I wish." She gave a sigh that came from deep inside, from the part of her where each of her babies had once lived. "Because of where the tumor's located, it's inoperable."

"You're kidding! So what happens in a case like this?"

"I think they'll try radiation treatments. I have to get a second opinion."

Jeffrey gave a groan and started pacing again. "More doctors, more money. Please don't tell me you're not coming home. Please don't say this is just going to go on and on—"

"Jeffrey!" Elizabeth exclaimed, her eyes growing teary. "I know you've got problems, but you could be more sympathetic about what I'm going through."

He stopped. "It's hard to be sympathetic when you've got alligators snapping at your ass." The trace of a smile softened his face. "But I am glad you're coming home. At least I won't have to pay Maria to take care of the kids."

"I wish that were true," she said sadly, "but we'll need someone to take care of the kids and help me. Mom can do some of it, but she can't—"

"You're too sick to take care of your own kids?" he said sarcastically.

"Yes," she answered. "The left side of my body is partially paralyzed. I can't stand or walk alone, and I can barely move my left arm. I would have told you sooner, but with all the problems you've had..." Elizabeth stopped when she noticed the way JT eyed her with a hateful glare.

"I can't believe you're doing this to me," he said. "Haven't I got enough on my plate? I can't take care of me and the kids. How am I supposed to take care of an invalid?"

"I'm not an invalid," she answered indignantly. "I've got a problem, and hopefully in time it will—"

"Are you nuts? Out of whatever mind you have left? If you can't stand, walk, or move from one spot to another, you're an invalid!"

"Don't say that! There are plenty of other things I can do. Anyway, Mom and Dad will help out."

"Help out with what?" JT asked angrily. "Help play with the kids? Help take away the last drop of privacy I've got? Help you nag me about what a failure I am? No, thanks! If they want to help, your daddy can give me the loan I need. Other than that, I don't need their help. And I don't want them at my house!"

"Maybe not," Elizabeth answered, "but I do."

"Then go home with them. Go back to their house, and let them take care of you until you're well enough to come home! They can afford it!"

JT stomped out the door before Elizabeth could explain the seriousness of her condition. To warn him that she might never again be able to care for their children, dance with him, stand in line at the supermarket, or clean the house. The precious ordinary everyday things she'd taken for granted were now gone.

When Elizabeth's parents returned, Charlie asked, "Where's JT?"

43

Elizabeth wanted to lie, to hide the embarrassment and hurt of being cast aside as worthless, but what purpose would that serve? They'd learn the truth tomorrow or the next day. In time she'd have to confess she'd be going home with them, not to her own house, to her children, to her husband.

"He left. He had to open the store."

"Did you tell him?" Charlie asked.

Elizabeth nodded. She waited, trying to swallow the tears, then said, "He's having a really hard time dealing with the pressure of all this—the bills, the store, taking care of the kids. He thought maybe it would be better for me to go back to your house when I leave the hospital."

"Our house?" Claire said quizzically. "Well, we'd certainly be glad to have you, but aren't you anxious to get home to the kids?"

"Of course I am. And JT will bring them over to spend time with me. But right now I can't even take care of myself. How can I take care of them? JT thinks it would be better this way. If it weren't for all these money problems, he could hire somebody…"

She looked at her father. "Can't you just give JT the loan he needs?"

"I've already given him several loans, Liz. If he needs more, why doesn't he ask his parents?"

"He already asked them, but they said no. They spent most of their savings to buy that place in Florida."

"Did JT put you up to this?" Charlie asked. "I know him; he'll stop at nothing to get what he wants. JT told you to ask me, didn't he?"

"Not specifically," Elizabeth replied. "But I know he's behind on our mortgage payments and worried about all the bills."

"When he finished complaining about his problems," Charlie said sarcastically, "did he have anything else to say?"

"Not much; you know JT." Elizabeth shrugged with her right shoulder.

Charlie shook his head in disgust. "It's high time he started remembering what's important."

"His store *is* important," Elizabeth said defensively.

"Nothing is as important as a man's family!" Charlie's words had an unusually sharp tone. "I have no respect for someone who values money more than his wife. Jeffrey's a poor excuse for a man!"

"Daddy, that's an awful thing to say."

"No, it's not. I know he's your husband, but he's using you to get to me. I'll bet he said if I give him the loan, you can come home. Right? That's what he said, wasn't it?"

A tear fell from Elizabeth's right eye.

"I knew it. That's the kind of man he is." Charlie's voice suddenly got louder and angrier. "Well, no more. I wouldn't give him a dime if he were standing on the corner with a tin cup. He's a bum, a good-for-nothing bum!"

"Charlie," Claire interrupted, "stop yelling at Elizabeth."

"I'm not yelling!" Charlie shouted. "But I'm not going to allow that bum to mistreat my daughter! I will see him bankrupt before I give him one cent of financing for that travesty he calls a business."

After that, no one talked about JT or the reason for Elizabeth not returning to her own house.

Charlie eventually left for the office, and Claire once again began plumping the pillows and straightening blankets.

"I know you're disappointed," she said. "But try not to let it get to you. Sooner or later JT will figure this out by himself."

"I hope so," Elizabeth said. "I surely hope so."

"He will. In the meantime Daddy and I will take care of you, and you won't have to contend with his grouchiness."

Elizabeth only could manage a fragile smile

A week later, on the same day Elizabeth left St. Barnabas to return to her parents' house, Christian was also released from the hospital. JT carried him home and handed him to Maria Ramirez, along with David and Kimberly. From that point on, he stopped calling Elizabeth altogether. She telephoned him countless number of times to ask if he'd bring the children but his answer stayed the same.

"Too busy," he'd say. "I'm taking care of three kids and trying to run a business."

"If you can't come, let the kids come," Elizabeth begged. "Mom will pick them up and bring them home."

"No way."

"Why not?"

"Because I said so."

Elizabeth noticed that each time they spoke his voice sounded sharper, his resentment more pronounced. Claire knew when those conversations took place because for the remainder of the day and sometimes for days following, Elizabeth was red-eyed and locked within herself. To cheer her, Claire would ask, "Would you like a cup of tea? We can watch *How the World Turns.*"

"No, thanks," Elizabeth would answer gloomily. "I already know how the world turns."

Claire, who at times could become emotional over a broken teacup, stood firm as a rock. Never once did she reveal the agony inside her. Instead, she forced herself to be cheerful. To pull happy thoughts from the air and hand them to Elizabeth. In return, she got a fractured smile, halfhearted at best. Claire knew nothing could restore the magical laugh Elizabeth once had, but still she tried.

Without her children and Jeffrey's arms to hold her, Elizabeth's pain increased. She woke thinking of them. Fell asleep with them on her mind. Maybe constantly asking that he come for a visit drove him away. But how could she not? For the past eight years they stood side-by-side, weathered storms, endured hardships, shared joys. How could she give up trying to resurrect such a relationship? True, JT had moods. He could be difficult, even impossible at times, but without him she felt like half of her old self.

The worst happened when the discussion turned to blame. In those conversations the realization that JT no longer loved her hit Elizabeth head on. Regardless of how much she had given, regardless of how much she still had to give, he no longer loved her.

"Please come over," she said, "even if it's only for a little while. I really miss you and the kids."

"Let's not go through this again."

"Don't talk like that. I don't like this situation either. I know it's hard on you. It's hard on me too."

"I doubt that!"

"Well, it is. At least you've got your health and the kids—"

"And you've got Daddy-Big-Bucks," he snapped. "This whole situation is his fault—"

"Stop it!" she said. "Stop acting like Daddy is to blame for your financial problems. He's not. He's no more to blame for your problems than I'm to blame for getting sick. It happened, that's all there is to it! Let's stop arguing about who's to blame and get back to loving each other."

"Screw you!" Jeffrey said and slammed the receiver down so hard it left a ringing in her ear.

That afternoon, for the first time, Elizabeth shared her pain with her mother.

"I don't understand how it can end this way," she sobbed. "How he can stop loving me just because I'm sick. What about our kids? What about all the things—" She fell into her mother's arms and wept like a child. "It's unfair, so unfair…"

"Yes, it is," Claire said. "But Jeffrey's the one to be pitied. He's got a cancer far worse than yours. His eats the soul and lets the body walk around more dead than alive."

She put her hand beneath Elizabeth's chin and tilted her face upward. "Try to understand, Jeffrey's not mad at you. He's mad at himself. He looks in the mirror and sees a man who's failed at life. He can't do anything about those failures, so he gets angry and smashes the mirror."

"But," Elizabeth sobbed, "I still love him."

On the second Tuesday in September Claire took Elizabeth to Sloan Kettering for a consultation. That same afternoon JT visited Charlie at his office, asking again for a loan and upping the ante to twenty-five thousand.

"No," Charlie said flatly without apologies or explanation.

"No?" JT repeated with a slit-eyed expression. "No?"

"That's right, no."

"Didn't Liz talk to you? Didn't she explain? I gotta have that money to keep going. How am I supposed to support my family if the store goes bankrupt?"

"That's not my problem," Charlie answered. "I imagine you'll have to get a job like most other men."

"A job doing what? I'm a retailer. Women's clothing, that's what I know. I'm no good at anything else."

Without lifting his eyes from the ledger sheet in front of him, Charlie said, "Well, since your store is about to go under, you're probably not very good at retailing either. Maybe it's time to consider a change."

JT slammed his hand on the desk. "I need that money! It's not just the store, I've got bills! I can't pay the mortgage, how am I supposed to pay for food, gas, electricity, and a babysitter for those three kids? You got any idea how much babysitters cost?"

"Liz has been begging to see her kids. Bring them to our house, and Claire will watch them for free."

"If Liz gets the kids during the day, will I get the loan?"

"No."

"I've got more than babysitting bills! What about all the other things, food, gas, electricity? What am I supposed to do about those?"

Charlie's sympathy was long gone. Although he never mentioned it, he knew of the telephone conversations that left Elizabeth in tears.

"As I suggested," he said icily, "get a job." He handed the classified section of the *Newark Star Ledger* to Jeffrey. "This should help."

JT whacked the paper aside. "Don't push me."

"Or what?" Charlie said. "What can you do?"

JT didn't answer. He whirled on his heel and stormed out of Charlie's office, slamming the door so hard the walls shook. As he crossed through the outer lobby of the bank he muttered loudly, "You'll find out what, old man! I'll fix you and your whole damned family! Just wait!"

Elizabeth Caruthers

Some days I hate Jeffrey. Other days I realize I'm still in love with him; then I hate myself. I want to stop thinking about him, but I can't. Forgetful as I've become, why can't I forget him for even a minute? In the darkest part of the night, when everyone else is sleeping, I lie here remembering his warm breath in my ear, the weight of his body circling me like a protective shell. I can picture mornings when the kids climbed in bed with us and wriggled around until we looked like a spaghetti bowl of arms and legs. Memories like that are so painful, I almost convince myself that it would be a blessing to drift into that black hole and remain there. In the light of day I can think more rationally and then I accept that those memories are what I have to hold on to, if I'm to keep my sanity and make it through this.

Jeffrey wasn't always this way. At one time our life together was absolutely wonderful. Things began to change about a year after he bought the store. At first he'd come home bubbling with enthusiasm. All through dinner he'd talk about how great business was, how he was gonna upgrade his merchandise and expand the store, how he'd change the look of Westfield.

Failure, that's what changed Jeffrey. He's always expected everything to be storybook perfect, even people, and especially himself. After all that pursuit of perfection, look where we are now. Both of us are broken—his spirit, my body.

Mom's right when she says JT hates himself. He hates himself and me too, because neither of us are what we once were. I understand his anger, but that doesn't make it any less painful.

The problem is Jeffrey can never settle; he always wants more. He wanted a store that would make him the envy of all the merchants in Westfield. Instead of trying to have more than everybody else, I wish he could've seen we already had everything that mattered. Try telling that to JT, and he'd think you were ninety-nine cents short of a dollar.

He's not one to take suggestions from anybody. Daddy tried to tell him he was getting in over his head, but he said Daddy had a negative attitude. JT developed this nasty streak when the business didn't pan out.

There's only one thing JT hates more than being wrong, and that's Daddy being right. One time I suggested maybe he should have listened to Daddy's warning, and JT nearly went ballistic. At that point I backed off and started giving him some space. I figured he'd calm down once the expansion was finished and business picked up again. Besides, with two kids I had more than enough to keep me busy.

Before we were married Jeffrey said he felt just as I did about having a large family, so I thought he'd be glad we were expecting a third child. I thought maybe it would take his mind off of his business problems, but it was just the opposite. He said we had trouble enough and didn't need any more babies. I've always felt children were a blessing. Until you hold your baby in your arms, you can't begin to imagine the size of the love inside of you.

When I was ten, maybe eleven, I had two best friends, Jeanne and Emily. Jeanne wanted to be an actress, Emily a model. "How about you, Liz?" they'd ask. "What do you want to be?"

"A mother." That's what I'd say, every single time. While Jeanne and Emily were busy reading movie magazines, I'd be down the block watching Missus Tillinger's babies for free.

Of course nothing ever turns out the way you think it will. Jeanne went to Hollywood, but last I heard she was a secretary. Emily married a forest ranger and moved to Canada. And me? I'm back at my parents' house allowing some stranger to care for my three babies.

Maria Ramirez is nice enough but she's still a total stranger, and it kills me to think she's the one mothering my children. It ought to be me. Me or Mom—at least she's their grandma. Of course that's not likely to happen; Jeffrey has made it obvious he doesn't want Mom around. Before I came home from the hospital, she'd help out with the kids whenever she could. Then JT told her to stay away. It's a shame, because David and Kimmie both adore her. Christian, well, he's still an infant. The first few months of a baby's life is when they come to know the touch and smell of people. If Jeffrey continues to keep the kids from us, how can Christian ever get to know Mom? Worse yet, how can he get to know me?

Jeffrey's trying to force Daddy to give him the money he wants, and he's using our kids as leverage. Unfortunately, the one who suffers most is me. Me and Mom. I haven't seen David and Kimberly since the week after Christian was born, and I haven't seen Christian since we left the hospital. As much as I miss Jeffrey, I miss the kids a whole lot more.

You'd think Jeffrey acting that way would be cause enough for me to hate him, but I don't. It's not that easy to stop loving someone. You feel hurt and angry, you sizzle like there's a bonfire inside of you, but at the end of the day you're still in love. If Jeffrey came to me tomorrow, wrapped his arms around me and asked me to come home and be his wife again, I'd do it in a heartbeat. I might say I'd do it because of the kids, but that would be a half-truth. I want my life back—a husband who loves me, my kids close by, all of us living together, breathing the same air. If I had Jeffrey and the kids alongside of me, I know I could defeat this monster inside my head.

Mom and Dad aren't quite so forgiving. They really hate JT these days. It's obvious by the way they speak his name, like it's something with a bad taste. That's why I don't tell them everything. They'd only hate him more than they already do.

I'm sure Mom knows anyway. Times like that she starts her "Let's-cheer-Liz-up" act. "You look lovely today," she'll say. "Lots more color in your cheeks." She doesn't want me to know she's worried about me, so I play along. It's our own little game. She pretends I look better, and I pretend to feel better.

Next week, I start the radiation treatments that will hopefully shrink this tumor. I pray it works. Let me live long enough to see my babies grow up, I ask. Then I'll go willingly. I want my children to know how much I love them. I want them to soak up the smell and touch of me, because that will stay with them long after I'm gone.

I wish I could tell you I'm not afraid, but I'm so scared that at times I can barely breathe. I know I've got an uphill battle on my hands, but I'm going to give it everything I've got so I can live long enough to raise my children.

Pray for me.

November 1984

Elizabeth returned to St. Barnabas Hospital for her radiation treatments. Most people traveled back and forth, arrived in the morning, got a quick zap of radiation and were home by supper. But the complications of Elizabeth's case meant someone had to watch over her night and day. Her progress had to be monitored in minute increments.

On the second Tuesday of the month, Claire packed a bag containing five cotton nightgowns, a bathrobe, slippers, and the book Elizabeth would probably never read. Then together they left for the hospital. Moments after Elizabeth arrived, a transport aide whisked her off to an icy room where she lay in a coffin-like machine that growled and clicked as they ran several new CT scans. The technicians measured her from the tip of one ear to the other, from the bridge of her nose to the top of her head. They analyzed those measurements crossways, at right angles, and upside down until finally they concurred on the precise spot for placement of the powerful radiation beam.

On Thursday, the day of Elizabeth's first treatment, Claire arrived early carrying a huge pot of yellow chrysanthemums. She placed the flowers on the windowsill, angled them toward the sun, then suggested, "Why don't I run out and get us a container of that good coffee from the diner?"

"No, thanks." Elizabeth wrinkled her nose and shook her head.

"How about a bagel? With cream cheese?"

"Unh-unh."

Before Claire could suggest Taylor ham on a roll, the breakfast tray arrived: orange juice, oatmeal, and runny eggs. Elizabeth pushed it away.

"Eat something," Claire said. "You've got to keep up your strength." She opened the napkin and handed it to her daughter. "Maybe a little bit? Just a bite or two?"

"Later." Elizabeth dropped the napkin onto the tray, leaned back, and closed her eyes. "There is one thing I'd like. Would you call JT and ask him to bring the kids to see me?"

"Sure," Claire answered, although she knew how he would answer. What to do, she wondered—ease away from the issue or let her daughter be disappointed as she'd been disappointed so many times before?

"Actually," Claire said, "you're in the acute care wing now, and in this area they have strict rules about not allowing children to visit."

"Oh." Elizabeth slumped deeper into her pillow.

"But I suppose it wouldn't hurt to check."

Elizabeth opened her eyes and smiled, just a slight curve on the right side of her mouth.

Moments later the nurse came to take her to Radiology.

Two days after the third radiation treatment, Cyndi, the day nurse who had just started her shift, noticed Elizabeth's skin glistening with perspiration, yet to the touch she felt cool, clammy almost.

"Are you warm?" Cyndi asked.

Struggling to slow her breathing, Elizabeth shook her head.

"Any pain?"

Elizabeth nodded and placed her hand on her chest.

Within minutes she was on her way back to the radiology department, where they found a blood clot snaking its way toward her heart. Elizabeth's last memory came as a blur of faces hovering over her and the sound of a faraway voice calling for oxygen.

When she awoke Elizabeth was in a cavernous room with bright lights glaring against white walls. A monitor beeped as neon green lines rose and fell with her heartbeat. There was no television, no chair for visitors. The only sounds came from the whirring and whooshing of machines, the click of heels against a tile floor, and the drone of muffled voices.

Elizabeth lifted the oxygen mask from her face. "Where am I?" she asked Lucinda, the nurse next to her bed.

"The Intensive Care Unit," Lucinda answered and continued writing on Elizabeth's chart. "You've got to leave this on," she added and carefully replaced the oxygen mask.

With her right hand Elizabeth lifted the bottom edge of the mask. "What happened?" she asked, then replaced the mask.

"You suffered a pulmonary embolism."

Elizabeth's blue eyes began to fill as she mouthed, "What now?"

Lucinda tenderly touched Elizabeth's shoulder. "Don't worry. Doctor Sari found the clot before it had time to do any real damage. He's got you on blood thinners to prevent a recurrence."

She adjusted the IV drip, then smiled. "Your job is just to relax and get some rest. We'll take care of everything else."

For the eight days Elizabeth remained in the Intensive Care Unit, Claire was the only visitor. She arrived early and held her daughter's hand for the full twenty minutes visitors were allowed. Then she left the ICU, sat in one of the gray plastic chairs lining the hallway, and waited for two hours until the next visiting session. Claire was the first visitor to enter the Intensive Care Unit in the morning, and she stayed until the ICU doors closed at night.

"Daddy said to tell you he loves you," she whispered into Liz's ear. "JT knows what's happened and he's promised to come, as soon as he can find someone to watch the store." Claire lied about JT coming to visit, but she said it to encourage Liz and lift her spirits.

She'd driven to the house to tell Jeffrey of Liz's condition. When no one answered the door, she penned a quick note and left it in the mailbox. So what she'd said wasn't a complete lie. Claire thought that once Jeffrey learned the seriousness of Elizabeth's condition, he'd visit.

It never happened.

On the very same day as Elizabeth's pulmonary embolism a sheriff's deputy delivered a summons notifying JT he was being sued for non-payment of rent. He had sixty days to come up with eight-thousand dollars. If he didn't, the door of Caruthers Couture would be closed.

For weeks JT had suspected this might happen, so he'd begun to cart home some of the merchandise—velvet dresses, satin shawls, fringed evening gowns, even a large jewelry display case. He had no idea what he might do with those things but figured they were better off in his possession than with a pack of bill collectors. When he finally received the summons his guestroom already held racks of clothing, dozens of sequined purses, and a trunk full of glittery rhinestone jewelry.

Once the threat of losing his store became a probability, JT sunk into the blackest mood imaginable. Day after day he'd leave the children with Maria Ramirez, then hurry into Caruthers Couture to wait for cash-carrying customers. Every day grew longer than the one preceding it. Since he had little to do, he focused on his growing hatred of Charlie McDermott and counted the days until his store would be padlocked.

Finally, when JT reached a point of desperation, he visited Liz. He had come up with a plan to refinance their home. With a new mortgage, he could get enough money to tide him over.

"The house is in both names," Harold Bollinger, the loan officer at United Trust, told him. "You'll need your wife's signature for refinancing."

"Can't I just sign for her?" JT asked.

"No, absolutely not," Harold replied. "It's against the law unless you've got power of attorney. Do you have power of attorney?"

"Uh, sort of." The minute the words left his mouth, JT knew he had blown it. He'd stumbled over the words and sounded like a man lying.

Harold Bollinger narrowed his eyes and looked down his nose. "There's no 'sort of' with loan applications. Either you produce a notarized document stating that you have power of attorney, or you get your wife's signature."

"Uh, my wife's more than willing to sign these papers," JT replied nervously, "but unfortunately she's in the hospital and can't get here."

"No problem. We'll prepare the paperwork, and you can take it to the hospital for her to sign."

Harold Bollinger, a banker for some thirty years, noticed the nervous twitch in Jeffrey's left eye and added, "Of course, her signature will have to match the signature we have on file."

JT had planned to copy Elizabeth's signature onto the bottom of the loan application, but Harold Bollinger's warning made him nervous. For days he practiced signing her name, but each time it appeared shaky, loopy where it shouldn't be and squiggly at the tail end of certain letters. He searched the house until he came across a document bearing her signature, then he taped it to the glass window and tried tracing her name through a ray of sunlight. He did this with four different pens and a fat black marker, but nothing worked. The signatures looked so different that even a half-blind monkey would know it was a forgery.

After days of trying, JT finally decided to go to Saint Barnabas and ask Elizabeth to sign the loan application. He hated the idea of going there; just the thought made the hair on the back of his neck bristle. The possibility of running into Charlie McDermott—or Claire—made it worse. As far as JT was concerned, Liz's illness was destroying his life as well as hers. The McDermotts were forcing him to beg for something that was rightfully his.

His hatred of Charlie simmered and came to a slow boil. Day after day, hour after hour, JT reminded himself that if Charlie had given him the loan he needed, he wouldn't have a summons hanging over his head. He wouldn't need to refinance the house. And he wouldn't be facing this confrontation with Liz.

By the time JT worked up enough courage to go to Saint Barnabas, Elizabeth had been transferred from the Intensive Care Unit back to her old room with the yellow chrysanthemums on the windowsill. Just as he'd feared, both Claire and Charlie were there. They stood alongside Liz's bed with somber looks.

Doctor Sorenson was also there. She gave Jeffrey Caruthers an icy nod. "I assume you got my message. I'm glad you could make it."

Jeffrey had not gotten the message, because ten days earlier he'd stopped retrieving messages from an answering machine that offered nothing but bad news and foreclosure threats. Nonetheless he returned her nod.

Elizabeth smiled at her husband and stretched out her right hand. The left lay limp in her lap. "Hi," she said, glad to see him.

JT gave her a nod but remained where he was, standing out of reach with his hands locked behind his back.

"I'm glad everyone is here today," Doctor Sorenson began, "because I have some unpleasant news, and I believe Elizabeth will need the support of her *entire* family." She shot an accusatory look at JT, then continued.

"I've decided to terminate Elizabeth's radiation treatments. It's been seven weeks, and unfortunately there's no indication that the tumor is responding." She slid two X-ray films onto the light panel. "This is Elizabeth's first CT scan, where we can see the size of her tumor before radiation treatments." She pointed to the dark mass.

"And this scan"—she directed their attention to the next X-ray—"was taken two days ago. As you can see, the size of the tumor has actually increased."

Elizabeth eyes grew teary.

JT stepped back, edging himself a bit closer to the door.

Charlie asked, "What now? Chemotherapy?"

Doctor Sorenson shook her head. "Afraid not. Chemotherapy is a shotgun approach. We can't target just the cancerous cells, so the toxic drugs kill the good cells as well as the cancerous ones. Elizabeth is too weak to tolerate that."

The word "cancer" caused Claire's knees to buckle, forcing her to grasp Charlie's arm. "What then?" she asked, fighting back her tears. "What do we do now?"

"There's not much we can do," Doctor Sorenson answered. "The tumor is inoperable because of where it's located, and the radiation treatments have been unsuccessful. Of course we'll continue to treat Elizabeth's symptoms so that she's comfortable and relatively pain-free. But with a tumor this aggressive, only a miracle drug…" She shrugged.

For the second time in two months, Elizabeth looked at Doctor Sorenson and asked, "Am I going to die?"

The doctor took a deep breath and sighed. "Unfortunately Elizabeth, this is a terminal situation."

"How long?" Elizabeth finally asked.

"Maybe months, maybe years. It depends on how rapidly the tumor grows."

With every question JT moved further back until eventually he was pressed up against the far wall.

"Mister Caruthers, do you have any questions?" Doctor Sorenson asked pointedly.

JT shook his head side to side.

"I do," Claire said. "You mentioned a miracle drug. Is there one that might stop the tumor's growth?"

"Yes and no," Doctor Sorenson answered reluctantly. "There have been reports of a new regimen, but it's a long shot. I'm almost hesitant to subject Elizabeth to it without a more substantial analysis of the success ratio."

Charlie asked, "What kind of treatment is it?"

"It's a group of drugs. They've been individually approved and used for other applications, but not in a combination therapy and not specifically for inoperable brain tumors. Right now the regimen is undergoing clinical trials and showing positive signs, but it's still considered experimental."

"Are they chemotherapy drugs?" Elizabeth asked.

"Yes. The regimen is called Five F U. But this application works differently than most chemotherapy drugs."

"How?"

"Instead of killing cells, it segregates the tumor and starves it of the blood nutrition it needs to grow."

"I don't understand," Claire said. "Don't all chemotherapy drugs kill the good cells?"

"Yes, if taken individually. But this regimen bonds the drugs together so they're drawn to only the cancerous cells. The drugs create a barrier around the cells to prevent the normal flow of blood nutrition."

"Is Elizabeth strong enough for this kind of treatment?"

"I believe so. Her healthy cells won't be affected. Five F U attaches itself to *only* the cancerous cells. Theoretically, if we could isolate that area of her brain and deprive it of nourishment, we might be able to slow or possibly stop the tumor's growth."

"Is there a downside?"

Doctor Sorenson nodded ever so slightly. "Unfortunately," she winced at yet another use of the word, "these drugs are quite expensive. Because the regimen is not yet recognized as an approved therapy, it's not covered by insurance."

Without hesitation Charlie said, "We'll take care of the cost."

"There's more," Doctor Sorenson replied. "While I doubt use of this regimen could cause further deterioration, there's also no guarantee it will work." She turned to Elizabeth and asked, "Do you feel this is something you really want to pursue?"

"Yes, absolutely." Her eyes rimmed with tears as she stretched her right hand toward JT again. "I know it will work. It's got to. JT and the kids are counting on me to get well."

When he didn't come to her, Elizabeth lowered her hand and gave him a frail smile. He remained stone-faced, emotionless as the wall behind him.

Charlie glared at JT with contempt, then turned back to the doctor. "When can Elizabeth start these treatments?"

"As I said, this is a long shot at best. The regimen is still in clinical trials, and I'm not certain we can get clearance to use it. Before we even try, I'll need several other tests to establish whether Elizabeth is a candidate for consideration."

"I can deal with a few more tests," Elizabeth said.

"This means you'll have to remain in the hospital," Doctor Sorenson warned.

"It kills me to be away from my kids for so long, but I'll do whatever I have to do to get well."

A long moment of silence followed, the kind of silence that thickens the air and allows fear to creep into people's hearts. Charlie felt it as did everyone else. He noisily cleared his throat and asked more questions. Claire also asked questions; so did Elizabeth. But JT remained silent. When there was nothing more to be said, Doctor Sorenson left.

Cyndi, Elizabeth's day nurse, stood outside the room listening to the exchange. When Doctor Sorenson came out, Cyndi followed and struck up a conversation.

"I couldn't help but hear," she said. "Elizabeth Caruthers is my patient. Terminal, huh? Tough break. She's so young."

"Yes," Doctor Sorenson said, "and they have three small children."

"Her husband is the one who owns that big clothing store over in Westfield, right?"

Doctor Sorenson nodded absently and began writing a prescription order.

"How's he handling his wife's illness?"

Rebecca Sorenson paused. Forgetting her resolve never to discuss the personal affairs of a patient, she said, "It's odd. He seems almost removed from the whole thing. He doesn't visit her very often, and when he does he acts like a stranger. I think he's not accepting the reality of this situation."

"Yeah, that's what I was thinking too," Cyndi mumbled. Then she turned and walked away, wearing the slightest trace of a smile.

As she passed by Elizabeth's room for a second time, Cyndi distinctly heard JT's voice saying, "I want out!" She wanted to hear the rest of the conversation, but just then another patient called for her from his room.

Charles glared at JT and growled, "What the hell are you talking about?"

"I've gotta walk away from this," JT answered, shaking his head. "I'm sorry Liz's sick. I'm sorry things are the way they are, but there's not a damn thing I can do about it. I've got my own problems, and I can't take on the responsibility of hers."

"Responsibility?" Charlie echoed. "What responsibility have you—"

"I've got three kids and a business going down the tubes. That's more than I can handle. I gotta take care of me and the kids. There's no way I can care for Liz. She's your daughter, you've got the money, you take care of her."

"We enjoy having Elizabeth with us," Claire said, checking her anger, "but she wants to be with you and the kids."

"I can't help that. I'm up to my ass in bills. I got problems with no answers, and I don't want Liz coming back to my house!"

"How dare you!" Charlie snapped. "That house is as much hers as yours. More perhaps. She's got every right to—"

"No, she doesn't!" Jeffrey's voice grew belligerent.

"We'll see about that!" Charlie answered.

"Try it. I'm telling you right now, you bring her back to my house and I'll walk out. I'll take all three kids with me, and she can sit there and die alone!"

Charlie took a step toward JT. "You rotten—"

Elizabeth's eyes darted from father to husband, husband to father.

"No, Daddy!" she screamed.

Charles stopped and turned to his daughter.

"You can't make Jeffrey want me if he doesn't," she said. She closed her eyes and pictured JT's blue Buick—a car he had adored, a car he waxed and polished until it sparkled like a diamond—but once he got a dent in the rear fender, it became a car he could no longer stand to drive. Within weeks he had replaced the Buick with a new Pontiac.

She remembered the Bulova watch that kept perfect time but was tossed away when JT discovered a hairline crack in the crystal. The green cashmere sweater she'd bought for him while they were on their honeymoon, gone because of the smallest snag imaginable. Flawed as she had become, Elizabeth knew he wouldn't hold on to her.

When she opened her eyes again, he had left.

Later that afternoon Cyndi telephoned her sister, Kelsey, a single mom who, along with her two-year-old terror, had moved into Cyndi's one-bedroom apartment. To say the apartment was unbearably overcrowded would be a gross understatement. Kelsey had arrived with five suitcases, several sacks of toys, and a tricycle that had a battery-operated siren attached to the handlebars.

"I've nowhere else to go and no money," she'd complained.

Against her better judgment, Cyndi agreed to let her sister stay a few days. That was five months ago. Kelsey promised to get a job and find another place to live, but as days stretched into weeks she became more settled. Now she occupied every corner of every room, and she no longer bothered to flip through the "Help Wanted" section of the newspaper. Something had to be done.

The telephone rang six times before a groggy voice said, "Hello."

"Kelsey?"

"Yeah." She yawned.

"Were you sleeping?"

"Yeah. Me and Dumpling were napping."

"At four o'clock in the afternoon?"

"Well, there's nothing else to do."

"I've got a thought for you," Cyndi said. "I know how you like money and nice things. You know that big dress shop in Westfield, the one on Main Street?"

"The one next door to The Bootery?"

"Yup. The guy who owns it, his wife is here in the hospital, and she's got a tumor…"

The next morning Kelsey, wearing a tee shirt that made skin saggy by comparison, trotted into Caruthers Couture and asked for a job.

"I'm not really hiring right now," JT said, even though he could scarcely take his eyes from Kelsey, a younger, healthier version of Liz.

"I'd be willing to work for almost nothing." Kelsey sighed and leaned across the counter so her face was inches from his. "I'm real interested in learning the business."

"Oh." JT made no effort to move back.

"I'd be a trainee. And I could model some of your beautiful clothes. Show them off to their best advantage."

"That's a point," JT mused. "Yeah, that's a point. Seeing someone like you wearing the outfits might encourage customers."

"I'll try on a few things. You can see what I mean."

Before he could object, Kelsey scooped up an armful of gowns and headed for the dressing room. Moments later she came out wearing a blue satin sheath that reflected the color of her eyes and slid across her body like the cascade of a waterfall.

JT smiled. "Now that's how a woman should look."

Within the hour Kelsey had a job at Caruthers Couture. Although the store was just weeks from being padlocked, JT rationalized that Kelsey modeling clothes would bring an influx of customers.

Elizabeth stopped asking if Jeffrey would come to visit, but she continued to ask for the children. "Please," she begged Claire, "make him bring them to see me."

Three weeks after Jeffrey had stormed out of the hospital, when she could no longer stand by and listen to her daughter pleading to see her children, Claire began telephoning the Caruthers house. She called early in the morning, too early for Jeffrey to have left for work. She called throughout the afternoon and at dinnertime. Her final call was at ten o'clock in the evening, a time when all three children should have been tucked in their beds. Not once did Jeffrey answer the telephone. Eventually she tried calling the store.

"Caruthers Couture," a woman's voice chimed.

Claire, taken aback by the feminine voice, asked, "Is this Caruthers Couture?"

"Yes, it is."

"Is Jeffrey Caruthers there?"

"Yeah, sure, hold on a sec." The woman sounded young. And happy.

As she waited, Claire heard the woman say, "Honey, you've got a phone call."

Honey? What kind of employee calls the boss honey? Claire wanted to ask JT that question but never got the chance. After a giggly conversation at the other end, a conversation too muted for her to catch, someone hung up the receiver.

Claire called back twice, but no one answered either time.

The next morning before heading to the hospital, Claire drove to the Caruthers house. She parked her car in the driveway, walked to the front door, and rang the bell. She heard a flurry of footsteps and whispered voices inside, but no one answered the door. Claire slipped around to the side of the house and peeked into the garage window. JT's car stood there, and a red Nissan sat alongside it. More determined than ever, Claire returned to the front door and continued ringing the doorbell.

After almost twenty minutes, she knew JT wouldn't answer. She returned to her car and headed for Saint Barnabas. On the way she stopped at the bakery and bought a dozen of the Neapolitan cookies that Liz loved.

Charlie McDermott

I realize Elizabeth is no longer a child. She's a woman with three children of her own. But as far as I'm concerned, she's still my little girl. I'm her father, so of course I feel protective. Any father would feel the same way. How can they not?

We grow up understanding that fathers are the protectors, the ones who slay the dragon to keep their family safe from harm. Let me tell you, I'd trade this insidious monster inside Liz's head for a good, old-fashioned dragon any day. I look at her lying in that hospital bed and see my own inadequacies. I'm her father; I should be able to do something. Instead I fumble around, helpless as a baby. The money, that's nothing. I'd give everything I own to buy back Elizabeth's health.

Thank God for Claire; she's a tower of strength. Somehow she can move past the fact that Elizabeth is practically paralyzed and focus on pleasantries. She'll start talking about something of no importance whatsoever and next thing you know she has Liz laughing at the silliest things, like a bird pecking at the window or the long hair that stuck out of some doctor's ear. To watch her you might think Claire doesn't realize how serious the situation is, but I hear her crying at night and asking God to find a cure for Elizabeth.

I wish I could be more like Claire. When I'm visiting Elizabeth, I stand there with my hands stuffed inside my pockets. I ache to say something, but what can I say to make things better? A father should have all the answers, should take care of his child. All I can do is stand there, looking useless. To escape my own inadequacy, I go to work and let my share of the responsibility fall on Claire's shoulders. How cowardly is that?

For most of Elizabeth's life, I was there whenever she needed me. I was somebody to keep her safe from harm, ease whatever hurts came her way. She was a colicky baby who'd scream and carry on until you'd swear she'd have a convulsion. Even Claire couldn't stop her crying. But I could. I'd cuddle her and walk the floor for hours until she finally drifted off to sleep, her tiny little body curled up against my chest. I lost a lot of sleep, but what I got in return was well worth it.

I taught her how to ride a two-wheel bike, even though falling terrified her. I ran alongside her and steadied the seat until she got enough confidence to ride on her own. That's what a father does, keep his daughter safe—safe from falling, safe from getting hurt. I did all those things for Elizabeth, but God forgive me, I also gave her to Jeffrey Caruthers.

The day they were married, Elizabeth looked like an angel floating on a cloud. She was so happy and so in love. I got caught up in her happiness and when Pastor Howell asked, "Who gives this woman?" I answered, "I do," without considering all the reservations I had.

Jeffrey wasn't much more than sixteen when he started dating Liz, so I wasn't concerned about the seriousness of their relationship. I figured he was just some gawky kid scratching the itch of puppy love. Most every night he was sprawled out on our living room floor, and I watched how he followed Elizabeth everywhere she went. He hung on to her like she was a blue ribbon show dog, but still I didn't worry.

I should have, because that was the time to set things straight. Once she came home with a diamond ring on her finger, it was too late to start voicing my concerns. That diamond was way too big for someone of his age to have afforded. I wondered where he got the money for it, but Claire warned me against asking.

All the signs were there, I simply didn't pay attention. It was my responsibility to take care of Elizabeth, and I didn't. I allowed her to marry someone I had serious misgivings about, giving them my blessing and a good part of the down payment on their house.

Now when Jeffrey should be helping Liz get through this, he wants to be rid of her. Jeffrey only cares for Jeffrey. That's how he is, how he's always been. I don't generally think ill of people, but Jeffrey, well...

If I had my way, I'd go at him with every ounce of strength I've got. But that's not what Elizabeth wants. I suppose, in time, Jeffrey will get what's coming to him. I sure as hell hope so.

December 1984

Three weeks before Christmas the weather took on a chill, holiday decorations sprang up, and the fragrance of fresh-cut pine trees wafted from every street corner and vacant lot. Elizabeth had fared well with her first treatment of the "wonder drug." No serious side effects, no unusual reactions. Doctor Sorenson claimed to be "optimistically hopeful," although it was too soon to know whether the tumor had stopped growing. On the first Friday of the month Elizabeth was to have her second treatment. If she tolerated that one as well as the first, she'd go home for Christmas—well, at least back to the McDermott house.

Thursday morning Claire instructed Charlie to stop on his way home and buy a tree. Claire wanted it fully decorated before the weekend.

"Make sure to get a big one," she said, "at least seven, maybe eight feet."

"Okay," Charlie nodded and hurried out.

Before he left the driveway, Claire bolted from the house. "And lights," she called out. "Get some extra lights." Charlie nodded, backed into the street, and pulled away.

For what was probably the twentieth time, Claire ran through her mental list of things to prepare for Elizabeth's homecoming. The bedroom was ready and waiting: redecorated with fresh paint, cheerful curtains, a peony comforter, a brand new twenty-one inch television with a large button easy-to-use remote, a bedside bell to summon people, and portrait-sized pictures of David and Kimberly on the dresser.

The Christmas presents waited to be put under the tree Charlie would buy. Weeks ago Claire scoured the stores and carried home an armload of gifts: nightgowns, a bathrobe, slippers, talcum powder, perfume, and nail polish. She'd wrapped everything and tagged it with Elizabeth's name.

By ten minutes after nine Claire was on her way to the hospital. Normally the drive took seventeen minutes but today, stuck behind a Buick that had rear-ended a garbage truck, it took twice as long. Claire sat drumming her fingers against the steering wheel, trying to figure out what the new jitteriness inside her chest was telling her. By all accounts she should be feeling good about things. Elizabeth seemed to be doing better, and she was coming home. So what, Claire wondered, would cause her to be jumpy as a cat in a thunderstorm?

She left the car on the second level of the parking garage and hurried to the hospital. Halfway there she remembered the magazine she'd brought for Elizabeth, laying on the back seat of the car. For a brief moment she considered turning back, but something made her feet move forward. Across the street, past the glass door entranceway, through the lobby, and into the elevator, all the while still thinking she should go back for the magazine.

Claire pushed the fourth floor button and waited. When the elevator doors opened she stepped into the hallway and walked by the nurses' station. Suddenly she saw a number of nurses rushing in and out of room 416. Claire broke into a run.

Elizabeth sat in the chair sobbing, her yellow nightgown torn and covered with cabbage-sized crimson stains. Even if Claire had mistaken the source of the stains on Liz's nightgown, she could not mistake the dry blood crusted on her daughter's face and arm. Nor could she miss the blood splattered across the floor and patterned with rubber-soled footprints. Cyndi, the nurse on duty, and four other people bustled about the room. One of them, a candy-striped aide, hurriedly tugged blood-stained sheets from the bed and tossed them to the floor.

"Oh, my God!" Claire shouted. She tromped across the sheets and knelt alongside Elizabeth. Cyndi was sponging streaks of blood from Liz's arm.

"What happened?" Claire asked.

"I'm sorry," Cyndi said apologetically. "Elizabeth got out of bed and fell."

"Wasn't anyone here to help her?"

"She didn't call for help."

"Or you just didn't hear!" Claire replied angrily. "Elizabeth understands her paralysis. She wouldn't try to get up by herself!"

Before Cyndi could explain, Elizabeth sobbed, "I did forget, Mom. I did." She began to tremble.

"It's my fault," Claire said. "I should have been here." She wiped away the tears on Liz's cheek. "Don't cry. Everything's okay now."

"No, it isn't," Elizabeth replied sadly. "Nothing's okay. Look at what I've become."

"Don't talk like that, Liz. Yes, you're sick, but you'll get better. And then—"

Elizabeth looked at Claire with the expression of a hurt child trying to understand. "Then what? Then I'll be able to remember I'm paralyzed?"

Claire wrapped both arms around Liz and held her close. At a time like this even a mother could only whisper words of comfort and offer hopeful promises.

After a long while Elizabeth's sobbing subsided, and she succumbed to weariness. Leaning heavily on Claire's arm, she climbed back into bed and before long was asleep.

"What really happened?" Claire asked.

"It happened just as Elizabeth said," Cyndi answered. "Her short-term memory comes and goes. She needed to use the bathroom and tried to get out of the bed. It was instinct. She probably didn't remember being paralyzed."

"If it was only a fall from the bed, then why was there so much blood?"

"Because of the blood thinner she's taking, even the smallest cut bleeds profusely."

"Why is she taking—"

"She needs it to prevent a second embolism." Cyndi shrugged. "It's unfortunate, but what helps one thing sometimes hurts another. When Elizabeth fell the IV was pulled from her arm, the vein punctured, and the injection site lacerated."

"All that blood from the IV coming out?"

"Yeah," Cyndi answered. "The IV wasn't just removed; it was ripped loose from her arm. Most of the blood Elizabeth lost came from the punctured vein. She was lucky we found her just a few minutes after she fell."

"If you hadn't come in right away…"

"She could have bled to death."

When she heard that, Claire decided Elizabeth would never be left alone again. What Liz couldn't remember, Claire would remember. When Liz couldn't call for help, Claire would. Never again, she vowed, would her daughter be without someone to lean on and a hand to hold.

Claire kept her word. That same day she had Elizabeth moved to a larger room with space for a reclining chair. All night, every night, Claire sat in that chair. Sometimes she slept; often she did not. If she did sleep, she kept one eye open and her ears perked for the slightest sound of movement. When it became necessary to return home for a quick shower and change of clothes, she hired Loretta, a private nurse, to sit in the chair. Even though she was gone for just a few short hours, thoughts of Elizabeth crowded her head and urged her to return.

When the yellow chrysanthemums died Claire decorated the window sill with a tiny Christmas tree, and she placed Elizabeth's gifts around it. On Christmas morning when people all over town opened presents she sat beside Elizabeth encouraging her to open one gift after another. On the last day of the year when the grandfather clock in their hallway at home chimed midnight, Claire didn't hear it. She drank bubbly ginger ale from a plastic glass as she and her daughter toasted each other.

"Here's hoping nineteen-eighty-five is a better year," Elizabeth said.

"Amen," Claire replied. "Amen."

Claire McDermott

I don't trust Cyndi. Don't ask me why, because I can't say. Sometimes you just sense people are up to no good. That's how I feel about Cyndi. Most of the nurses take time to chat with Liz— about the weather maybe, a television show, their kids, things like that—but not Cyndi. She walks in and out, all business. Never looks me square in the eye. She's like a scrub brush, all bristle and no bend.

It could be that I'm misjudging her. Maybe she's got her own problems. People like Cyndi tend to believe their problems are worse than anyone else's, so they're long on self-concern and short on sympathy.

Personally, I doubt anyone has it as tough as Elizabeth. All the joys of life have been taken from her, but she manages to smile. Cyndi ought to thank God she's up and walking around. All Elizabeth can do is lie in bed and pray this new drug therapy works.

Liz is braver than I'd thought possible. It kills me to watch her going through this. If I could change places with her, I'd do it in a heartbeat. Believe me, it's far worse to watch your child suffer than to bear the pain yourself.

Charlie doesn't say it all the time, but I know what he's thinking. I can practically see the thoughts pressing up against his forehead when he pretends to read *Business Week* and stares at the same page for hours. He struggles with saying what's on his mind, especially when he's talking to Liz. That's because he can't give her what she needs to get well.

Charlie's used to fixing things. Give him a problem that's fixable, and he'll get it done. But this is something he can't fix. So he hides inside himself to keep from facing the God-awful truth.

He has plenty to say about Jeffrey and, trust me, not one word of it is good. If Jeffrey's name pops up, Charlie spends an hour going over his umpteen shortcomings. Last week down on Main Street, Charlie saw the padlock and the sheriff's notice on the door of JT's store and came home happier than I've seen him in months. It's hard to imagine how he'd react if he knew what I know.

Jeffrey is having an affair. Despite what he thinks, Liz is still his wife. I've struggled with whether to say something and finally decided not to. If I told Liz or Charlie, what good would that do? Charlie couldn't possibly hate Jeffrey any more than he already does, and Elizabeth is too sick to care. On second thought, I guess she does care but she's too sick to do anything about it, so why torture her with the truth?

Last week was Valentine's Day, a day when husbands generally give their wife flowers and candy, but Jeffrey didn't even send Liz a card. You'd think he could muster up enough love to send a card! Or at least send one from the kids. He didn't. Liz watched the aides pass by with bouquets for other patients, but she never said a word about how disappointed she was. She didn't have to; I could see it in her face.

While she was napping, I called Melanie down at the Garden Patch and ordered a dozen pink roses sent to the hospital. Pink roses are Elizabeth's favorite. Put in a card, I told Melanie, one that reads "We miss our Mommy," and sign it "With lots of love from David, Kimberly, and Christian." I said Kimberly, not Kimmie, because that's what Jeffrey calls her, and I wanted Liz to think he was the one who sent the flowers.

The roses weren't delivered until almost dinnertime, but when the aide brought them in Liz beamed.

"That was sweet of JT, wasn't it, Mom?" she said.

"It certainly was," I answered, but that's not what I was thinking.

March 1985

In early March the weather turned unseasonably warm, and tiny green buds suddenly appeared on the branches of winter-ravaged trees. Claire put her parka in the closet and began wearing sweaters. For almost two weeks, every day was as warm and sunny as mid-May.

At the same time Elizabeth had a string of good days. Days when her memory was sharp and the brain-rattling headaches disappeared. She still had little ability to move her left side, but after only six treatments of the wonder drug Elizabeth looked and felt better than she had in months.

The previous month, two days after her third treatment, the CT scan indicated Elizabeth's tumor had stopped growing. The technician checked the film several times, then reported his finding. The tumor measured the same size as the previous week.

Doctor Sorenson raised a dubious eyebrow. "Repeat the scan."

He did. The second scan confirmed what he'd seen on the first.

"This could be a fluke," Doctor Sorenson told Elizabeth. "Let's see what happens next week."

They waited. Liz received another treatment and then another CT scan.

"Excellent, this is excellent," Doctor Sorenson mumbled, as she slid the latest film onto the light box. She turned to Elizabeth with a smile. "It looks like your tumor is starting to shrink."

She slid a second film alongside the first. "Right here." She pointed to the outside edge of the dark mass. "It's almost, but not quite, a millimeter smaller."

Elizabeth gave a lopsided smile from the right side of her face. "I knew it," she said. "I just knew it."

"There's definitely been improvement." Doctor Sorenson found it hard not to smile back. "But we still don't know if it's a long-term solution."

"I don't understand," Elizabeth said. "You can see it's working, my memory is better, the headaches are gone and—"

"Yes, and as we move ahead with the treatments, hopefully you'll continue to improve," the doctor said. "But right now we're looking at a millimeter of shrinkage. A millimeter is about one-twenty-fifth of an inch."

"It'll keep working, I just know it," Elizabeth answered. She happily leaned back into the pillow.

On that same morning, a morning so sunny and warm even a sweater wasn't necessary, Claire stopped at the Garden Patch and bought two purple hyacinths on the verge of blossoming, one for her kitchen window and the other for the hospital.

"Spring is officially here," she said, setting the hyacinth on Elizabeth's tray table.

"It's beautiful," Liz answered. "Too bad I won't be here to see it bloom." She feigned a look of sadness.

"What—what are you talking about?"

The alarm in her mother's voice made Elizabeth give up the charade. "Doctor Sorenson said I can go home Friday."

"Wonderful!" Claire shrieked, hugging her daughter without regard for the hyacinth crushed between them.

"I still have to come back for treatments," Elizabeth said. "Two days every other week."

"Two days, that's nothing! It'll be wonderful to have you home, where I can take care of you. We'll have a chance to do things together. And wait until you see your old room! It's completely redecorated. Lots of pink just like—"

The look on Elizabeth's face diffused Claire's explosion of happiness.

"The stairs!" Claire smacked her hand to her forehead. "Of *course* I know you can't go up and down stairs! What I meant is your *new* room! Daddy and I decided to turn that useless old living room into a guest suite."

"Mom—" Elizabeth twisted the right side of her face into an expression of doubt, but Claire continued.

"There's no sense discussing it, the decision has already been made. The living room is going to be a girl's dorm. There'll be a place for you and for me. That way I can sleep downstairs with you any time I want."

The "any time" sounded casual, but in truth Claire already knew she'd sleep in that room with Elizabeth the first night, the second night, and every night from then on. And on those nights when Elizabeth returned to the hospital for treatments, Claire would return to the recliner alongside Elizabeth's hospital bed.

Later that afternoon while Elizabeth napped, Claire called the Goodwill Thrift Shop.

"I've got a lovely living room set for you," she said. "Sofa, chairs, tables, lamps, everything, but it has to be picked up tomorrow morning."

"That's not possible," the volunteer answered. "Our pick-up schedule is set weeks in advance."

"It has to be tomorrow," Claire stated firmly. "If you don't want it, just say so and I'll give it to the Salvation Army."

It took several minutes of negotiation before the volunteer finally agreed to have their truck there the following morning. Still determined to have the last word, he added, "In the future, call earlier."

Next Claire called a medical supply house and made arrangements for rental of a hospital bed, a walker, and a wheelchair.

"Make certain," she added, "it's one of those portable wheelchairs that will fit in the trunk of a car."

Her third call was to George Gardener, a handyman skilled at everything imaginable.

"I need the living room painted and some bedroom furniture moved down from upstairs," she said. "Can you do it tomorrow?"

"Not tomorrow," he answered.

"It has to be tomorrow."

"Can't. You gotta get somebody else."

"I don't have anybody else. Please, George," she begged. "Liz can't climb the stairs, and we're bringing her home from the hospital on Friday. We're turning the living room into a downstairs bedroom, and it's *got* to be ready."

"I still can't do it tomorrow." He paused a moment. "It's for Liz, huh?"

George had known Liz for almost twenty years—ever since, as a freckled-faced kid, she'd knocked on people's doors asking if they'd buy a box of Girl Scout cookies.

"Okay," he conceded. "I'll start tomorrow evening and finish up the morning after."

When Elizabeth awoke, Claire sat in the recliner smiling with satisfaction.

"I've got a number of things to take care of at home," she said. "I probably won't be here tomorrow and most of Thursday, but I'll get Loretta to spend both days with you."

"That's not necessary," Elizabeth said. "I don't need a nurse looking after me every minute of the day."

"Maybe not," Claire answered. "But Loretta has two kids going to summer camp, and she needs the money."

Loretta arrived bright and early Wednesday morning. "Be sure to take good care of my little girl," Claire said, happily dashing out and disappearing down the hospital corridor.

81

By the time Elizabeth arrived home on Friday afternoon, the McDermott living room had been transformed into a larger version of her bedroom. The walls blushed with a rosy hue, and a gossamer cascade of curtains replaced the damask draperies. Gone also were the sofa and overstuffed chairs, the bookcase, and a clutter of end tables. In their place was an arrangement of familiar furniture— gracefully carved oak nightstands, a dresser with an oval mirror, a tall chest with stacking shelves, and drawers enough for everything.

Elizabeth had grown up with this furniture, and it held memories of happier times. In the center of the room sat the hospital bed, its practicality disguised by the peony-covered comforter and a cluster of throw pillows. Discretely pushed against the far wall was the small day bed for Claire.

Leaning into the rented walker, Elizabeth looked around the room from one thing to another—Girl Scout awards hanging on the wall, the giant-sized television, the bouquet of flowers on the night stand, pictures of her children on the dresser. "Oh, Mom," she sniffed tearfully, "it's beautiful!"

Because his daughter was returning home, Charles telephoned the bank and said he wouldn't be coming to work. It had been a long while since he'd spent time with Liz, since he'd sat beside her and talked without awkwardness. In hospitals there seemed so little to say, shallow little courtesies, the kind that left an aftertaste in his mouth. After hello and how-are-you, all he ever did was fumble with his keys.

He waited until Liz slipped into her brand new cotton nightgown, then helped her into the bed. "How about I read to you? Would you like that?"

Elizabeth nodded.

"*Catcher in the Rye*? How's that sound?"

She nodded again and allowed a happy but tired smile to settle on her face. Her father could have read anything—an encyclopedia, a dictionary, the telephone book. She just wanted the loving sound of his voice.

Before Charles turned the third page Elizabeth was sound asleep. He closed the book and tiptoed from the room.

Claire had to do something she didn't want. Charlie would staunchly oppose it, but she had to do it nonetheless.

"Can you stay here and keep an eye on Elizabeth?" she asked as Charlie settled into reading the latest copy of *Business Week*.

He looked up and smiled.

Claire shrugged on a brown sweater, dug the car keys from her purse, and descended the steps leading to the basement and garage. She made her way toward the back of the basement and the furthermost area to Charlie's workshop. For several minutes Claire looked around; then she picked up a large sledgehammer, stashed it in the back seat of the car, and slid behind the wheel.

As Claire drove she thought about the last words she'd heard from Jeffrey. "I want out," he'd said. "You take care of her!" Claire had tried any number of times to speak to him since, but he refused to answer the telephone and the doorbell. She'd seen cars in the garage and people moving behind the drawn shades, but not once had he acknowledged her. Today he would have to.

This was not a snap decision; the thought had rumbled through Claire's mind for days. She considered discussing it with Charlie but decided against it. He would have stopped her. In fact, she would have stopped herself if she had an alternative. But she didn't. Not when JT refused to talk.

Claire reasoned Jeffrey deserved whatever he got. *What kind of man walks away from a wife who's sick? Only the lowest of the low!* The anger swelled in Claire like rising dough, the thoughts coming so rapidly they pillowed over one another. It was time somebody stood up for Elizabeth.

"Enough is enough," she grumbled. Jeffrey would no longer prevent Elizabeth from seeing her children. She gave birth to those kids, and she had every right to see them!

Claire was seething by the time she turned into Jeffrey's driveway. A light glowed upstairs and shadows of people moved. She climbed from her car, slammed the door, stomped around to the side of the house, and peered through the garage window. The red Nissan stood alongside JT's Chrysler.

"Enough!" she yelled, then stormed back to the front door and jabbed the bell.

Whispers came from inside, then silence. Claire pressed the bell a second time.

"Jeffrey Caruthers, you'd better answer this door!" she screamed. "If you don't open it right now, I'll knock it down!" She continued to ring the bell for several minutes then stopped, stomped to the car, and returned with the sledgehammer.

At first Claire thought brandishing it would be enough. But her anger slipped out of control, and she found herself attacking the door. The heavy sledgehammer took considerable effort to lift and swing. Once Claire got in motion it came crashing against the brass knocker, tearing it and several chips of paint loose from the door. Seconds later, Jeffrey yanked open the door and faced her with a menacing glare.

"You do that again," he screamed, "and I'll call the police!"

"Apparently it's the only way to get your attention," Claire answered. "We have things to discuss. Let's go inside and talk."

"You're not coming in my house!"

"It's not your house! Half of it belongs to Liz!"

"Well, she's not here, and when she's not here it's *my* house!"

Claire reminded herself this was not why she had come. "Forget about who owns the damn house," she said. "Let's not stand out here and air our dirty laundry in front of your neighbors."

"I don't give a shit. Air what you wanna air! Just get outta here and leave me alone!" JT began to close the door, but Claire wedged herself between the door and the jamb.

"Get out!" he shouted and pushed harder.

"No," she answered, holding firm although the door dug into her thigh. "I came to ask about some things, and I'm not going to leave until you listen."

"Then you'll go?"

"Yes," Claire answered, maintaining her hold on the doorway.

"Go ahead," JT said, easing off the door but still standing firm.

"I need to get Elizabeth's things. Now that she's home from the hospital, she wants her clothes and jewelry, photo albums, personal stuff. It means a lot to her—"

"Home from the hospital?" JT repeated.

"Yes," Claire answered.

"Elizabeth's okay now?"

"Not one hundred percent," Claire said, relaxing her guard. "Apparently this new treatment is working, and Liz's feeling much better. She's had such a positive reaction that Doctor Sorenson said she could come home and—"

"But she's still dying, right?"

"Everybody's gonna die sometime—"

"But Liz is dying right now!" he said angrily. "Are you people blind or stupid? Do you really think pumping her full of these crapshoot drugs is gonna change things? It's not! All it does it prolong my agony!"

"*Your* agony?" Claire snorted. "*Your* agony?"

JT began to exert pressure on the door again, but Claire held her ground. "I'm not leaving until I get what I came for!"

Again he eased the pushing. "Okay, you can have the lousy clothes. I'll send them over when I can. What else?"

"You have to let the kids come visit Liz."

"I'd rather burn in hell," JT sneered. "There's no way she's seeing the kids! They're finally getting used to her being gone. You think I'm gonna let them get attached to her all over again? No way! She's dying, accept it! Get on with your life! That's what me and the kids are trying to do!"

85

"They're not just your kids," Claire argued. "Liz gave birth to those kids, she's their mother, she deserves—"

"She deserves to die for doing this to us!" JT screamed and gave Claire a violent shove, sending her tumbling from the doorstep.

Before she could gather herself from the ground, he slammed and bolted the door.

Claire knew she'd get nothing more from JT. She could take the sledgehammer and pound on the door until it was a pile of splinters, but Jeffrey still would not answer. She returned to her car and sat there watching until the lights turned off and she saw no further sign of life inside the house. Then she backed her car out of the driveway and went home.

Later that night Claire told Charlie, "I stopped by to see Jeffrey."

"Oh," Charles answered, waiting for bad news.

"I told him Liz would like to have her clothes and jewelry and personal stuff now that she's home from the hospital. He said okay. He'll bring them over."

"He agreed?" Charles gave a sigh of relief. "Good. Maybe he'll come around. One step at a time, Claire, that's all we can hope for. One step at a time."

She struggled with whether to tell Charlie what JT had said about not allowing Liz to see the kids, but in the end decided against it. Jeffrey had agreed to bring the things Liz needed and there was always a chance he would change his mind about the kids, especially after he saw how well she was doing.

Although Elizabeth's left side remained paralyzed, she began to take interest in things she'd ignored for months. She slept less, listened to radio talk shows, and read—books, magazines, even the daily newspaper's advertising inserts. Each night she'd cream her face with moisturizer and in the morning apply lipstick as pink as the peonies on her bedspread. She hadn't done these things in the hospital. Her smile returned, rosy as the glow of the walls in her new bedroom.

Claire told her daughter Jeffrey would bring her clothes, and Elizabeth tried calling on the pretext of thanking him. He never answered. Instead of giving way to depression, Elizabeth began telephoning friends she'd not spoken with for months and asking if they'd come for a visit.

After just one week at home, she said, "Nancy's coming over this afternoon. I hope you don't mind."

"Mind?" Claire smiled. "Why, I'm delighted."

That afternoon when Claire heard the ripple of Liz's laughter, she began to believe in the impossible. Somehow, some way, the tumor's size would continue to decrease. She imagined it shrinking, shriveling to the size of a pea, and then disappearing altogether. Claire still heard the far-off echo of Doctor Sorenson's warning, "Not a cure," but it disappeared beneath the sound of her daughter's laughter.

The Following Month

For the first ten days of April Westfield awoke to an abundance of bright sunshine, each morning more glorious than the previous one. Then on the eleventh day, a Saturday, it began to rain. It started before dawn and grew heavier as darkness puddled into a watery gray morning.

Claire heard the rain pinging against the gutters and sensed this would be a bad day. Damp weather always brought a flare-up of the arthritis in her back, but she had the premonition of something far more troublesome waiting to happen. For a long while she lay there listening to the rain and trying to convince herself she was being foolish. Suddenly a loud crash splintered her thoughts.

She jumped from her bed shouting, "What happened? What—" But before an answer came Claire saw the puddles of water and shattered glass strewn across the floor.

Elizabeth was already becoming teary.

"I'm sorry," she sniffed. "I was trying to pick up that glass of water, but something's happened to my hand!"

"Don't cry," Claire said, moving across the floor without regard for the shards of glass. "It was an accident; accidents happen."

"But I don't understand," Liz said, sobbing. "What's happened to me?"

After making an obvious effort to lift her left arm, she finally reached across with her right hand and lifted the useless arm.

"Look at this!" she screamed. "I can't even move my arm!"

Suddenly Claire realized Liz had no memory of her paralysis. She wrapped her arms around her daughter and gently explained,

"You're sick, sweetheart. There's a tumor pressing against the side of your brain, and it causes this type of temporary paralysis." Claire weighed each word carefully so she could explain without discouraging Liz.

"Actually, the treatments you're taking have helped a lot. Why, in no time you'll probably be back to your old self."

Elizabeth looked at her mother, saying nothing.

"Do you remember the chemotherapy treatments?" Claire asked.

Still wearing a blank expression, Elizabeth shook her head side to side.

"Do you remember the hospital? Or Doctor Sorenson?"

"Oh." A flicker of recognition suddenly registered. "Yes," she said moments later, "of course I remember."

Claire smiled. "See, you're doing much better. You're not expected to remember every single thing, that's why—"

"But how could I possibly have forgotten something as important as this?"

"Doctor Sorenson told us these temporary memory lapses are to be expected. Once you're better, they'll stop."

"I've done this before?"

"Only a few times. Never for more than a minute or so."

Liz hesitated a moment, then brought her right hand to her face and covered her eyes.

"Oh, my God," she moaned. "Now I remember. I remember it all."

"Well, then, you know this is no time for feeling down," Claire said. "You've made good progress, but you can't expect to be totally self-sufficient—that's why you've got this little bell alongside your bed. Jingle it, and I'll help with whatever you want."

"What I want," Liz said, a stifled sob in her breath, "is to be free of this horrible thing. I want to do things for myself, get my own glass of water, stand without someone to hold me, walk through my own front door, pick up my babies, and hug them. I want to clean house and do laundry—"

A well of heartache and frustration broke and poured itself out in a cascade of tears.

"Don't cry, honey," Claire whispered, gently rubbing the back of her daughter's quivering shoulders. "Please don't cry. We'll get through this together. Everything will work out. Give it time, Liz. Give it time."

She wrapped her arms around Liz and held her close until the sound of sobbing disappeared beneath the rat-tat-tat of rain against the window. After a long while, Claire helped Liz into her bathrobe then into the wheelchair. On good days Elizabeth thumped from room to room using her walker. But on bad such as this, she slumped into the wheelchair and allowed herself to be pushed from one place to the next.

By early afternoon the rain had become a drizzle with an occasional splotch of sun pushing through. In the early afternoon Liz gave in to a nap. Claire sat beside her trying to focus on a magazine, hoping she'd already seen the worst of this day but remembering that misfortunes generally came in sets of three. First there was the rain, then Liz's accident. What next, Claire wondered?

A little while later she heard noises outside: the rumble of an engine, the sound of men yelling. She left Elizabeth napping and stepped outside. A black pickup truck stood in the driveway, older perhaps than Claire and certainly in worse condition.

"Get a move on!" the driver yelled to the man standing in the truck's flat bed. "Toss 'em out."

"They're gonna get wet."

"Just do it!" the driver commanded. "We don't get paid for dry, we get paid for delivering!"

"Wait a minute!" Claire shouted as she ran toward the truck. "I think you're making a mistake. We're not expecting any—"

By then the man in the flat bed had heaved two large black garbage bags onto the driveway and had a third in his hand.

"Your name McDermott?" the driver asked.

"Yes," Claire answered. "But—"

"Then we got the right house," he answered. "I told JT, twenty bucks if we dump the stuff in the driveway. We don't carry it inside for no twenty bucks!"

Dumfounded, Claire stammered, "What's Jeffrey got to do—"

But by then the truck had already backed away, leaving behind five soggy garbage bags in the driveway.

Bewildered by the situation, Claire opened the first bag: Elizabeth's clothes. Had she not recognized the pink suede suit her daughter wore Easter before last, Claire would have mistaken it as laundry. Coats, suits, dresses, shoes, underwear—none of it sorted, folded, or stacked, everything damp and crumpled. Clothes Liz had been meticulous about now looked like a bunch of rags set aside for dusting furniture or polishing the car. All five bags were the same, each worse than the one before. The injustice of it suddenly overwhelmed Claire.

"How could he?" she cried and burst into tears.

After she'd cried for nearly twenty minutes, Claire thought of Liz. Determined that her daughter should never learn of the callous disregard Jeffrey had shown, Claire hauled the five bags into the garage. From the upstairs bedroom she gathered an armful of hangers and a hairdryer. She returned to the garage and began to sort through the bags. Piece by piece, she shook loose the wrinkles and fanned the hairdryer back and forth until each garment appeared to have been dry cleaned. She hung the slacks, skirts, suits, and dresses on hangers and put the blouses, nightgowns, pajamas, and underwear in baskets. Claire expected to come across Liz's jewelry and treasured photo albums beneath the other things, but they were not in the first, second, third, or fourth bags.

The fifth bag contained mostly shoes that she sorted into pairs, setting aside three shoes that had no mates. Once she'd completed the task she looked around, wondering if she'd overlooked something. She gave each bag a vigorous shake, then checked inside every purse. Nothing. Jeffrey had sent clothes. Only clothes.

No photo albums, no jewelry, no fur coats, no camera, not a single item of monetary value. He'd sent only what he wanted to get rid of.

With a heavy heart Claire carried the things into the house and arranged each in their proper place. She put the folded things in the bureau, dresses and such hung in the closet, and beneath the hanging clothes lined up rows of pumps and sandals like colorful soldiers on parade. With everything in place, Claire sat down to wait for the tinkle of Elizabeth's bell.

When Elizabeth awoke, Claire informed her that her clothes had been delivered.

"Now you have no reason to lazy around in that bathrobe," she said cheerily.

Elizabeth's eyes brightened ever so slightly. "JT was here?"

"No, he had a courier service bring the things. Jeffrey probably would have come himself, but maybe he's working."

"Yeah, maybe," Elizabeth answered with little conviction.

In an effort to redirect the discussion, Claire flung open the closet door. "Look at these lovely outfits! This suit was always my favorite. You look so beautiful in—"

"Mother," Liz interrupted, "that suit is a size six. It wouldn't fit me anymore. Not since I've gained all this—"

"Then it's time for some new clothes," Claire said, ignoring the look of protest on Liz's face. "Every woman needs clothes that fit, clothes she feels comfortable in. If you feel up to it, we'll go shopping tomorrow. Tuesday's a good day. The mall is never crowded on Tuesdays. I'll put your wheelchair in the car, and when we're finished shopping we can have lunch at that cute little—"

Liz closed her eyes and leaned back into the pillow.

"What's wrong?" Claire asked.

"Nothing," Elizabeth answered. But tears rimmed her eyes. "What about my wedding ring? Did JT send my wedding ring? Or my engagement ring? The Rolex he gave me for our first anniversary? Did he send any of my jewelry? My picture albums? Did he say when he'd bring the kids over?"

"Not yet," Claire answered. "But he'll most likely—"

"No, he won't," Liz said in a brittle voice. "He'll never bring the children to visit. And he won't send any of those things. You know it, and I know it. We're only fooling ourselves."

"Not necessarily," Claire replied. "We don't know—"

"I know." Liz opened her eyes, and the truth hidden behind them became painfully obvious. Somehow she'd known all along. "He sold everything I owned and is keeping me from ever seeing my kids again as payback for what I've put him through."

"But how do you know that? What did you put him through?"

"JT claims it's my fault Daddy has refused to lend him any more money. He's convinced it's on account of the hospital bills. You know, Mom, JT actually hates our whole family. He said we're to blame for all his problems and we're gonna pay."

"What did he mean?" Claire asked. "Pay how?"

"JT came back to the hospital that night last November. At first I figured he came back to apologize. But he just stood there for a while. Finally he slammed some papers from the bank down on my tray and said he was gonna lose the store if I didn't sign for a second mortgage on the house."

"Did you?"

"No," Elizabeth answered wistfully. "I started to. I had the pen in my hand, but in the end, I didn't. I thought if I helped JT get the money he needed, he'd love me again. I picked up the pen and was ready to start signing when I suddenly remembered the house wasn't really mine to give. It belongs to our family, our children. Deep down, I knew it was foolhardy to let JT take chances with it. As soon as those loan payments became problematic, he'd dump the house just like he's dumped everything else, including me."

"What did he say when you wouldn't sign?"

"He was really mad, the maddest I think I've ever seen him. He said if I wasn't willing to help him get the money, he'd figure a way to get it, and it was gonna be a way I wasn't any too fond of. And I know that meant he would keep the kids from visiting. He knows that's one way to get back at all of us."

"He can't prevent you from seeing those kids. You're their mother."

"But what can I do, fight Jeffrey?"

"That's exactly what you can do! If you really want to see your kids, you've got to be willing to fight for them."

Elizabeth rolled her eyes. "I can't even get out of bed by myself. How am I supposed to take on someone determined as Jeffrey?"

"Be more determined than he is," Claire answered. "If you love those kids, demand to see them! Take Jeffrey to court and force him to bring them over here."

"Do you think I could?"

"Yes, I do. Daddy and I will help. You're not in this alone."

They talked for a long while afterward. They shared secrets they'd kept, secrets that had been too painful to reveal.

"I wanted to spare you the heartache," Claire said.

Liz laughed. "And I didn't want to worry you."

They both agreed if Liz would ever see the kids, something had to be done and right away.

"If we take Jeffrey to court, he'll be very hostile. Can you deal with that?"

"I'll do what I have to do," Elizabeth answered. "Not because I've come to hate Jeffrey, but because I love my children more."

Without thinking she smoothed the hem of the sheet with the pinkie finger of her left hand

.

Claire McDermott

Jeffrey Caruthers is the most contemptible person I've ever come across. It may seem strange that I'd say that about someone I once considered a son, but there's no other way to describe a man who takes such obvious pleasure in doing hateful things. For him to send Liz's clothes stuffed into garbage bags as he did was downright despicable. I know he was getting back at me. You say something Jeffrey doesn't like, and he'll look daggers through you. Once you cross him, you can be sure he'll get even.

I know Jeffrey has a grudge against Charlie because of the money. That is what it is, but he has no reason to act hateful with me and Liz. Okay, me maybe, because of my taking a sledgehammer to his door, but Liz? Most men pray for a wife like her. She's smart, beautiful, and devoted. Jeffrey's none of those things. I never even understood what Liz saw in him, but after all that's happened she still loves him.

With the meanness in Jeffrey there's no telling what he'll do. Taking Liz's babies from her is way beyond having a lack of love. It's a cruelty that's nearly impossible to measure. Any mother understands that; how can she not? A mother would sooner give up her right arm than one of her babies. I know, because that's how I feel about Elizabeth.

Long before Liz was born, I made plans for all the things she might do. I dreamt about her first day of school, her recitals, her graduation, her wedding day, and even the babies she would someday have—all this before I even held her in my arms. So is it any wonder that Liz should feel the same about her babies?

The worst part of any day is when Liz starts thinking about how much she misses the children. One minute she'll be laughing about something the kids have said or done, then all of a sudden she'll sink into an unmistakable gloominess. If I ask what's wrong, she'll say nothing. She pretends nothing is wrong, and I pretend to believe her. I suppose it's a way to get through the day without both of us falling apart.

Even though I try to stay strong and positive-minded for Liz, there are days I feel I'm losing the battle. I don't talk about those times, just as I don't mention the ugly things Jeffrey says and does. I know I promised to be more forthcoming with the truth, but what good would it do for Liz? She already has more than enough to contend with.

I keep thinking back to the men who dumped those bags in our driveway. I wanted to chase down the truck and tell those men they'd burn in hell for the awful thing they did. Then I realized they were just the messengers. Jeffrey was the one responsible, and I couldn't do anything to get back at him. That's why I cried the way I did, because of the anger and frustration. I wasn't just crying about the clothes, I was crying over the hundreds of hurts Liz has suffered and, if I'm really honest, also about some of my own.

Until that day I had hope Jeffrey would change his mind about bringing the kids to visit. I thought maybe he'd come by with her clothes, see how well she's doing, and rethink everything. Now I know he'll never do it. Not unless he's forced to, which is why we're gonna need a lawyer.

Three days later

By the time Charles returned from his business trip, Claire was firmly entrenched in her decision to go after Jeffrey. For several months he'd doled out bits of hope, promising to bring the children and disappointing Elizabeth time after time. Now he no longer pretended. Claire knew unless they did something drastic, Liz would never again see her children.

Claire still hadn't mentioned the red car in Jeffrey's garage. Maybe he had a girlfriend; maybe not. It was possible the car belonged to a cleaning lady, a babysitter, or a buddy—possible maybe, but not probable. Something about the drawn shades and the figures moving about the bedroom said Jeffrey was having an affair. But his affair wasn't the real problem.

Claire simmered with things to tell Charlie, but after almost thirty years of marriage she'd learned not to pounce on him when he walked through the door so she said nothing except, "Hello, dear."

He stopped, kissed her cheek, then asked about Liz.

"Doing much better. She did have one forgetful episode this week, but only for a minute or two. What's more important is that I actually saw her move two fingers on her left hand. Not much, but a little bit. When I asked Liz to do it again, she couldn't but I think that was mostly because she was pressuring herself."

"That's good, right?" Charlie replied. "Isn't it an indication her paralysis is—"

"Not necessarily. I called Doctor Sorenson's office and told them Liz had some movement in those two fingers, but the nurse said that's not unusual. Apparently at some point the left side of the brain starts to compensate for the right's lack of function and starts sending movement commands. The nurse said it's not something you can force, it happens when it happens."

"But just the fact that it's happening, isn't that what's important? Anyway, has Jeffrey brought the kids to visit yet?"

Claire, busy breading a chicken cutlet, gave a cynical glance. "Of course not. But we'll get to that later."

Although no one mentioned Jeffrey at the dinner table, he was on everyone's mind. Claire knew what she had to say, but it had to wait until Elizabeth wasn't around. Liz knew firsthand the ugliness of her husband's behavior, but hearing it only deepened the wound.

Once she cleared the dinner table and helped Liz into bed, Claire approached Charlie.

"We need a lawyer," she said.

"A lawyer?" He peered across the top of the newspaper.

"Yes." Claire lowered herself into the chair facing his. "I went to see JT thinking I might convince him to be more reasonable. Liz calls and pleads to see the kids. He says okay, he'll bring them on Sunday. She waits all week, and when he doesn't come or call she spends the day crying. Now that she's doing better, I thought he'd at least let her see the kids."

"And?"

"He won't. It's worse than ever. Jeffrey said he'd sooner burn in hell than let any one of us see the kids. He pushed me down the steps and slammed the door in my face."

Charles set the newspaper aside. "Pushed you down the steps?" he repeated quizzically.

"Yes. He said he'd call the police if I came back again."

"Police? He has no cause to—"

"He said I was destroying his property."

"Destroying what property?"

"The front door. Not the whole door, just the brass knocker and a little bit of wood."

Charlie's face had a question all over it. "What did you—"

"I hit it with your sledgehammer, okay? I didn't plan to do it, it just happened. I took it with me. If Jeffrey had answered the door, I would never have done it. I just wanted to talk to him. I thought maybe we could—"

"Wait a minute. Let me get this straight." Charlie still looked bewildered. "You hit Jeffrey's door with the sledgehammer?"

"Yes, but just so he would open the door. When I saw that flashy red car in the garage and him moving around upstairs, I lost my temper."

"Why didn't you just ring the doorbell?"

"I did, for nearly twenty minutes. When he wouldn't answer, I hit the door with the sledgehammer. Only once," she added. "To show him I meant business."

"Once, twice, or ten times is unimportant," Charlie said. "It's still against the law."

"But if I didn't do it, he wouldn't have opened the door." Claire then proceeded to tell how she'd asked for Liz's personal belongings.

"JT said okay, but all he sent were her clothes bagged up like sacks of garbage and dumped in our driveway."

"He didn't send anything else?"

"No." Claire related Jeffrey's conversation with Liz in the hospital, told how he'd tried to get her to sign the house over, and the threat he'd ultimately made.

"He intends to make good on that threat, because in those bags there was not one thing of value. None of the fur coats, not Liz's engagement ring, not her Rolex, not one piece of jewelry, not even the leather luggage we bought for her."

"That's what this is about? You want to sue Jeffrey because of Liz's jewelry?"

"No, those things mean a lot to her, but they're not the issue. If Jeffrey's doing what he threatened, he's probably already sold the jewelry. We need a lawyer so we can force him to let Liz see the children."

"How can he not let her see the kids?" Charles asked angrily. "She's their mother. Jeffrey might decide he's not going to allow us to see the children, and we'd be helpless to do anything about it.

But for one parent to take children away from the other parent without a court order is illegal."

"Illegal or not, he's doing it."

Before she could say anything else, Charlie picked up the telephone and began to dial.

"Dudley," he said, addressing his long-time friend, "we've got a confrontational situation with Elizabeth's husband, and we need some legal help." Charlie explained how after delivering Christian and leaving the hospital, Liz had come back to live with him and Claire. "Now her husband refuses to allow the children to visit their mother."

"On what grounds?" Dudley asked.

"No grounds. He just ignores her requests to see the kids."

"Have either you or Claire approached him about this?"

Charles swallowed hard. "Claire has."

"And what was his response?"

"He said he'd sooner burn in hell than have the kids see Liz."

"Whew, that's quite a response," Dudley said. "Has he got any credible reason for feeling that way? Abuse, anything like that?"

"Good Lord, no! Liz is a wonderful mother. The kids adore her, but Jeffrey claims that seeing her would not be in their best interest."

"Why?"

"Because Elizabeth—" The remainder of the words stuck in Charlie's throat. He hesitated for a moment then continued, "—has a brain tumor that's terminal."

"Elizabeth?" Dudley gasped. "What? How?"

"They discovered a malignant growth last summer."

"But surely they can do something to—"

"No, they can't," Charles said. "The tumor is located on the hypothalamus, so it's inoperable."

After an uncomfortable moment of silence, Dudley stammered a string of sympathies. "I'll help you in every way I can," he said, "but family law is not my specialty."

"I'm aware of that," Charlie answered. "But you've known Liz for most of her life, and I can't think of anyone I'd sooner trust to look out for her best interest."

"That much, I can guarantee you." Dudley scheduled a meeting for Monday morning. "I'll move on this immediately and petition the judge for accelerated action. Can you give me some idea of how long Elizabeth's got?"

The question came at Charles like a thunderclap. For more than a year he'd struggled through the days, crowding his hours with lengthy business meetings and conferences, never daring to consider the future, never facing that there could be a last and final day of Liz's life. Elizabeth was seriously ill—okay, terminal. But terminal was not definite. It was vague, a shadow loitering on the far edge of the future, not something that forced a father to predict the remaining number of days in his daughter's life.

"Why would you ask such a question?" he stammered.

"I'm sorry," Dudley apologized. "I only ask because it would help if I could show the court our need for expediency."

"Oh." Charles again hesitated. It was impossible to guess, so he simply parroted Doctor Sorenson's words. "It could be a year, two years, maybe more. It depends."

"Great," Dudley said. "Great."

The following morning Charlie told Elizabeth they'd made an appointment with the lawyer.

"Dudley's confident we'll be able to force Jeffrey to let you see the children," he said.

"Wonderful," Elizabeth said wearily.

"Wasn't that what you wanted?"

"Yes, but…"

"Is there something you want to talk about?"

For a long while Elizabeth said nothing.

"It breaks my heart to think this is the only way I can get to see my children," she murmured. "It may not seem so now, but

Jeffrey and I were once very much in love. Now he wants no part of me—not my broken body, not even my heart. If we could create these beautiful children together, how is it possible that he can hate me as he does?"

Charles eased his arm around Elizabeth and gently drew her to his chest.

Speaking with a deep sadness Elizabeth said, "It's hard to accept that Jeffrey's grown so hard-hearted that a lawyer has to force him to let me see my babies. I never dreamed—"

"It's the things we think can never happen that hurt the most," Charlie whispered. He held his daughter close so she wouldn't see the tears in his eyes.

On Monday morning Claire's eyes popped open two hours before dawn, and she immediately began making a mental list of the things she'd tell Dudley Grimm. First of all, Jeffrey Caruthers was mean, selfish, and ill tempered. He was also unemployed and flaunting an underage mistress in front of his children. To Claire's way of thinking, any one of those things provided sufficient cause for a judge to award custody of the children to Liz. And it was common knowledge that the court almost always awarded custody of children to the mother, in which case she would assist Liz and happily care for all three children.

Kimberly, she reasoned, could go into Liz's old bedroom, David in the guestroom, and the sewing room could become a nursery for Christian. Naturally they'd need to redo those rooms, buy children's furniture, night lights, toy boxes, stuffed animals, and such. That wasn't a problem. To the list of necessities, Claire added a rocking chair and a baby monitor.

As she lay in bed waiting for daylight to creep across the horizon, Claire began to envision the smile that would brighten Liz's face when the children bounded into the room to kiss her good morning. Claire had no doubt that asking for full custody of the children was the right thing to do. Children belonged with their mother. They belonged with a family who would teach them to love, not a father who'd use them as a means of fulfilling his own vendetta. By the time they arrived at the law offices of Cooper, Fletcher, and Grimm, Claire felt better than she had in weeks.

"Good morning, Dudley," she sang out happily.

Dudley Grimm, a small dark-haired man with the expression of an undertaker, answered, "Good morning."

Charles nodded and followed them into the conference room.

They settled around the table and Dudley opened his writing tablet. "Let's start with an overview of everything that's been going on."

"The long and short of it," Charles answered, "is that Liz's husband refuses to allow the children to visit their mother."

"For how long?"

"It began shortly after Liz started chemotherapy treatments late last year. She saw the kids once in October, and after that Jeffrey stopped bringing the children to the hospital. In November he broke off all communication, even phone calls. Then last month he told Claire he'd rather burn in hell than allow anyone in our family to see the kids."

Dudley began writing. "Did he give any explanation for this behavior?"

"Jeffrey told Liz he thought it would be better for the kids if she didn't spend time with them. He claimed he was trying to wean the children so they wouldn't be so traumatized when she dies. That was last fall. Liz has probably seen the kids once or twice since then."

"You realize," Claire interjected, "that such an idea is ridiculous, especially since Liz is doing extremely well. A terminal diagnosis doesn't necessarily mean a person is at death's door. It simply means that whenever the person does die, it will probably be from that illness."

"Oh. And Elizabeth," he said, still scribbling notes. "Is she awake, coherent, able to converse with the children?"

"Of course," Charles said emphatically. "Liz occasionally has short memory lapses, but it's mostly insignificant, everyday things. When it happens, it only lasts a few minutes. She might not remember the name of a color or what to call a food, but she remembers everything about the kids. Even when she can't tell you what day of the week it is, she can tell you what Christian weighed when he was born and the name of Kimberly's favorite doll."

"Good," Dudley said without glancing up. "Very good. So am I correct in assuming what we're looking for here is a court-mandated schedule of parental visitations for Elizabeth?"

"Oh, Liz would like more than just visitation," Claire said. "What she wants is full custody of all three children."

For the first time, Dudley stopped writing and looked up. "Wants custody?"

Charlie turned to Claire, astonished. "Custody?" he repeated. "Liz never said—"

"She might not have said it in so many words," Claire countered. "But I know for certain it's what she intended."

"I don't understand," Dudley stammered. "If Elizabeth's condition is terminal, who's going to—"

"Me," Claire answered. "Our house has plenty of room, and I'm perfectly capable of taking care of Liz and the children."

"Even if that's true," Dudley said, "no court will award custody to—"

Harsh words did not come easily to Dudley Grimm so he hesitated, trying to find a tactful way to say what he had to say. When none came to mind, he reluctantly finished the statement. "A mother who's dying."

"Liz isn't dying," Claire replied sharply. "She's learning to live with her disability. Surely the court will understand that. If they have a concern about her ability to care for the children, then let them assign custody to us."

"Us?" Charlie echoed. "Why, we've never even discussed—"

"That won't happen anyway," Dudley said. "You're grandparents. Unfortunately, grandparents have no legal standing, except in rare instances where both parents are deceased, and there is no specific—"

"What about if the father is an unfit parent?" Claire asked.

"Unfit how?"

"He's mean, intolerant, selfish, has no job, has a girlfriend living with him—"

"Does he abuse the children in any way? Neglect their care? Leave them unattended?"

"I can't say that exactly."

"Then you have no case," Dudley said apologetically. "Without specific proof of such actions, the court automatically awards custody to the natural parent."

"Well, what about if we say—"

"Claire!" Charlie interrupted. "That's enough! Let's get on with what we came here to do, which, in case you've forgotten, is to get Liz visitation with the kids."

Dudley Grimm breathed a sigh of relief. "That, I think, is quite doable."

He asked a number of questions about Jeffrey: his home address, his last place of employment, any known childcare arrangements, and whether he had retained a lawyer to fight this action. Writing furiously again, Dudley asked about the children, the state of their health, and their previous relationship with their mother. Just before the meeting came to an end, he requested the name, address, and telephone number of Elizabeth's doctor.

Thus it Began

On the second Tuesday of May the Caruthers' doorbell chimed early in the morning, so early that JT was still in bed. Believing it to be Claire, he squeezed his eyes shut and tugged the blanket over his head. A few minutes later he heard the knock—a knock much too heavy for Claire, unless she'd come back with the sledgehammer. He bolted out of bed and flew down the stairs ready for a fight.

"I warned you—" he screamed as he yanked open the door.

"Jeffrey T. Caruthers?" the sheriff's deputy asked.

"Yes, but if this is about the store—"

The deputy handed him an envelope, politely said, "Have a nice day," and turned toward his car.

"Wait," JT cried out. "What's this?"

The deputy didn't bother looking back. He climbed into the patrol car, pulled out of the driveway, and disappeared down the street.

"What the—" JT looked at the envelope, addressed to him but with a return address of the Union County Courthouse. Still groggy and bewildered he stumbled back inside, flopped down on the sofa, and tore open the envelope.

At the top of the first page a line of bold black letters shot through him like bullets:

Motion to Compel Parental Visitation
Caruthers v Caruthers

"No way!" he screamed and slammed the paper down. The noise startled Christian who woke crying, which hardly concerned Jeffrey since he'd launched into a full-blown rage.

"This is Liz's doing!" he ranted. "Her and that crappy family of hers! Troublemakers, that's what they are, big-time troublemakers! Their life is miserable, so they think they're gonna make mine miserable too! Well, this time they ain't getting away with it!"

He angrily kicked over the coffee table and sent a stack of magazines flying. "If they want a fight, I'll give it to them! I'll make them wish they never heard of me! I'll—"

Suddenly JT noticed Kimberly on the stair clutching Ballerina Bear. "Daddy, are you mad at me?" she asked tearfully.

"Oh." Jeffrey saw the fear in his daughter's eyes, and shame overcame him. "No, sweetheart, Daddy's not mad at you. I just bumped into the coffee table and knocked it over."

"Were you yelling because it hurt?"

"Yes, Kimberly," he replied. "It hurts a lot."

He stood there for a few moments, saying nothing. Then he righted the table, picked up the magazines, and headed for Christian's room. After changing the baby's diaper, he dressed David and Kimberly and herded them downstairs for breakfast.

"There is no French toast," he patiently explained as he poured milk over two bowls of Captain Crunch and set them in front of the children. He scattered a handful of Cheerios on the highchair tray and began to spoon strained applesauce into Christian's mouth.

As Jeffrey performed each task his mind churned with thoughts of how he could get back at Elizabeth and her family.

Once the children were settled in front of the television, Jeffrey called Missus Ramirez. When she arrived, he went into the family room and locked the door.

Jeffrey's first call was to Harry Hornzy, a man who'd been arrested seven times and not once convicted. "I'm gonna need some legal help, so I thought of you."

Harry gave a raucous guffaw. "Yeah, well—"

"I hear tell your lawyer is pretty good at winning cases, so I figured—"

"He's good; he ain't cheap."

"Good is what I'm looking for. I'll pay what I gotta pay. I want a bloodthirsty shark—you know the type—somebody who'll chew my wife to pieces and spit out the remains."

"Walter's your guy. Walter Petrecca. You gotta tell him I sent you else he plays it straight and narrow, you get what I mean?"

"Yeah. He sounds like what I'm looking for."

Jeffrey's next call was to Walter Petrecca. "Harry Hornzy suggested I call. I've got a problem, and I need a lawyer."

"What kinda problem? Assault? Break and enter? Car jack—"

"No, no, nothing like that. It's a custody battle."

"Custody? That's a family dispute. I do criminal law."

"You gotta help me," JT said, desperation threading his voice. "My wife's using her family to bury me. I need somebody vicious enough to destroy the bitch."

"Oh," Petrecca said. "One of those. My ex, she's the same."

"Okay, so you know what I mean."

"Yeah. I feel for ya, but I still don't do family law. If you want, I'll give you the name of the lawyer who handled my divorce. It's a woman, but don't let that fool you. This one's a killer. My ex wanted the house plus one-hundred-thou alimony. Noreen whacked her down to ten."

That was enough to convince JT. He took Noreen Sarnoff's telephone number and called her next.

On Friday morning Jeffrey Caruthers met with Noreen, a six-foot-tall blonde with razor sharp features. He handed her the notice he'd received, along with a check for eight thousand dollars.

"I trust you can take care of this," he said.

She raised an eyebrow as if to question his doubt. "Isn't that what you're paying me for?"

They rehashed Jeffrey's reasons for not allowing the children to visit their mother. Noreen studied the Motion to Compel Visitation.

"Looks like this is going to Judge Brill," she said. "He's a softie. The probability is he'll be sympathetic to the dying mother."

"What kind of crap is that?" Jeffrey snapped. "Elizabeth's dying! She's got a brain tumor! That's one step away from being a vegetable. How can anybody have sympathy for a vegetable?"

"Hold on a minute. Are you saying your wife is incapable of recognizing or conversing with the children?"

JT shrugged. "She's probably not that bad."

Noreen again raised her eyebrow. "Okay, let's clarify this. Is there any actual medical proof your wife is incoherent, mentally incompetent, or violent enough to cause physical damage?"

He shook his head.

"Too bad," Noreen replied. "That would have given us a real edge."

JT smiled. Petrecca was right: she was a killer.

When Jeffrey left Noreen Sarnoff's office the corners of his mouth had turned up and he was whistling.

Two days later Noreen telephoned Jeffrey at home.

"I spoke to your wife's doctor," she said. "A Rebecca Sorenson. She acknowledged that Elizabeth's tumor has been diagnosed as terminal but also indicated that the chemotherapy treatment your wife is undergoing has resulted in a marked improvement. According to Sorenson Elizabeth still suffers from left-side paralysis and occasional memory lapses, but otherwise she's perfectly coherent and capable of restricted motion activities. In fact, she suggested that seeing the children would be extremely beneficial for Elizabeth."

"Of course she'd think that, she's being paid by—"

"Regardless," Noreen interrupted. "The bottom line is Doctor Sorenson can hurt, but not help, your case."

"So what do we do?"

"We find our own medical expert, someone who's more attuned to our way of thinking. And we have to do more than answer your wife's motion. We need to go back at her with an aggressive counter complaint."

"For what?"

"We'll file a motion requesting sole legal custody of all three children based on her limited life expectancy. That will give you the authority to make decisions concerning what is or isn't in the best interest of the children."

"Sole legal custody," JT repeated. "That's good, real good."

Five days later Claire McDermott stood at the front door of her house and signed for the registered letter sent from the family law division of the Union County Court. Even before she'd closed the door, Claire could sense bad news seeping through the paper. Registered letters were almost always bad news. Friendly mail waited in a mailbox until a person had time for it. Bad news was something Elizabeth could do without, Claire reasoned. She carried the envelope into the kitchen and slit it open. The document inside read:

Caruthers v Caruthers
Petition for Sole Legal Custody of Three Minor Children

"This is ridiculous," Claire grumbled. "He's already got custody!"

She slapped the paper down on the counter and walked into the dining room. For several minutes she stood there staring out the window, seeing nothing but the words: sole legal custody. Finally she turned back to the kitchen, picked up the paper, and began to read.

Apparently Jeffrey wasn't only seeking custody of the children, he was also asking the court to deny Elizabeth's request for visitation rights because it was not in the best interest of his children and would cause them undue emotional distress.

"*His* children," Claire huffed. "*His!* That's so JT, acting as if Liz had no part in the birth of those babies!"

For a good two minutes Claire stood there talking to herself, giving voice to her anger. Finally she picked up the telephone and called Charlie at his office. "You can't imagine what he's done now."

"What who's done?" Charlie replied.

Claire gave an audible huff. "You know who I mean. Jeffrey!"

"Oh." Charlie sighed.

"He's filed a petition asking for custody of the kids."

"Hasn't he already got custody?"

"He wants *sole* custody! He wants to deny Liz visitation rights!"

"That's ridiculous! No court is going to—"

"Maybe not," Claire interrupted. "But we can't take a chance that—"

"We're not going to," Charlie answered. "Call Dudley, and let him know what's going on. He'll handle it."

"Are you sure Dudley can—"

"Of course he can. He's a lawyer!"

Claire hung up the telephone wishing she felt more certain of Dudley Grimm's capabilities. He was such a mild-mannered man, so soft-spoken and small, so slender and only inches taller than Claire herself. She would have preferred someone with a booming voice and powerful girth, someone capable of striking fear into the opposition.

That evening Claire met Charlie when he came through the door. "Don't mention this to Liz," she whispered. "She doesn't know."

"Doesn't know?" Charles echoed. "Why?"

"I don't want to worry her right now. She's had a good day, so why spoil it?" Claire went back to preparing dinner.

Two days later Dudley Grimm telephoned Claire.

"Judge Brill called a conference with me and Jeffrey's lawyer," he said.

"Why?"

"My guess would be that his docket is overloaded. He's probably going to ask that we come to a mutually agreeable resolution out of court."

"The judge can conference all he wants, but I'll never give up Liz's right to see her children nor will I agree to Jeffrey having sole custody."

"Claire," Dudley said, "you don't get to make any of the decisions in this case. These actions concern only Elizabeth and Jeffrey. As far as the court is concerned, you and Charles are basically bystanders."

"Excuse me?" Claire's voice was riddled with indignation. "We are not simply off-the-street bystanders. We're the children's grandparents!"

"But as I explained, in the state of New Jersey grandparents have no legal standing in a custody battle. The only exception would be a case where both parents are either deceased or declared unfit to raise the children."

Claire sputtered a few more objections, but when she hung up the telephone she knew the time had come to tell Elizabeth.

Judge Brill didn't tolerate squabbling lawyers and frivolous actions, something he made perfectly clear before he'd settled into his seat.

"I see no reason why I should have a case such as this on my docket."

"Your Honor," Dudley Grimm said mildly. "My client is a dying woman who has asked for nothing more than a few personal mementos and access to her three children."

"Reasonable enough request," Judge Brill commented. He turned to Noreen Sarnoff. "Why does your client have a problem with that?"

"Well, Your Honor." Noreen sighed in the breathless way that caught men off guard. "The children in question are young and extremely impressionable. The father feels that seeing their mother die in front of them would cause extreme emotional trauma." She gave another sigh. "Then there's the issue of the grandparents—"

"The grandparents," Dudley cut in, "are responsible and upstanding parents who have stepped in to care for their terminally-ill daughter because her husband refused to do so. Understandably, they are concerned about the welfare of her children."

Judge Brill looked to Noreen.

"Not so, Your Honor," she said. "The grandmother exhibits a tendency toward violence. That became obvious when she attacked my client's house with a sledgehammer."

Judge Brill gave an impatient huff and rolled his eyes. "Is there any chance that these people can reach an out-of-court agreement through mediation?"

Both lawyers shook their heads.

"My client adamantly refuses to allow visitation," Sarnoff said.

Dudley Grimm added, "My client feels equally strong about her right to spend time with her children."

Seeing no hope of settlement, Judge Brill mandated a psychologist's examination of all parties involved as well as the attending physician's report on Elizabeth Caruthers' medical status.

"Let's find out exactly what we're dealing with here," he said. He rose and left the room.

A Summer of Madness

On the hottest day ever recorded, a day when most people did nothing but gulp down glasses of iced tea and wait for the weather to break, Claire and Charles McDermott trekked across an asphalt parking lot in Newark, New Jersey.

"I still don't see why the judge is making *us* talk to the psychologist," Claire grumbled. She fanned the sheet of directions in front of her face, but the small breeze it gave off hardly made a difference.

"You ought to get rid of that attitude before we go in here," Charlie suggested. "That's the sort of negativity the psychologist is going to be looking for."

"Whose side are you on?" Claire started fanning herself again.

"It's not a question of sides," Charlie replied. "Remember, we're not doing this for ourselves. We're doing it for Elizabeth."

"We shouldn't have to do it at all."

Doctor Belleau's office was on the third floor but because of the extreme heat the elevator, like most everything, had stopped working. After trudging up three flights of stairs, both Charles and Claire arrived at his office red-faced and soaked with perspiration.

"I'm sorry for the inconvenience," Doctor Belleau apologized, extending a cool, air-conditioned hand.

Despite the clamminess of her hand in his, Claire forced a smile.

"These things happen," Charles gasped, still red-faced and trying to catch his breath.

"And at the most inopportune time." Doctor Belleau laughed.

Although he had a pleasant enough smile, Claire thought the doctor seemed terribly young. He had the appearance of someone she'd expect to find jogging through the park, not delving into a person's innermost thoughts.

"Have you been in this business for long?" she asked, trying to sound friendly and not overly critical.

Doctor Belleau laughed again.

"Thirteen years. But I get that question often. I should be thankful for looking younger than my years, but in this profession a youthful appearance can be a detriment."

Claire smiled. It was going to be more difficult to dislike Doctor Belleau than she'd originally anticipated.

"What I'd like to do," he suggested, "is speak with each of you individually. Afterward we'll all sit down together." He led Claire back to his office, leaving Charles to wait in the reception room.

Once in his office, Doctor Belleau sat Claire in a high-backed leather chair and placed himself across from her. "Are you comfortable?" he asked.

She nodded.

"Okay then. I'm going to record our session. Why don't we start with you telling me a little bit about yourself?"

"Well, um," Claire stammered. She wasn't prepared for this— she'd figured on questions about Liz, about the children, even about Jeffrey, but she'd not anticipated telling her life story.

"There's not all that much to tell," she finally said. "I'm a wife and mother. I live for my family. Elizabeth, she's my only child, and I can't imagine what my life would have been like if someone had taken her from me the way Jeffrey has taken the children from Elizabeth."

"Are you angry with Jeffrey for keeping the children away from your daughter?"

"Yes, I'm angry. Wouldn't you be if someone took your kids?"

"Unfortunately, I don't have any children," he answered, which, as far as Claire was concerned, was not much of an answer. She began to feel less inclined to like the young Doctor Belleau.

"Why do you think Jeffrey wants to keep the children away from their mother?"

"Does it matter why? It's wrong!"

"Would you still feel it was wrong even if he were doing it for their good?"

"He's not! He's doing it for the good of himself. So, yes, it's wrong." Claire hesitated just long enough to gain control of her anger.

"No one has the right to take children away from their mother. Jeffrey is not just keeping them away from Liz. He's also keeping them away from me and their grandfather."

"How would you feel if Jeffrey agreed to allow the children to see their mother but not you?"

"That's ridiculous," Claire snapped. "I'm their grandma. Why would he do a thing like that?"

Doctor Belleau shrugged and waited for her to continue.

"Spite," she finally said. "Pure spite. Jeffrey is a mean-spirited person. He's the type who would do something hateful like that. Why else would you take little children away from a grandma who loves them?"

"Do you think Jeffrey feels spiteful toward you?"

"Yes."

"Why?"

"I don't know," Claire answered, "but he does. Maybe he realizes I'm onto him. Maybe he's worried I'll tell people about his chippie girlfriend."

"Would you?"

"No, but not because of him," she said. "I wouldn't do it because it would hurt Liz more than it would hurt him."

"If you had the chance to hurt Jeffrey without upsetting Liz, would you?"

Claire turned away and didn't answer.

"Okay then," Doctor Belleau finally said. "Let's talk about your grandchildren. Since they're so young and impressionable, do you think their mother's condition might upset them?"

"Christian is an infant. He wouldn't know the difference."

"What about the older children?"

"David and Kimberly have seen Liz sick before. She went through a rough time when she was carrying Christian, and she was sick quite often."

"More than morning sickness and headaches?"

"Yes. Sometimes she was bed-ridden for days on end."

"Who cared for the children then?"

"I did, of course," Claire said. "I'm their grandma."

"And now that Jeffrey has someone else taking care of the children, how does that make you feel?"

"How should it make me feel?" Claire said angrily. "I'm the grandmother! A mother should be there to care for her daughter's children, not locked out of the house like some stranger!"

"Have you tried to telephone the children?"

"Of course. Elizabeth and I have both tried, but Jeffrey doesn't answer the phone. If he does happen to answer, he says they're sleeping or playing outside. He makes up any excuse to keep us from talking to the kids."

"Have you considered that they might actually be sleeping?"

"They're not," Claire replied disdainfully.

Doctor Belleau continued to ask difficult questions, making Claire believe he was trying to trick her into saying things she had no intention of saying. Gradually her answers slipped into brief one word statements—yes, no, perhaps. Once that happened, Doctor Belleau suggested it was time for him to talk with Charles.

The doctor escorted Claire to the reception room. Claire planned to warn Charles of the doctor's trickiness, but there was no chance. Doctor Belleau waited while Charles replaced the magazine he'd been reading, and then the two of them disappeared down the hall together. After that Claire could only sit and worry as the minutes ticked by.

Eventually they called for her to join them. The moment she entered the room, Claire noticed Charlie's calm demeanor had given way to the gruffness she'd expect if he'd gotten a speeding ticket or had an exceptionally bad day at the office. Claire settled into the third leather chair and before she had time to cross her legs, Doctor Belleau turned on the tape recorder again.

"I understand that your daughter, Elizabeth, now resides at your home and you care for her, is that correct?"

"Yes," Claire answered. "She wanted to go back to her own house where she could be with her husband and her children, but Jeffrey wouldn't hear of it. A sick wife was supposedly too much for him to deal with."

"But isn't it true that Elizabeth isn't simply sick, she's dying?"

Charles angrily spoke up. "So are you. You're dying, I'm dying, we're all dying, every last one of us. It's only a matter of time."

"Yes, but wouldn't you say Elizabeth's death is imminent?"

"No one but God knows when someone will die. Life doesn't come with guarantees. In the blink of an eye you could be struck by a car, hit by lightning, shot by an intruder." Charles stared square into the doctor's face. "How imminent is your own death when you consider that these things can happen?"

"Isn't there a difference in that those are unexpected occurrences, whereas based on Elizabeth's medical condition, her death is expected?"

"Expected when? A year? Five years? Ten years? Nobody knows. Right now the growth of that tumor has stopped, and she's doing quite well. Maybe next week or next month some pharmaceutical company will announce a miracle drug that can get rid of the tumor altogether."

"Do you believe that will happen?" Doctor Belleau asked.

"Can you swear it won't?" Charles answered.

Doctor Belleau checked the time and waited to see if Charles would say something more, but he didn't.

"Well," the doctor finally said rising. "Our time is up, so let's leave it here."

Claire and Charles took one last gulp of cool air; then they walked back down the three flights of stairs, climbed into their sweltering car, and drove home.

"When do you think this weather will end?" Claire asked, fanning her face.

Charlie shrugged and cranked up the air conditioning to maximum. "Is that better?"

"A bit," she answered, although her face still felt flushed and her blouse soaked through with perspiration.

They talked about stopping for milk, paying the paperboy, and that evening's television programming, but neither of them said a word about Doctor Belleau's questions.

Two days later the telephone rang while Claire folded laundry in the basement, so Elizabeth answered it.

"Missus McDermott?" the caller inquired.

"No, this is her daughter," Liz said.

Doctor Belleau then identified himself and explained that he had actually hoped to speak to her.

"The court has requested that I interview all parties involved in your plea for visitation," he said. "I was hoping you'd have a few minutes. Of course, if you'd prefer to do this in person—"

"No, no," Elizabeth answered nervously. "This is fine."

They talked for several minutes, and then Doctor Belleau asked why Elizabeth thought her husband refused to let her see the children.

"Do you know I have a malignant brain tumor that's terminal?" she asked.

"Yes, I am aware of that."

"Well, that's why. He claims he wants to wean the children away from whatever attachment they have to me so they won't notice when I die."

"Not notice? Is that what you think?"

"No, that's what Jeffrey said."

"What about you, how do you feel?"

"I believe my sweet babies need every good memory of me that I can cram into their heads. Then when I'm gone, they'll be able to remember how much their mother loved them."

For several heartbeats Doctor Belleau said nothing. Finally he cleared his throat and asked if Elizabeth thought she was physically strong enough to hold the baby or care for the older children.

"I'd have to sit to hold Christian," she answered. "Mom and Dad are here to help me, so I don't think that's a problem. David and Kimberly adore Mom, and they'd be no trouble at all."

"Your mother seems quite stressed," he said. "Do you think she could handle taking care of you and the children at the same time?"

"You don't know Mom," Elizabeth replied laughingly. "She could run a hospital and a nursery school at the same time if she had a mind to."

"Ah, yes," Doctor Belleau said, chuckling. "I know what you mean. My mother raised five sons, and she's the same—tough as nails but soft as an old shoe."

Elizabeth laughed again. "You've got it."

They talked for a few minutes more, not about Jeffrey or the plea for visitation, but about Liz's love for her children and how she missed them. Eventually the doctor thanked her for her time and hung up.

When Claire came from the basement carrying her basket of freshly-folded sheets and towels, she asked, "Was that the telephone?"

"Yes," Liz answered, "but it was for me."

Claire smiled and continued upstairs with her basket.

Elizabeth Caruthers

This hateful thing inside my head is tearing my family apart, piece by painful piece. Mother and Dad think I don't see this, but I do. In the evening they sit across from each other for hours without speaking. That's not like either of them. It used to be that Mom would chatter endlessly—telling Dad about all the things he needed to repair, gossiping about a neighbor, making plans for the weekend. Now she's got nothing to say, because of me. She and Daddy think about me all the time but it's too painful to discuss, so they sit there and say nothing.

The irony is if you measured my tumor it would be small enough to hold in your hand, like a bird's egg or crabapple maybe. But inside your head it becomes enormous, bigger than anything you could ever imagine. It takes over your life and spreads itself into the center of everything. People start edging their way around it, the way they would an elephant standing in the middle of the room. We all know it's there, but given its size and capacity for destruction we pretend not to notice. We don't even speak of it because calling attention to it might unleash its fury.

Dad's worse than Mom in some ways. He's convinced himself there's a cure right around the corner—a new drug or some miraculous regimen of chemotherapy they're hiding from us. Me, I know better. I know if such a thing existed, Doctor Sorenson would have given it to me.

I feel sorry enough for myself, but I feel even sorrier for Mom. I'm her whole life. She's been like that as far back as I can remember. Most moms shoo their kids out to play, but not my mom. If I asked to make cookies, she'd stop whatever she was doing just so we could make cookies together. I can't remember a single instance when she was too busy to spend time with me or my kids. So I keep asking myself, what is she gonna do with all that empty time when I'm gone? Hopefully, she'll be able to spend time with the kids. My babies are the only part of me she'll have left.

I know JT believes seeing me will upset the children, but I can't understand why he wants to keep them away from Mom. She's never done anything except love and care for them. But, no, Jeffrey would rather pay Missus Ramirez to watch them and then complain about how he has no money.

I suppose he can't comprehend the meaning of a close family. He distrusts everybody and thinks if somebody does something good, they're after something. His parents are that way too. His mom reminds me of an icy statue. She's totally aloof and has no use whatsoever for children of any size. I guess that's why he's the way he is.

I know I should feel a ton of hatred for Jeffrey, and plenty of times I do. Other times, I actually feel sorry for him. You'd think he has nothing but meanness inside of him. But truthfully, I think that meanness is just his way of covering up the hurt. With all the time I spend lying in bed, I've given this a lot of thought.

It's impossible for me to forget how close Jeffrey and I once were and how many thousands of times he's said how much he loved me. That's why I find it hard to believe his heart is as callused as he pretends. I think he's afraid to face the fact that I'm dying, so he tries to convince himself that he doesn't care. I pray Jeffrey comes to his senses while I'm still alive because if he lets this drag on until after I die, the guilt of it will haunt him for the rest of his life.

The sad truth is that I am going to die. I know it. I'm not giving up, I'm simply being realistic. I can feel this thing pressing against the inside of my brain again, and over the past two weeks the headaches have started coming back. I haven't told anyone yet, not even Mother. Before I tell her I want to talk to Doctor Sorenson and see what she has to say about it. She's the one person who will tell me the truth, even if it isn't what I want to hear. I believe she's fighting this thing almost as hard as I am.

For several months I was getting better; it felt almost like the tumor was gone. I'm still taking the chemotherapy treatments, but something has changed. I worry that one of these days I might slide into an awful oblivion and never come back. What if I never have a chance to say goodbye to the people I love? That thought scares me the most.

Every night I ask God to please let me spend some time with my babies before I lose what's left of my mind. I want to be able to tell each of them how very special they are and how much I love them. Tomorrow I think I'll write each of them a long letter that they can keep after I'm gone—but of course, a letter is nowhere near as sweet as whispering those things in your child's ear.

Several Weeks Later

Judge Brill began sorting through his mail, a stack of documents that would have been half the size were it not for frivolous actions and over-zealous lawyers—lawyers who thought delaying tactics could enable their clients to get away with almost anything. After two hours into the task he came across the envelope from Doctor Peter Belleau.

"About time," the judge grumbled. He slit the envelope open and thumbed through the contents.

"Elizabeth Caruthers appears extremely well-adjusted given the prevailing circumstances," the first report read. It continued for almost two pages and ended with, "Based on my telephone interview of Elizabeth, I have concluded that she exhibits deep and sincere feelings for her three children. It is therefore my recommendation that the court grant visitation as her request appears to be reasonable, well-intentioned, and without malice."

The second report was on Charles.

"In a situation such as this it is not unusual for those involved to hold on to an unrealistic expectation of cure, which is precisely what Charles McDermott is doing. This expectation has pushed him into a state of denial regarding Elizabeth's impending death. The court must therefore consider whether such a mindset might ultimately influence the three minor children and cause them to experience a higher level of anxiety at the time of their mother's demise."

The report stated that other than this singular concern, Doctor Belleau thought Charles even-tempered and genuinely concerned about his grandchildren's welfare.

Claire's report followed.

"Claire McDermott exhibits the behavioral tendencies of a mother bear defensive of her cub. Although there has been an incident of violence I believe that to be an isolated occurrence, precipitated by the son-in-law's aggressive behavior toward Elizabeth. Claire does harbor considerable animosity toward Jeffrey Caruthers, but I am confident that her devotion and fierce loyalty to her daughter and the three children will prevent this anger from adversely influencing those relationships."

When Judge Brill finished reading the report on Claire, he began looking for what Doctor Belleau had to say about Jeffrey Caruthers. Twice he rifled through the papers, and twice he came up empty-handed. Judge Brill had no tolerance for inefficiency, so he lifted the receiver and dialed Peter Belleau's office.

"Where's my report on Jeffrey Caruthers?" he growled. "I got your other reports, but there was nothing on Caruthers."

"Well," Belleau said, "we've got a problem there."

"What kind of problem?"

"Mister Caruthers canceled the first two appointments we had and was a no-show for the third. I've tried to reschedule, but he doesn't return my calls."

"We'll see about that!" Judge Brill growled and slammed down the receiver.

The judge chewed three maximum-strength Tums and then placed a call to Noreen Sarnoff.

"Counselor," he said firmly, "I hope you can explain why your client has failed to show up for the psychologist's evaluation ordered by this court."

"Well—"

"Because," the judge continued, "if you are unable to provide a satisfactory explanation, I will hold both you and your client in contempt of court. Have I made myself clear?"

"Yes, sir," Noreen answered without a hint of promiscuousness. "Unfortunately," she added, trying to pull thoughts from the air, "my client has been extremely ill for several weeks. It's a very bad case of stress. He's torn apart by this situation and—"

"I don't want to hear it!" Judge Brill snapped. "If he's too stressed to see Doctor Belleau, then he's too stressed to make decisions for three minor children! Either I have Doctor Belleau's analysis of him on my desk by the end of this week, or I will award custody of those children to the mother!"

"But the mother is—"

Judge Brill banged down the receiver.

Within the hour, Jeffrey Caruthers telephoned Doctor Belleau's office and scheduled an appointment for that afternoon.

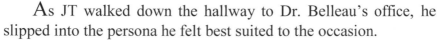

As JT walked down the hallway to Dr. Belleau's office, he slipped into the persona he felt best suited to the occasion.

The moment Doctor Belleau entered the room JT flashed a toothy smile and stuck out his hand. "I apologize for missing our previous appointment."

"Actually, you've missed three," Peter Belleau answered.

"Ah, yes, and I truly regret that. But please bear in mind that my first and foremost concern is my children and caring for them. Unfortunately doing this all by myself leaves very little free time. "

Feeling no sympathy after the way Judge Brill had lit into him, the doctor gave an insincere smile and led Jeffrey Caruthers back to his office. Once they were seated in the brown leather chairs, Peter Belleau suggested Jeffrey give a bit of background on himself.

"There's not much to tell," JT said pleasantly. "I'm a dedicated husband and father, and that's pretty much it."

"Oh," Doctor Belleau mused. "My understanding was that you refused to allow your wife to return to your house once you learned she had a terminal condition. Is that true?"

"That's my mother-in-law's version of what happened. It was nothing like that."

"What was it like?"

JT uncrossed his legs and then re-crossed them. "Well, I never actually refused to allow Liz to return home, I only said it would be difficult for me to take care of her."

"Did you say difficult or impossible?" Doctor Belleau asked.

"Hmm," JT stalled, giving the appearance of trying to remember. "I can't say."

"If I told you that your in-laws are prepared to provide a live-in helper to care for Elizabeth, would you be willing to have her return to the house?"

The possibility caused Jeffrey to become visibly agitated; suddenly his foot began bouncing up and down. "No. I would not allow her to return to the house."

"And why would that be?"

"Why?" Jeffrey repeated angrily. "Don't ask me why when you already know! Liz is sick. She's worse than sick, she's dying! I love my kids, and I don't want them exposed to all that sickness and death!"

"Aren't they Elizabeth's children also?"

"She's dying. Do you not understand? Dying means she's on her way to being dead. What's a dead woman gonna do with kids—drag them into the coffin alongside of her? No way. Not my kids. They don't need that kind of heartache."

"What kind of heartache?"

"You're the shrink, you tell me!"

"I could argue that it would be beneficial for children to establish a relationship with their mother before she—"

"Are you kidding?! You're supposed to be a psychologist, and you're telling me it's a good thing for kids to bond with a mother who's got one foot in the grave? Why, so they can have nightmares about her death?"

"Is it possible that, given time to understand, they might ultimately be more accepting of her death?"

"No, it's not possible," Jeffrey answered, turning his face away.

"And why is that?"

"You think you know so much, but all that psycho mumbo-jumbo doesn't mean squat to little kids. With them it's out of sight, out of mind. They haven't seen Liz for almost ten months, and pretty soon they'll just quit asking about her."

"Do they ask now?"

"Sometimes. Not often. Christian just turned one; he's never known his mother, so he's never gonna ask about her. The other two, they'll forget in time."

"What about Elizabeth, do you think she's forgotten her children?"

"Obviously not," JT replied disdainfully, "or she wouldn't be putting me through this torture."

"Do you think she's doing this just to torture you?"

"Probably."

"Isn't it possible that she simply wants to see the children?"

"If she really cared, she'd spare them the agony."

"What if she believes that losing their mother without ever having a chance to say goodbye is a far greater agony?"

"Who cares what she thinks? I know what's good for my kids."

"What about your in-laws? As I understand it, you won't allow them to see the children either. Is that true?"

"Don't get me started on them. That miserly old skinflint and his trouble-making wife are never gonna see my kids again. Never. You got that?"

"Obviously you have some anger issues with your in-laws. Why?"

JT gave a loud exasperated huff then sat there for a full minute before answering. "Because of them my life is totally screwed up. Everybody thinks they're so good because they're always volunteering to help this cause or that cause, and when they're not volunteering they're going to church or saying prayers for somebody. Well, I say charity begins at home and when I needed money to keep my business from going belly-up, Liz's old man thumbed his nose at me."

"Is it possible that he didn't have the money to give you?"

"No way. He had it. He just didn't want to give it to me. If it was something for his precious daughter, well, now, that would have been a different story."

"Don't you think he might consider providing for Elizabeth's family the same as providing for her?"

"You just don't get it do you? He hates me. He's always hated me. Right this very minute he's probably reminding Liz how he always said I didn't know squat about retailing."

"Retailing, is that the business you're in?"

"Was! Because old man McDermott refused to lend me a little dab of his precious money, I lost my store. Some great life, huh? No store, no job, no money, a stack of bills that could choke a horse, and three kids to take care of."

"Are you currently looking for a job?"

"Doing what? Retailing, that's all I know."

"Is it possible you could find a job in that field?"

"I suppose the McDermotts told you to ask me that," JT sneered. "Well, I'm not gonna go from being a business owner to clerking in some five-and-dime. I've already lost everything else. Now they're trying to take away my kids and what little pride I've got left."

"Who's trying to take away—"

"The McDermotts!" JT shouted angrily. "Are you not hearing me?"

"I hear you, but I'm confused as to why you think the McDermotts are at fault."

"They're doing everything they can to force me out into the street. They think if I've got no way to support my kids, they can take them away from me."

"Isn't it possible they're only interested in seeing the children?"

"Ha! Shows what you know. I don't suppose they told you how they got Liz to ask for all her jewelry back. I want my Rolex and my engagement ring, she tells me, like she's got someplace to wear those things. Well, she's not getting them, know why?"

Doctor Belleau shook his head.

"Because they're gone. Sold. I used the money to pay the mortgage and put food on the table. What's more important, a dead woman wearing a diamond ring or me and my kids having a place to live and something to eat?"

"Perhaps Elizabeth agrees. Have you discussed this with her?"

"How can she agree when her money-hungry parents are telling her to get the jewelry back?"

"Perhaps Elizabeth simply wants these things because they have meaning for her, sentimental value. Isn't that possible?"

"Yeah, sure. And the moon is made of green cheese."

Seeing that nothing could be resolved, Doctor Belleau changed the subject. "Tell me about the children," he said.

"What's to tell? I take care of them as best I can. I'm not all over their back for every little thing they do wrong. They got it a lot better than I had."

"Meaning what?"

"Look, I'm not Liz. She's all over them with that huggy-kissy stuff. You know where that gets you? No place, that's where. I give the kids what they need, nothing less, nothing more."

"And what is it you think they need?"

"Beds to sleep in, food on the table."

"Do you think that's enough?"

"Well, I ain't asking them to jump through hoops to please me."

Doctor Belleau scribbled something on his notepad then continued. "Do you care for the children by yourself?"

"I've got a lady friend who lends a hand, and there's Missus Ramirez. She babysits now and then."

"This lady friend, does she live with you?"

"Why, is that what my mother-in-law said?"

131

"She's of the opinion that you have a girlfriend."

"See what I mean!" JT shouted. "I can't take it anymore!" He jumped to his feet and began pacing in front of the doctor. "It's not enough that I've lost everything, the McDermotts are looking to destroy me. They pretend to be goody-good, but the truth is they're exactly like my old man. All they want to do is tear me down! They'll say anything, do anything—"

JT flung himself back into the chair and started sobbing.

"What do they want from me?" he wailed. "Did I make Liz sick? Did I ask for any of this? Do they think I want this?"

Doctor Belleau handed JT a box of tissues as tears streamed down his face.

Before the session ended Jeffery had poured out his story of the father he adored who was stony-hearted and impossible to please.

After JT left the office, Peter Belleau sat at his desk and composed his final analysis.

"Jeffrey Caruthers has a genuine but rather misdirected sense of protectiveness for his three minor children, and he has convinced himself that seeing their mother will destroy whatever peace of mind and security he has been able to provide. I believe he has deep-seated issues with his father, and this is the root source of his insecurities.

"While Jeffrey's wife, Elizabeth, was previously a bastion of comfort offering unbridled acceptance, her illness has now positioned her as the ultimate challenger to his emotional stability. Because he has been deprived of what was previously his safe place, Jeffrey feels certain that everyone is adversarial and every situation is dangerous. Coincidence has become conclusion, and he is confident that all misfortunes are a result of his in-laws attempts to punish him for his failures. This insecurity has escalated into a state of free-floating anxiety so great that he perceives every setback to be yet another crisis."

Peter Belleau went on for several pages, describing the specifics that led to this conclusion. He ended the report by writing, "Although I am of the opinion that Elizabeth Caruthers is an intelligent, caring individual who is well-qualified for visitation privileges with the three minor children, I caution the court not to push Jeffrey Caruthers beyond his emotional limits because of his fragile emotional state."

Peter Belleau read through the report once again. Then he slipped it inside an envelope and dropped in into the mailbox as he left the building.

September 1985

Judge Brill read through Peter Belleau's analysis of Jeffrey Caruthers; then he reread the phrases that troubled him. Certain words jumped off the page and stuck out. "Overwhelming sense of insecurity"; "beyond his emotional limits"; "fragile emotional state." Judge Brill thought back to six years ago, when Jack Wallner, a man much like Jeffrey Caruthers stood before him. Jack Wallner, a man who'd returned to the courthouse steps and discharged a bullet into his brain just hours after the judge had awarded Alma Wallner custody of their two girls.

The judge knew he had been justified in that decision. After all, Jack was unstable, "stretched beyond his emotional limits," in the words of the psychologist who'd conducted his interview. Judge Brill had no reason to doubt that awarding Alma Wallner custody was the right decision, yet for months afterward he could see Jack's desperation in every pair of eyes that came before him. For a while he'd considered leaving the bench and returning to private practice where he could deal with the cut-and-dry issues of embezzlers and negligent landlords.

When he could no longer tolerate the agony of sleepless nights, Judge Brill took a three-month leave. He rented a camper and drove cross-country with his wife and her pocket-sized Chihuahua. Only after they'd watched sunsets from atop the Blue Ridge Mountains, strolled the tropical beaches of the Florida Keys, fished for salmon off the coast of Washington, and basked in the California sun, was he able to forget. Until now.

After several minutes, he lifted the receiver and dialed Dudley Grimm's number.

"Counselor," he said, "I realize we've already discussed this, but I'd like to ask again if there is any possibility you and the opposing counsel can reach a compromise."

"It's highly unlikely, Your Honor. My client is flexible on the return of her jewelry, but she's been diagnosed as terminal and before she dies she wants to spend time with her children. There's no chance she'll back down on that."

"Have you offered the jewelry concession to opposing counsel?"

"Yes, at our last conference. But her client flatly refuses to budge on visitation. Even though Jeffrey Caruthers realizes his wife is dying, he's adamant about not allowing the children to see her."

Judge Brill gave an exasperated sigh.

"Elizabeth Caruthers is a dying woman," Dudley said. "She should at least have the opportunity to say goodbye to her children. Do you think that's unrealistic?"

"In cases like this it becomes near impossible to determine what is realistic or unrealistic," Judge Brill said sadly. "Everything simply becomes a point of argument."

"Your Honor, if anyone is being unrealistic and uncooperative it is the opposing counsel. She knows that time is critical to my client, and she's employing every delay tactic conceivable."

"Miss Sarnoff claims the grandparents are an issue."

"That's nothing but a red herring. They figure Elizabeth Caruthers is quasi-bedridden and lives with her parents, so there's no way the children can visit their mother without exposure to the grandparents. If they ask to keep the kids away from the grandparents, it effectively eliminates any visitation with the mother."

"Point taken," Judge Brill replied. "I'll have another chat with Miss Sarnoff to see if she can't move this along."

Judge Brill called Noreen Sarnoff.

"May I assume you've read through Doctor Belleau's report on your client?" he asked.

"Yes, Your Honor, I have," Noreen replied.

"Given Doctor Belleau's evaluation of your client's emotional state, would you agree that a long, drawn-out trial is not in his best interest?"

"Yes, but—"

"I suggest approaching him about allowing the mother a reasonable visitation schedule."

"The problem is—"

"I'm not interested in what his problem is. In my opinion the plaintiff's request is well within reason. And since the court calendar is already overcrowded, I fail to see any purpose in allowing this to drag on."

"But, Your Honor, my client refuses to—"

"That's why I am speaking to you, Counselor. I'm asking that you take another shot at finding acceptable grounds for compromise."

"Okay, Your Honor," Noreen said. "But I doubt I'll have much success. Mister Caruthers refuses to allow the mother or grandparents access to the children."

"You might want to remind him that he's got a very weak case. Both Doctor Belleau and her attending physician have issued statements claiming Elizabeth Caruthers is quite capable of visiting with the children. In fact, they've suggested it would be beneficial."

"We have our own medical expert who suggests—"

"Miss Sarnoff," he said abruptly. "I believe that I've made my request perfectly clear. I've asked that you find grounds for a compromise, not provide me with a litany of excuses for why you cannot!"

"Yes, Your Honor," Noreen replied.

Minutes later, Noreen picked up the telephone and called Jeffrey Caruthers. "I just heard from Judge Brill."

"What now?" JT replied curtly.

"You're not gonna like it," Noreen warned, "but he's pushing us to talk compromise. He indicated that your wife's request is—"

"I don't give a crap what he thinks, or what you think, or what anybody else thinks! I'm not letting Liz or her goody-two-shoes parents near my kids! I'm the one responsible for them. I'm the one who's gonna have to deal with their nightmares and hysteria when Liz dies, and there's no way I'm putting them through that torture! Do I make myself clear?"

"I understand your position, but—"

"I'm not discussing this anymore!" With that he slammed down the receiver.

It had been a long and aggravating day for Noreen Sarnoff, and it wasn't over. She began to draft a Motion for Continuance. She didn't expect it to help, but if she could delay things long enough, maybe they'd get lucky and Elizabeth Caruthers would die before the case went to trial.

When Judge Brill arrived at the courthouse the following morning, the motion lay on his desk.

"Figures," he said, sadly shaking his head. The judge had hoped to settle this case without a trial, in a way that didn't rip out someone's heart and leave them with only a desire for death. Obviously, that wouldn't happen.

Judge Brill allowed his coffee to grow cold while he reread the case file and then reread it again. Finally when he could find no other way to resolve the dilemma, he told his clerk to contact both attorneys and advise them he would hear oral arguments in his office the following morning at ten o'clock.

That afternoon Judge Brill received a second motion. It was a Motion to Dismiss, filed by Dudley Grimm on behalf of the plaintiff. In his brief Dudley stated that in view of the plaintiff's imminent demise, Jeffrey Caruthers' Motion for Sole Legal and Physical Custody was legally meaningless intended only to harass Elizabeth Caruthers and cause undue delay in the proceedings.

The following morning as Judge Brill drove across the Pulaski Skyway a truck carrying an oversized load of gravel slid out of control and slammed into the guard rail, causing the nine drivers following to rear-end each other. The judge was number eight, so his car was hammered in front and back. Traffic in both directions inched forward. Northbound travelers found it impossible to squeeze by the pile-up of cars, and southbound travelers, craning their necks to see what happened, slowed movement to a crawl. By the time Judge Brill finally reached the courthouse, he was in the foulest possible mood.

Noreen Sarnoff and Dudley Grimm sat in his office when Judge Brill arrived. With few pleasantries, he settled himself behind the desk and opened the case file.

"Okay, Counselor," he said, giving a nod toward Noreen. "Let's hear why you need another continuance."

"We need additional time for discovery. My client believes the mother's ability to physically and emotionally handle being with the children is in question, and to establish proof of this we need to depose a number of nurses who were on duty during Elizabeth Caruthers' stay at Saint Barnabas Hospital. We also need time to obtain a full medical history and a more in-depth psychiatric examination."

"Your Honor," Dudley interrupted, "they are already in possession of Doctor Sorenson's report on Elizabeth's condition."

"But we have not had an opportunity to depose the doctor, nor have we had access to any of the nurses who attended Missus Caruthers."

"Your Honor," Dudley said, "this is beating a dead horse. They have the doctor's signed statement, so why would further discovery be necessary? We've stipulated agreement as to Elizabeth's medical limitations and the terminal prognosis."

"There is also the issue of a full psychiatric examination," Noreen argued.

"And why," Judge Brill asked, "is that considered relevant?"

"Your Honor," Noreen said, "we have no way of knowing whether the tumor pressing against Elizabeth Caruthers' brain has in any way altered her mental capacity. So before the court considers any type of visitation, we would like to see documentation attesting to her stability."

"Do you have reason to believe she might in some way harm the children?"

"Not at this moment, but in a situation such as this—"

"Miss Sarnoff is creating a hypothetical that has no relevance here!" Dudley argued. "First off, we have stipulated that Elizabeth Caruthers does have blackout periods, but they are infrequent and limited in duration. Secondly, she lives with the grandparents of the three minor children. These people are her parents, one of whom is always in attendance and readily available should she require assistance. The truth of this matter is that Miss Sarnoff realizes time is of the essence, and she is determined to delay these proceedings until the outcome is decided by my client's demise."

Judge Brill turned to Noreen. "I'm inclined to agree with Counselor Grimm. You're in possession of Doctor Belleau's psychological evaluation of the plaintiff, and you have Doctor Sorenson's statement. Therefore, I am going to deny your request for further depositions but will allow a two-week continuance."

"But—"

"There are no buts," Judge Brill said emphatically. "I expect this trial to be on the court's calendar before the October recess." He initialed his denial and handed it to the clerk in attendance.

"Next issue," the judge, said turning to Dudley. "Your request to dismiss Mister Caruthers' plea for sole custody."

"Again, we feel that the custody motion is another of the plaintiff's attempts at creating undue delay," Dudley said. "This is a meaningless motion, since Jeffrey Caruthers already has physical custody of the children. Once his wife dies he will automatically inherit sole legal and physical custody. In the interim, there is no evidence of parental misconduct that would preempt Elizabeth Caruthers from retaining her custodial right for visitation."

Judge Brill gave Noreen a nod. "Miss Sarnoff?"

"We of course oppose the request for dismissal, Your Honor," she answered. "My client's plea for sole legal custody was made to avoid any potential interference or entanglement created by the children's maternal grandparents. It is well documented that there is considerable friction between Mister Caruthers and the grandparents. Giving Mister Caruthers sole legal custody would avoid any potential issues that might arise after their daughter's death."

"Unless there is evidence of parental abuse," the judge said, "the grandparents have no legal standing in the custody issue."

"Perhaps not, but they can engage my client in a time-consuming and costly lawsuit."

The judge raised a doubtful eyebrow. "Given the existing circumstances, I tend to agree that this is a frivolous petition. So, although I am denying Mister Grimm's motion for dismissal, I am going to hold this petition in abeyance until the court has reached a decision on the issue of visitation."

"Thank you, Your Honor," Noreen and Dudley echoed simultaneously.

Room 110
Union County Courthouse

The courtroom split straight down the middle so that warring parties need not sit shoulder-to-shoulder. When Judge Brill entered the room, the clerk called out, "All rise. Court is now in session, the Honorable Judge Theodore Brill presiding." The judge sat, and everyone else followed.

In the past two months, Elizabeth Caruthers' headaches had increased in both number and intensity. Some days she found it difficult or nearly impossible to pull herself from bed. Elizabeth had heeded Doctor Sorenson's words—"Undue stress will only serve to worsen your condition"—and stayed home. In her place Claire and Charles McDermott sat at the plaintiff's table with Dudley Grimm.

On the opposite side of the room, Noreen Sarnoff and a solemn-faced Jeffrey Caruthers sat at the defense table. Dressed in a black suit with a skirt that ended well above her knee, Noreen had her mouth painted in a perfect pout, the kind men found hard to resist. She had considerable concern about the strength of this case, so she'd put together her most alluring look and planned to use it to full advantage.

For two days she'd practiced her opening statement. She'd added precisely the right amount of pursing her lips, raising her brows, and leaning into her words, and now she was ready. She would start with the sad-eyed comparison of a mother who would use the children to satisfy her own need as opposed to a father whose unselfish motive was simply to save the poor darlings from the separation anxiety that would surely accompany her death. After that she would—

"Since I am well aware of the claims and counter-claims of this case," Judge Brill said, "I suggest we forego opening statements in the interest of expediency."

"Fine with me, Your Honor," Dudley said.

The judge looked at Noreen. "Counselor?"

No way would Noreen let go of the opening statement she'd perfected.

"The defense believes that it is extremely important to reiterate the critical issues involved in this plea for visitation," she answered. "Without opening statements, the full and explicit intentions of both parties may be misunderstood or misinterpreted."

Under other circumstances Judge Brill may have overruled a lawyer's request to proceed with opening statements that simply wasted the court's time, but the memory of Jack Wallner's wild-eyed plea for his children remained at the forefront of the judge's mind. Jeffrey Caruthers had that same look of angry desperation. Rather than risk another stretch of endless months wondering whether he'd made all the right decisions, Judge Brill answered, "Very well." He gave Dudley Grimm a nod and said, "Please proceed, Counselor."

Dudley stood, buttoned his jacket, and began to speak.

"My client's request is quite simply the plea of a dying mother to spend time with her children and be allowed the opportunity to bequeath to them certain possessions that she has treasured. She is the birth mother of these children and, up until the time she was diagnosed with a terminal brain tumor, was their full-time caregiver. Elizabeth Caruthers was a stay-at-home parent who spent most of her waking hours attending to the needs of her children, whereas Jeffrey Caruthers, their father, spent very little time with them. He was the proprietor of a business that required his undivided attention six days a week, plus an untold number of late evenings.

"Your Honor, Elizabeth Caruthers has proven herself to be a caring and dutiful mother and as such has both the natural and legal right to see her children—a right that the defendant has denied her. He has taken the law into his own hands by denying his wife access to most of her personal possessions. Without regard for their sentimental value, Jeffrey Caruthers decided that a dying woman doesn't need jewelry or any material assets.

"Worse yet, he has refused her access to her children, either by telephone or in person. He alone decided Elizabeth should not be allowed to see or speak with her children because bonding with her would make death more painful for them to endure. In short, Your Honor, Jeffrey Caruthers has set himself up as both psychological expert and dispenser of justice."

Dudley stopped for a moment to let that thought hang heavy in the air. Then he continued.

"Elizabeth Caruthers has done nothing that can in any way be misconstrued as harmful to her children, yet her husband insists that spending time with her would not be in their best interest. Without benefit of professional guidance, Jeffrey Caruthers decided the children would suffer undue trauma if allowed to *bond* with their mother."

He turned to face Jeffrey as he spoke.

"Only a father who has been emotionally absent for much of their life could make such a foolhardy decision. Doesn't he understand that his children have already bonded with their mother? She's nursed them when they were sick, fed them when they were hungry, taught them to walk, talk, share, and love. It's physically impossible for a child not to have bonded with such a parent."

Dudley turned back to Judge Brill.

"Mister Caruthers has also refused to allow the three minor children to see Claire and Charles McDermott, their maternal grandparents. Again, this was done without any justifiable reason other than their biological relationship to his dying wife. The only thing achieved by Jeffrey Caruthers' unwarranted actions is that he has separated the children from the people they are closest to, people they already know and love—their mother, their grandmother, and their grandfather.

"If he is allowed to continue along this path, the youngest child, Christian, will never have a chance to experience the same affectionate family relationships in which David and Kimberly thrived."

Dudley spoke briefly about Elizabeth's medical diagnosis and her emotional state of mind, assuring the judge that neither of these presented a threat of harm to the children.

"On the other hand," he said in closing, "if Elizabeth dies without ever letting David, Kimberly, and Christian know how much she loves them or saying her final farewell, the children might suffer from emotional scars for the rest of their lives."

He promised the opinion of Alexander Rupert, a well-known expert in the area of child psychology, "a far more credible opinion than that of Jeffrey Caruthers," he added. Dudley Grimm returned to the plaintiff's table and sat alongside Charles McDermott.

Noreen Sarnoff, who had busily scribbled rebuttal notes on each point addressed by Dudley, stood before her opponent was fully settled in his seat.

"Your Honor," she began, strutting to the center of the courtroom. "Mister Grimm would have this court believe my client has acted inappropriately and, I quote, 'taken the law into his own hands,' but in actuality Jeffrey Caruthers has done what any caring father might do to protect his three small children from the anguish of their mother's death.

"Mister Grimm has also suggested that the Caruthers children are being isolated from loving family relationships, whereas the truth is that they are being shielded from the anger and hatred that Elizabeth and her parents now feel toward my client. When Jeffrey Caruthers found his business in trouble he turned to the McDermotts for help, but they refused. In addition to that refusal they continue to hold him responsible for the business failure and his resulting inability to provide nursing care for their terminally-ill daughter."

Noreen took a deep breath and brushed back the wisp of hair tickling the side of her face.

"I intend to show that the loving grandmother the plaintiff's attorney has described is actually a violent ill-tempered woman who attacked the home of my client with a sledgehammer. How can we possibly fault Jeffrey Caruthers for wanting to spare his children the agony of such exhibitions?"

Claire's heart rose into her throat. She wanted to crawl beneath the table or, better yet, disappear entirely. Were it possible to go back in time, she gladly would have. She'd go back and grovel at the doorway begging for Jeffrey to answer. If he chose not to answer she'd back away meekly, certainly not take a sledgehammer to the door.

"The plaintiff's attorney," Noreen said, "has also faulted my client for the long hours he spent working to build a business that could provide the income necessary for his wife's extravagant lifestyle. A three-bedroom bungalow was not good enough for Elizabeth Caruthers. She wanted a big house and expensive jewelry, jewelry that my client ultimately had to sell in order to provide for his children."

Elizabeth never wanted those things, Claire wrote on a slip of paper and passed it to Dudley. He gave her a quick nod.

Noreen walked back to the defendant's table, picked up a document, and flamboyantly waved it in the air.

"We have in our possession a notarized statement from Doctor Hans Wolfburger, a highly respected child psychologist who specializes in separation trauma. In this document, Doctor Wolfburger states that children who have been removed from exposure to a parent then returned and removed for a second time will suffer severe and long-lasting trauma frequently resulting in neurosis and a rejection complex.

"Since the Caruthers children have not seen or had interaction with their mother for almost ten months, she no longer plays a role in their day-to-day existence. To restore that relationship would ultimately force them to undergo the loss of their mother for a second time, precisely the scenario that Doctor Wolfburger refers to."

Noreen paused and then launched into a detailed account of Elizabeth's paralysis and blackout periods, stressing Elizabeth's physical weakness and questioning whether it would put the children in physical danger.

"It is the responsibility of the court," Noreen said emphatically, "to see that these questions are adequately addressed before any change is made in the custodial issues pertaining to these three minor children."

She returned to the defense table where Jeffrey Caruthers sat with a malicious grin curling the corners of his mouth.

Judge Brill rapped his gavel and declared that the court would take a ten-minute recess. Once everyone returned, Dudley Grimm proceeded with his case and called Claire to the witness stand.

Claire placed one hand on the Holy Bible and swore she'd tell the truth then settled into the witness box.

"Missus McDermott," Dudley began, "you are the mother of Elizabeth Caruthers and the maternal grandmother of David, Kimberly, and Christian Caruthers, is that correct?"

"Yes," Claire answered nervously.

"And prior to your daughter's illness, how often did you see those grandchildren?"

"Every day. I'd stop by for a visit in the afternoon, and I'd stay with the children when Jeffrey and Elizabeth had an evening out."

"And how would you describe your relationship with your grandchildren?"

"Wonderful," Claire answered promptly. "Those kids love me every bit as much as I love them. David, he's the oldest, loves to have me read stories. He generally asks for the tales about King

Arthur and his knights. Before I can finish one story, he's already asking for another one. He's heard the same stories at least one hundred times, but he never gets tired of listening to them."

"What about Kimberly?"

"She was two years old when Liz first got sick, but that little tyke sure had a mind of her own. Elizabeth taught the children that they had to take turns choosing the story, and if David asked for a King Arthur story on Monday, then on Tuesday, Kimberly would insist on Goldilocks. Even though she was only two, she knew how to keep track of when it was her turn."

"And Christian?"

"He was born after Elizabeth got sick, so I never really had the chance to spend time with him."

"Why is that?"

Claire lowered her eyes. "Jeffrey told me to quit stopping by in the afternoon, because I was disrupting his household."

"With Elizabeth in the hospital, didn't he need someone to watch the children while he was working?"

Claire nodded. "Yes, but he'd rather pay Missus Ramirez to babysit than have me do it for free."

"Were you aware of Jeffrey Caruthers' financial difficulties at that time?"

"Yes. He'd already asked Charles for another loan."

"Another loan? Had he borrowed money on other occasions?"

"Yes. Five times before."

"And did your husband give him the money he was asking for?"

"He did the five times before, but not this time."

"Was that the reason Jeffrey Caruthers no longer allowed you to see the children?"

"Objection!" Noreen called out. "Calls for speculation on the part of the witness."

"Sustained," Judge Brill answered and with a nod to Dudley he said, "Rephrase your question, Counselor."

"Very well," Dudley answered. He turned to Claire and asked, "Did Jeffrey Caruthers ever give a reason for not allowing you to visit with the children?"

"Yes and no."

"Please explain."

"He said we were to blame for all his problems, even Elizabeth's illness. But he never explained why he thought that."

Dudley nodded and stood there for a moment fingering his chin. He finally said, "Missus McDermott, this court has heard how you attacked the defendant's house with a sledgehammer. Is that true?"

Claire cringed. "Yes," she finally stuttered. "That's true, but it's not the way it sounds."

"Please explain."

"It happened just after Elizabeth was released from the hospital. Jeffrey had already told us she couldn't go back to his house because he couldn't take care of her, so Liz came to stay with us. She'd been asking to see the kids, plus she wanted some of her clothes and personal belongings. I tried telephoning Jeffrey to ask if I could come by and get her things. I can't even guess how many times I called. Dozens maybe. But he wouldn't answer the phone.

"Finally I drove over there and knocked on the door. There were lights on in the house and I could see him moving around inside, but he wouldn't answer the door either."

"So you tried to break it down?"

"No," Claire answered indignantly. "I didn't really plan to use the sledgehammer. I only brought it because I thought it might scare Jeffrey into opening the door. I figured if we could have a face-to-face conversation, I'd be able to reason with him. After I stood outside for twenty minutes ringing the bell and he still didn't answer, I hit the door one time—just one time and not even hard enough to make an actual dent in the wood."

"Did Jeffrey then answer the door?"

"Immediately."

"Had he not answered, would you have continued your sledgehammer attack?"

"No. After that one moment of anger, I pretty well came to my senses."

"Once Jeffrey opened the door, did you ask him for your daughter's clothing and personal belongings?"

"Yes, and he agreed to bring them over."

"Did he bring them over?"

"No, he didn't. He tossed some of her clothes into garbage bags and had a pickup truck dump the bags in our driveway. It was raining really hard that day, so most of the clothes got wet and smelly. When I first opened the bags, I thought it was just rags, but then I saw Liz's pink suit…" Claire tearfully lowered her face into her hands.

"I'm sorry, Missus McDermott. I know this must be painful."

"Yes, it is." Claire sniffed.

"Do you need me to ask for a ten-minute recess?"

"No," she answered sadly. "Just go on."

"Missus McDermott, when you opened the bags sent by Jeffrey Caruthers, did they include any of Elizabeth's jewelry or the other items she'd asked for?"

"No. Just clothes and shoes."

"At the time you went to the Caruthers' house to ask for Elizabeth's belongings, did you also ask if the children could come to visit Elizabeth?"

"Yes."

"What was the answer?"

"Jeffrey said he'd burn in hell before he'd allow Liz or any of her family to see his kids. Then he pushed me off the stoop and slammed the door."

"When Jeffrey Caruthers pushed you off the stoop, did you take the sledgehammer to the door again?"

"No."

"Was that because you'd already realized it was a mistake to resort to violence?"

"Objection!" Noreen shouted. "He's leading the witness."

Dudley offered to rephrase the question. He turned back to Claire. "If this situation presented itself again, would you repeat the attack on his door?"

"No. I'm sorry I did it the first time. I know it was wrong. But at the time, I was frustrated because he wouldn't talk to me. I knew how much Liz wanted to see the children, and I didn't know of any other way to get Jeffrey's attention."

"So you did it for your daughter, Elizabeth." Dudley hesitated a moment then asked, "What else would you do to help her?"

"What kind of a question is that?"

"Well, would you lie about her mental and physical abilities so that this court will feel sympathetic and grant visitation, even if it's not in the best interest of the children?"

"Of course not," Claire answered. "I love those children the same as I love Liz. I'd never do anything that might harm them."

"Can you say with complete honesty that your daughter is strong enough mentally and physically to have regularly-scheduled visits with her three young children?"

"I can and will say it. I swear before God that those children would be perfectly safe with Elizabeth. It would be good for both the children and Elizabeth to spend time together. Liz loves those children more than most people can understand, and the kids feel the same way about her. I don't for one minute believe that David and Kimberly have forgotten their mother, and I think they deserve the chance to spend time with her while they can."

"Missus McDermott, how do you feel about your son-in-law?"

"At one time," Claire said sadly, "I loved Jeffrey the same as I would a son. But now—well, now he's a different person. He's bitter and mean beyond belief. Liz gave him everything she had to give, an abundance of love and all of her good years. But he has nothing to give back during this last bit of her life. How would you feel about someone like that?"

150

Dudley gave a sympathetic nod. Then he said, "One last question. Have you or would you say anything derogatory about Jeffrey Caruthers within earshot of your grandchildren?"

"No, I never have and never would. Regardless of my feelings about Jeffrey, he's their father and one of these days he'll be their only living parent, so why would I say anything that could destroy the children's faith in him?"

Dudley smiled, then turned to Noreen and said, "Your witness."

Before Noreen could take the courtroom floor, Judge Brill rapped his gavel. "It's getting close to noon, so let's stop here and take a forty-five-minute recess for lunch."

Claire breathed a sigh of relief and stepped out of the witness box.

The Trial Continues

As they left the courthouse, Noreen and Jeffrey turned to the left and disappeared around the corner. The McDermotts and Dudley went in the opposite direction. Claire was full of questions. But with the men walking at a brisk pace in long strides it was all she could do to keep up, so she waited until they'd settled into a back booth at the Crooked Spoon and ordered their lunch.

"How'd I do?" she asked.

"Fine," Dudley said. "But the tough part is ahead of you. Noreen is a razor-sharp lawyer. Whatever you say, she's gonna turn it around and rephrase it in the negative. So make certain to watch for that, and don't let her lead you into saying something you hadn't intended."

"Like what?"

"For instance, she gets you to admit that you love Elizabeth more than life itself. Then she'll rephrase it to sound as if your concern for your daughter will override any concern you might have regarding the welfare of the children."

"Oh dear," Claire said.

"Noreen's good. She'll make you believe she's very sympathetic, but when she gets what she needs she'll pounce."

"Oh dear," Claire repeated.

"Don't worry," Dudley said. "You can get around that. Just keep your answers short as possible, one word if you can. Don't give her anything to work with. And most importantly, don't let her get you riled. If I know Noreen, she'll drag out that sledgehammer incident and use it to make you look like a raging hothead, so be careful."

By the time their sandwiches arrived, Claire's stomach was knotted with fear. Her grilled cheese grew cold as she listened to Charles and Dudley.

"I'll call you to the stand right after Noreen finishes her cross of Claire," Dudley told Charles. "I'm going to concentrate on the financial aspect of your relationship with Jeffrey, and I'll ask you to tell the court about his reaction when you wouldn't give him the money."

"But this isn't about the money."

"But if we show that his actions were brought about because you refused to lend him the money he wanted, we can prove his motive for keeping the children away from you and Elizabeth is vindictiveness rather than the belief it's in their best interest."

Charles nodded and chomped down on his sandwich.

When they settled back into the courtroom, Claire nervously glanced at Noreen Sarnoff.

"Claire McDermott," the court clerk called out, "please retake the stand for cross examination. Remember, you have already been sworn in."

Noreen rose from her seat and in a few long strides stood facing Claire. "Missus McDermott, do you love your daughter?"

Claire remembered Dudley's warning about the lawyer's trickery.

"Yes," she said tentatively.

"Do you also love your three grandchildren?"

"Yes."

"Who do you love more, your daughter or your grandchildren?"

"Objection," Dudley called out. "That has no relevance—"

"Your Honor," Noreen interrupted, "I'm trying to establish the witness's priorities in relationship to the wellbeing of the children."

"I'll allow it," Judge Brill said. "But watch where you're going, Counselor."

Noreen smiled and turned back to Claire.

"I love them equally," Claire finally said.

"Well, what if they were all trapped in a burning building and the fireman said it was only possible for him to rescue either your daughter or her three children. Who would you want him to save?"

"How can you ask a mother that question?" Claire said suddenly, forgetting Noreen's sharp-edged tongue. "It would be impossible for any mother to choose one child over another, and every one of my grandchildren is as dear to my heart as my own child."

"But if you absolutely were faced with such a choice?"

"My grandchildren," Claire said. "They're babies, just starting their life. My Elizabeth is on the doorstep of ending hers."

A stream of tears began to flow from Claire's eyes, so Judge Brill called for a five-minute recess so she could compose herself.

Once Claire returned to the stand, Noreen began in a much more sympathetic tone.

"I can see how much you love your grandchildren. So you want what is best for them, true?"

"Yes."

"Does that include living in a non-combative environment?"

"Yes."

"Do you believe attacking their father with a sledgehammer is part of such an environment?"

"I didn't attack him, I hit the door," Claire said. "But I shouldn't have. It was an unfortunate choice, made in a moment of anger."

"A moment of anger," Noreen repeated with a self-satisfied nod. "And how often do you get that angry?"

"Never before, and I would venture to say never again."

"But suppose you were to get that angry again. Might you take it out on one of your grandchildren? Hit them? Push them down a flight—"

"Objection!" Dudley shouted. "There are no grounds for such an assumption!"

"Sustained," Judge Brill replied, giving Noreen an edgy glare.

Wanting to pull her thoughts together and cover up her increasing concern about the case, Noreen walked back to the defense table, shuffled through several papers, then turned back to Claire.

"You claim your daughter, Elizabeth, is mentally and physically capable of having visitation with the children, yet she is conspicuously absent from this courtroom. Why is that?"

"Elizabeth is too sick to sit in this courtroom and listen to people argue about whether or not she's entitled to see her own children."

"If she's too sick to fight for her children, isn't it possible that she's also too sick to care for them during visitation?"

"No, it isn't possible," Claire answered. "Someone else is almost always with her—myself, Liz's dad, or a nurse."

"Almost always," Noreen repeated with another cynical nod. "But have you considered what could happen to the baby if Elizabeth lost consciousness during one of those *almost* times?"

"We'll guarantee that someone will always be there when the children are with her."

"Even if someone is there, what would happen if Elizabeth were to pass out or have a seizure? Wouldn't that person be busy attending to your daughter instead of watching over the children?"

"We can make certain there are always two people when Elizabeth has the children with her."

"You've already acknowledged that it's possible Elizabeth could have a seizure. Don't you think that would be a horrific thing for her children to experience?"

"Objection," Dudley said with an air of disdain. "Miss Sarnoff is badgering the witness, and she's asking for a speculative opinion on a hypothetical situation."

"Sustained," Judge Brill said. "Move on, Counselor."

Noreen suppressed a sigh of frustration. "Very well," she said, switching tactics. "You've made numerous statements indicating that you have an extremely low opinion of your son-in-law, isn't that true, Missus McDermott?"

"How can I not have that opinion of him?" Claire answered, forgetting Dudley's advice. "He's a greedy, mean, selfish person who has gone out of his way to be cruel to Elizabeth! Any mother would feel as I do when someone hurts their child."

"And your daughter, has she expressed the same opinion about her ex-husband?"

"Husband," Claire corrected. "They're still married. And, yes, she has."

Dudley grimaced.

"With all of this animosity directed toward Jeffrey Caruthers, you still expect the court to believe that your entire household can project a positive impression of the children's father whenever they're around?"

Sensing that the damage was already done, Claire answered, "We can and will!"

"I'd say that is highly unlikely," Noreen replied.

Before Claire could argue the point, Noreen bellowed, "No further questions," and returned to her seat.

Dudley stood and called for Charles McDermott to take the stand. As planned he asked about the amount and number of loans he'd given Jeffrey.

"So," Dudley said, pausing for emphasis, "in total you have given your son-in-law one-hundred-and-ten thousand dollars in loans to shore up his failing business, is that correct, Mister McDermott?"

"Correct," Charles acknowledged.

"And has he repaid any of this money?"

"No," he answered, shaking his head.

"When was the last time Jeffrey asked you for a loan?"

"September of last year."

"And how much was he looking for?"

"Twenty-five thousand."

"Did you give it to him?"

"No," Charles answered. "With all of Elizabeth's expenses we couldn't afford it."

"How did Jeffrey react to that?"

"He was furious. He said his business would go down the tubes unless he got the money to revitalize it."

"How did you respond to that?"

"I said he ought to think about getting a job."

"And?"

"He behaved like a raging bull, called me a self-centered jackass, and stormed out, slamming my office door so violently I thought the glass would break."

"Since the time of that incident have you or your wife seen or spoken to any of the Caruthers children?"

"No," Charles answered sadly.

"Has Elizabeth seen or spoken to the children since that time?"

"Last October Jeffrey brought the children to the hospital. He came to ask Elizabeth if she could get me to change my mind about giving him the money. Since then, she hasn't seen or spoken to the children."

Dudley thanked Charles then said he had no further questions and returned to the plaintiff's table.

Noreen's cross examination of Charles only touched on whether Jeffrey Caruthers had actually threatened to withhold access to the children because he was denied the loan he'd requested.

"No," Charles answered. Noreen indicated she had nothing more.

Dudley's third and final witness was a well-known child psychologist who had authored a paper on childhood separation anxieties.

As soon as the silver-haired doctor was settled, Dudley said, "For the court record, please state your name and credentials."

"Alexander Rupert. I hold a doctorate of philosophy from New York University and a master's of counseling from Johns Hopkins. I am a licensed marriage and family therapist with a specialization in child development and education. Working under a Vanderbilt University grant, for the past five years I've been conducting a clinical research program to assess and develop treatment for childhood behavioral conditions resulting from depression, anger, and resentment."

"How old are these children?"

"Our studies consist of both male and female subjects, ranging from two years to fifteen years of age."

"In these studies," Dudley asked, "were you able to identify the root source responsible for the development of those specific conditions?"

"Yes. Over sixty-seven percent of the cases studied were a result of the child being separated from a parent, either by divorce, death, or abandonment."

"Would you please explain your findings in those cases where death was the causative factor?"

"Children who had a parent taken from their life suddenly and without explanation suffered the deepest and longest-term trauma. This includes feelings of abandonment and loss of life from sudden heart attacks, automobile accidents, and suicide."

"Why is that, Doctor Rupert?"

"Unfortunately, the child often believes the loss of their parent is a result of something they have done. They mistakenly blame themselves and try to change some element of their behavior or appearance, thinking it will cause the missing parent to return."

"Even if that parent is deceased?"

"Yes. This is especially true of children under the age of ten. It is quite possible for a child to understand death when they are adequately prepared, but a child who is simply told that their mother or father has passed away tends not to believe the story. They convince themselves the parent is in fact alive and simply does not want to return to them."

"What is the end result of such a situation?"

"The child is generally anxious and insecure, always fearful that the remaining parent will also disappear from their life. A good percentage of the children who grow up with that type of anxiety will, as young adults, end up in therapy."

"When a parent is diagnosed with a terminal illness, is it more advantageous to allow a child to witness the reality of that illness or shelter them from the truth and possible ugliness of it?"

"It is unquestionably better to expose the child to the events leading to the loss of a parent. Fortunately, the young mind does not fully grasp the concept of long-term suffering. They understand sick, sicker, sickest, dying, and finally dead. So in the long run they come to expect and ultimately accept it. However they do not, as we adults do, agonize over the day-to-day suffering that brings a loved one to that final destination."

"One last question, Doctor Rupert. Would it be harmful to the Caruthers children to spend time visiting their mother who has been diagnosed with a terminal brain tumor?"

"Absolutely not. It would be far more disastrous for them to have her removed from their life without explanation. To take that final goodbye from a child replaces the normal course of grieving with anger and guilt."

"I have nothing more," Dudley said.

Noreen had a number of questions for Doctor Rupert, most of them repetitive.

"Are you trying to tell this court that children do not understand pain? That if they skin their knee or cut their finger they don't bleed? They don't hurt?"

Doctor Rupert, unruffled by her badgering, answered, "I did not say they do not understand pain, I said they do not comprehend the anguish of long-term suffering. Pain is a purely physical and somewhat temporary condition where children are concerned. They hurt only as long as the injury in question is painful. The long-term anguish of suffering is something only adults can understand."

"If a child were to see their dog crippled by a car, do you not believe they would understand suffering?"

"They would likely experience short-term anguish. Then, best-case scenario, the dog's leg would be amputated and the child would be quite happy with their three-legged dog. Worst-case scenario, the dog would die and be buried in the back yard. The child would still suffer only short-term anguish because he saw the dog die and be buried, so while he is saddened by the loss he does not have a sense of abandonment."

It went on that way for a full twenty minutes. Finally with a rather impatient huff, Noreen announced she had no more questions.

After Noreen sat, Dudley took the floor again. He introduced three exhibits—the first, a certified copy of the medical report from Doctor Sorenson, the second, a copy of psychologist Peter Belleau's opinion of Elizabeth's mental stability based on his telephone conversation with her.

"As you will note, Your Honor," Dudley said, "Doctor Belleau agrees with Doctor Sorenson that visitation time with her three children would be most beneficial for Elizabeth Caruthers."

The third exhibit was simply a list of the jewelry and other items that Elizabeth had requested. At the top of the list was Liz's two-karat diamond engagement ring. No one actually anticipated that it would be returned, but Dudley had put it on the list as something for negotiation.

The Defense

Noreen had three people listed as witnesses. The first was Doctor Hans Wolfburger, a man with a good part of his face hidden behind a bristly red beard. Doctor Wolfburger spoke with a thick accent, replacing W sounds with Vs and Ss with Zs. When asked what the potential effect of reuniting the Caruthers children with their dying mother might be, Doctor Wolfburger answered, "You vill zee da younzeers have much zrezz und turmoil."

"Excuse me," the court stenographer said. "Could the witness please repeat that?"

Doctor Wolfburger repeated his answer.

"Come again?" the stenographer said.

After she asked a third time, Judge Brill leaned forward and whispered, "I believe he said that we will see the youngsters have much stress and turmoil."

"Oh," the stenographer answered, turning back to her machine.

It continued that way throughout much of Doctor Wolfburger's testimony, but Noreen established that in a qualitative study, children separated from one or both of their parents then reunited and removed for a second time frequently suffered a rejection complex. The testimony took several go-rounds with Judge Brill often serving as interpreter.

Doctor Wolfburger, apparently as frustrated as the court stenographer, finally asked, "Vhat zeems to be zee problem?"

Taking into account the stenographer's problem deciphering Doctor Wolfburger's words, Dudley Grimm structured most of his cross examination with questions that could be answered yes or no.

"A qualitative study," Dudley asked. "Isn't that one which draws in-depth information from a relatively small number of participants?"

"Ya." Doctor Wolfburger nodded.

"The number of participants in your study, was it less than one hundred?"

"Ya." Doctor Wolfburger nodded again.

"Under fifty?"

Another nod.

"Between thirty and fifty?"

"Nein."

"Between twenty and thirty?"

"Ya." The doctor gave another nod.

"And was this study conducted within the past ten years?" Dudley asked.

"Nein." The doctor shook his head and waved a hand indicating further back.

"So the study was conducted over ten years ago, right?"

The doctor nodded.

"And in that study," Dudley asked, "can you recall what number of those children separated from a parent or parents for the second time lost the parent to death as opposed to divorce?"

Doctor Wolfburger scratched at his beard for several moments, then he held up two fingers.

"Only two of the twenty or thirty children in the study lost their parent to death?"

"Ya."

"So, your assumption that the Caruthers children will be psychologically harmed by restoring their relationship with their dying mother is actually based on a decade-old analysis of two children, correct?"

Doctor Wolfburger sat there staring straight ahead.

"Please answer," Dudley said.

"Dat conclusion leaze much confusion."

"Not to me," Dudley answered. Before Noreen could jump up and object, he said, "I have no more questions."

Noreen's second witness, oncologist Doctor Frank Bowden, testified that patients with a malignant brain tumor often suffer severe headaches, memory lapses, or complete blackouts.

"By complete blackout," Noreen asked smugly, "do you mean that the patient passes out and loses consciousness?"

"Yes," Doctor Bowden answered. "Although these blackouts sometimes last only a few minutes, they can also extend into the comatose or quasi-comatose state, which frequently precedes the patient's death."

When Noreen returned to the defense table, Dudley said any cross would be unnecessary because they had already stipulated that there was a possibility such a thing could happen.

Judge Brill smiled, dismissed the doctor, and moved on to Noreen's third and last witness: Jeffrey T. Caruthers. He wore a dark blue suit, a crisp white shirt, and a gray tie with narrow bands of red on it. A look of sadness clouded his eyes and the corners of his mouth tugged down just far enough.

Once he was sworn in, JT looked at Noreen.

"While your wife Elizabeth was in the hospital," Noreen asked, "did you bring the children to see their mother?"

"Of course," JT answered. "We all visited Elizabeth in the hospital. I brought the kids to see Christian in the nursery a few days after he was born."

"When was the last time you took the children to see your wife?"

Jeffrey gave a deep sigh. "Almost ten months ago. I took David and Kimberly to visit their mom in October of nineteen-eighty-four. I'm pretty certain it was October, because in November Elizabeth suffered a pulmonary embolism and she was in the Intensive Care Unit for quite some time."

"Did you bring the children to see her while she was in Intensive Care?"

"No. Children aren't allowed in Intensive Care."

"During that time did you visit Elizabeth?"

"I wanted to." JT conjured up another sigh, this one deeper than the first. "But unfortunately, with caring for the children, I didn't have much free time."

"We've heard testimony that your mother-in-law volunteered to watch the children for you. Why didn't you take her up on that offer?"

"Because I felt it wasn't in the best interest of my children."

"Why is that?"

"Claire McDermott has a violent temper. She's the kind of person who without provocation takes a sledgehammer to your door. And she bad-mouths me to my kids. Neither she nor my father-in-law have one nice thing to say about me. They say I've turned my back on Elizabeth because I've accepted that she's dying. But what else can I do? I've got a responsibility to my kids. We have to move on with our life. We've got to keep living, because if we don't we'll be buried alongside Liz."

"Jeffrey, you mentioned that the McDermotts have a negative opinion of you. Is that a guess, or have they actually told you?"

"It's a fact. When I asked for a loan," JT said, his voice crackling with fragments of anger, "Charlie McDermott not only refused to help, he said flat out that I was a failure. He told me I shouldn't even be in retailing."

"At the time you asked for that loan weren't you in danger of losing Caruthers Couture, the store which was your family's sole source of income?"

JT cast a vengeful eye across the room to the plaintiff's table. "Yes."

"And did you ultimately lose Caruthers Couture?" Noreen asked.

"Yes," JT repeated with increasing bitterness. "It went belly-up, because I couldn't meet the financial obligations."

"So what income have you and your children lived on since the store closed?"

"None. We've survived on what little money I had left in the bank and some personal possessions I've been able to sell."

"Those personal possessions," Noreen prodded, "did they include the jewelry that your wife, Elizabeth, has asked to have returned?"

"Yes. Her engagement ring was a two-karat diamond. I figured it was more important for me to provide for our children than for Liz to be buried with that ring on her finger." Wistfully he added, "I had hoped she would understand."

"Did you ever discuss your financial situation with Elizabeth and ask for her assistance?"

"Yes. When her father refused to help out, I suggested that we get a second mortgage to tide us over until I could get situated in some new business. She wouldn't sign the papers."

"She *knew* that you and the children had no money to live on and *still* refused to sign the papers?"

"Yeah," JT said with an air of disgust. "She knew, her whole family knew."

"Did it make you angry when Elizabeth and her parents not only refused to help but refused to acknowledge your predicament?"

"Sure it made me angry, I'm only human."

"Is that anger why you finally decided not to allow the children to see Elizabeth or her parents?"

"Of course not," JT answered indignantly. "I decided that the children shouldn't be around Liz for their own good."

"What prompted you to come to that decision?"

JT raised his hand to his chin and sat like he was deep in thought for almost a full minute.

"It wasn't a sudden decision," he finally said. "It was just a bad situation that eventually decided itself. Liz got so much worse, and I could tell it was painful for the kids to see her that way. Then in December she had an incident where she forgot about being paralyzed and took an ugly fall in the hospital. Claire was upset and called and said I ought to get over there. She said the IV had been torn loose from Liz's arm, and there was blood all over the room."

"Did you go?"

"I couldn't. There was nobody to stay with the children, and I certainly wasn't going to let them see their mother like that."

"Is that when you decided it would be better for the children not to see Elizabeth anymore?"

"I suppose so. They hadn't seen her since October and they weren't asking to go." JT gave a forced chuckle. "You know kids, out of sight, out of mind. Anyway, I figured for the time being it would be better for them not to go, I didn't want to have them walk in on something horrible like what had just happened."

"Over time, Elizabeth started to show some improvement. What happened then?"

"The improvement was very slight, and the diagnosis was still the same. She was dying. By then the kids had stopped asking to visit her, and it seemed as though they'd begun to accept her absence. I figured it would be better for them to leave it that way."

"But wasn't Elizabeth asking to see the children?"

"Sure, because that's what would make *her* happy. Me, I was more interested in doing what would be best for the kids."

Noreen said she had no further questions and turned him over for Dudley's cross-examination.

"You claim you visited your wife in the hospital and brought the children to see her," Dudley said. "Can you recall how many times?"

"How many times I visited her?" JT asked.

"Yes," Dudley answered. "During the period when your wife was hospitalized, how many times did you visit her?"

"It's difficult to remember."

"Would you say it was more or less than fifty?"

"Probably less."

"More or less than twenty?"

"I don't know," JT answered impatiently.

"Would it surprise you to know the actual count was nine?"

"Yes," JT said, fumbling to pull his thoughts together. "It would surprise me. I figured it was more. Of course, I had problems with getting someone to watch the store and paying a babysitter, so I guess that's why I didn't—"

"On those nine visits, do you recall the number of times you brought the children to see their mother?"

"No, but I'm sure you're going to tell me," JT answered flippantly.

"Six," Dudley replied. "Three times prior to Christian's birth, once to see him in the nursery, once the day he was released into your care, and once when the primary purpose of your visit was to elicit your wife's assistance in asking your in-laws for a loan. Six times in almost eighteen months. Is that your idea of devotion?"

"Objection," Noreen called out. "Counselor is badgering the witness!"

"Mister Caruthers is a hostile witness," Dudley countered, "and I'm trying to clarify the issue of visitation brought up in direct."

"I'll allow it," Judge Brill said.

"You went to visit your wife on three other occasions," Dudley said. "Do you recall the reason for any those visits?"

"Hmm," Jeffrey said, stalling for an answer. Suddenly his expression brightened.

"Now, I recall. There was a conference with Liz's doctor. I was going to visit anyway, but I was able to time it so that I could be there to talk with the doctor."

"That's right," Dudley replied. "You were there for that one conference. But you missed all of the others, didn't you?"

"What do you expect? I was working at the store all day and taking care of the kids all night!"

"Right, you mentioned that," Dudley said sarcastically. "But let's move ahead to your next visit. That one was solely for the purpose of asking Elizabeth to sign for the second mortgage you wanted to take out, wasn't it?"

"No." JT glared at Dudley.

"Elizabeth refused to sign that mortgage application, because she was concerned about her children not having a home. Aren't those the same children you claim to be protecting?"

"I *am* protecting them!"

"And on another of your so-called visits wasn't your intent solely to ask Elizabeth, who had just been diagnosed with a brain tumor, to play upon her father's sympathy and suggest he give you the necessary funding for your store?"

"I didn't want him to *give* me the money," JT answered. "I wanted a loan."

"A loan?" Dudley repeated. "A loan like the other loans he'd given you? But doesn't the word loan infer that it's something to be repaid?"

JT's mouth curled into a hateful sneer.

"The answer is yes," Dudley said. "Yet on five previous occasions you obtained loans from Charles McDermott, loans totaling one-hundred-and ten-thousand dollars, and never repaid one cent of that money. Isn't that true?"

"I intended to," JT said defensively. "That's why I needed another loan, so I could keep Caruthers Couture afloat. Without that store, I can't repay anything."

"But didn't your store operate at a deficit from its opening?"

"Only because I didn't have the money to expand the way I should have."

"Wasn't that ongoing deficit the reason Charles McDermott refused to give you the loan you asked for last September? Wasn't that also the reason he suggested you consider some other line of work?"

"He doesn't know squat about fashion!" JT shouted. "What right does he have to tell me what business I ought to be in?"

"So," Dudley said, jumping on the opportunity, "Charles McDermott's comments made you quite angry, didn't they?"

"Yeah, they made me angry. Anyone would get angry if somebody ran them down the way he did me."

"In fact, you were so angry you decided to get even, didn't you? You decided to stop Charles McDermott, his wife, and his daughter from ever seeing your children again, isn't that true?"

"No, it isn't!" JT shouted.

"I think it is. I believe you used your children as a weapon to inflict pain and heartache on the family that you blamed for all your problems, a family already burdened by their own sadness. You got even by refusing to allow Elizabeth or her parents access to the children. You did it because you were driven by the desire for revenge!"

Despite Noreen repeatedly shouting, "Objection!" JT bolted from his seat.

"You're friggin' nuts!" he screamed. "I didn't want Liz or her parents around because I felt it was better for the kids! That's all, better for the kids!"

"Mister Caruthers! Sit down and refrain from such outbursts," Judge Brill warned. "We can take a short recess if you need to compose yourself."

JT sat down and said nothing.

"Mister Caruthers, do you blame the McDermott family for your problems?" Dudley asked.

"I don't hold them one-hundred-percent responsible, but it wouldn't have killed Charles to help me out financially. Maybe then I wouldn't have lost the store."

"So you don't blame them for your problems?" Dudley waited for JT to shake his head.

"Well, then, can you explain why you told Doctor Peter Belleau, the court-appointed psychologist, that the McDermotts were responsible for all of your problems, including the gene that caused Elizabeth's illness?"

"I didn't mean it. I suppose I was just venting."

"Were you? Or was Charles McDermott's refusal to lend you the money the final and most influential factor in your decision to keep the children away from Elizabeth's family?"

"I said it had nothing to do with it."

"It didn't? You've already told the court that you brought the children to see Elizabeth six times at the hospital. After she was released from the hospital and forced to move into her parents' home, did you ever bring the children to visit her?"

"No, but that's just a coincidence."

"Do you honestly expect this court to believe it's coincidental that you decided it would be harmful for the children to see their mother and their grandparents just days after Charles McDermott refused to give you yet another loan?"

"Believe what you wanna believe, but I'm telling the truth."

"Then please tell the court exactly what did prompt you to decide it would be harmful for the children to see their mother?"

"Do you not understand dying?" JT said antagonistically. "Liz is dying! She's gonna be out of their life soon enough, so why would I want the kids to get more attached to her? The more attached they get, the harder it's gonna be losing her."

"But aren't the children already attached to their mother?"

"Less now than when she first went into the hospital. When she was first hospitalized, they cried all the time asking when Mommy was coming home. Now they don't do that anymore."

"What about as the children grow older? Isn't it quite possible that they'll wonder why they never had a chance to say goodbye to their mother? Don't you think that even after she's been removed from their life, they might take comfort in knowing how much she loved them?"

"I'll deal with that when the time comes."

"You heard Doctor Rupert's earlier testimony. He feels that when a parent is taken away from a child without adequate explanation or understanding, the child often experiences a sense of rejection. Have you considered that possibility?"

"I don't agree with his opinion."

171

"But Doctor Rupert is a professional, whereas you're—"

"I'm their father!" JT cut in sharply.

"Yes, you are," Dudley answered. "And Elizabeth is their mother. If you have the right to decide what's best for the children, shouldn't she be allowed to have her say about seeing them?"

"No. I'm not dying; Liz is. I'm the one who's gonna have to take care of those kids after she's gone, so what I say is what counts."

"You said earlier, and I quote, you 'need to get on with your life.' Does getting on with your life include having a lady friend who spends quite a bit of time at your house and with your children?"

"Why? Is there a law against my having a friend?"

"There's no law against it, but I question whether this woman is a factor in your decision to keep the children away from their mother."

"No," JT answered angrily. "She's not!"

"So you say," Dudley replied. "What about Charles and Claire McDermott? What's your reason for not allowing them to see the children?"

"I said it before," Jeffrey answered. "It's going to be hard enough to raise three kids on my own without having some busybody in-laws bad-mouthing everything I do or say. The McDermotts don't like me. They never did like me. They don't trust me, and I don't trust them. So the bottom line is I don't want my kids exposed to that kind of negativity."

"You claim the McDermotts have never liked or trusted you, yet Charles McDermott gave you loans totaling over one hundred thousand dollars and he never once asked you to sign a note. Isn't that trust?"

"He only did it because of Elizabeth."

"But Elizabeth had no ownership of Caruthers Couture. That store was owned by you and you alone, correct?"

"Yeah," JT answered begrudgingly.

"If Charles McDermott were to reconsider your loan request, would you allow Elizabeth and her parents to spend time with the children?"

Noreen bolted from her seat. "Objection!"

"Sustained," Judge Brill said. He gave Dudley a look of annoyance.

"No more questions," Dudley stated and resumed his seat.

"Any re-direct?" Judge Brill asked Noreen, but she answered no.

"Judging by the testimony we've heard over the past two days, I must tell you this is an extremely complex case with many side issues. Therefore, before we proceed with summations, I personally would like to interview Elizabeth Caruthers, since she will be a key factor in my decision."

Dudley stood. "Your Honor, with all due respect, Elizabeth would find it extremely difficult to make an appearance in court."

"I understand that," Judge Brill answered. "So I'll interview her at the McDermott home. Ten o'clock tomorrow morning. The attorneys can be present, but you will not be allowed to question the witness and there will be no other participants." The judge turned to his clerk. "Make arrangements for a stenographer."

Moments later the judge stood, and the clerk announced, "Court is adjourned until ten a.m."

173

In Elizabeth's Words

Dudley arrived first at the McDermott house. By the time Noreen rang the doorbell he'd already downed a cup of coffee and explained why Claire could not sit in on the judge's interview with Elizabeth. Judge Brill and a young dark-eyed court stenographer arrived minutes before ten, then all four of them—the two lawyers, the judge and the stenographer—disappeared into Elizabeth's room, closing the door behind them.

Realizing he couldn't do anything, Charles headed to the office. Claire, however, stationed herself at the kitchen table to catch what was said through a vent she'd left open.

The interview started with Judge Brill thanking Elizabeth for her cooperation and promising to keep the session brief as possible.

"The primary purpose of our being here," he explained, "is to provide you with an opportunity to explain your side of this case. Respecting the fact that your stamina is rather limited, I will be the only person asking questions. The attorneys are here as observers. If either attorney feels they have a pertinent issue, they have been instructed to direct the question to me and I will decide whether or not to pursue it."

"Okay," Elizabeth answered and gave a right-side-of-the-face smile. Wearing gray slacks and a light blue sweater that matched her eyes, she sat atop the bed with her back propped against a pile of pillows.

"Why don't we start with you telling me a bit about yourself?"

Elizabeth laughed. "I suppose what you see is what you get. You already know that I have three children and a husband who's fighting to keep them from me. I live here with my mother and father because Jeffrey won't allow me to come back to our house. Oh, and I also have a tumor in my head that's squeezing the life out of me."

"Well, that certainly cuts to the chase of things," Judge Brill said. "But I'd like to hear a bit more about the children and why you feel it would be beneficial for them to spend time with you."

"Have you ever lost someone close to you?" Elizabeth asked. "I have. I've lost all four grandparents, and I never even knew them. My father's parents lived in England, and my mother's parents died in a car crash two months before I was born. So my whole life, I've wondered about them. All of my friends had grandparents who loved them, but not me.

"Something like that can make a child feel terribly insignificant. I don't want my babies to feel that way. I want their little hearts to be filled with the knowledge of how much my parents and I love them. I want them to understand that I didn't just disappear from their lives, our Lord and Savior called me home."

Judge Brill leaned closer soaking up every word. "But do you think it's possible that your children might be too young to understand such a concept?"

"Not if they have a chance to experience it with me, to be part of what's happening, to see death through my eyes and understand it's not something fearful. It's part of God's plan for our life. Every person who lives is destined to someday die. It would be awful for the children to go through life seeing death as some ugly monster that snatched away their mother without a word of goodbye."

What started out as trial testimony turned into a conversation—a conversation between two people well acquainted with the most heartbreaking aspects of life. Noreen and Dudley stood silently at the far side of the room. During a few lulls in the conversation the only sound came from the stenographer's machine.

"Do you have any thoughts on why Jeffrey is fighting so hard to keep the children away from you and your parents?"

"Jeffrey can't deal with life, let alone death. He believes that this situation is life's way of getting back at him. He's angry because he lost the store. He's angry with my dad because he didn't get the money he wanted. He's angry with Mom because she loves me, and he equates that with disliking him. But most of all, he's angry with me. Jeffrey hates broken things, and to him I'm not only broken but I'm also to blame for getting sick and forcing him into a situation where he has three kids to look after and all these financial problems."

"But, why would he—"

"Jeffrey's not a man of faith. He wants to believe he's got a better plan than God. When his plan fizzles, he's got nowhere to go and no one to turn to."

"Have you spoken with him about—"

"Many times. But Jeffrey's set in his way. Something is either perfect or it's broken, and if it's broken he wants to get rid of it."

Elizabeth allowed the right side of her mouth to curl into a sad smile. "One time I told Jeffrey, 'Nothing's perfect. Life is like a sidewalk leading to heaven. We're bound to come across a few cracks in it.' Know what his answer was?"

Judge Brill shook his head.

"He told me, 'When you find cracks in the sidewalk, it's time to look for a new house.'"

"And how do you view those cracks in the sidewalk?"

"They're God's way of moving life's cement. He's giving us a chance to let something new grow."

A long minute passed before Judge Brill asked another question. "Do you feel you're physically able to handle all three children at one time?"

"I doubt that I could do it by myself. But my parents are almost always nearby, and they're happy to lend a hand."

"That might not be the ideal situation, since your husband believes the children will be adversely affected because of your parents' dislike for him."

"He might think that, but it's not true. They're disappointed because of the way Jeffrey's treated me, but Mom and Dad are not vindictive people and they'd never dream of saying something negative about Jeffrey in front of our children."

Judge Brill continued chatting with Elizabeth, first about her years of living with Jeffrey, and then about her relationship with her parents. After that exchange he asked what type of visitation she wanted.

"Unfortunately, I have no way of knowing how long I have, so to me every day is precious," Elizabeth said. "If I could be with my babies every day, I'd be deliriously happy."

"But you realize that probably won't happen, right?"

"Yes, but you asked what I wanted, not what I thought might actually happen."

Judge Brill laughed. Then he tenderly placed his hand over Elizabeth's, promised to be fair, and said goodbye. As the small entourage left the McDermott house, the judge told the attorneys that he would hear their summations Friday morning at ten o'clock.

Noreen winced. That gave her one evening for preparation, hardly enough time to structure an argument to convince herself, let alone Judge Brill, that spending time with this woman could be harmful to any child. Noreen had anticipated finding a frail, dreary-faced woman, a pathetic person too irrational and far too morbid to be with impressionable young children. Unfortunately, Elizabeth Caruthers was exactly the opposite with gentle words and crystal clear reasoning. Even in the face of adversity, she appeared strong and sensible. Worse yet, she was genuinely believable. Elizabeth had convinced the judge that she was a loving mother deeply concerned about the wellbeing of her children.

Noreen's hopes for a plaintiff who would rant about her hatred of the defendant were gone. Elizabeth Caruthers had expressed sympathy for him and nothing more. She'd left no loopholes and pretty much slammed the door on most of the closing arguments Noreen had in mind.

As soon as Noreen arrived at the office, she called Jeffrey Caruthers to explain the details of Elizabeth's testimony. Jeffrey was ready for war long before Noreen suggested they agree to supervised visitation twice a month.

"I'll agree to nothing!" JT shouted. "Nothing!"

"I'm not suggesting you give in," Noreen argued. "But if we're forthcoming with a reasonable offer of terms for visitation, there's a good chance Judge Brill will go along with what we're proposing. On the other hand, if we remain confrontational, there's a distinct possibility he'll issue a visitation order the way Elizabeth requested it."

"How's that?"

"She told Judge Brill she wanted to see the kids every day, and judging by the look on his face I got the impression he was listening."

"You gotta be kidding!"

"I'm not."

"What kind of half-baked lawyer are you?" JT screamed. "You're supposed to win this, not give in! I told you what we were up against and you said we could win! You said—"

"Knock it off, Mister Loud-mouth!" Noreen finally yelled back. "I'm sick of hearing about what I said. You told me your wife was a half-dead invalid, incapable of thinking or caring for her children. That, my friend, is a gigantic, bold-faced lie! Elizabeth Caruthers is very much alive. She's also likeable and articulate! Face facts, your wife was a very credible witness. Whatever argument we had regarding her rationality is gone, vanished, down the drain!"

"Excuse me," JT said in a cynical but much more even tone. "I thought you were supposed to be on *my* side."

"I am on your side," Noreen answered. "But it's time to get real and work with what we have."

"And what's that?" JT asked.

"You've got a problem with your in-laws, so maybe we can get supervised visits that exclude them from seeing the kids. We can possibly limit the number of visits and the duration, but I seriously doubt we can win outright."

JT said nothing for a long time. Then he told Noreen, "I don't care what you think. I'm sticking with my plea for no visitation. None. Not for Liz or her parents. That's it, end of story."

Without any further discussion he hung up the telephone.

Friday morning, Dudley began his closing argument by thanking the court for interviewing Elizabeth Caruthers at her home.

"But perhaps I should correct myself," he said, "since Elizabeth was not actually interviewed at her home. She was interviewed at her parents' home. Unfortunately, after she was diagnosed with a brain tumor, her husband, Jeffrey Caruthers, the father of her children, the man she devoted her life to, would not allow her to return to their home. Because Elizabeth is unable to function independently, she was forced to go to the one place where she was welcome—her parents' house. Even that measure of cruelty was not enough to satisfy Mister Caruthers' quest for vengeance. He also took away the thing his wife treasures most— her children."

Dudley's words brought tears to Claire's eyes and as she fished through her pocketbook for a handkerchief, Charles pulled his from his pocket and handed it to her. She wiped the tears from her eyes, then eased her fingers into the curve of Charlie's hand.

"The saddest part of this story," Dudley continued, "is that Jeffrey Caruthers' primary motivation is to wreak revenge on a father-in-law who refuses to give him any more money. I say give rather than lend, because lend would infer there was some intention to repay the debt. Jeffrey Caruthers never had such an intention. Not only did he not intend to repay his one-hundred-and-ten-thousand-dollar debt, but he became enraged when Charles McDermott drew the line and said no more."

JT and Noreen sat side by side at the defense table, him staring blank-eyed into nothingness, her scribbling notes as Dudley spoke.

"Ever since the day Charles McDermott pulled the plug on his funding of the defendant's failing business," Dudley said, giving JT an accusatory glance and then turning back to the judge, "no one in the McDermott family has been allowed access to the Caruthers children. Not even Elizabeth, the mother of these children. The truth is obvious. He is using Elizabeth's love for her children to gain revenge against his in-laws.

"Jeffrey Caruthers claims he is doing this for one reason: because it is in the best interest of his children. How can any parent believe it to be in the best interest of their child to deprive them of their mother's love as well as the love of their grandparents?

"Elizabeth Caruthers is a dying woman with a singular motive, which is to leave her children with a legacy of love. She is a devoted mother who wants and deserves to spend time with her children so they can approach adulthood with the knowledge of how much she loved them.

"In earlier testimony, Doctor Rupert, a highly-acclaimed child psychologist, provided this court with clinical study results indicating that children are less likely to blame themselves for the loss of a parent and have fewer long-term psychological problems when they understand the causative factors in the death of that parent. The same study indicated that the sudden and unexplained removal of a parent substantially increases the child's risk of psychological problems.

"The defense would have you believe Elizabeth Caruthers is mentally incapable of spending time with her children—too bitter, they say, too maudlin. But it is easy to see that she is none of those things. She is instead a woman of great faith. A woman who wants to share her acceptance of God's will with her children so that as they grow older, they can be free to celebrate her life rather than live with recriminations of her death.

"Your Honor," Dudley continued, "this court has met with and interviewed Elizabeth Caruthers, so I need not go into lengthy detail about her sincerity and genuine love for the children. Although the defendant has taken from her that which she holds most dear, she bears him no malice and is not asking the court for redress. Elizabeth Caruthers asks only that you right the wrong taking place. She is well aware that this tumor has affected her motor skills and causes sporadic memory loss, but she is still quite capable of dealing with the emotional needs of her children. As for her physical infirmities, she has assured the court that one of her parents will be on hand to offer assistance whenever the children are present.

"In closing, Your Honor, we respectfully request that the court grant Elizabeth Caruthers visitation with her children four days each week. And in light of the uncooperative posture taken by her husband, Jeffrey Caruthers, we also ask that the court order these visitations scheduled for specific days and duration times."

Dudley gave the judge a polite nod, then returned to his seat.

Noreen stood and smoothed her skirt, regretting that she'd dressed in a black suit that gave her the look of a hard-edged, uncaring person. This morning she'd thought it projected an air of professionalism, but now she wished she'd worn something a bit more feminine—a silk dress or a light-colored suit. With Dudley playing all those sincerity, goodness, and sympathy cards, she might come across as some sort of ogre if she launched an all-out attack on Elizabeth. Noreen took two steps forward.

"Your Honor," she said hesitantly. "Like this court, Jeffrey Caruthers is absolutely and totally committed to any action that is solely in the best interest of his three young children. He has exhibited his level of dedication by setting aside his personal interest in the retail establishment of Caruthers Couture to remain at home and take care of the children that his wife, Elizabeth, can no longer care for."

Dozens of thoughts whirled through Noreen's head. She knew the summation she'd practiced based on the psychological damage the children could suffer from exposure to their dying mother wouldn't work now. On the spur of the moment she decided to shift strategies and target Claire and Charles.

"Your Honor," Noreen said, her voice commanding, strong and upbeat. "Although Jeffrey Caruthers is deeply saddened by his wife's medical condition, he still has three children to look after. These children deserve as much stability as possible despite these tragic circumstances. The McDermott household does not offer either a stable or tranquil environment. We've heard Elizabeth Caruthers testify that she accepts and understands the reality of her death and wants her children to do the same. However, the McDermotts, who are part and parcel of any visitation, are in complete opposition to her way of thinking. Instead they preach and predict a cure.

"Charles McDermott told the court-appointed psychologist that he, meaning the healthy thirty-two-year-old doctor himself, could quite possibly die before Elizabeth. Charles and Claire McDermott have both voiced this commitment to the idea that some yet-undiscovered miracle drug will come along in time to save their daughter."

"What we have here," Noreen gestured toward the plaintiff's table, "is a house divided. A family where the mother will whisper the reality of death into the children's left ear while the grandparents shout fantasies of cure into their right. The children will have one figure of authority dispensing hope, the other dashing it.

"Reality, fantasy," Noreen said, turning her palms upward and using them as measuring scales. "Reality, fantasy," she repeated. "How can we even hope to understand the weight of that on a young mind? In such an environment, it would be almost impossible for any child, even a child of considerable maturity, to avoid the confusion that inevitably leads to emotional problems."

Noreen paused, walked back to the table, and took a long drink of water. The expression of concern sliding onto Judge Brill's face said she was driving home her point. *Good,* she thought and continued.

"In addition to all of this emotional turmoil, the children will also be exposed to Claire McDermott's potential for violence. We've already heard how she took a sledgehammer to my client's door. Who's to say such an incident won't happen again? Next time it could be one of the children who become her target of outrage."

Noreen noticed a frown cross the judge's face, so she stopped any further exploitation of Claire.

"Over the past months," Noreen said, "Jeffrey Caruthers has tried in the gentlest way possible to wean the children away from their mother, to lessen their connection and their dependence upon her. Was he trying to be cruel? Absolutely not! He was doing what, as a loving father, he felt compelled to do so that when Elizabeth Caruthers finally leaves this earth, her children would be spared the heartbreak and trauma he has had to suffer.

"Such an action has been hard on Jeffrey Caruthers. It has cost him his business, his financial stability, even his relationship with his wife and her family. But to him it was worth it, because he was protecting the tender hearts of his children who with the careful guidance of their father have now reached a point where they no longer cry for their mother, where they no longer beg that she come home. They've reached a point where she's gradually fading into a sweet memory. It would be unthinkable to take this progress away from them.

"Jeffrey Caruthers is not a saint, and I don't purport to picture him as such. He is, however, an extremely devoted father who tries to protect and care for his children. It's regretful that other relationships have faltered because his focus has been on doing what is best for his children. He could have salvaged those relationships by catering to the needs of his wife and in-laws. But he chose to concentrate on his children. Jeffrey Caruthers did what he believed was best for them, and if he had to make that choice again he would do exactly the same thing.

"We ask that the court endorse these efforts by denying any visitation to the McDermott household, which unfortunately includes Elizabeth Caruthers."

Noreen turned back to her table and sat down.

Judge Brill thought for a moment before speaking.

"I am extremely cognizant of the need for an early decision in this case, but there are many complex and tragic issues, all of which I must take into consideration before rendering my verdict. Before ten o'clock Monday morning both attorneys will receive my decision."

With that he rapped his gavel, then left the courtroom.

Samuel E. Brill

Judge Brill left the courthouse Friday afternoon with stooped shoulders, his head tilted forward, and his eyes downcast. Placing one foot in front of the other, he propelled himself across the parking lot. In his right hand he carried a brown briefcase swollen with papers, a load so heavy it caused him to list to that side.

After hearing the summations of Caruthers v Caruthers, he'd sat through eight more tales of family strife—brother against brother, daughter against mother, child neglect, spousal abuse and violence…such terrible violence. On their faces Judge Brill saw the tracks of bitter tears and in their eyes stories of heartache piled upon heartache. It seemed as though there was no limit to the amount of bitterness and hatred a person could feel toward someone they'd once loved.

Some cases were clearly black or white. They had no shades of gray, no shadows of doubt lurking around the corner, and no recriminations waiting to haunt Sam Brill should he dare to sleep. In cases where right and wrong were easily defined, Sam Brill dispensed justice in a fair and efficient manner. Once decided, those cases were packed away in manila envelopes and filed alongside thousands of others. They remained at the courthouse when Sam Brill went home at night.

But there were others too painful to seal inside an envelope. Those cases burned their way into Sam's memory and poked a fiery finger at his brain. In each of those instances he'd rendered the decision he thought just. But Sam knew justice was blind, incapable of understanding the bond between children and their parents.

Sam Brill had resolved eight of the nine cases he'd heard that day. The only one left pending was that of Caruthers v Caruthers. It should have been a relatively easy decision. If he went strictly according to the law, Elizabeth Caruthers had every right to be with her children. She was a principled woman, a good mother, a person who trusted in the will of God, and would certainly do her children no harm. But Sam Brill had to consider her husband, Jeffrey Caruthers, a self-centered man, irrational, obstinate, divorced from reality—a man with the same look of desperation and wild-eyed ferocity as Jack Wallner.

When Sam ruled the Wallner girls had to be returned to Alma, Jack flew into an uncontrollable rage, screamed a string of obscenities, and shook his fist in the air. Then before anyone realized what was happening, Jack flung himself across the defense table and came at the judge. Luckily the court deputy tackled him before he made it across the courtroom. Sam could have had Jack Wallner carted off to jail, and he regretted not doing so. It would have saved the man's life.

Sam reminded himself that he allowed Jack Wallner to walk free because he'd felt compassion for a man stretched beyond his emotional limit. He'd tried to be merciful, but something had gone terribly wrong. From that day forward Sam couldn't rid himself of the picture of Jack Wallner lying dead on the courthouse steps— part of his face gone, and those frenzied eyes forever accusing.

On Friday evening Sam had little appetite. He ate a few bites of chicken, worked a handful of peas into his mashed potato, then claimed he wasn't very hungry and left the table. After dinner he settled into the recliner to watch television, but after flipping channels for nearly an hour he found nothing worth watching and went to bed.

Bed, but not sleep. Sam climbed beneath the sheets and stretched out on his back, but there in the ridges and swirls of ceiling paint he could see Jack Wallner's face. He turned on his right side but that didn't work, so he turned to the left. Nothing helped. The face was everywhere—angry eyes glinting through the silver of a mirror, peering into windowpanes, accusing, accusing, endlessly accusing. The pale shimmer of morning edged across the sky before Sam Brill finally fell asleep.

On Saturday he agreed to accompany his wife, Maggie, to the Plainfield Craft Fair, even though it was something he disliked doing. But he needed a place to escape the thoughts and images of Jack Wallner. They walked through aisle after aisle of vendors selling handmade wares—ruffled aprons, painted teapots, crocheted doilies. Maggie stopped in front of a woman selling potholders stitched into the shape of people.

"Aren't these adorable?" she said, turning to Sam.

He gave an obligatory nod.

"Which do you like best?" she asked, holding two chubby-faced potholders—one decorated with a blue apron, the other with green.

Sam, in no mood for decision making, said, "Get both."

"They're exactly the same," Maggie answered with a pout. "Why would you suggest that I buy both when they're exactly the same?"

"Blue," he said to end the discussion. Maggie smiled and went to pay for her purchase. Sam walked on, past the clowns painted on velvet, past a booth filled with lacy toilet paper covers. Did life have to be this way, he wondered. Did everything have to revolve around his decisions? It was never ending—big decisions, little decisions, unimportant decisions, life or death decisions, choose wrong and a child's life was ruined, choose wrong and a father puts a gun to his head, choose wrong and that decision haunts you for the rest of your life.

Maggie caught up with him and took hold of his arm. "I'm glad you chose blue," she said. "I liked that one best."

Sam felt a jolt of annoyance. If Maggie liked blue, then why had she asked him to decide? Why didn't people simply make their own decisions? Suddenly Sam felt tired, worn threadbare by the difficult questions that continuously picked at the fiber of his soul.

"Remember the camping trip we took six years ago?" he asked nostalgically.

Maggie gave him a smile and nodded.

October 9, 1985

At nine-fifteen Monday morning a messenger left the Union County Courthouse carrying two large brown envelopes. Despite the way Sam Brill had labored over his decision, he realized it would probably not satisfy either recipient. Elizabeth Caruthers was a reasonable person, someone Judge Brill hoped might accept his ruling and understand how he had come to such a decision. Jeffrey Caruthers would not. He was a dark soul, someone with layer upon layer of anger folded inside of him, a person Sam believed capable of unthinkable deeds. Hoping to avoid a replay of the Wallner tragedy, he'd spent half the night composing a lengthy document that wove heartfelt advice though the bitter reality of a court order.

At nine-thirty, the first envelope arrived at the law office of Simmons and Grimm. The receptionist carried the envelope into Dudley's office and handed it to him.

"I believe this is what you're waiting for," she said.

Some cases, Dudley knew, were little more than points of law to be argued, but this case was different. Charlie McDermott and Dudley were lifelong friends. They'd gone to school together, attended each other's weddings, and welcomed new babies into their families. Dudley thought of his own daughter, two years younger than Elizabeth and a mother herself. Yes, this case meant a lot to Dudley. It meant a lot because he wanted to win, not for himself but for Elizabeth. Dudley stared at the envelope for several minutes before he garnered enough courage to slit it open.

Three times he read through Judge Brill's decision. When he had gleaned all there was to be had from the lengthy court order, he telephoned Elizabeth. "I've got good news and bad news," he told her.

Claire listened on the extension.

"What's the good news?" Elizabeth asked.

"The good news is that Judge Brill's order states Jeffrey has to allow all three children to visit you. He also gave us a court-appointed schedule for the visits."

"That's wonderful," Elizabeth said.

"So what's the bad news?" Claire asked apprehensively.

"I'm afraid the bad news in part involves you. Rightly or wrongly, Judge Brill has acknowledged Jeffrey's concern that you and Charlie might give the children an unrealistic expectation with regard to Elizabeth's condition. He's ruled that all visits with the children must be supervised."

"By who?" Claire asked.

"Jeffrey or a court-approved guardian."

"JT is going to bring the children?" Elizabeth said brightly.

"He probably will. I don't have an acknowledgement from his attorney yet," Dudley answered. "Judge Brill's order states that Jeffrey has to deliver all three children for a visit every Sunday morning from nine o'clock until noon. And he also has to allow you to telephone the children three times a week."

"Starting when?" Claire asked.

"Visitation will most likely start this coming Sunday, phone calls possibly as soon as tomorrow. I'll know more after I speak with Noreen Sarnoff."

They spoke for a few minutes longer, but Elizabeth's head already buzzed with excitement. Before she hung up Elizabeth cooed, "Thank you, Mister Grimm, thank you so very, very much."

At nine-forty, the second envelope arrived at Noreen Sarnoff's office. Without a moment's hesitation she tore it open and read through Judge Brill's decision. The words "Jeffrey Caruthers is ordered to deliver the three minor children for weekly visitation" virtually jumped off the page.

Noreen grimaced. Losing was never fun, but at least visitation was limited to once a week and she'd gotten the visits supervised, which she reasoned counted for something.

She poured herself a second cup of coffee, then sat behind her desk considering just how she would give JT the news. At ten-fifteen she reluctantly telephoned Jeffrey Caruthers.

"Good news," she said. "Elizabeth didn't get what she was looking for. Judge Brill limited her visitation to once a week, and he ordered that those visits be supervised either by you or a court-approved guardian."

"Good news?!" JT screamed. "Are you nuts? I said *no* visitation! Did you not understand that no visitation means none? None! Zero, nada, zilch—"

"I realize that's what you wanted," Noreen interrupted, "but we're lucky to come out of this with a split decision when—"

"Don't give me that split decision crap! I paid good money because you said we'd win. A slam-dunk, that's what you said, a slam-dunk."

Noreen's temper finally flared and she shouted, "Enough! If you think screaming in my ear is gonna change things, you're sadly mistaken. You're lucky to get what you got! Personally, I think the court went easy on you. Why, I don't know."

"Oh, great," JT snarled. "Now you're on *her* side!"

"No, stupid, I'm on your side. Face facts, you were a lousy witness. You came across as vindictive and ticked off at the world. Elizabeth, on the other hand, was great. She was sincere and believable, and more importantly she didn't try to bury you, which she probably could have."

"Look, I said no visitation and that's what she's getting, none. I don't care what you say or that judge says or anybody in the entire state of New Jersey says, I'm not allowing my kids to step one foot inside that house."

"You haven't got a choice."

"Oh, yes, I do! I can take the kids and—"

"Don't say it," Noreen warned. "Because if you tell me you're planning to kidnap those children that's a crime, and attorney-client privilege goes out the window when it comes to prior knowledge of a crime about to be committed."

"I'm just saying—"

"Don't," Noreen warned again. "And let me give you this little piece of free advice. If you do try something stupid, you'll end up in the slammer for a good long time and the probability is your in-laws will be the ones to raise your children. Don't think they wouldn't love to see that happen!"

"They can't take my kids away from me, I'm their father."

"The court can and will if you even *think* about kidnapping those children."

"So I'm supposed to just march myself over there every Sunday and hand my kids over to that bunch of crazies? Who's to say they won't take off with the kids?"

"Judge Brill ordered supervised visits," Noreen reasoned. "You can stay there with the kids, or you can obtain a court-approved guardian to accompany them on visits."

JT snorted. "Some concession that is."

"It's better than nothing."

"What if the kids don't want to go? What if they're sick or something?"

"If the kids are sick, you call your wife, explain the situation, and arrange an alternate time for visitation."

"How am I supposed to deal with this?" JT asked, desperation permeating his voice.

"It's once a week," Noreen said unsympathetically. "Just do what the court ordered so you don't risk losing your kids altogether."

"What about after Liz dies, do Claire and Charlie still get to see the kids?"

"No, the court order only applies to the children's mother."

"Then I'm off the hook? I don't have to bring the kids over there anymore?"

"Not unless the McDermotts bring another lawsuit to request their own visitation."

"Can they do that?"

"They can, but I doubt it would be successful. New Jersey has no real statute governing visitation for grandparents."

"So this is only until Liz dies?" JT said.

After that Jeffrey tried to talk Noreen into giving him a reduction on her fee since she didn't get him the decision he wanted. When she told him that he had a better chance of seeing pigs fly, he slammed the telephone down.

Noreen Sarnoff sat behind her desk shaking her head in amazement. Not much surprised her, because she'd seen the worst of them—knife-wielding gang members, sleazy crooks, swindlers of every sort, wife beaters even—but never anyone as callous and unyielding as JT Caruthers. She knew she had to watch her step with him, cover all bases. Noreen Xeroxed Judge Brill's court order and attached a letter detailing what was expected. At the bottom of her letter she wrote in bold-face type, "This visitation schedule is effective immediately, and you have been instructed to bring the three minor children to visit their mother, Elizabeth, starting on Sunday, October fifteenth."

Elizabeth could hardly wait to talk to the children, and for all of Monday afternoon she could do little but think and rethink what she might say to them. It had been almost a year. A year was forever in the life of a child. In a year a baby learns to stand and walk, a toddler becomes a little girl, and a boy goes from Robin

Hood to race cars. What would they be like now, these babies of hers? Would they remember the things they'd once done together? Would they ask questions she couldn't answer? Did they know of her illness and did they understand what was happening? How much, if anything, had Jeffrey told them? After the long months of wondering whether she would ever see her babies, it would finally happen. The joy of it made her heart feel light as the flutter of angel wings.

Elizabeth closed her eyes and pictured David, her first-born. With dark hair and eyes the color of a Hershey Bar, he looked like his father and in some ways he had Jeffrey's mannerisms. David was still a little boy but already knew how to flash a smile that got him most anything he wanted.

And then there was Kimberly with her constant calling of "ommy, ommy." While learning to talk, Kimberly lopped off the first letter of almost every word. Now she was three, no longer a toddler but a little girl. Elizabeth pictured her a bit taller, perhaps more wiry, but still blessed with silky blond curls. Kimberly loved stories about a prince and princess who marry and live happily ever after. Elizabeth recalled when she herself loved those stories. She'd believed in them until—

A wave of sadness emerged but Elizabeth turned her thoughts to Christian, the child she had never really known. She'd last seen or held him five weeks after he was born. Now his first birthday had come and gone along with those baby experiences—the first peals of laughter, tiny hands grappling for whatever they could reach, a first tooth, a first word, learning to sit, to stand, to trust, precious moments every one of them, but regretfully not hers to share.

How would he react, this child who had never known her? To him she was a stranger. That thought struck hard. Christian would need time, and she had to allow him that. She would have to hold back the desire to snuggle his face to hers. She would have to wait until he felt ready to come to her.

In time it will happen, Elizabeth assured herself. *In God's own time, it will happen.*

Although it took all the willpower she could muster, Elizabeth waited until three-thirty Tuesday afternoon to telephone the children. She dialed Jeffrey's number and listened as it rang and rang. For a full eight minutes she sat there listening to the hollow echo of that ring before she finally hung up.

"It's fairly warm today," Claire suggested. "Maybe JT's taken them to the park."

"Sure, that must be it," Elizabeth said.

At six o'clock she tried again, but still no answer. She tried again at seven and then at eight. There was still no answer.

"Do you think something might be wrong?" Elizabeth asked her father, but Charlie said he doubted such was the case.

"What then?" Elizabeth asked earnestly.

Charlie shrugged. "JT's not one who likes losing. Maybe he thinks he can weasel out of the ruling."

"He can't do that," Claire declared. "It's illegal! The court order said he had to let Liz talk to the children. If the court ruling says that's what he has to do, then he has to do it!"

"The likelihood," Charlie said, "is that JT won't out-and-out defy the court order. But he'll probably do everything possible to push his limits."

"Can he get away with it?" Elizabeth asked apprehensively.

"Maybe, maybe not," her father answered. "It all depends on what we do. If we believe he's deliberately defying the judge's visitation order, we can take him back to court."

"What good will it do?" Claire asked. "If he doesn't obey the court order the first time, what makes you think he'll obey it the second time?"

"If we take him to court for disobeying the first order, the judge will probably hit him with sanctions. A fine, possibly even jail time."

"Dad," Elizabeth said. "Isn't it a little too premature to be thinking of that? After all, he didn't answer the phone for one day. That doesn't mean he's never going to."

"I hope not," Charlie said gravely. "I certainly hope not."

For the remainder of the evening there was no further discussion about JT. Claire worked on an afghan she was crocheting, Charles watched the second World Series game, and Elizabeth pretended to read. For almost an hour Elizabeth flipped through the pages of *Better Homes and Gardens*, looking at roasted turkeys and chrysanthemum arrangements clouded by the haze of tears plaguing her eyes. At ten o'clock, when her eyes had grown weary and her heart exhausted, Claire helped her into bed.

Charles said nothing that night. He had seen the tears in Elizabeth's eyes and understood the heartache she felt, but he was at a loss for words. When morning came he left the house at eight-thirty, but instead of turning toward the bank he traveled through a maze of streets until he came to the Caruthers house. He parked the car, pulled a sheet of notepaper from his briefcase, and began writing. Once finished, he stepped from the car, carried the folded paper to the house, and slipped it through the mail slot in the front door. After that he drove off.

The Warning

Jeffrey despised the shaft of sunlight that sliced across the bedroom and interrupted his sleep. On Wednesday morning he woke to that blinding glint of light and the sound of David relentlessly calling his name. Jeffrey turned over and tugged the blanket above his ears. Moments later David tromped into the bedroom and began poking his back.

"Wake up, Daddy," David said, "I need you to read my letter."

"Later," JT answered wearily.

"No, now."

JT turned to face the boy. "I'm trying to sleep. Go back downstairs and play. We'll read your book later."

"It's not a book," David answered peevishly. "It's my letter from Grandpa."

JT sat up. "Your letter from Grandpa?"

David nodded.

"Go get it."

David thumped down the stairs and came back carrying the note Charles had written. He handed it to JT. "Read," he commanded.

JT unfolded the note and scanned the first few lines.

"Jeffrey," the note began without any salutation and written in the tight script that JT recognized as Charlie's.

"Where'd you get this?" he asked the boy.

"Grandpa gave it to me."

"He was here? In the house?"

"Grandpa was outside," David said. "He saw me in the window and put my letter in the letter hole. Now read, okay?"

"Okay," JT answered. "But after I read it to you, I have to keep the letter and put it in a safe place because it also has a message for Daddy, okay?"

"Dear David," he began, making up the words, "I hope you are being a very good boy and minding everything your daddy tells you to do. Your daddy has a lot of responsibility, and he needs you to help him. You must eat whatever he gives you for dinner and don't hit your sister. Love from Grandpa."

"That's all?"

"Unh-huh," JT nodded. "Just that and a business message for me."

"Read me the business message."

"Nope, little boys don't need to hear grown-up messages." JT turned David around and gave him a pat on the behind. "Now scoot. Christian was up half the night, so let me sleep a while longer."

"Okay," David answered. He ran into Kimberly's room hollering about how he'd gotten a special letter from Grandpa.

Once the boy had left, JT opened the note again.

"Jeffrey," it read, "Either you answer the telephone this afternoon and allow Elizabeth to talk to her children, or we will be headed right back to court. I also expect you to deliver all three children to our house for a visit with their mother this coming Sunday at precisely nine o'clock—not one minute later. This is the one and only warning I will give you. If you cause my daughter another minute of unnecessary anguish, I will notify Judge Brill that you are in defiance of his court order and we can take it from there.

Charles Francis McDermott."

There was no longer any chance of sleep for JT. He stood and paced the room for several minutes thinking of how to handle this. When he heard Kelsey's car pull into the garage, he tore the note into tiny pieces and flushed it down the toilet.

"Okay, Charlie," he grumbled. "Start threatening me, and we'll see who wins." As far as JT was concerned nothing would louse up his relationship with Kelsey—including spending Sundays with Liz. He pulled on a pair of jeans and headed downstairs.

Kelsey stood in the kitchen pouring milk over a bowl of Cheerios. The expression on JT's face softened as soon as he saw her. He crossed the room and folded her into his arms. This was the sort of woman he needed, a woman full of life, who stood straight and tall, a woman with the face of an angel and the lithe body of a teenager. He pressed his face into the nape of her neck and breathed in the scent of jasmine.

Before JT could take full advantage of the moment, David ran into the kitchen. "Bobby won't give me back my race car!"

"So what?" JT said. "Let him play with it for a while."

"But it's mine."

"Enough!" JT snapped. "Sit down and eat your breakfast."

"Bobby's not eating."

"He will," Kelsey cooed. "Come on, dumpling, it's time for breakfast."

Bobby did bear a strong resemblance to a dumpling in that he was squat, round, and dimpled. He came as a package with Kelsey. She might have looked like a teenager, but she was actually a twenty-one-year-old single mom struggling to make ends meet since she'd lost track of dumpling's daddy.

"Don't worry," JT had assured her. "After Liz dies, we'll get married."

"Why not now?"

"Because a divorce costs. If I divorce Liz, she gets half of everything. If I wait for her to die, I keep it all."

That conversation had taken place weeks ago, but Kelsey had little patience and kept asking how much longer it would take. Jeffrey didn't want to lose Kelsey, so he'd gone to great lengths to placate her. First he'd given her Liz's sapphire ring, then it was the Rolex, and after that a bracelet embellished with three solid gold Spanish doubloons.

With the bright red race car still clutched in his chubby little hand, Bobby scooted himself onto the chair closest to Kelsey and began stuffing Cheerios into his mouth. David, glowering at the car, snorted, "This ain't fair."

"Get used to it," Kelsey said when JT went upstairs. "Bobby's gonna be your brother."

When JT returned with Kimberly and Christian, David asked, "Is it true, Daddy? Is Bobby gonna be my brother?"

"Well, yes, I suppose so," JT answered nervously, "sooner or later."

"It had better be sooner," Kelsey said.

Later that morning, when Bobby and Christian had gone down for a nap, Kimberly and David were watching cartoons, and Kelsey was deep into the October issue of *Vogue*, JT slipped away. He went into his study, closed the door, and dialed Noreen Sarnoff's number. The telephone rang six times, and eventually a recording answered.

"This is Jeffrey Caruthers," he said after the beep. "I've got a problem. Call me back."

When Noreen heard JT's message later that afternoon, she cringed. She'd thought with the trial over and the court order executed, she'd heard the last of Jeffrey Caruthers. But he was back again with the sound of urgency in his voice.

JT's name came at the top of the list of clients Noreen disliked. She debated about calling him or simply erasing the message. In the end her sense of ethics won out, and she dialed his number.

"What now?" she asked when he answered on the very first ring.

"Liz's father is threatening me," JT said. "Isn't that illegal?"

"Threatening you?"

"Yeah, he says he's gonna take me back to court."

"For what?"

"Because I didn't answer the telephone when Liz called."

Noreen started putting the pieces together. "Exactly how many times did you not answer?"

"I don't know exactly—"

"More than five?"

"Probably."

"More than ten?"

"Maybe."

"Did she leave messages?"

"Yeah."

"Did you return her calls?"

"No, and I'm not going to."

"Judge Brill's ruling stated that you had to permit your wife to speak to the children three times a week. If you don't, you're in defiance of his order and Charles McDermott has every right to ask the court for sanctions."

"What happens then?"

"You could be fined, spend time in jail, maybe even lose custody of the children."

"That's stupid," JT said.

"No," Noreen replied, "*you're* stupid for defying the judge's order."

"So what do I have to do?"

"As soon as we hang up, call your wife and let her talk to those kids. And make certain you get them over there Sunday morning."

"I don't have anybody to bring them."

"Oh, pleeese," Noreen groaned. "If there's no family member available to take them, go yourself!"

"And sit there for three hours watching Liz die?" JT asked, but Noreen had hung up.

"Some lawyer," he grumbled.

JT didn't call Liz when he hung up. Instead, he unplugged the telephone and waited until seven o'clock that evening to return her calls. When he finally did, Elizabeth's father answered the telephone.

"Is Liz there?" JT said. "David wants to talk to her."

"Hold on please," Charles answered, his voice cold but civil.

Moments later, Liz picked up the phone.

"Jeffrey," she said, trying to sound healthier than she felt. "Thanks for calling me back."

Without acknowledging her words, JT handed the receiver to his son. "Hi, Mommy," David said.

Elizabeth had waited so long to hear those two words. She opened her mouth and a sigh escaped, carrying away the anguish of lost time. "David, honey," she said, "Mommy's missed you so very, very much."

"I miss you too, Mommy. Are you in heaven?"

"No, honey, Mommy is at Grandma's house." Elizabeth started to ask why he thought that, but she heard David's voice recede slightly.

"Daddy," the boy yelled. "Mommy's not in heaven, she's at Grandma's house!"

A stab pierced her heart, but she moved on. "Would you like to come and see Mommy?"

"Unh-huh. Can Kimberly come too?"

"She sure can. You can come and Kimmie can come, and Christian can come too. We'll have a party with milk and cookies. And guess what else? Stories! Mommy's got three new story books, and I'll read each of you a special story. Would you like that?"

"Are they Robin Hood books?"

"Robin Hood?" Liz said, feigning surprise. "Why, I thought Peter Rabbit was your favorite."

"Peter Rabbit is for babies," he said indignantly. "I like Robin Hood."

"Well, then," she laughed, "it's a good thing I got a new Robin Hood book."

"Robin Hood is Christian's favorite too, so you have to read two stories."

"Two stories!" Elizabeth exclaimed. "Don't you think maybe Christian would rather hear a Peter Rabbit story?"

"No, he likes Robin Hood."

"Did he tell you that?"

David giggled. "Silly, Christian doesn't know how to talk. He's a baby. He says Daddy and milk, that's all."

David's first word was Mommy, as was Kimberly's, but Christian was a child who had never known a mother. Elizabeth choked back the urge to cry.

"Well, then," she said, moving past the momentary sadness. "How do you know Christian doesn't like Peter Rabbit?"

"I know," David said with the guile of a six-year-old, "because when I show him both books, he points to Robin Hood."

"Oh," Elizabeth said. "Well, then, I guess I'll just have to read two Robin Hood stories."

"Hooray! Can we come to Grandma's house tomorrow?"

"Not tomorrow, but Daddy's going to bring all three of you to see me on Sunday. Sunday's only two more days after tomorrow."

"Daddy," David called out. "Are we going to see Mommy on Sunday?"

Elizabeth heard Jeffrey answer, "We'll see. Now hang up and come take your bath!"

"Daddy said I've gotta hang up," David reported.

"I heard him. Baths are important, so do what Daddy said. Go take your bath. I'll talk to Kimmie for a little while."

"She can't talk. She already went to bed."

"Oh," Elizabeth said, momentarily stumped. "Well, then—tell Daddy to please have Kimmie call me tomorrow."

"Daddy gets mad if anybody calls her that. He said her name is Kimberly, not Kimmie."

In the background Elizabeth heard JT shout, "One minute!"

"I can hear your daddy calling you, sweetheart, so you'd better go."

Liz hesitated a second, then said, "I love you, David." By then he was gone.

On Thursday there was no call from Kimberly, nor was there a call on Friday. Both days Elizabeth called the house any number of times, but the telephone rang without an answer. By Saturday morning Elizabeth grew quite discouraged and began to wonder if JT would ever allow her to talk to or see the children. She tried calling three times, but still no answer. On the fourth try Kimberly answered in her high-pitched little girl voice.

"Hi, Kimberly," Elizabeth said, a swell of affection catching in her throat. "Do you know this is Mommy?"

"Yes," Kimberly answered. She sounded far more grown-up than Liz remembered. "You're at Grandma's house, not in heaven."

"Yes, I'm at Grandma's. But that doesn't mean I don't think of you and miss you every day. Tomorrow is going to be very special. So special it will be almost like Christmas."

"Why?"

"Because you and David and Christian are coming to see me! Isn't that wonderful?"

"Will you buy us toys?"

"What toys do you want?"

"A Baby Tears doll with her own baby carriage and a highchair, and a ball for Christian, and a race car for David and—"

"Whoa, isn't that an awful lot to be asking for?" Elizabeth laughed. "Where would I get all that money?"

"From Grandpa."

"What makes you think Grandpa has that much money?"

"Grandpa has a lot of money," she said. "He stole Daddy's money."

Elizabeth stopped laughing. "What makes you think Grandpa stole Daddy's money?"

"Daddy said so. He said he doesn't have enough money to buy us toys because Grandpa stole it all."

It took Elizabeth a moment to gather her thoughts. "Kimberly, sweetheart, I think you might have misunderstood what Daddy said. Grandpa would never ever steal anything, especially not from you or your daddy. Grandpa loves all of us, even your daddy. People don't steal things from somebody they love."

"Then who stole Daddy's money?"

"I don't think anybody stole Daddy's money, I think maybe he just lost it. Remember when you lost your red mittens?"

"Unh-huh."

"Nobody stole them, you just lost them. They might have fallen out of your pocket or maybe you left them at the playground but they were lost, not stolen. And that's probably what happened to Daddy's money. It got lost."

"Doesn't Grandpa have enough money to buy us *one* toy?"

"We'll see. I'll try to get something special for when you come to visit. Would you like crayons and a Cinderella coloring book?"

"Yes, yes!" Kimberly shouted. "I love Cinderella. And don't forget, Christian needs a ball 'cause sometimes he takes David's, and David gets mad."

"Well, we can't have that, can we?" Elizabeth teased.

They continued to talk for several minutes. Kimberly chattered on telling her mother stories of Christian—what made him laugh, how he was learning to walk, and how he could almost say her name. Listening to the way she spoke about her baby brother made Kimberly seem older, too adult for a child of her years.

"He's the cutest baby ever," she cooed, her words so motherly Liz was torn between laughter and tears. Her little girl, still a baby herself, had blossomed into a big sister with an abundance of love to share.

Before long, she heard JT calling for Kimberly to hang up, so Elizabeth told her daughter how very much she loved her then let her go. After that, Liz began to count the hours until all three of her babies would be with her.

Waiting

As Elizabeth recalled the conversation with her daughter, thunder cracked so loud it caused her bones to rattle. Right behind the thunder came spears of lightning and after that a torrential downpour.

"A storm like this can't possibly last for long," she said optimistically.

"No telling," Charlie answered as he watched a waterfall cascade off the roof and puddle on the front lawn. "You might want to consider staying in."

"No way," she replied. "I need to go shopping."

"Make a list and I'll go for you."

Elizabeth smiled. "I know you would, but this is something I want to do. I've finally got a reason to buy books and toys. I don't want to miss that."

Charlie shrugged. "Whatever you say."

By three o'clock Saturday afternoon the thunder and lightning moved on, and the rain slowed to an intermittent drizzle. Charlie loaded Elizabeth and her wheelchair into the car and off they went.

"You make sure she doesn't catch a cold," Claire warned, even though she knew that was beyond her husband's control.

Inside the toy store it seemed as if every child in town had arrived with their weary mothers hoping to entertain them on a too-rainy-to-play-outside afternoon.

"Isn't this exciting?" Liz murmured as she rolled past a group of boys eyeing a rack of baseball mitts. She hesitated, wondering if perhaps that was what she should buy for David. After a few moments of watching the boys she moved on. Maybe next year, she thought. If there was a next year.

Two rows back a dozen little girls clustered around the Suzie Homemaker display with its array of miniature brooms and toy-sized appliances. Watching a toddler cling to the harried mother trying to pull free caused Elizabeth's heart to lurch. She remembered living that same scenario. All too often she'd rushed through those moments, anxious to move on to chores calling for her attention—chores that would always be there. *How absolutely foolish,* she thought.

The books and games display in the back of the store drew Elizabeth's attention. She'd been there dozens of times before. She could picture David standing on tiptoes to reach for his first Robin Hood book and Kimmie—who would always be Kimmie, as far as she was concerned—sitting on the floor with a Three Little Pigs pop-up book.

With Elizabeth revisiting special memories, the shopping expedition took almost a full two hours. The cumbersome wheelchair crowded the aisle so she moved slowly, taking time to ponder each item, holding things in her hand until she sensed they were perfect. A race car for David, a baby doll for Kimberly, a red ball sized to fit the hand of a baby. Piece by piece she gathered together a collection of storybooks and a gift for each of the children. When they left the store the rain had stopped. Elizabeth barely noticed; a sense of contentment missing for many long months filled her.

Sunday morning Elizabeth's eyes fluttered open when the first whisper of daylight shimmered across the bottom edge of the window shade. Just before waking she had floated in the gauzy space that surrounds a dream. In this one she'd seen Kimberly as a bride with an older, silver-haired Jeffrey beside her and her brothers close by. A young man stood at the altar with an aura of goodness about him. Elizabeth couldn't see herself, but she could sense her presence.

Had it been any other day, Elizabeth would have gladly lingered in the sweetness of that imaginary world, but this day was wonderful beyond a dream. She would see her children again.

"Mother," she called softly, "I'd like to get up."

Claire had trained her ears to hear even the slightest whisper, so she woke without hesitation. "Okay."

Since the paralysis had worsened Elizabeth could no longer pull herself up without someone's help. She'd tried on three separate occasions to reach for the metal walker next to her bed, and she'd fallen all three times. Now she had to call for help, or stay in bed forever. As she fought the physical cruelties of her illness, she thought of how it also robbed a person of their dignity and independence.

Elizabeth slid her arms into the new sweater she'd saved for this occasion. Once dressed, she sat at the vanity and smoothed a thin film of cream over the puffy contours of her face. A dusting of powder and a few strokes of a rose-colored blush to brighten her cheeks with an artificial look of health came next. Using only her right hand, she applied lipstick and then eased it back into its cap. The simplest of movements were arduous for Elizabeth.

Once finished she took hold of her walker, inched her way into the living room, and lowered herself onto the sofa to wait. It was barely seven-thirty.

She sat there, watching the grandfather clock slowly tick off the minutes, each one seemingly hanging in the air longer than its allotted sixty seconds. Eventually it was eight o'clock and then, after an excruciatingly long stretch, eight-thirty.

"Come, let's have breakfast," Claire said.

But Elizabeth wasn't the least bit hungry.

"Skipping breakfast isn't healthy," Claire warned and turned toward the kitchen.

The clock ticked off another minute, then another and another. Before too many minutes had passed Claire came into the room carrying a tray with two mugs of coffee and a dish piled high with David's favorite raisin cookies.

"You remembered," Elizabeth said with her half smile.

"Well, of course," Claire answered with an air of pretended indignation. "Do you think you're the only one who's missed those children?" She laughed and sat down. "Here, try one," she said, handing Elizabeth a cookie. "I want to make certain they're good enough for my grandchildren."

As they talked the clock ticked minute after long minute until it struck nine. "They should be here any minute," Elizabeth said.

But it wasn't any minute—and not any of the next sixty minutes. The clock chimed ten loud gongs, then moved on. Elizabeth and her mother waited, neither of them mentioning the unthinkable.

"Could be he's stuck in traffic," Claire said.

"Or maybe an accident on the highway," Elizabeth added.

"David can be hard to get moving in the morning."

"And Kimmie takes forever to eat."

Finally at seventeen minutes after the hour the doorbell dinged.

When Claire opened the door, David and Kimberly burst into the room with an explosion of energy. "Mommy, Mommy!" they shouted in unison. After climbing on Elizabeth and hugging her with such force she nearly toppled from the sofa, they showered Claire with the same level of affection. In all the excitement Elizabeth didn't think to ask about Christian until after Jeffrey left.

Jeffrey had followed them in, but after a quick glance at Elizabeth he'd turned around and stepped outside. It was late October, and winter had already shown itself with icy cold rain and winds that tore the leaves from trees. He tugged his collar up around his neck, then sat down on the step and lit a cigarette.

Seeing Liz had taken him by surprise. She sat on the sofa and laughed like this was some kind of party. She looked almost *healthy.* He took a long drag of the cigarette.

It's unfair, he sulked. *She's sitting there like the Queen of Sheba while I'm struggling to make ends meet.* He tossed the cigarette on the sidewalk, stomped it out, then lit another one.

For the first half-hour of their visit, both kids bubbled with questions. Was Mommy all better? When was she coming home? Did she have surprises for them? Could they have more cookies? Eventually, Elizabeth would have to tell them the truth about what was happening, but not today.

"Mommy's still sick," she said, "but the doctor is trying to make me better."

"Daddy could give you medicine," Kimberly volunteered. "When I was coughing, Daddy gave me medicine and I got better."

Turning the thrust of conversation from herself, Elizabeth prompted, "Did you also have a sore throat?"

"Yes," Kimberly nodded, "but it's all better. See?" She stretched open her mouth.

"Daddy says you'll never get better," David said.

"Nobody but God knows that for certain," Elizabeth answered. "Do you remember what I taught you about God?"

"Yeah. He lives up in heaven."

"And what does He do in heaven?"

"He watches over little kids."

"And what are you supposed to do so that God knows to watch over you?"

"Say my prayers," David answered dutifully.

"And do you say your prayers?"

"No," Kimberly exclaimed. "He doesn't."

"Do you?" Elizabeth asked her daughter.

"Sometimes," she answered tentatively. "When David doesn't bother me."

211

Jeffrey stomped out the second cigarette and lit a third. He could hear the excited voices inside. He knew they were laughing at him and the way he shivered on the cold cement step while they stayed warm and comfortable and had a fine time. Liz wanted people to feel sorry for her, but he was the one who deserved their pity. He was the one up to his knees in bills. He was the one responsible for taking care of three kids—kids who, judging from the sound of their laughter, enjoyed being with Liz more than him.

He tossed his cigarette onto the walkway then twisted and ground it until it was nothing but shreds of tobacco. He stood, took two steps across the walkway then two steps back. Once, twice, then again and again, pacing as the anger inside of him swelled and pushed against his skin.

At first he didn't notice the rain, but when the wind pushed the icy drops inside the collar of his jacket, he moved beneath the overhang. Now closer to the door, he heard their words clearly. Charlie told David he'd take him to a Yankees game in the spring.

"Over my dead body," Jeffrey grumbled as a frigid droplet slithered down his back. The rain began to fall harder and wind gusts blasted his face. He moved closer to the door until his back pressed against it.

Suddenly the door opened and Jeffrey tumbled inside, landing on his back and looking up at Liz leaning on her walker.

"What the hell are you trying to do, cripple me?"

"I'm sorry," she said. "I just wanted to ask if you and the kids could stay for lunch."

Scrambling to his feet, he gave her an angry glare and snarled, "No." He heard David and Kimberly already at the dining room table.

"You've got forty minutes," he said, eyeing his watch. "Then we're out of here."

"But, Jeffrey—"

212

"Twelve noon!" he said, tapping the face of his watch. "You've got the kids until twelve noon, not one minute longer!"

"That's not fair," she argued. "You were late getting here, and you didn't even bring Christian. Judge Brill said—"

Jeffrey took a step forward and jabbed a finger at Elizabeth's face. "Don't start with me. You think because your daddy's got money, you can bully me around?Try it and see what happens!"

"I wasn't trying to bully you into anything. I only thought maybe we could spend some time together as a family."

"Spend time together?" His face crumpled in disbelief. "You're crazy! Only a crazy person would ask me to spend time with someone I hate."

"You don't really mean that."

"Yes, I do! I can't even stand to be around you! You know what I wish? I wish you'd hurry up and die so me and the kids can get on with our life!"

Tears rimmed Elizabeth's eyes.

"Jeffrey," she whispered.

But he stormed down the walkway. She bit her lip as she watched him, his steps crashing against the cement, his body hunched against the cold, his movements deliberate and unrelenting.

"Are you all right?" Charlie asked from behind Elizabeth.

Torn between sorrow and shame, Elizabeth tried to force a smile.

"It was nothing," she said. "You know Jeffrey. He can be a hothead at times."

"We'll see about that!" Charlie moved toward the walkway.

"Don't," Elizabeth said softly.

The muscle in Charlie's jaw twitched as he stepped back inside the door and wrapped his arms around his daughter's trembling shoulders.

"He's not worth it," he whispered, pushing back his own anger to comfort his daughter.

Together they stood there for several minutes, until Elizabeth lifted her head from his shoulder and said, "We'd better get back to the kids."

Charlie nodded, saying nothing more even though he'd already decided what had to be done.

Claire McDermott

I'm not deaf. I heard every word Jeffrey said, but what could I do with David and Kimberly sitting at the table waiting for me to pour milk? I tried to pretend the commotion was nothing and covered it up by asking if they wanted cookies. I know both kids heard Jeffrey screaming, but they didn't mention it. They didn't have to; the frightened looks on their poor little faces made it obvious. Kimberly's only four so she probably didn't understand the maliciousness of her father's words. David understood. I know he did, because he ducked his head like a child who'd already learned to hide from anger.

Hearing one parent speak to the other in such a way is something kids don't forget. It roots itself in their impressionable minds and leaves an ugly mark. Kids exposed to such behavior eventually accept meanness as the way of the world, and they pass it on to others. It's unthinkable that any father would offer his babies such a heritage.

I can't imagine what Judge Brill was thinking when he awarded Jeffrey custody of the children. Only someone who's evil through and through would say the mean things Jeffrey said. I wish I'd recorded that conversation with Elizabeth. If Judge Brill got an earful of JT saying those things, I bet he'd make some pretty different decisions.

Jeffrey told Judge Brill it's not revenge. He said he just wants to get on with his life. If so, why doesn't he let me watch the kids and he can look for a job? Because he doesn't want a job, that's why. He just wants to make Elizabeth as miserable as possible. After JT left, Charlie said he was gonna ask Dudley if it's possible to get a court order to prohibit him from talking to Liz. Liz never mentions a word of what's transpired, but I see the hurt in her eyes. Let me tell you, there's no pain on earth worse than watching your daughter's heart be broken.

A Man of Defiance

On the second Sunday of scheduled visitation, Jeffrey brought Christian but claimed the other two had the sniffles. When Jeffrey arrived an hour and forty-five minutes late, Elizabeth's father opened the door and growled, "You're supposed to be here at nine o'clock, and you're supposed to bring all three children!"

"You ought to be glad I'm here with this one," Jeffrey answered and shoved the squirming baby into his grandfather's arms.

"Where're David and Kimberly?"

"They're home sick, and I'm not going to drag them out in this weather so they can get worse colds."

"They've both got colds? Like Christian had a cold last week?"

"Yeah. Just like that." Jeffrey started down the walkway. "I'll be back at noon."

"Don't bother," Charlie said. "Liz has three hours visiting time, so I'm not answering this door until one-forty-five!"

Charlie parked Christian on Elizabeth's lap, then called Dudley. "He got here late again," Charlie said. "I did as you suggested."

"Good," Dudley answered. "Was there any problem?"

"Not yet, but I'm betting there will be."

"I'll be there within the hour," Dudley said.

When Charlie returned to the living room, Elizabeth was on the floor with Christian.

"Good grief!" Charlie exclaimed. "What happened?" He bent to help Elizabeth up.

"No, no," she said happily. "I want to stay here. We're building a tower."

With her back braced against the sofa, she handed the baby another bright red block as he squealed with delight. "Go ahead," she said, guiding his chubby little hand. "Put it right here on top of the yellow one." He waved his hand back and forth eventually bouncing himself into the stack of blocks, which sent it tumbling and caused Christian to burst into giggles.

"How'd you get down there?" Charlie asked.

"Mom helped me."

Claire gave a guilty shrug and smiled.

A look of concern appeared on Charlie's face. "Do you think she should be doing this?" he asked Claire.

"I think it's the best medicine in the world," Claire whispered back. "Look how happy she is."

Elizabeth smiled and laughed as she had not done in many months. Every time the baby laughed or squealed, her smile grew brighter. And if Claire watched closely, every so often she could see a slight bit of lift on the left side of Elizabeth's face.

Charlie lowered himself into a chair and watched as the baby scampered back and forth across Elizabeth's legs retrieving blocks, stacking them, and then happily squealing when they tumbled.

"Give the block to Mama," Elizabeth coached. "Give it to Mama."

"Eeeeeeeee," Christian answered and handed the yellow block to Liz.

"Ma-ma," she repeated. "Say Ma-ma."

"Liz, just look at how he's taken to you," Charlie said. "He already knows you're his mama."

After almost an hour of stacking and tumbling, Christian crawled into Elizabeth's lap. He leaned his head against her stomach and stuck his thumb in his mouth.

"Somebody's sleepy," she said. With her right hand she began to rub his back in tiny little circles using the same motion she'd used when Christian was still inside of her. Minutes later he fell asleep.

"Are you comfortable?" Charlie asked.

"Very." Elizabeth smiled and continued to rub the baby's back. They remained that way for a long while until the chime of the doorbell woke Christian and he started crying.

"Am I in time?" Dudley asked.

Charlie nodded. "He's not back yet." Just then Charlie spotted Jeffrey's car turning the corner. "That's him now."

"You go back in," Dudley said. "I'll take it from here."

Charlie returned to the living room and snapped on the television. "Maybe," he said with a forced joviality, "Christian would like to see some cartoons!" He began flipping the channels until he finally came upon a trio of dancing pigs. "This looks good. Want to see this, Christian?"

"Eeeeeeeeee," the baby squealed.

JT stood a good head taller than Dudley, but Dudley made up for the difference by sheer determination.

"See this?" he said, waving a copy of the court order in front of Jeffrey. "This says you're to be here at nine a.m.! It means nine o'clock sharp! It also states that Elizabeth is to have three hours of visitation with her children. Children, not child!"

"Get that thing out of my face," JT snarled.

Dudley told JT he'd find himself back in court if he didn't wise up. "You've already had five instances of defying this court order. One more, and that's it!"

219

"*Five*? What are you—"

"The first was last Sunday when you came late. The second was when you brought two children instead of three. The third was when you removed the children without allowing Elizabeth the specified three-hour visitation. The fourth was when you arrived late again today, and the fifth was when you showed up with just the baby instead of all three children."

"That's a load of crap!"

"No, those are documented instances of your failure to abide by the court-ordered visitation schedule. And I haven't even started on the number of times you failed to allow Elizabeth her telephone calls. Let's see now, that was—"

"Okay, okay. So what are you looking for?"

"First, leave here, and don't come back until Elizabeth has spent three hours with the baby. Next, make certain she receives three telephone calls from the kids every week. Not every week you feel like doing it, but every single week. Lastly, make damn certain you're here on time every Sunday and that you've got all three children. Not one, not two, but all three!"

"And what if they're sick?"

"I don't care if you've got to bring them in an ambulance, bring them!"

"What if there's some perfectly logical reason for—"

"Don't even go there. The next time you fail to adhere to the court-ordered visitation schedule, I go back to Judge Brill with a petition for sanctions."

"Big deal."

"Maybe it's no big deal to you," Dudley answered. "But it would be to someone who doesn't want to spend time in jail."

Jeffrey turned and walked away. "Don't think you scare me, you pompous jerk!" he yelled as he climbed into the car. After he'd gunned the motor several times, JT gave Dudley a dark-eyed stare. Dudley returned it and added the reproachful look of an annoyed parent.

The eye-to-eye threats continued for several minutes before JT floored the gas pedal and rounded the corner with a screech heard seven blocks away.

Jeffrey didn't come back at one-forty-five, nor did he come at two or two-thirty. At nearly three o'clock Kelsey rang the doorbell and said, "I'm here to pick up Christian."

"Who are you?" Charlie asked.

"JT's friend."

Charlie looked beyond the girl and spotted Jeffrey waiting in the car. "Friend or no friend, I'm not giving Christian to anyone other than his father."

Kelsey rolled her eyes. "Geez. You gotta make this difficult?"

"I suppose so," Charlie answered, then said they'd get the baby ready while she went to fetch Jeffrey. He closed the door.

"Jeffrey's here to pick up the baby," he told Elizabeth.

She sighed. "So soon?"

Claire scooped Christian from the floor and bundled him into his snowsuit. "Tell Mama bye-bye," she prompted. "Bye-bye, Mama."

Christian squealed, "Byeeeeee."

"Ma-ma," Claire repeated.

"Byeeeeee."

"Close enough." Claire handed the baby to Charlie.

As they walked away, Christian looked back at Liz and cried, "Maaaaaaa-ma!"

The following Tuesday Elizabeth received a telephone call from David and Kimberly. They were allowed to talk for five minutes but no longer, since their father was supposedly setting supper on the table. David said his cold was all better and

Kimberly started to say she didn't have a cold, but David pinched her and she began to cry.

"It's okay," Elizabeth said, comforting her daughter. "I'm sure David was only playing. He didn't mean to hurt you—"

"Yes he did," Kimberly sniffed. "He did it 'cause Daddy said to tell you we was sick, but we wasn't sick!"

"Well, Kimberly, you're right, and David is wrong. Children shouldn't lie, even if somebody else tells them to. It makes Jesus sad when little children tell lies."

"See, Gooney!" Kimberly called out. "Mommy said we ain't 'posed to tell lies!"

"But brothers and sisters aren't supposed to fight, either."

"We ain't fighting," Kimberly said. "David's just being mean to me."

"Okay, then I'll tell David to stop being mean to you."

"Could you tell Kelsey not to be mean to me too?"

"Is Kelsey your friend?"

"No. Kelsey's a grown-up. She's Daddy's friend."

"Oh." Before Elizabeth could say anything, someone hung up the telephone.

There were no more telephone calls that week, and Elizabeth's calls went unanswered. On Sunday, Jeffrey didn't come at nine o'clock despite Dudley's warning. By noon, Elizabeth accepted that neither Jeffrey nor the children would come.

At twelve-thirty Charlie got behind the wheel of his car and drove to Jeffrey's house. He parked in the driveway, walked to the front door, and rang the doorbell. No one answered. He stood there for almost fifteen minutes and then followed Claire's footsteps and walked around to look in the garage window. Two cars sat parked side by side—Jeffrey's and a red Nissan.

Charlie returned to the front door and began ringing the bell, this time with a vengeance. Still no answer. Suddenly Charlie could think of nothing but the hurt, the heartache, and the pain his daughter had suffered, and he angrily raised a fist to pound on the door.

Something made him hesitate, and in that split second he realized the foolishness of such an act. It was the very thing Jeffrey was hoping for. Another act of violence, he'd claim, and try to convince the court that it was right to keep Liz's children from her.

"Not this time," Charlie grumbled. "Not this time." He climbed back into his car and returned home.

Elizabeth spent most of the afternoon in tears. Claire spent most of the afternoon trying to comfort her daughter. Charlie had a lengthy telephone conversation with Dudley.

The envelope from Simmons and Grimm waited for Judge Brill when he arrived at the Union County Courthouse on Monday morning. Sam Brill groaned as he slit the envelope open.

"I knew it," he grumbled as he read the petition for sanctions citing the numerous occasions on which Jeffrey T. Caruthers had deliberately and willfully defied the court.

His first telephone call was to Noreen Sarnoff. "Have you seen this petition yet?" he asked.

"What can I say, he's an odd duck, that's for sure."

"Does he realize that I can have him incarcerated for failure to obey the court order?"

"I've explained it any number of times, so either he's too dense to understand or too contrary to care."

"Well, Counselor," Judge Brill said, "I want to see you and your client in chambers tomorrow morning at nine-thirty."

"Let me call and make sure he's available."

"I didn't say I want you to *try* to be here. If either you or Jeffrey Caruthers fail to show, I'll send a squad car to bring you in!"

Noreen already regretted her decision to defend JT, but now she was stuck with him. She dialed Jeffrey's telephone number and listened to it ring for at least five minutes. Then she got in her car and headed for his house.

Jeffrey had learned to ignore the sound of the doorbell since it was generally somebody looking for money or one of the McDermotts trying to make his life miserable. Bill collectors never waited longer than five minutes. Liz's parents might stay for twenty. But the person bonging the bell had been there for a half-hour, which is why Jeffrey finally looked out the window and saw Noreen standing on the stoop. He opened the door.

"Sorry," he said. "I didn't hear the bell."

"You've got to be kidding!" Noreen pushed past Jeffrey into the living room. "I warned you! I said keep it up and you'll land in jail, but you're too bullheaded to listen!"

"I don't know what—"

"Don't give me any of that crap! You violated the court order, and Judge Brill is pissed! He wants us there tomorrow morning at nine-thirty. Don't show this time, and there'll be a cop on your doorstep!" Noreen jabbed her finger into Jeffrey's chest. "And trust me, he's not gonna stand there ringing the damn doorbell!"

"I missed one lousy Sunday," Jeffrey said. "For that they're gonna crucify me?"

Noreen turned and leaned into his face. "Shut up! I may have to defend your stupidity, but don't for one minute think I believe your lies. It's all here." She waved the petition in his face. "Twenty-seven counts of failure to comply with court ordered visitation. Twenty-seven counts!"

"I couldn't possibly—"

"Oh, but you did!" Noreen snapped. "Now we've both got to answer for it. I'm tempted to tell Judge Brill you were thinking of kidnapping those kids and let him toss your miserable ass in jail!"

"You can't do that, you're my lawyer."

"Don't remind me."

"There were extenuating circumstances—"

"I'll bet."

"I was sick."

"Unless you had two broken legs and were in the critical care ward at the hospital, nobody, including Judge Brill, is gonna believe you."

For the first time Jeffrey sounded concerned. "Okay, okay. So what do we do to fix this?"

"Not we," Noreen replied, "you. Judge Brill isn't going to send me to jail, but he's likely to send you."

"I can't go to jail. I've got kids to take care of."

"You should've thought of that sooner."

"You're my lawyer, you've gotta do something!"

"No, I don't. I don't have to defend somebody who blatantly defies a court order. But I want to get this thing over, so I'll tell you this. Your story might be more believable if you said the kids were sick."

"Well, they were," he said immediately.

Noreen rolled her eyes. "And do you have a reason for missing the phone calls?"

"Uh, yeah." Jeffrey waited for Noreen to give him a good excuse.

"Well, what is it?"

"Um, the kids were too sick to talk. So I unplugged the telephone because I didn't want it to disturb their sleep."

"If Judge Brill goes along with that lame-brained excuse, he's gonna want some sort of assurance that this is not going to happen again."

"I'll give him my word it won't."

Noreen gave a cynical sneer. "Your word?"

"Yeah. What else can I do?"

"Your word is as good as nothing."

"If you say that, for sure he's not gonna believe me."

"I'm not going to repeat it in front of Judge Brill, but let me give you fair warning. You'd better be on time, and you'd better look extremely contrite."

"Oh, I will. I will."

The following morning Jeffrey was already at the courthouse when Noreen arrived. He wore the same suit and tie he'd worn at the trial. "How do I look?"

"Fine," Noreen answered. "I hope you've given some thought to what you're going to say."

Before he had the chance to run through it, they were called into the judge's chambers.

Judge Brill's eyes were narrow and he impatiently shuffled papers from one side of his desk to the other. Almost three minutes passed before he looked at Jeffrey.

"You have willfully defied the court order pertaining to your wife's visitation rights. Is there any reason why I should not remove those children from your custody and have you incarcerated for the next thirty days?"

Jeffrey swallowed hard, and his voice came out high-pitched and squeaky. "I'm sorry. My children were all sick with colds, and I was beside myself. I had thought about calling Elizabeth earlier in the day, but with David throwing up and Kimberly running a fever, I got busy taking care of them and forgot. By the time I got all three kids in bed, I figured it was rather late to be telephoning."

Judge Brill shook his head. "Mister Caruthers, you are a test of a man's patience. I find it extremely difficult to believe that in each of these twenty-seven instances you experienced such dire circumstances that you could not perform your court-ordered responsibilities."

"Judge, you've gotta believe me, that's exactly what happened. And Elizabeth, she's just looking for me to do something wrong so that she—"

"Stop right there. I would suggest you carefully consider what you say, since I already have affidavits attesting to the negative aspects of your behavior."

"Your Honor," Noreen said sweetly, "I apologize for my client's behavior. Unfortunately, he sometimes allows his emotions to cloud his judgment. But he does earnestly care for his children and has given his word that going forward he will comply with all aspects of the court's ruling."

Jeffrey simply nodded.

"Very well, Counselor. I will allow Mister Caruthers one more chance. But be advised, if I am forced to address this issue again, he will go to jail regardless of what hardships it causes his family."

"Thank you, Your Honor."

Once outside the courthouse, Jeffrey grinned at Noreen. "Good work."

"Wipe that stupid smile off your face and listen up," she replied. "You may think because I'm a woman I'm a pushover, but you'd better think again. You remember Walt Petrecca, the criminal lawyer who suggested you call me?"

"Yeah."

"Well, Walt owes me, and he's got some pretty rough friends. If I have any more trouble with you, one of Walt's friends is gonna pay you a visit, and trust me, his friend won't stand on the stoop waiting until you get ready to open the door."

"Are you threatening me?"

"Warning," Noreen replied. "I'm warning you."

December 1985

Four weeks passed without incident. Jeffrey came every Sunday, sometimes at nine, sometimes nine-thirty, but never later. Every week he brought all three children. In the fifth week, he showed up with only Kimberly and Christian. David, he claimed, was attending a playmate's birthday party.

"If this is gonna cause you to go off the deep end," he told Charlie, "I'll get him and drag him over here."

Charlie told Jeffrey not to bother but to make certain David telephoned Elizabeth the next day.

The living room floor became Elizabeth's playground. Whenever the children arrived she'd be settled in place, her back braced against the sofa and a collection of books and toys within easy reach. The floor acted as a level playing field, where she did not have to rise or stand or walk. The children scooted back and forth across her stretched out legs, vying for the closest position but not questioning the strange arrangement.

The two weeks before Christmas filled Elizabeth with such great happiness that she could almost forget the pounding in her head and the constant ache in her lower back. Although she could no longer make trips to the toy store, she made a list and allowed either Claire or Charlie to do the shopping.

Christmas appeared everywhere. Red candles surrounded by pinecones became centerpieces, candied fruit appeared in glass dishes, and gaily-wrapped presents crowded the hall closet. On the seventeenth a chunky chair disappeared from the living room and a Frasier Fir replaced it, sweetening the room with the scent of a forest. That evening Claire made a pot of hot chocolate and Charlie carried six boxes of decorations up from the basement. Elizabeth, in her wheelchair, joined the tree-trimming party and sang along as Bing Crosby wished for a white Christmas.

Using only her right hand, she wrapped most of her own presents. For Claire, there was the crystal perfume bottle that she'd had Charlie buy and for him the briarwood pipe Claire bought. For the children there was any number of books and toys. She'd gotten almost everything they'd asked for, except the one thing Kimberly wanted most.

"Mommy," she'd said, "would you help me write a letter to Santa? I want a Cabbage Patch baby with yellow hair."

"Okay," Elizabeth answered. "But do you think maybe Daddy is going to buy you a Cabbage Patch Doll?"

"He's not." Kimberly's face had a knowing look far too grown-up for any four-year-old. "Daddy said they're ugly."

"Even the ones with yellow hair?"

Kimberly nodded.

"Well, then, we'd better hurry up and write a letter to Santa!"

"Thank you, Mommy!" Kimberly cried and threw herself onto Elizabeth's lap. With her tiny little arms hugging as hard as possible, she added, "You're the best mommy in the whole world."

As it turned out, finding a Cabbage Patch baby became an impossible task.

"Have you tried Toy Mart?" Liz asked.

Claire nodded. "Yesterday."

"What about Steiner's Toys?"

"They don't have it either."

"The Drug Emporium?"

"Sold out."

Elizabeth began to telephone stores—somebody had to have a yellow-haired Cabbage Patch doll. She called toy stores, variety stores, department stores, discount stores, and drug stores, but every store had sold out weeks earlier. She began to pray for a miracle.

Ten days before Christmas Elizabeth called all the stores back. "I thought maybe there was a chance you'd gotten more in," she said.

"Don't I wish," one shop owner replied. "I could sell another fifty!"

Elizabeth began leaving her name and telephone number. "If you get one with yellow hair, please call me," she said. But no one called.

Two days before Christmas, when the stores were crowded to bursting, Elizabeth had Claire load her and her wheelchair into the car and head for Tykes N' Teens in Westfield. After a painstaking ninety minutes, Elizabeth emerged with three dolls—a stand-up little girl nearly as tall as Kimberly, a baby with painted yellow hair, and a bald-headed baby wrapped in a pink bunting—none of which resembled the full-cheeked Cabbage Patch Kids.

That year Christmas fell on a Wednesday, and Elizabeth had hoped to give the children their gifts the Sunday before, but Jeffrey called and said he wouldn't bring them. "They're all sick," he said. "Some kind of flu, they're puking all over the place."

"Sick, huh?" Charlie said.

"Yeah, sick. If you don't believe me, I can bring over a bucket of puke and prove it!"

"That's not necessary," Charlie said begrudgingly. "Just make sure you get all three of them here next week so Liz can give them their presents."

"Yeah, sure."

Christmas morning dawned with a gray sky promising snow and a bitter wind toppling plastic snowmen and whisking outdoor wreaths from their hooks. Elizabeth had listened to the ominous howl of the wind through much of the night and when she finally did fall asleep she dreamt of pudgy-faced Cabbage Patch kids running away from her. She slept right through Claire's sausage pancakes and didn't stir until nearly noon. By then the snow had begun to fall.

"It looks so beautiful," Elizabeth said with melancholy in her voice.

"It's only three more days until the kids will be here," Claire said. "Why don't we wait and celebrate our Christmas with them?"

Elizabeth's eyes brightened. "What a great idea!"

"I'm all for it," Charlie added.

Claire set aside the turkey and prepared a meatloaf. At five o'clock that afternoon the McDermott family had a simple family dinner. After they'd eaten, Elizabeth, who'd been nursing a headache for three days, returned to bed.

The Christmas snow had disappeared by Thursday morning, but gray skies hovered overhead.

"It looks like we'll get more snow," Elizabeth said apprehensively.

"I doubt it," Charlie replied. "It's too cold for snow."

But late Friday afternoon it began to snow again. By nine o'clock almost two inches had fallen. At ten o'clock Charlie pulled on a parka, tugged a wool cap over his ears, and shoveled the walkway. When he returned to the house stomping snow from his boots he commented, "It's a light snow, nothing to worry about."

On Saturday morning Westfield awoke to eighteen inches of snow piled high against doors. It covered walkways and brought travel to a standstill. Walt Berringer, the weather forecaster, explained how an unexpected storm front had drifted down from Canada and stalled overhead.

"That front has finally moved on," he said, pointing to a glob of gray on the map, "but there's a mass of cold air following it, so it looks as if this snow will be with us for a while."

"How long?" Elizabeth said wearily.

As if answering her question, Weatherman Walt said, "By mid-week we should see a warming trend."

"Oh dear," Elizabeth murmured. "The kids are supposed to come over tomorrow."

"I wouldn't count on it," Charlie said. "Not with all this snow on the roads."

Claire gave him a reproachful glare, a warning to say no more.

On ten o'clock Sunday morning the telephone rang. Elizabeth, sitting on the sofa, answered.

"Guess what, Mommy," David said. "We had a big snowstorm!"

"I know," she answered. "We had it too."

"Today Daddy's gonna take us sleigh-riding."

"That sounds like such fun. Did you get a sled for Christmas?"

"Yeah," he answered, then said nothing more about sleigh-riding or that Bobby, and not he, had received the sled. Quickly changing the subject, he parroted, "We can't come to Grandma's house today because there's too much snow."

"I know," Elizabeth said. "I miss you and Kimmie and Christian, but I wouldn't want your Daddy to have an accident driving in the snow."

"You're not supposed to call her Kimmie."

"That's right, I forgot."

"Daddy said you forget a lot of things because you're sick. He said pretty soon you're gonna forget us. Is that true?"

"It's true that I forget things. That's because Mommy has a boo-boo inside her head. But I could never forget you or Kimberly or Christian. The three of you are not just inside my head, you're inside my heart. When someone is inside your heart that means you love them so much you'll never, ever forget them."

"Daddy," David yelled, "Mommy said she's not ever gonna forget us!"

"What else did you expect her to say?" Jeffrey answered, then told David to give the phone to his sister.

Elizabeth wanted to tell David Christmas just didn't seem like Christmas without seeing him, but before she had the chance Kimberly voiced a sniffling hello.

"What's the matter?" Elizabeth asked.

"I wanna go to Grandma's house, and Daddy won't bring me."

"Sweetheart, I'm disappointed too," Elizabeth said tenderly, "but it's not safe for Daddy to drive the car when there's so much snow on the road."

"I don't care, I wanna come anyway."

"I know, honey, but I wouldn't want Daddy to have an accident where you or one of your brothers might be hurt. You be a good girl and mind what Daddy tells you, and then as soon as this darned old snow melts he'll bring you over and we'll have a wonderful Christmas together."

"Did you get me presents?"

"Yes, indeed. Lots of presents."

"A Cabbage Patch baby with yellow hair?"

"No, Kimberly. Mommy tried to order one from Santa, but he didn't have any."

"Grandpa could buy one in the store."

"Grandpa and Grandma and Mommy tried every store we know of, and nobody had a single Cabbage Patch Baby left."

"Oh." Kimberly sighed, her disappointment obvious.

"But do you know what Mommy is gonna do?"

"What?"

"I'm going to keep looking until I can find a yellow-haired Cabbage Patch Baby, and then I'm gonna buy it specially for you."

"You mean for my birthday?"

"Nope. I mean the very minute I find it, I'm giving it to you."

"Honest?"

"Cross my heart."

"Enough, Kimberly!" Jeffrey yelled. "Get off the phone."

"No!" she answered defiantly.

"Kimberly," Elizabeth scolded. "It's not nice to say no to your Daddy like that. He loves you and wants to do what's best for you."

"No, he doesn't. He only loves David and Bobby."

"Bobby? Who's Bobby?"

"He's gonna be our brother."

"Brother? Who told you such a silly—"

233

"Kelsey. She said when you die Bobby is gonna be our brother. Please don't die, Mommy. I hate Bobby, and I don't want—"

"That's enough!" Jeffrey screamed. A moment later someone slammed the phone down.

Elizabeth did not see her children until January 5th of 1986. Although the Frasier fir had lost most of its needles and two strings of lights had gone dark, Christmas was wonderful for Elizabeth as she sat in her wheelchair watching the children open their presents.

And thus begins 1986

In the early part of January, Elizabeth went back to Saint Barnabas for her regular chemotherapy treatment.

"I wasn't happy with your last report," Doctor Sorenson remarked. She ordered multiple scans before and after Elizabeth's treatment.

"This time I want you to stay here for three days," she told Elizabeth. "We'll need to run additional tests."

That Friday Doctor Sorenson came into Elizabeth's room carrying an armful of charts and X-ray films. Her solemn expression told everyone that something was terribly wrong.

Claire edged closer to Elizabeth. Doctor Sorenson nervously slid her eyeglasses back onto the bridge of her nose.

"Have the headaches been getting worse?" she asked.

Elizabeth nodded.

"Any vision problems? Pain in your back or legs?"

Elizabeth nodded again.

Claire was shocked. "Liz, why didn't you say something about—"

"It wouldn't have helped," Doctor Sorenson interrupted. "The chemotherapy treatments are no longer working. Elizabeth's tumor has become extremely aggressive and has almost doubled in size over the past four weeks."

Claire gasped. "What can we do?"

"Unfortunately nothing. We've run out of options. There are no more miracle drugs. The only thing we've got left is possibly the power of prayer."

Rebecca Sorenson took Elizabeth's hand. "I'm sorry," she said, her voice cracking.

"Sorry?" Claire repeated, tears pooling in her eyes.

"What about increasing the chemotherapy treatments?" Elizabeth asked.

Doctor Sorenson reluctantly shook her head. "I'm afraid not. Your tumor has developed a resistance to the drugs, so they're no longer effective against it. If we escalate the treatments it might actually stimulate the tumor's growth, because cancer cells become more aggressive as they struggle against chemotherapy drugs."

"What then?" Claire asked. "Does Liz just wait to die?"

"Knowing Elizabeth," Doctor Sorenson answered, "I believe she'll choose to live life to the fullest for whatever amount of time she has left."

"And how long is that?" Elizabeth asked. "How long do I actually have?"

"There's no way of telling. It could be months, a year, maybe two. It all depends on how rapidly the size of the tumor increases."

After that there was nothing more to be said, but Doctor Sorenson did not hurry away. She stayed for nearly a half-hour assuring them that she would be there for whatever they needed. She told them she would make certain Elizabeth was kept comfortable and pain-free. Before leaving the doctor handed Claire two prescriptions.

"When the pills aren't enough to control the pain, let me know," she said. "I'll arrange for a morphine drip."

The Sunday before Valentine's Day Elizabeth and the children pasted red hearts on lace doilies. They dunked heart-shaped cookies in strawberry milk and listened to a story about Gertrude and the Lost Valentine. Elizabeth hugged each of the children to her chest and said nothing about the pain, but once they left Charlie had to carry her to the bed.

That was the last day she played on the floor. As Doctor Sorenson promised, the pills eased the pain but also caused such drowsiness that Elizabeth often fell into a sleep that lingered through much of the day and night. Still determined to spend time with her children, she took the pills from Sunday afternoon through Saturday morning and turned them away on Saturday evening so that she might be alert when the children came to visit.

The following Sunday and each Sunday thereafter, the children visited in the bedroom. Christian curled into his mama's lap and Kimberly cuddled so close that a breeze couldn't pass between them. But David began positioning himself on the far side of the room, turning a deaf ear to his mother's words as he played with Lincoln Logs and Tonka trucks.

Kimberly made up for David's lack of enthusiasm. She begged and pleaded for story after story.

"Tell about when I was a baby," Kimberly would say, snuggling closer.

The request lightened Elizabeth's heart, and even on those days when pain shot through her head she would stretch her memory to recapture the minutest details of some special day. Each story was a gift for her children tied together with her ribbon of memories.

Time and again she tried to draw David into the group. "Do you want to hear about when you were a baby?" she'd ask. But he'd turn his attention to some toy and pretend not to have heard.

Such sullenness bothered Claire, and twice she confronted the boy.

"Do you hear your mother talking to you?"

The first time she received a half-hearted shrug. The second time David added another Lincoln Log to his fortress and then purposely knocked it over.

Although David claimed no part of the story-telling, Elizabeth still included tales of his childhood. Despite a feigned disinterest in the middle of one story David said, "*Daddy* was the one who bought me that rocking horse!" With that he shot an accusatory look at his mother.

No one could change David's behavior, and week after week he grew more withdrawn and sullen. Several times Claire took him aside to ask what troubled him.

"Nothing," he'd answer, then stand there with his eyes narrowed and an expression of distrust stretched across his face. The moment she paused for a breath, he'd slip away.

In the first week of April the temperature became milder, and Elizabeth asked her father to take her out in the wheelchair. For nearly an hour they traveled up one street and down another, past newly-greening lawns, potted tulips, and freshly-painted fences. But the warm day of sunshine and promise faded into a night with pain pounding through Elizabeth's head and into her spine.

For three nights in a row she couldn't sleep even though she swallowed double doses of the pills. The fourth morning Claire called Doctor Sorenson and asked for something stronger. That afternoon Elizabeth began taking morphine, which brought restful sleep and oblivion. On Sunday she slept through most of the children's visit and was still asleep when the time came for them to leave.

"Your daddy's waiting in the car," Claire said. "Give Mommy a kiss goodbye and put your sweater on."

"No," David said, refusing to kiss his sleeping mother.

"Shame on you," Claire scolded.

"Mommy's contagious," David grumbled. He kicked a toy car, and pieces of plastic flew across the room. "If I touch her, I'll die too."

"That's ridiculous!" Claire answered. "Where on earth did you get such a silly idea?"

David didn't answer.

"David," Claire said, her voice stern and unrelenting, "answer me! Who told you your mother was contagious?"

Begrudgingly he answered, "Kelsey."

"That's absolute foolishness," she grumbled. "You shouldn't be listening to some kid—"

"Kelsey's not a kid," he argued. "She's a grownup."

"No grownup would ever say such a thing—"

"Kelsey did! She said Mommy's gonna poison me!"

"That's not true! It's the silliest thing I've ever heard! Your mother loves you and would never do anything to hurt you."

"She's contagious!"

"Nonsense. Your mother has a tumor on her brain. A tumor is not contagious."

"I don't want to get a tumor in my brain."

"Oh, David, stop being so silly and get your sweater on. I'll straighten this nonsense out with your father."

"No!" David shouted defiantly. "Daddy doesn't want to talk to you!"

"I don't care what your daddy wants," Claire answered with an air of impatience. She turned to zip Christian's jacket.

"I hate Mommy!" David shouted and darted from the room.

Before Claire could stop him, the boy was out the door and running toward his father's car. Her first impulse was to confront Jeffrey and demand to know why the boy would say such a thing. But she hesitated, reasoning that with everyone on edge it might be better to wait until David settled down a bit.

As Claire handed Christian to his father, she waved goodbye to David who turned his face away.

From that day forward, Elizabeth spent most of her time sleeping. After each dose of morphine she fell into a deep sleep lasting for hours. She only woke when a bolt of pain rattled through her body, reminding her it was time for another dose of the mind-dulling drug. All the while Claire stayed by her daughter's bedside, watching as she slept and praying for even the slightest improvement.

When David, Kimberly, and Christian came for their weekly visit, Claire forced herself to smile. She closed Elizabeth's bedroom door and steered the children into the living room, suggesting they play there while Mommy slept.

"Mommy's always sleeping," David complained, his tone echoing his father's cynicism. "Why doesn't she play with us?"

"Mommy needs a lot of rest so she can get better," Claire answered.

After several weeks of restlessness, Elizabeth finally drifted into a sound sleep and slept for three days without waking. Claire believed it was simply a case of exhaustion, but Charlie insisted they call the doctor.

That evening Doctor Sorenson visited and told the McDermotts that Elizabeth had slipped into a coma.

"But she's been sleeping so peacefully," Claire said. "How could this have happened?"

"A person in a comatose state often seems asleep. Elizabeth most likely was sleeping, but at some point she slipped into the deeper level of unconsciousness that's considered a coma."

"Will she wake up?" Charlie asked.

"Maybe, maybe not. Given the situation with Elizabeth's tumor, it's impossible to predict what will happen."

As Doctor Sorenson evaluated Elizabeth's vital signs, Charlie and Claire stood there saying nothing. Claire nervously picked at a spiral of thread hanging from the corner of the bedspread, and Charlie stared at the floor with the right side of his mouth twitching furiously. Neither of them dared look at one another or at their daughter.

Finally Charlie spoke. "Is Elizabeth aware of what is going on?"

Doctor Sorenson grimaced ever so slightly, then held her finger to her mouth. Once she concluded her examination she motioned for the McDermotts to follow her out of the bedroom.

After they'd moved to the living room, the doctor said, "I believe it's best not to allow the patient to hear conversations of this nature."

"So Elizabeth understands what we're saying?" Charlie said.

The doctor hesitated. "A comatose state encompasses a wide range of alterations in consciousness. Some are not much more than a deep sleep; others are so severe that neither sound nor physical stimuli can be processed by the patient. In cases such as Elizabeth's, where the patient is somewhere in the middle of those two extremes, we believe there is some level of receptivity to sound and touch stimuli. The patient might seem to be unresponsive, but there are documented instances where recovered patients recalled conversations that took place while they were comatose."

"Then Elizabeth does hear us?" Charlie repeated. "But she's unable to respond?"

"It's feasible that she hears your voice, but as far as the degree of perceptive awareness, well..." Doctor Sorenson ended with a questioning shrug.

"Is Elizabeth experiencing any pain?" Claire asked, recalling all the tearful nights she'd spent beside her daughter.

"If she is it's unlikely the pain is intense or prolonged. Without a response, it's impossible for me to give a definite answer. But I'll set Elizabeth up with a timed morphine drip. That way she'll have the right amount of medication to keep her comfortable. At least pain will be one thing she won't have to deal with."

"Thank you," Claire said wearily.

Charlie rubbed his fingers back and forth across his forehead several times. Then he spoke slowly and with sorrow. "How bad is Elizabeth?"

"I wish I could say she's getting better," Doctor Sorenson said. "But the truth is she's failing."

Failing? The word hit Charlie like a bucket of cold water. He'd never been good at comforting someone, so he'd left that to Claire. When he arrived home from the office Liz was generally sleeping. He'd tiptoe into her room, plant a kiss on her cheek, and whisper how much he loved her. He'd concentrated on making enough money to pay for her care, and until now he'd turned a blind eye to the inevitable.

But Claire had lived with it for months as she'd watched Elizabeth lose a bit more mobility each day, as she listened to the soft moans that came when the headaches grew worse, and as she prayed for her daughter's pain to give way to restful sleep. Yes, Claire was aware, constantly aware, of her daughter's failing health. It was a dark shadow hovering night and day, an evil voice hissing in her ear, a heavy weight crushing her spirit and pulverizing bits of hope.

But she was far from ready to acknowledge the terrible loss that lay ahead. How could a mother ever be ready for such a loss? Claire lowered her face into her hands and began to weep. Charlie moved closer and tried to provide the comfort of his arms, although his heart was also shattering.

A Change of Plans

On a Sunday David rolled a racecar across the living room floor and announced he didn't want to go to Grandma's house.

"Too bad about what you want," Jeffrey snarled. "I don't feel like being hauled into court again, so shut up and put your jacket on!"

"No!"

Jeffrey threw the jacket in the boy's face. "Put it on!"

David batted the jacket away. "I'm not going."

Jeffrey grabbed the boy by the arm and yanked him to his feet. "You're going whether you like it or not! If you don't want to go see your mother, tell her!"

"I can't," David sniffled, rubbing his arm.

"Why?"

"Because she's dead."

"Dead?" Jeffrey stared at the boy in disbelief. "What do you mean dead?"

"She doesn't wake up anymore."

"He's lying!" Kimberly screamed. "Mommy's not dead, she's sleeping!"

"She doesn't wake up anymore?" Jeffrey repeated. "Ever?"

"Never," David answered glumly.

"So what do you do when you're there?"

"We watch TV or play with stuff. Grandma gives us cookies, but we're not allowed to go in Mommy's room."

"Because Mommy's sleeping!" Kimberly squealed.

"Yeah, I bet," Kelsey commented snidely.

"You keep out of this," Jeffrey growled. He turned back to the children. "When was the last time you actually saw your mother?"

David shrugged but avoided looking into his father's face.

"Was it last week?" Jeffrey asked.

"Yes!" Kimberly shouted.

"No, we didn't!" David said eyeing his sister.

"Did so!"

"Did not!"

"Enough!" Jeffrey screamed. "Kimberly, shut up and let your brother answer." He turned back to the boy. "Have you seen your mother since Christmas?"

David nodded but didn't look up.

"Since Valentine's day?"

"I don't know."

"He's lying!" Kimberly shouted. "Mommy made Valentines."

Jeffrey gave her a silencing glare, then turned back to her brother. "Is that true?"

David nodded again.

"Have you seen your mother since then?"

"Yeah, in bed."

"Awake in bed? Or sleeping?"

"She used to be awake. Now she's asleep."

"So you haven't seen or spoken to your mother for a while?"

"I told you, we're not allowed in her room."

"And she never comes out of the room?"

"No!" David answered emphatically.

"Ain't you the chump," Kelsey chided. "You been suckered into hauling the kids over there to visit your in-laws!"

"Shut up!" Jeffrey screamed. "It's enough I gotta deal with them without having to listen to your stupidity!"

"Hurry up, Daddy," Kimberly whined. "I'm hot."

"We're not going anywhere, so you can take that stupid jacket off!" Jeffrey screamed. He turned and stormed out of the house alone. Kimberly wailed about how she wanted to go to Grandma's house. Kelsey began to think about what style bridal gown she would wear.

Jeffrey drove around for fifteen minutes, fuming. None of it made sense. If Liz was dead he would have been notified, unless she died and they somehow managed to keep it a secret. The McDermotts, he reasoned, could be shrewd enough to try something like that. Sure, they'd trick the poor dumb husband into thinking his wife was still alive, then get some pig-headed judge to order weekly visitations.

Clever, real clever. They're probably looking to alienate my kids, take them the way they took my store. They think they'll get away with it because they're so high and mighty. They figure me for an idiot, a schnook who can be tricked into believing their dead daughter is still alive. I'll bet they're laughing at me this very minute—well, no more!

Without signaling, Jeffrey made a sharp U-turn and headed for the McDermott house. He screeched into the driveway, climbed out of the car, and angrily marched to the door.

"Where are the kids?" Claire asked when she saw Jeffrey standing alone.

"They're not coming!" he said. "I'm here to see Liz."

"She's sleeping, and I don't want—"

"I don't give a crap about what you want!" Wild-eyed, Jeffrey jostled Claire aside and headed for Elizabeth's room. Before she could stop him, he slammed the bedroom door open.

Charlie heard the commotion and came running. He entered the room just as JT grabbed Elizabeth's shoulders and began shaking her.

"Wake up!" Jeffrey screamed angrily. "Wake—"

In an explosion of anger, Charlie threw his right arm around his son-in-law's neck and yanked him away with a force that propelled both of them backward into the wall. The nightstand went flying and a sprawl of medicine bottles scattered across the floor.

"I'll kill you if you touch my daughter again!" Charlie shouted.

"Are you crazy?" Jeffrey screamed, driving his shoulder hard into Charlie's chest. "She's practically dead! You're keeping her alive, but she's a vegetable!"

Charlie punched Jeffrey to the floor, then jumped astraddle his chest and began hammering his face with blows. He hit him again and again, bouncing his head against the floor, bloodying his nose.

"Stop it!" Claire screamed. "Stop this craziness!" She rushed to Elizabeth's bedside and eased the blanket up around her daughter's bared shoulders.

Her voice halted Charlie's barrage and allowed Jeffrey to break free. Scrabbling to his feet, he screamed, "You broke my nose, you idiot—"

"That's not all I'm going to break if you don't get out of here!" Charlie answered. "Get out and don't ever come back, or so help me I'll—"

"Oh, I'll get out," Jeffrey said mockingly. He turned toward the door with his hand clasped to the rush of blood cascading from his nose. "But take a good look, 'cause you ain't never gonna see me or my kids again!"

"I'm warning you!" Charlie roared.

Jeffrey hesitated, gave Charlie a look that promised the worst was yet to come, then turned and walked away, kicking aside a stray medicine bottle.

Claire still hovered over her daughter.

"It's okay," she whispered. "Daddy and Jeffrey had words, but that's all over now so don't you worry." She smoothed back a lock of hair that had fallen across Elizabeth's face.

Eleven messages waited for Judge Brill when he arrived at the courthouse on Monday morning—five from Jeffrey Caruthers, three from Noreen Sarnoff, two from Dudley Grimm, and one from his sister-in-law, Ida, saying that she and Harold planned to come for a visit. Sam Brill pocketed Ida's message, then spread the others across his desk. *What now?* he wondered as he began to dial Dudley's number.

"The McDermott family is asking for a restraining order to keep Jeffrey Caruthers away from their daughter," Dudley explained.

"Last I heard the man had no interest in even seeing his wife."

"Well, apparently that's changed, because yesterday he stormed into the McDermott house and attacked Elizabeth in her bed."

The image of Jack Wallner immediately flared in Sam Brill's head. "Was anyone hurt?"

"No, but Charles McDermott had to forcibly eject him from their house."

"Not good," the judge mumbled. "Not good." He said he'd have a conversation with the other side and get back to Dudley.

Judge Brill called Noreen next. "Counselor, are you aware that the McDermotts want a restraining order against your client?"

"For what?"

"They claim he attacked their daughter."

"That's not true, Your Honor. The only thing my client did was try to discover the truth, which to the best of my knowledge is not considered a crime."

"During this supposed quest for truth, did he attack his wife?"

"Attack, no. He did, believing her asleep, give a gentle shake that was intended to simply wake her."

"Explain."

"David, the eldest of the Caruthers children, complained the grandparents were not allowing him and the other children to see their mother. Every time they came for a visit, they were told she was asleep. My client, understandably concerned about the welfare of his children, went to check it out and discovered his wife,

Elizabeth, was in a coma. Naturally, he was upset because he hadn't been notified."

"Did he behave aggressively toward Charles McDermott?"

"On the contrary, Mister McDermott attacked him!"

"Elizabeth's father?" Judge Brill asked with astonishment.

"Yes! He broke Jeffrey's nose and—"

"And I suppose your client also wants a restraining order against the McDermotts?"

"No. In light of the mother's current condition, he's asking the court for relief on the existing visitation order."

Judge Brill heaved a sigh. "Have him in my office at three this afternoon, and I'll listen to arguments." He hung up, tossed all five of the messages from Jeffrey Caruthers into the wastebasket, and telephoned Dudley Grimm and instructed him to bring the McDermotts at three o'clock.

Judge Samuel Brill had a full docket and a desk piled high with the folders of people waiting for decisions. He pushed back his chair, closed his eyes and once again remembered Jack Wallner. If only he could trace things back far enough, he might somehow discover where he went wrong.

Sam Brill was never late, so when he failed to appear his clerk hurried back to chambers and rapped on his door. When she got no answer, she called out his name and eased the door open. He sat behind his desk, his head tipped back as if sound asleep. When she went to wake him, he wasn't breathing. On his desk lay a brochure depicting the serenity of the Grand Canyon.

Claire McDermott

The pain of giving birth is nothing compared to the pain of watching your child die. Birth is a joyous pain that brings promise, but this is a hell worse than anything you could possibly imagine. Some days I can actually feel my heart being cored from my soul and shredded into confetti. I want to scream and cry out, but I don't. I can't. I have to stay strong for Elizabeth. So I push back the ache in my heart and listen for the sound of her breathing. I pray that something will change, that the Lord will have mercy on my child.

I believe Elizabeth hears my voice and understands what I'm saying, so I talk to her all the time. I read aloud for hours on end—magazines, books, and quite often the Bible, Psalms mostly. I tell her I understand this terrible thing she's going through and try to sound convincing when I say it's a temporary setback. But I can't even fathom what it's like to be trapped inside the prison of your own mind. I worry she might be frightened, and I try to ease her fears by acting as normal as possible. I want to take her in my arms and comfort her as I did when she was a child, but that time has gone.

We haven't seen or heard from any of the children since the day Charlie and Jeffrey had the fight. I miss the kids more than words can say. But right now I've got to focus on Elizabeth—she's the one who needs me most.

I'm tired to the bone, but I seldom sleep. I doze off for a few minutes from time to time, but I always wake startled and anxious to make certain Elizabeth is still okay. I've heard her speak words twice. The first time she called for her daddy, and the second time she talked about David. It wasn't actual conversation, just loose words like the rambling of someone caught up in a dream. That's partly why I don't sleep: I'm hoping she'll call for me, and I want to be there to answer.

The nurse comes once a day. She monitors Elizabeth's condition, checks her feeding tube, things like that. She's generally here less than an hour but during that hour I rush upstairs, shower, and change my clothes. The minute she leaves, I hurry back to sit beside the bed.

In situations like this Charlie acts as if he has five thumbs and no fingers. Seeing Elizabeth hurts him as much as it does me. The only way he can cope is to shield his eyes, turn away and not look directly into the bright light of truth. I wish I could tell him what to do, but I myself don't know. Nobody does. We're the blind leading the blind, cripples leaning on other cripples, lost souls praying for guidance.

Visitation Revisited

In the wake of Judge Brill's death the case of Caruthers v Caruthers was assigned to the Honorable Margaret Thumper, a newcomer to the bench and a woman determined to prove herself by making quick work of the sizeable caseload dumped on her desk. She zipped through the files of troubled teens and violent spouses, giving little more than a cursory glance at documents that told of malicious behavior patterns and mental instability. Within two weeks of the tragedy, she had begun to hear cases.

Although given only two days' notice, both Dudley Grimm and Noreen Sarnoff were informed that Judge Thumper would hear arguments in her chambers at three o'clock sharp on Wednesday. Margaret Thumper was determined not to be tagged "the junior judge," so to compensate for her youthful appearance she wore her blond hair slicked back in a tight chignon and a pair of wire-rimmed glasses perched on the tip of her nose. She aimed her words like spears, and she had developed her stern demeanor to the point where she could go for days without smiling.

"Sit," she said when the two attorneys entered the room. Without looking up she opened the file folder in front of her. "You've each got five minutes, so get right to the point and state your case quickly. I'll hear from the plaintiff's attorney first."

Dudley said, "Your Honor, this request for a restraining order against Jeffrey Caruthers is entered on behalf of my client, Elizabeth Caruthers, and the parents with whom she currently resides. On April nineteenth, Jeffrey Caruthers physically attacked his wife while she was lying in a sickbed. Based on this behavior, we ask that the court prohibit him from entering the McDermott house when he delivers the children for their weekly visit."

Dudley glanced at his watch and began to speak faster. "We are also asking for sanctions against Mister Caruthers, because for the past three weeks he has failed to present the three minor children for their court-ordered visitation. And this is the third time we have had to take Mister Caruthers back to court because of failure to abide by the specified visitation orders."

"Rebuttal?" Judge Thumper said, glancing at Noreen.

"Yes, of course," Noreen answered quickly. "In response to the first complaint, my client did not attack his wife. He saw her in bed, believed her to be asleep, and used a gentle shake to wake her. Unfortunately, Elizabeth Caruthers was in a coma. My client had no knowledge of her condition when he approached her. I find it ludicrous that the plaintiff should be requesting a restraining order since it was Mister McDermott who attacked Jeffrey Caruthers. He suffered a broken nose and needed six stitches to close the gash in his chin!"

"Two minutes," the judge said, again checking her watch.

Noreen began to speak more rapidly. "The reason Jeffrey Caruthers has not delivered his children for visitation is because he believes it not in their best interest to see their mother in such a deplorable condition. The visitation ordered by Judge Brill applied only to the mother. It explicitly excluded the grandparents since they have no custodial rights in the state of New Jersey."

Margaret Thumper tapped the face of her watch and Noreen ceased talking. The judge looked at Dudley, "At the time of the alleged attack, was Elizabeth Caruthers comatose?"

"Yes, Your Honor."

"Is she still comatose?

"Yes, Your Honor."

"Has the husband made any further attempts to approach or harass his wife or her parents?"

"Well, he hasn't been bringing the children—"

"No long-winded explanations, just yes or no."

"No."

The judge turned to Noreen. "Is your client requesting anything other than relief of the visitation order previously issued by the court?"

"No, Your Honor."

"Very well, petition granted." She turned to Dudley. "I'm giving you the restraining order you requested but denying sanctions against the defendant. And I suggest that you don't waste the court's time with any further motions for visitation."

"But, Your Honor," Dudley stuttered. "There is a distinct possibility my client will come out of this coma, and if she—"

"How long has she been comatose, Counselor?"

"About seven weeks, but she shows signs of—"

"If she snaps out of it, you can re-file." With that Margaret Thumper stood.

A stunned Dudley Grimm walked slowly down the hall while Noreen hurried to call her client with the good news.

The Long Hot Summer

Summer came early that year with a blast of heat that sent people in search of air conditioners and oscillating fans. Claire pushed back the curtains and opened the windows in Elizabeth's room hoping to catch a cross breeze. In the fourth week of June the air hung hot and heavy as an August day.

Claire lifted her daughter's head and slid a fresh, cool pillow beneath it. Elizabeth's face and hair were damp, her eyelids fluttering.

It's this heat, Claire reasoned, as she folded back the sheet and the lightweight blanket. She telephoned Charlie and asked him to bring home an industrial-sized fan so they could get the air in the room circulating. Afterwards she went into the kitchen and returned with a large bowl of ice water and a soft square of terrycloth. She dipped the cloth in water, twisted it lightly to remove the falling droplets, then ran the cloth across her daughter's face, neck, and arms. Elizabeth's skin grew cool and comfortable to the touch.

"Doesn't this feel refreshing?" Claire asked rhetorically, using the same gentle tone she'd used for nearly two months. "With the weather as hot as it's been, there's little else we can do to keep cool. Daddy is going to bring home…"

She continued for hours with a steady stream of conversation to accompany the gentle sponge bath. Each time the ice melted, Claire went back for another bowl. Eventually Elizabeth seemed to settle into a more restful sleep.

That night Charlie stood a huge fan in the corner of the room, stretched an extension cord across the room, and turned it on. "How's that?" he asked.

"Better," Claire answered, grateful for the darkness that cooled the room to a tolerable level.

When the sun rose the next morning, the heat was worse and the humidity so thick a person could feel it crawling across their skin. Claire had fallen asleep on the day bed, but when she woke Elizabeth seemed more restless than the previous day. Her fingers twitched from time to time, and she jerked her head from side to side. Claire felt her brow, which was clammy and damp with perspiration.

She adjusted the fan so that it moved a flow of air across the room but did not blow directly on the bed, and then she went for another bowl of ice water.

Throughout the long hot day Claire continued to wipe her daughter's skin with icy cold cloths. When night came she continued until the air cooled to where a person could breathe comfortably. After she emptied the last bowl of water, she stretched out on the daybed.

When a person's soul is as weary as their body, sleep overtakes them—so Claire slept. And she dreamt. In her dream a little Elizabeth ran, played, called out to her...

"Mother?" The voice sounded weak and far away. "Mother?"

Claire jumped to her feet, startled.

Elizabeth's eyes were open. "Mother?"

"You're awake!" Claire gasped, folding her daughter into a joyous embrace. "Thank you, Lord," she murmured. "Thank you."

Elizabeth's eyes darted about, and she looked confused. "Where's—"

"I know it's a bit bewildering," Claire said, tracing her hand along the contour of Elizabeth's face. "You've been asleep a long time."

"Oh." Elizabeth closed her eyes again and drifted off to sleep.

Claire watched and waited for her daughter to wake but she slept silently through the day, through the night, and through two more days. Claire continued the sponge baths, crediting them with the miracle. On the fourth day Elizabeth again opened her eyes, slowly, sleepily, and for less than a minute.

Claire felt certain Elizabeth would soon regain consciousness, so she filled the room with bright, colorful flowers. "I want Liz to see something pretty when she opens her eyes," she told Charlie and reminded him that once Elizabeth could sit up they would need to have Dudley file a new petition for the children's visitation.

Charlie said, "I think you're being overly optimistic." He knew the truth. The first time Liz opened her eyes and spoke a few words he'd been every bit as excited as Claire, but then he'd spoken with the doctor. He spoke with Doctor Sorenson once a week, sometimes more often.

"Elizabeth is wavering on the shallower edge of a comatose state," Doctor Sorenson had explained. "It's not at all uncommon for a patient in that state to drift in and out of consciousness. It can happen any number of times. Enjoy it for what it is—a few extra moments of time with your daughter. Believe me, it is not a harbinger of what is to come."

Consciousness came and went throughout the sweltering summer. Elizabeth opened her eyes dozens of times, although seldom for more than a minute or two. She spoke a few words here and there, generally slurred and confused in thought. Nonetheless, Claire's spirits soared, and she continued to feel encouraged. Confident the icy sponge baths had caused the improvement, she insisted Charlie replace the large fan with an air conditioner that kept the room as cold as the inside of a refrigerator.

"I'm certain it's helping Liz," she said, bundling herself in an alpaca sweater.

On the last Sunday of August Elizabeth's eyelids fluttered as Charlie bent to kiss his daughter good morning; Claire said, "Say good morning to Daddy."

Suddenly a whisper-thin voice answered, "Good morning, Daddy."

Elizabeth eyes remained closed.

"You're coming along beautifully," Claire gushed, gingerly embracing her daughter.

Charlie smiled, patted Elizabeth's hand, planted a gentle kiss on Claire's cheek, and then left the room before Claire could see his tears.

That afternoon Claire read aloud for hours. She finished the final chapters of *To Kill a Mockingbird,* then moved on to the book of Revelations. Close to five o'clock she set the Bible aside and stood to check on Elizabeth.

"How are you doing, sweetheart?" she asked. A hand to her daughter's head revealed a damp brow, icy cold but slick with beads of perspiration.

"My goodness," Claire exclaimed. "It feels as though you've got a fever."

Elizabeth's face appeared restful and unusually calm with just the slightest trace of a smile. Her eyelids fluttered ever so slightly.

"I'm sorry to be so much trouble, Mother," she whispered.

"Nonsense," Claire answered. "You're no trouble at all!" She gently smoothed Elizabeth's hair back from her face. "We need to break this fever. I'll get some ice water."

It took Claire less than two minutes—just long enough to empty a tray of ice cubes into a bowl, fill it with water, and hurry back—but when she returned Elizabeth's breathing had slowed.

Claire gasped and cradled her daughter in her arms. As she held her in a close embrace, the last bit of air rattled from Elizabeth's chest.

When Charlie came home two hours later, Claire still held Elizabeth.

"I was her mother," she wailed, "but I couldn't save her."

After the funeral dozens of friends and neighbors streamed through the McDermott house. They came with saddened faces and carried casseroles, trays of meat, fruit, cakes, pies, pastries. They embraced Claire and Charlie as they offered condolences and spoke of what a wonderful person Elizabeth was, but in the far corners of the room ugly whispers asked, "Where is her husband? Where are her children?"

The night his daughter died, Charlie called Jeffrey and left a message on the answering machine. The following day he drove to the house and slipped a note through the mail slot. But no one from the Caruthers family came to say goodbye to Elizabeth. The church generally reserved the first pew for the grieving family, but Claire and Charlie sat alone. Charlie held her hand. Claire stared straight ahead, her eyes blinded by misery.

In the weeks that followed, Claire allowed grief to consume her. It lived in every thought, in every word, in the river of salty tears flowing from her eyes. It shunned the touch of anyone who reached out and closed its ears to words of sympathy.

Although the rental company came and took back the hospital bed Elizabeth had used, the remainder of the room stayed exactly the same. Claire continued to lie on the narrow day bed night after night, seldom sleeping.

"You can't go on like this," her friend, Mildred, said, but Claire turned her face to the wall. Who was Mildred to give such advice? How could she possibly understand, when she had three daughters, all of them alive and well?

When Charlie suggested she return to their bed, she ran into Elizabeth's room and slammed the door in his face.

"Please," he begged, but she had already closed her ears to such a suggestion.

Eventually Charlie began staying at the office later and later. He'd stop at the diner for a bite to eat, then go home to a dark, silent house, a house where his wife had locked herself in her dead daughter's bedroom. Many a night he'd wake to the sound of

Claire sobbing, then in the morning he'd see her red-eyed and puffy.

"Perhaps if we took a vacation, got away for a while," he suggested to no avail. "Or move," he offered. "We could find a new house, without so many memories."

But Claire drew back from the thought as if scalded.

In October, shortly after the leaves began to fall, the phone rang. When Claire answered the telephone, the caller said, "Good news! I've got it!"

"Excuse me?"

"I finally got it, the blond Cabbage Patch doll you wanted."

"I'm sorry, I think—"

"Is this Elizabeth Caruthers?"

Claire's breath caught as she suddenly remembered the doll Liz promised to get for Kimberly.

"My daughter Elizabeth passed away," she said quietly, "but she ordered that doll for her little girl, and I'd very much like to pick it up."

"I'm so sorry," the caller stuttered, "if you don't want—"

"Oh, but I do. Finding that doll was something my daughter had her heart set on. Now it's the only thing I can still do for her."

"There's plenty of things you can do," the caller said. "I'm a grandma myself, and I know how much kids need their grandma. I'm certain your daughter will find great peace in knowing you're looking after her little one."

"Three," Claire replied. "Elizabeth has three. Two boys and one girl."

"Oh, well, then, you've got your work cut out for you." She gave the address of her shop and said she looked forward to meeting Claire.

"Me too," Claire replied. Oddly enough, she meant it.

That night Claire didn't sleep in Elizabeth's room. She sat in the recliner and thought about the three children who now needed her more than ever. Before daylight crawled into the sky she decided to go to Jeffrey. She would do whatever she had to do— beg, grovel, apologize, anything. And if the only way to break down this wall between them was to give him money, she would force Charlie to give him whatever he wanted, right down to their last cent.

Claire closed her eyes, convinced that her purpose on earth was to care for Elizabeth's children, which was why she'd been left behind even though she'd wished to go with her daughter.

The Following Day

Claire awoke filled with purpose. First she planned to pick up the Cabbage Patch doll and buy presents for the boys. Then she would drive to Jeffrey's house. She'd ring the doorbell and wait patiently until he got good and ready to open the door. She would not make a scene of any sort. She'd simply park herself on the stoop and wait. Sooner or later he had to use the door, and if she had to wait until tomorrow then she would wait.

"You look better this morning," Charlie said.

"I feel better." She smiled and poured herself a cup of coffee.

The drive across town was uneventful, although a garbage truck blocking her way made the trip slower than necessary. Claire parked in front of Todd's Toys and hurried inside. The Cabbage Patch doll sat on a ledge behind the counter, and a note stuck to the box read, "Hold for Elizabeth Caruthers." Claire flashed back to the memory of Liz telephoning store after store to find the doll, and for a moment she feared the tears would start again.

"You have got to be Elizabeth's mother!" Nora Todd came from the back of the store carrying an armful of teddy bears.

Shaken from her reverie, Claire answered, "Yes, I am."

Nora dropped the teddy bears onto the counter and wrapped her arms around Claire. "I feel for you. I know what it's like to lose a child."

"You do?"

Nora nodded. "Walt and I lost our Tommy when he was only twenty-eight."

"How awful."

"Yes, indeed. Tommy was our baby and smart as could be."

"How did he—"

"Car accident. A drunk driver ran a stop light and hit him."

Claire gasped. "Oh, no."

"Yes. He died before they got him to the hospital. Tommy left a wife and four little boys, every one of them as good looking and smart as he was."

Claire gasped, clutching her hand to her heart. "How on earth did you get over—?"

"I had to, for the boys. Every time I'd look at one of them, I'd see my Tommy. I finally came to realize Tommy wouldn't ever be completely gone, not as long as I had those boys. Of course, they grew up faster than weeds." Nora laughed. "I was wishing they'd be babies forever, but life moves on whether you want it to or not."

"Isn't that the truth. Liz's oldest boy is already in first grade."

"Tommy's oldest just went off to college."

"It's wonderful that you were able to remain close with them," Claire said wistfully.

"It wasn't easy. Tommy's wife remarried and I was afraid they'd shut us out, but Walt and I just kept turning up like a couple of bad pennies. Eventually everybody accepted that the kids had three sets of grandparents instead of the standard issue two." Nora smiled and began straightening the jumble of teddy bears. "You never forget, but in time you get past the heartache."

Claire returned the smile. "I hope so."

"You will," Nora said confidently. "Those grandchildren will be a constant reminder that you've still got an important part of your daughter right here with you."

When Claire left the store, the conversation looped through her mind. She knew Nora was right. David, Kimmie, and Christian were a part of Liz, the part Claire could hold on to. She and Charlie had to provide those children with all the love Elizabeth would have given them. Claire began picturing the face of each child and picking out what features most resembled Liz. Kimberly definitely had Liz's personality, and her smile, and the tilt of her…

Lost in thought, Claire failed to notice when the traffic slowed, so her foot was still pressing the gas pedal when she hit the Buick in front of her. Seconds later the delivery truck following her slammed into the back of her car.

A brawny man with a beard the color of a carrot climbed from the Buick and tromped toward Claire.

"What's the matter with you?" he growled. "You blind? You can't see I'm stopped?"

"Oh dear, I'm sorry, terribly sorry. No question it's my fault. Instead of paying attention, I was thinking—that is, my daughter passed away—"

"Oh," he grimaced, pulled back his anger, then turned to survey the damage. "I guess you've got insurance?"

Claire nodded.

After two hours of paperwork and formalities, the tow truck finally hauled away her smashed car and she telephoned Charlie.

When he heard she'd been in an accident, he gasped. "Are you hurt?"

"No," she answered. "But the car's in bad shape."

"Drivable?"

"No. You'll have to come pick me up."

When Charlie arrived, she stood on the street corner with a Cabbage Patch doll under her arm and a shopping bag from Todd's Toys dangling from her hand.

"You sure you're not hurt?" Charlie asked.

"Unh-huh."

"You want to stop at the hospital and let them check you over?"

"No," she answered. "But I would like you to take me somewhere else."

As Claire settled into the passenger seat, she launched into a full explanation of all that had happened—the telephone call, the doll, Nora Todd's loss of her son, and, lastly, her vow to make amends with Jeffrey regardless of cost.

"I know we both have a lot of resentment about the way he treated Liz," she said, "but for the sake of our grandchildren, we've got to set it aside and move on."

"That's easier said than done. After the way he—"

"You couldn't possibly dislike Jeffrey any more than I do. But regardless of what we feel, we've got to patch things up with him. If we don't, he'll never let us see the children!"

Charlie didn't disagree.

"Anyway, I was thinking if you came with me—"

"I don't know if that's such a good idea," Charlie said. "Especially given the last time I saw Jeffrey."

"All the more reason you should be there. It's important for him to see you're willing to bend, willing to ask his forgiveness."

"Seeing me might make him less inclined to listen."

"No, it won't, because the minute he opens the door I'll say we both regret whatever misunderstandings have come between us. That way he'll realize we're not looking to make trouble. I'll explain we're there to make amends and give him whatever financial assistance he needs. I'm not even going to mention seeing the kids until we get him on a friendly footing."

"What makes you think he won't slam the door in your face before you can say anything?"

"He won't, I just know he won't. I'll get down on my knees and beg him to listen if I have to."

"I don't know," Charlie said.

"It'll work. You'll see."

As they approached the Caruthers house, Claire pointed to the pot of chrysanthemums on the front stoop. "That's a real good sign."

"It is?"

"Yes, it indicates he's feeling a bit more optimistic."

"I fail to see how one has anything to do with the other," Charlie mumbled as he followed her up the walkway. Claire touched her finger to the doorbell and rang it just once. They waited several minutes, but no one answered.

"We'll just sit on the stoop and wait," she said.

"I'd rather not," Charlie answered. "Let's go for a bite of lunch and come back later."

They compromised, waiting for fifteen minutes then heading off to the diner.

After lunch they returned to the house and rang the doorbell a second time; still no answer. Again they waited, this time for nearly an hour. Claire lowered herself onto the stoop, and Charlie paced up and down the walkway. Finally he convinced Claire they ought to come back in the evening when Jeffrey was more likely to be at home.

It was dark by the time they returned. Upon seeing the lights of the house ablaze, Claire said, "He's obviously at home now."

Once again they rang the doorbell and waited, and this time it was only moments before the door swung open.

"Yes?"

Claire had never seen the brown-eyed woman before. "Are you the housekeeper?"

"I suppose you could say that," the woman said with a laugh. "I'm Fran Lombard."

"Oh." Claire stuck her hand out. "Pleased to meet you. I'm Claire McDermott, and this is Charlie."

"Yes…and?"

"We're the children's grandparents," Claire explained. "We're here to see Jeffrey."

"Oh," the woman chuckled. "You must be looking for Mister Caruthers, the previous owner."

Stepping closer to the door, Charlie said, "Previous owner? Jeffrey Caruthers and his children no longer live here?"

"Not for some time," Fran Lombard answered. "They moved before we bought the house, and we've been here for over a month."

"Where did they move to?" Claire asked in a high-pitched, anxious voice.

Fran shook her head. "I haven't a clue. We never even met the man. The real estate agent handled everything."

"Do you have the name of the agent?" Charlie asked.

"I'm pretty sure it was Elkins. Pamela, I think. She works for Somerset Realty."

"What about mail?" he asked. "Do you have a forwarding address?"

Fran shook her head again. "Sorry. I just give it back to the postman and say he doesn't live here anymore." She saw the look of distress on their faces and added, "But I'll bet the post office has a forwarding address, because he still gets a lot of bills coming to this address."

"Thanks," Charlie said. Then he turned and walked away with Claire, who was too tearful to say anything.

The following day the search for Jeffrey began. It started at the post office with a clerk who claimed they had no forwarding address for Jeffrey Caruthers, and if they did it would be illegal to give it out to an unauthorized party.

"I can only release that information to Mister Caruthers himself," she said.

"He already knows it!" Claire snapped.

The second stop was the Somerset Realty office. Pamela Elkins did work there, the manager said, and she had handled the sale of the Caruthers house. But she was on vacation in the Caribbean and not due back for three weeks.

"Do you have a forwarding address?" Charlie asked.

"Not in our files. It's possible that Pamela knows the new address but—"

"I know. She's on vacation."

"Right."

The next stop was Noreen Sarnoff's office.

"We're trying to get in touch with Jeffrey," Charlie explained. "But apparently he has—"

"Skipped town?" Noreen said sarcastically.

"I don't know if I'd say that," Charlie replied diplomatically, "but he has moved. He's sold his house and—"

"Skipped," Noreen repeated.

Claire registered a look of alarm. "Do you know where he went?"

"If I knew where that deadbeat was, I'd be collecting what he owes me."

"But you're his lawyer. Don't you have some way of contacting him?"

"Nope. He was there one day, gone the next. He never even put the proceeds of his house in the bank. He took the certified check, cashed it, and disappeared the same day."

"Have you spoken with Pamela Elkins?"

"Yeah. She knows something, but she's got a serious case of lip-lock. Whatever she does know, she's not going to tell."

"And there's no other way to find him?" Charlie asked.

"Through friends possibly or family. They won't talk to me, but they might be willing to tell you where he is. Other than that…" Noreen spread her hands in a gesture of helplessness.

"What about the court?" Claire asked. "Doesn't he have to tell them—"

"Unfortunately not. He's got sole custody of the kids, so he can take them anywhere he pleases without telling anyone."

Claire groaned. "They're our grandchildren. We've got to find them."

"You might try hiring a private investigator, but you'd probably be wasting your money. When somebody like Jeffrey decides to disappear, it's pretty hard to find them. And even if you do, you still can't make him let you visit the kids."

A stream of tears started to come from Claire's eyes. "Those children are all we have left of Elizabeth. We've got to find them."

"We will," Charlie promised. "We will." He put his arm around her and together they left the office, both of them hunched over with sadness draped across their shoulders.

Searching

For two weeks Claire remained in bed. In the morning she'd wake, remember she'd lost her grandchildren along with Elizabeth, and then drop back onto the pillow.

"Why bother?" she'd moan. "There's nothing to get up for."

The telephone went unanswered, uncollected mail jammed the mailbox, a thick layer of dust settled on tabletops, and Charlie went back to eating his dinner at the diner.

On Sunday he tried to coax her into going to church.

"The Lord's not interested in hearing from me," she said and turned toward the wall. When Charlie argued such a thing wasn't true, she rattled off a list of prayers that hadn't been answered.

"What about those? If He was listening, would He have let me lose Liz and then lose my grandbabies too?"

Charlie tried to remind her the Lord moves in ways we don't always understand, but Claire's ears closed tighter than her eyes. Finally he went to church alone.

"Where's Claire?" Pastor Tom asked. Charlie simply said she didn't feel well.

Mildred sauntered over. Mildred had known Claire since grade school, knew Claire inside and out, better perhaps than Charlie.

"Is Claire still home feeling sorry for herself?"

Charlie gave a sheepish grin. "She's a bit under the weather."

"Baloney! She's not sick. She's just feeling sorry for herself. I stopped by three times last week, but she wouldn't open the door. I'm her best friend, and she won't open the door!"

With a weary nod of his head, Charlie sighed. "It's not you, Mildred. Claire won't talk to anyone these days. She's crawled into a shell and she—"

"She doesn't need you feeling sorry for her, what she needs is somebody to drag her butt out of that bed!"

"As depressed as she is, I hardly think it would help for me—"

"Well, I'd do it if she'd open the door!"

When Charlie left for work Monday morning, the front door of the McDermott house was left unlocked.

Shortly after ten o'clock, Claire heard the doorbell chime but she remained in bed and tugged the covers up around her ears. The chime rang a second time and then a third. After that she heard the front door open and footsteps tromp up the stairs.

Fear slid through Claire's chest as she nervously called out, "Who's there?"

"Me," Mildred said, barreling through the bedroom door.

"How did you—"

"The door was open, so I figured you must've left it open for me."

"As you can see, I'm not up to having company." Claire dropped her head back onto the pile of pillows.

"What I see is a woman feeling sorry for herself for no good reason."

"I have a reason," Claire said defensively, then launched into the story of how Jeffrey had disappeared, taking her grandchildren with him.

"And you figure staying in bed is better than looking for them?" Mildred asked sarcastically.

"Did you not hear what I said?" Claire replied. "No one knows where they've gone!"

Mildred plopped down on the bed. "And you're willing to accept that without looking any further?"

"Where else can I look?"

"David's in first grade, so try checking the school. Ask some of the neighbors. You said Jeffrey had a girlfriend, try finding her. Go see Jeffrey's parents. Anything is better than lying here like a lump. You're so busy feeling sorry for yourself you haven't thought about anybody else. What if the kids are someplace they don't want to be? What if they're waiting for Grandma to find them?"

When Claire gave no answer Mildred said, "I guess they'll have to keep waiting, because Grandma is busy wallowing in self-pity!"

"I am not," Claire argued.

"Then prove it. Get out of that bed."

"I told you, I'm not well."

"Okay, I'll take you to the doctor."

"I'm not *that* sick."

"Then get dressed, and we'll start trying to find those kids!"

The thought of finding her missing grandchildren pried Claire from the bed. Then the two old friends set off on a mission.

Their first stop was David's elementary school where the records clerk assured them she had no knowledge of the children's whereabouts.

"Mister Caruthers picked up David's records himself," she said. "He didn't give any indication of what school David would be transferring to."

"If you hear anything—" Claire said.

"I doubt we will," the clerk replied, "and even if we did, that information is restricted. The law prohibits our releasing it to just anybody."

"I'm not anybody, I'm his grandmother!"

"That may be," the clerk replied, "but if Mister Caruthers wanted you to know where David is, I think he would have told you."

After leaving the clerk, Claire and Mildred went in search of room 208 where Carolyn Platt taught first grade.

"We miss having David in our class," she cooed. "How is he doing in his new school?"

"I wish I knew," Claire replied sadly. "Our son-in-law has taken all three of the children and disappeared."

"Disappeared?"

"Completely. No forwarding address, nothing." Claire's eyes began to grow teary. "I was wondering if David ever mentioned where they were going."

"No, he didn't," Carolyn said sympathetically. "As a matter of fact, his father pulled him out of class one day and that was that. I never even had the opportunity to say goodbye."

That evening Claire telephoned Jeffrey's parents in Florida.

"I understand your loyalty to your son," she explained, "but I'm not looking to cause trouble. I'm only interested in seeing my grandchildren and—"

Before she could mention helping Jeffrey with any financial problems, the irate Emma Caruthers began screaming in her ear.

"How dare you! What audacity! You have some nerve asking for my help after all the hateful things your family has done to my boy!"

"We've never done—"

"Don't think you can lie to me! Jeffrey's told me all about you and that miserly husband of yours!"

"I'm afraid you've been misinformed, Charlie actually helped Jeffrey to—"

"To drive him out of business! That's what he helped do!"

"Maybe we can make things right with Jeffrey," Claire said, sounding conciliatory. "If you could just give me his new address—"

Emma screamed, "Hell will freeze over first!"

No stone was left unturned in the search for the Caruthers family. Charlie spoke with banking associates and fellow members of the Chamber of Commerce, tactfully inquiring whether anyone had heard from Jeffrey or knew of his whereabouts. The answer was always a shake of the head. Claire and Mildred bundled themselves in sweaters and tromped up and down the streets questioning neighbors and conversing with children at play in hopes of finding David and Kimberly's new address.

271

Shortly after Thanksgiving the weather became blustery, playgrounds emptied out, and the last vestige of leaves disappeared from trees, but still there was no word of David, Kimberly, or Christian. When the frosty winds of December drove everyone inside Claire made telephone calls. She called the children's dentist, their pediatrician, even a children's wear shop on the far side of Union, but the answer was always the same. No one, it seemed, knew anything. The family had simply vanished.

Although Claire grew teary-eyed at the mere mention of grandchildren she clung to a thread of hope and followed every imaginable lead, none of which proved successful.

Then on a day when the wind rattled windows and upended garbage cans Louise Farley, a frail wisp of a woman well into her eighties, came knocking at the door.

"What are you doing out in this weather?" Claire said as she tugged the tiny woman inside.

"I came to ask a favor," Louise said in spurts, trying to catch her breath.

Claire took hold of her arm. "First sit down and have a cup of tea. You've no business being out in this weather."

Still shivering, Louise said, "This isn't so bad. In Minnesota over Thanksgiving it was so cold my bones nearly froze."

"Minnesota?" Claire said. "What in the world were you doing in Minnesota?"

"Visiting my sister, Clovis. Minnesota's a nice enough place but way too cold for the likes of me." Louise wrapped her bony fingers around the steaming cup of tea. "When you and Charlie go out there be sure to bring plenty of warm clothes, because you're gonna need them!"

Claire laughed. "Oh, I doubt we'll be going to Minnesota."

"You're not planning to visit the grandchildren?"

"You mean our grandchildren?" Claire asked.

"Yes," Louise answered, "David, Kimberly, and the little one—what's his name?"

"Christian."

"Yes, that's it, Christian."

Claire felt her heart jump. "You know where they live?"

"Not really. But they were at the Minnesota State fair when I saw Clovis in the fall, so I'd guess somewhere in Southern Minnesota or maybe Wisconsin."

Claire gasped. "You've seen them?"

"Not since September."

"Where?"

"The Minnesota State Fair," Louise repeated. "It's quite an event. There's livestock shows, a big Ferris wheel, kiddie rides, and every kind of food imaginable, even fried cheese. Can you believe—"

"You saw Liz's kids? Our grandchildren?" Claire asked again.

"Oh, yes. They were there, all three of them. They were with their daddy and some girl who looked to be half his age. David, he saw me before I saw him. He started waving and calling out 'Hi, Miss Louise,' but that girl yanked him and Kimberly away before I got a chance to talk to them." The old woman's face wrinkled with disdain. "That girl looked like a trashy sort."

Claire peppered Louise with question after question but got few answers. Yes, she had seen the kids. Yes, they all looked well. No, she hadn't had an opportunity to talk to them. No, she hadn't trailed them back to wherever they were living.

"It never dawned on me to do that; I didn't know they'd gone missing."

After nearly two hours of questioning, Louise finally got to the favor she'd come to ask about. "I was hoping you'd be willing to help me with my Sunday school class for the next six weeks."

Caught up in the euphoria of good news, Claire answered, "Sure."

That night Claire told Charlie of the conversation.

"Now that we know they're in Minnesota, we can get a private investigator to find them," Claire said.

Although he argued that trying to find five people who lived somewhere in the state of Minnesota or perhaps Wisconsin was like searching for a needle in a haystack, Charlie finally agreed to hire an investigator.

"But even if we get Jeffrey's address, it doesn't mean he'll allow us to visit the kids."

Claire didn't want to consider such a negative train of thought, so for the remainder of the month she happily planned their reunion with the children.

A Partridge in a Pear Tree

When Claire arrived at the church on Sunday morning, the last thing she expected to see was a room full of noisy kindergartners, twenty-seven in all. When Louise asked for Sunday School help, Claire had envisioned a class of adults like the Bible study she'd attended five years ago. She'd never considered that a woman in her eighties would teach children.

"I don't know if I can handle this many kids," she whispered in her friend's ear.

"Of course you can," Louise answered, then she shoved a tub of crayons toward Claire and told her to put a handful in the center of each table. "Mix them up so there's an assortment of colors on each table."

Louise turned to the whirlwind of kids who were talking, laughing, chasing one another, and, in one case, crouching beneath the table, and she clapped her hands—once, twice, slight pause, then three quick claps. Suddenly the noise stopped, and the children repeated the clapping pattern. Clap, clap, pause, clap, clap, clap. Once the room got quiet, Louise asked in a thin, delicate voice, "What time is it?"

Claire glanced at her watch, but a chorus of little voices shouted, "Learning time!"

With no word of direction, the children scurried toward the center of the room and sat on the floor. The only exception was the boy from beneath the table. He sat apart from the group, head hanging low and his back pushed against the wall.

Claire went and squatted beside the boy. "You look awfully sad," she whispered.

He nodded almost imperceptibly but kept his chin tucked to his chest.

"I'm sorry you're feeling sad," she said sympathetically. "Maybe if you tell me your name, I could do something."

"Adam."

"Well, Adam, do you want to tell me what's wrong?"

He kept his eyes focused on the floor and shrugged.

Claire wrapped her arm around the lad's shoulder. "If you tell me the problem, maybe I can fix it."

"My shoe's untied."

Claire squeezed his shoulder. "Well, that's easy enough to fix."

He pulled his right foot from beneath his leg, and she saw a brown shoelace flopping loose on both ends. Claire tightened the laces and looped the two loose ends into a bow.

Adam lifted his head and smiled.

"How about we go listen to the rest of Miss Louise's story?"

Adam nodded.

When Claire stood he took hold of her hand, and when he lowered himself into the crowd of his classmates he tugged her down alongside of him.

After the story there was a prayer and another round of clapping, then Louise announced it was time for pageant practice.

"Yea!" the chorus echoed gleefully.

"Can I be the partridge?" a voice called out.

"No, Brenda," Louise answered, "Sara is the partridge. You're a French hen."

"Why does Sara get—"

"Because she's smaller and the tree platform is only big enough for a very small person." Louise motioned to a group of boys. "Calling Birds, over here."

Adam still clung to Claire when Louise wriggled a finger at him. "You're a Turtle Dove. You should be next to Tommy." Adam slid his hand from Claire's and moved to stand alongside a dark-haired boy with round glasses.

"Okay," Louise said. "Now, everyone, stay with your group." She waved toward Claire. "You take the partridge, turtle doves, French hens, and calling birds. I'll get the rest."

"Take them where?"

"You don't *take* them anywhere." Louise chuckled. "Just teach them their parts of the song."

Claire stood there slightly petrified.

"It's easy," Louise assured her. "We start with the partridge sitting in the tree and she sings the first verse, then the turtle doves come on stage and they sing the second verse, and so on. Everybody joins in on the chorus."

"Okay," Claire answered nervously. She turned to the group in front of her. "Do you all know the song?"

The partridge nodded as did two hens, one calling bird, and one turtle dove. The remainder shook their heads.

"Well," she said, remembering how she'd once taught the refrain to Elizabeth, "this song is actually a story. It tells about all the wonderful Christmas presents a man bought for his true love. On each day of the Christmas season, he gave her a very special gift."

"Was he a prince?" someone asked.

"He might have been," Claire answered. "On the very first day, he gave his love a partridge in a pear tree. Sara, that's you. The pageant opens with you sitting in the tree and you get to sing, 'On the first day of Christmas my true love gave to me, a partridge in a pear tree.'"

"By myself?" a wide-eyed Sara asked.

"Yes, won't that be fun?"

Sara twisted her face into displeasure.

"How about we'll sing together until you get comfortable with doing it?"

"What if I never get comfortable?"

"Then the night of the pageant I'll hide behind the tree and sing along with you."

Sara smiled. "Really?"

277

"Cross my heart."

Once Sara began singing things moved along smoothly. The two calling birds added some wing-flapping to their verse and one of the French hens got the hiccups, which caused a lot of giggling. After what seemed like minutes, Louise repeated her clapping routine and announced that the dress rehearsal would be at seven o'clock on Tuesday evening.

"You'll need to try on your costumes, so be on time!" She turned to Claire. "You too."

"Me? But I'm temporary. I'm only helping out."

"You're directing the first four days of Christmas."

Claire hadn't planned on directing anything, especially a bunch of kindergartners with stage fright, but when she looked down and saw Adam beaming up at her, she answered, "Okay."

That afternoon Claire plopped down in Charlie's recliner and gave a sigh of relief. "I'm glad this is temporary," she said.

"Why?"

Claire thought about it but found she didn't have an answer. True, the time flew by, which was generally a sign a person was enjoying themselves, but she'd come away with an odd sense of sadness. It felt as if the hole in her heart left by the loss of their grandchildren had somehow grown larger. And singing that song, turning it into a story as she had with Elizabeth, brought back so many memories.

After a long while she answered, "I really can't say."

That's how it went for the next two days. One moment Claire would be troubled by the flood of memories pushing their way into her head, and the next she'd find herself wondering how to get Sara past her stage fright.

The children in the class were the same age as David and a number of boys also had dark hair and dark eyes, but Claire turned her attention to someone else. Adam had hair as light as corn silk and eyes the color of a cement walkway. He was timid and frail, nothing like her grandson. Yet something about the boy haunted Claire. She remembered him crouched under the table and sitting alone. There was a certain sadness in Adam's eyes, one that Claire simply couldn't forget. When she thought about how he'd sat with his head bowed as if the weight of the world pressed down on it, Claire could believe Adam's heart hurt as much as hers.

The night of the dress rehearsal Adam cautiously peered into the room, but once he spotted Claire he ran to her and wrapped his skinny little arms around her knees. He was a child she could so easily love, but Claire's heart warned, "He's not yours."

The funny thing about love is that sometimes it latches on to you when you're looking to run the other way. And apparently Adam had decided to love Miss Claire whether she wanted him to or not.

The night of the pageant the temperature plummeted to ten degrees, and even though the furnace was fired to its maximum the church auditorium remained colder than cold—frosty. Teeth chattered, hands were pocketed, and overcoats remained buttoned.

"I'm freezing!" the partridge said.

"Leave both sweaters on under your costume," Claire replied. "That will help."

"I'm too cold to sing."

"It'll warm up when the furnace gets going."

As she dabbed a bit of glue on the calling bird's loose plume, a masculine voice called, "Are you Miss Claire?"

The sound of an adult in the midst of all those children caught her ear. "Yes, I am," she answered as she turned toward him.

"I'm Dorothy's dad," he said. "Sorry, but Dorothy has the flu and can't come tonight." He handed Claire his daughter's French hen costume. "Hopefully you can get someone else to fill in."

"There *is* no one."

"Sorry," he repeated then left.

The partridge, who now had a stream of tears rolling down her face, repeated, "I'm still too cold to sing."

Claire gathered the little girl into her arms. "Sara," she whispered, "are you afraid you'll forget the words if you have to sing alone?"

The girl nodded.

"Okay," Claire said. "A promise is a promise. When the curtain opens and you're sitting in the tree, I'll be hiding behind it and I'll sing with you. That way you won't forget any of the words."

"Okay." The partridge smiled and flapped her wings.

"Good." Claire laughed. "Very good."

The backstage room of the auditorium was crowded with people, mostly kids, but Claire had yet to see Louise. She stood and looked across the sea of heads. With her snow-white hair Louise should have been easy enough to spot, but—

"I'm not gonna be a stupid hen!" Brenda shouted as she began to remove her costume.

Rushing over Claire asked, "What seems to be the problem?"

"I'm not gonna be a French hen. People will laugh at me."

"What makes you think they'll laugh?"

Brenda, the tallest and chunkiest child in the class, placed her hands on her chubby hips and stood there with a rebellious glare fixed on her face.

"Because the song says *three*!" she said angrily. "Three French hens, not two!"

"I'm trying to get a replacement for Dorothy. As soon as I find Miss Louise—"

"I wanna be the partridge!"

"Brenda, dear, I've already explained, the platform is too small to hold you—"

"I don't care!"

"Brenda," Claire bent and whispered in the girl's ear, "I chose you to be a French hen because they're the stars of the show. The French hens get to stand in the middle of the stage, right in front!"

Brenda smiled. "Really?"

Claire nodded. "Everyone in the audience is going to be busy looking at you, and they won't even notice if a hen is missing."

Brenda smiled and strutted off, waving her tail feathers.

Claire continued searching for Louise. Finally she spotted Pastor Branford edging his way through the crowd.

"Excuse me," she said, tapping him on the shoulder. "I haven't been able to find Louise Farley yet. Have you seen—"

"She's down with the flu and asked if you would take over the supervision of her group."

"Me? But I don't know—"

Pastor Branford, obviously preoccupied with something else, said, "Thanks," then moved on.

"Oh, dear," Claire murmured as she started through the room rounding up gold rings, geese, and swans. As it turned out one of the gold rings had his costume on backward, two geese were also home with the flu, and one swan had a broken wing.

"Five minutes 'til curtain," the pageant director announced.

Claire quickly scotch-taped the broken wing, reversed the gold ring costume, and went with four instead of six geese. She bunched each group together in the order of appearance on stage.

"I'll be behind the tree," she said, "so watch closely. When I give the signal, the group at the head of the line comes on stage singing. Now remember, you come onstage one group at a time, and you have to wait until I give the signal for your group. Okay?"

"Okay," they answered, but Claire felt a nervous bubble bouncing around her stomach.

"One minute 'til curtain."

Claire hoisted Sara onto the platform. "Are you okay?"

Sara nodded wordlessly.

The house lights dimmed, the curtain opened, and the music started, but not a sound came from Sara. Finally Claire, who had squatted behind the tree, began singing a flat and somewhat off-key rendition of the song.

"On the first day of Christmas my true love gave to me…"

A roar of laughter came from the audience.

Claire kept singing but turned her head, peeking through the grid of the tree to check on Sara. The partridge now stood on the platform flapping her wings.

"Sit down," Claire hissed as she signaled for the two turtle doves.

They came in on cue singing and moved to their assigned spot on the stage without incident.

The hens came next. Claire gave the signal but Brenda, preoccupied with a loose feather, failed to notice so the hens made a late entrance and Claire was already singing, "…three French hens…" The laughter from the audience sounded louder than before.

Claire peeked again. "Oh no," she moaned. It was bad enough to have two French hens instead of the required three, but Brenda was strutting across the stage like a bandy rooster.

The calling birds came next with a flawless performance. Claire sighed with relief and signaled for the gold rings. Four gold rings marched in but Brian, the lad with his costume backward, was missing. They had already moved on to the chorus when Brian came running in—his costume backward again.

The audience laughed louder with each mishap. Between the straggling gold ring and the geese who were two short of their number, it was impossible to tell when one uproarious stretch of laughter ended and the next began. When the seven swans came on stage Claire saw her repair had not held and one swan was dangling a broken wing. Thankfully the swans were her last group.

Miss Burgess, who taught the seven-to-twelve year-olds, stood in the wings. Her maids-a-milking, ladies dancing, and lords-a-leaping moved on stage without incident, and the audience applauded loudly. The eleven pipers marched in playing flutes, and the drummers followed with real drums.

When the song ended more than seventy children stood on stage, not counting Claire still crouched behind the tree. If there had been a trap door that would enable her to fall through the floor, Claire would have taken it. But there was none, so she stood and smiled at the audience. Then she lifted Sara from her perch and herded the group of children offstage.

When they reached the changing room, Claire turned to them and said, "You did a wonderful job. I'm very proud of you all."

"Even me?" Sara asked shyly.

"Especially you," Claire said, giving her a hug.

When the final chord of "Silent Night" faded from the auditorium, parents came to collect their children and the room became a whirlwind of activity. "Do you have your mittens?" mothers asked. "Where's your sweater?" "Hurry up, Daddy's waiting in the car."

Claire was looking for Luke's muffler when Adam pulled her aside.

"This is for you," he said. He handed her a small raisin box and then ran toward the doorway where his father waited. Halfway there he stopped, ran back, wrapped his arms around Claire's knees, and said, "Merry Christmas, Miss Claire." Before Claire could say anything he was out the door and gone.

Until that moment Claire had not considered any part of the season merry. In fact, she'd struggled through the days just hoping not to cry. She had expected it to be the saddest and loneliest Christmas ever. There was no Christmas tree at the McDermott house that year, no gaily-wrapped presents. Yet when Claire showed Charlie the raisin box, there was Christmas. Inside the box she found three marbles and a matchbox car—a gift that brought tears to Claire's eyes.

Charlie McDermott

What does a banker know about hiring a private investigator? Nothing, that's what. Okay, I've watched a few episodes of "The Rockford Files" and "Magnum, P.I.," but those guys deal with hardcore criminals. All I want is to find Jeffrey so we can see our grandchildren.

Claire thinks she's the only one who misses Elizabeth and the kids. I miss them just as much as she does, but I can't afford to let her know I'm hurting, or she'd fall apart.

The more sympathetic I am, the more depressed Claire gets. That's not good for anybody. Life won't stop and wait for a person to get over the pain. You've got to push past it and move on. If I don't help Claire do that, who else will?

Helping out in Sunday school has been good for Claire. It took her mind off herself. She says it's exhausting and she's glad it's over, but I'm hoping they'll call her back. For the past few weeks she's been sleeping at night, which is a lot better than wandering through the pitch-black house. It's a relief for me, because I worried that she'd fall down the stairs.

Anyway, about this private investigator, I finally got hold of one. Dudley gave me the name of a guy. Funny, I never thought of Dudley as the sort of lawyer who'd need a private investigator. He says this Frank Walsh is good at finding out things about people who are involved in messy divorces.

Walsh seems nice enough, but he's no Rockford. He's skinny, wears a three-button suit, and looks more like a stockbroker than a private investigator. I definitely can't imagine Frank Walsh crawling through drainpipes or popping bullets at someone.

I met with Walsh last Tuesday and gave him what information I had along with photographs of Jeffrey and the kids, at least the older two. Can you believe the only picture we have of Christian is the one taken in the hospital? Christian's two years old now. He's a blond-haired toddler, not a bald baby, so I doubt the hospital picture would be of any help.

Walsh seemed confident that he'd be able to locate the kids. Jeffrey's more than likely changed his name, so I asked if that decreased the probability of finding them. Walsh said no. Apparently, a man with three kids is easier to trace than someone who's traveling alone.

Even if Walsh finds them, it won't help unless Jeffrey's willing to let bygones be bygones. I can understand how hardships like losing Liz, then the store, and most probably the house can tear the guts from a man and make him resentful, but I'm hoping we can get past it. God knows I've got plenty of reasons to hate Jeffrey as much as he does me, but I'm ready to give it up for the sake of our grandchildren. I'm even willing to help him get back on his feet, if it lets us reassemble the pieces of Elizabeth's life. I'd do anything in the world for our daughter, and that includes making sure her family is cared for.

Moving On

The following morning Claire awoke with Louise and her ill health on her mind. For weeks, Louise had talked about nothing but the pageant. She'd sewn feathers on costumes, painted gold rings, and threaded together enough leaves to fashion a tree, so it was strange that she'd miss the pageant. Louise was getting on in years and now rather frail, the sort of person who shouldn't be living alone. If she had the flu, who would care for her? The flu could become serious. If her fever spiked she might stop eating; then what? For all anyone knew Louise could be—

Claire jumped out of bed, and within the hour she tromped across the street with a pot of chicken soup. She rang Louise's doorbell and waited long enough to consider going for help when finally she heard the shuffling of feet and the door opened.

"Oh, my goodness!" she exclaimed. "You look awful!"

Louise did look terrible. She shivered from head to toe and looked as green and bug-eyed as a frog.

"What do you expect," she said. "I'm sick!"

Claire pushed through the doorway and headed for the kitchen. She set the pot of soup on the stove, laid the potholders aside, and turned on a gas burner.

"This will be piping hot in no time," she said. "It's just what the doctor ordered."

"I don't think so," Louise replied, looking like someone about to throw up what they hadn't yet eaten. She turned and headed back to the bedroom.

Claire followed her. "You've got to eat something. You've got to keep your strength up. If you don't eat—"

Louise waved Claire off with a flutter of her hand and climbed back into bed.

In the past two years Claire had become an expert at distinguishing fever from flushed, and she could tell the seriousness of a person's sickness with little more than a glance. She placed her hand on Louise's forehead and gasped.

"You're burning up! You've got to get to the hospital!"

Louise protested, but by the time Claire stopped to listen an ambulance was already on its way.

When the medics loaded Louise into the ambulance Claire climbed in with her, and when they wheeled her into the emergency room Claire tagged along. Other than a sister in Minnesota, Louise had no one. She needed a friend, and Claire decided to be that friend.

She sat beside Louise throughout the day. She followed when they readied a room and moved Louise to an upstairs ward, and when Louise asked her if she would take care of teaching Sunday school for another week or two, Claire said yes.

Claire didn't leave the hospital until nearly eight o'clock that evening. The sky had gone dark and icy cold while sleet drizzled. She thought of telephoning Charlie to pick her up, but she didn't want to drag him out on a night such as this so she took a taxi. The ride usually took fifteen minutes at most, but when the taxi driver got to her street he stopped. Whirling lights from police cars and fire engines set the entire block ablaze, and the street was cordoned off.

"I'm gonna have to let you off here," the driver said.

Claire thought of Charlie. She handed the driver a twenty dollar bill, jumped from the car, and began running down the street. *No,* her heart screamed, *no, not Charlie, please, God, not Charlie!* Then from a distance she spotted him huddled with a group of neighbors, all of them shaking their heads mournfully.

"What's happened?" she exclaimed, running toward them.

Charlie pointed toward Louise's house—now little more than a blackened shell.

An image of the soup pot sitting on the stove flashed through Claire's mind and she fainted.

When Claire came to she lay on her sofa, but the image returned and she began to cry. "What have I done?" she moaned.

"You?" Charlie said, looking bewildered.

Claire explained how she was responsible for the fire, how she'd set the soup on to heat then forgotten to take it off the stove, how she carelessly left the potholders atop the stove and how—

"You're not to blame," Charlie interrupted.

"I know you're trying to be kind, but the truth is—"

"No, I mean, you're really not to blame. The furnace exploded, and that's what started the fire."

"The furnace?"

"No doubt about it. Everyone on the street heard the explosion. We all came running out and Harry called the fire department right away, but the house was gone before they got here."

"It was the furnace?"

"Yes," Charlie answered. "It was old, and with the weather as cold as it's been Louise probably had it turned up high."

"You're positive it was the furnace? The soup had nothing to do with it?"

"Absolutely nothing! In fact, you probably saved Louise's life by getting her out of the house before it happened."

Claire breathed a sigh of relief, then began worrying about where Louise would live once she came home from the hospital. With her house in ashes, there was no place unless...

Claire looked at Charlie and said, "Louise can live here. We've got that empty bedroom upstairs. It's the perfect solution.

"I've no objection, but she might not want—"

"She doesn't have family; where else can she go?"

"Doesn't she have a sister?"

"In Minnesota! If it's this cold here, can you imagine how cold it is there?"

The next morning Claire returned to the hospital with a heavy heart. It had fallen upon her to be the bearer of bad tidings. She found Louise sitting up in bed.

"You look a lot better." Claire forced cheerfulness into her voice.

"I feel a lot better," Louise replied. "And I have you to thank."

"Nonsense. What are friends for?"

Claire knew she had to tell her about the fire. "We're friends," she said, "and friends do whatever they can to help one another."

Louise smiled and gave Claire's hand an affectionate pat.

"For example, if my house were to burn down tomorrow, I just know you'd insist that Charlie and I come and live with you—and we would."

Louise laughed. "Then you'd be two fools. That drafty old house is a terrible place to live. It's cold all the time, and the windows rattle every time a breeze passes by. Soon as I can sell the place, me and Clovis are gonna get us a nice little house in Florida. We've done decided."

"You never said—"

"Well, I'm not one to go about blabbing my business, and besides who knows when it will happen. So far the real estate agent hasn't been able to find a buyer foolish enough to want the place, and I can't go until it's sold."

"You can't move," Claire declared. "What about your Sunday school class?"

Louise laughed. "I'm eighty-three years old. How much longer do you think I'm gonna be able to keep up with those kids?"

"What are they supposed to do without you?"

"They'll get used to having a new teacher. I figure after a few weeks you'll be—"

"Me? I'm temporary. I'm willing to do it for another few weeks, until you're back on your feet. But I'm not capable of—"

"It seems the Lord's decided you are capable. Just look at the way the kids have taken to you."

"Nonsense. Kids are kids. They'd be the same with anyone."

"Not true. Especially not true of Adam. Ever since his mother died he's been—"

"Adam's mother died?"

Louise nodded. "Four or five months ago. August, I believe."

"August," Claire repeated with a grievous expression of understanding, "is when my Elizabeth died."

"Perhaps that's why the Lord brought you and Adam together. He figured you both needed—"

"Not me," Claire cut in. "I don't need the responsibility of another child, much less a classroom full of them. I've got my grandchildren, or at least I will have as soon as we find out where they're living. Those three will take up every spare minute I've got."

Louise smiled and said, "You might not need Adam, but he certainly needs you."

"Well, as I said, I'll stay on as your helper, but eventually Pastor Branford is going to have to find someone who can take over."

Louise chuckled. "He doesn't need to worry about finding a teacher right now. The way things are going, it could be years before that house sells and I'm gonna stay put until it's sold."

"Ah, yes, the house."

Claire began by asking if there was adequate insurance, and when Louise answered yes she moved into explaining about the fire.

As Claire described how the fire department arrived too late to save the house and how they'd said she might have died had she been at home, Louise sat there wide-eyed. After Claire told her everything, Louise leaned back into her pillow and gave a deep sigh.

"Well, if that don't beat all," she said. "The Lord sure works in mysterious ways." She asked Claire to telephone her sister, Clovis, in Minnesota and tell her she ought to start packing.

After Louise left the hospital she spent three weeks living with Claire and Charlie. During that time she arranged her affairs, collected her insurance settlement check, and purchased enough new clothing to last for a month, perhaps two. Bypassing row after row of mufflers and wooly sweaters she said, "Why buy a bunch of winter things when I'll be living in Florida?"

Louise already had her plane ticket. First she would travel to Minneapolis where she'd spend a week or two helping Clovis pack up her possessions. Once that was done, they'd leave for Florida.

"Since you'll be in Minnesota for a while," Claire said, "I thought you could keep an eye out for our grandchildren."

"Well, sure," Louise said. Then she warned Claire not to get her hopes up since the Minnesota stay would be short. "Don't forget, it's winter," she added. "Cold as it is there, I doubt we'll do much running about town."

On the morning of February seventeenth, Louise Farley packed her belongings into one medium-sized suitcase and waved goodbye to New Jersey and the twenty-seven children of her Sunday school class. Before she left Claire promised to teach the class until Pastor Branford could find a replacement.

Two Days Later

Almost six weeks had passed since Charles McDermott had sent Frank Walsh in search of Jeffrey Caruthers and his children. Charlie received three telephone calls from Frank during that time. The first came to inquire about the make and model of Jeffrey's last known car. The second call came from Minnesota, a lakeside community called Orono.

"Looks like I've got a lead on him," Frank said.

The third call came the Wednesday after Louise left town.

"I've found him," Frank said.

He explained that Jeffrey had rented a house in Plymouth, a suburb of Minneapolis, and he worked as a waiter in Max and Martha's Waterside Café.

"Are the children with him?" Charlie asked anxiously.

"Yep. Only there're four of them. One belongs to a young woman he's passing off as his wife, but I can't find any record of them being married."

"Are the children okay? Healthy? Well fed?"

"I can't find anything to indicate otherwise. Jeffrey works nights, and the woman takes care of the kids while he's working."

Charlie asked a number of other questions, mostly relating to the area and whether David had been enrolled in school. Frank gave a brief overview of the situation, then said he'd come by Friday morning to pick up a check for the rest of his fee and provide a detailed report.

"How much?"

Frank answered, "Just shy of seven grand, but that includes expenses."

That same afternoon Charles McDermott transferred another ten thousand dollars from his savings account to his checking account, figuring that he'd need extra cash to cover the cost of their plane tickets to Minnesota.

Frank Walsh's report included five photographs. The first two showed Jeffrey loading the children into an unfamiliar minivan, and while the faces of David and Kimberly were easily distinguishable Christian's snowsuit left little more than a nose visible. In the third, David was playing with classmates in the schoolyard. The fourth was of Jeffrey leaving the restaurant where he worked. The final photo was a street shot of Jeffrey and the woman identified as Kelsey Grigsby with all four children.

In page after page, Frank Walsh recounted Jeffrey's new life. He no longer went by the name Caruthers, but now used his middle name, Thomas, as a surname, which had made him considerably more difficult to locate. He had little or no traceable assets other than the minivan purchased with proceeds from the sale of his house. His checking account had a minimal amount, and he always made cash deposits. He had rented a First Federal Bank safe deposit box, which Frank believed contained the cash from the sale of his house. And while he had not officially declared bankruptcy, he had left town owing substantial amounts to a number of creditors.

The woman living with Jeffrey called herself Kelsey Thomas but was Kelsey Grigsby. Her only known relative was her sister, Cyndi Grigsby, who lived in New Jersey and worked at Saint Barnabas Hospital.

The fourth child, a boy by the name of Robert, also used the Thomas surname, but on his birth certificate the father was listed as unknown.

David attended the Plymouth elementary school and was registered using the name Caruthers. All four children appeared in good health and adequately cared for.

At the end of the report Frank had included Jeffrey's address and telephone number, and he had attached an invoice for $6,848.

"I take it this is satisfactory," Walsh said.

Charlie assured him it was, then pulled out his checkbook.

When he was alone Charlie read through every word of the report, then he reread it again and again. Had he missed something? Passed over some small detail that might be important? He studied the pictures and the faces of his grandchildren looking for some telltale sign. Were they happy? Unhappy? Did they want to be found?

Charlie couldn't decide whether the right way to approach the situation would be a phone call first to explain his intentions, or whether he should just appear on their doorstep. Approach it the wrong way, he knew, and things could get out of control, possibly turn ugly. With a mix of emotions swirling through his head Charlie folded the report, placed it back in its original envelope, and slid it beneath the stack of file folders in the second drawer of his desk. Before telling Claire he needed time to think.

Once Louise was gone, the McDermott household settled back into a regular routine. That was fine with Charlie, who kissed his wife goodbye then trotted off to the bank. But for Claire it meant a return to long days of loneliness, to thinking again about the things she'd lost, and searching for answers that didn't come. Each morning she'd rise, dress, and think about how she might stretch a handful of errands into a full day's work. The pantry was already overstocked with canned goods and paper products, the closets were filled with freshly dry-cleaned garments, and she'd purchased enough birthday cards to last a decade.

Too edgy to sit and read a book, too discontented to watch soap operas about people with fabricated problems, Claire eventually turned to baking. On Monday she made four dozen cinnamon rolls then delivered them to a number of the neighbors. On Tuesday she made cupcakes and filled the freezer with them so she'd have a supply on hand when her grandchildren returned. On Wednesday she took out the ingredients for sugar cookies when the doorbell interrupted her.

"Thank God you're home!" A young woman charged through the door with a little girl sucking her thumb. "Chloe's lame-brained babysitter didn't show up again. It's the third time this month!"

Claire stood there dumfounded as she tried to recall where and when they'd met.

Noticing the bewilderment, the woman stuck out her hand and said, "Rita, Rita Matthews. Liz and I were friends. I live over on Bethany, the yellow house two in from the corner."

"Goodness yes," Claire said. "At first I didn't remember—"

"It's been a while."

"Yes, it has."

"I know this is last minute, Missus McDermott, but I'm desperate. Please, please, please tell me you can watch Chloe today."

"Well, I was planning on doing some baking."

"Chloe's an angel and I promise she won't be a bit of trouble, but if I miss work again I'm sure to be fired."

"Just for today?"

Rita nodded. "Please?"

"I suppose I could—"

Rita thanked her profusely and darted out the door. The sad-eyed little girl with her carrot-colored curls had the look of a Raggedy Ann doll. Still sucking her thumb, she watched her mother disappear down the walkway.

Claire looked at the child. "Would you like a glass of milk?"

Chloe shook her head.

"Would you like milk if I put chocolate in it?"

Chloe shook her head again.

"Do you like cookies?"

Chloe shrugged.

"Well, I was about to make some cookies. Do you want to watch?"

Chloe smiled and pulled the thumb from her mouth. "Can I help?"

"I don't know," Claire teased. "Do you have any experience?"

"Yes," she said with childlike earnestness. "I used to help my grandma."

Once she got started Chloe turned into quite the chatterbox, talking about things probably considered family secrets. As Claire tied an apron around her waist, the child told how her grandma had moved to Cincinnati because she'd married Grandpa Sam.

"He's not a real grandpa," she said, "but he's like a real grandpa."

By the time Rita returned Claire knew a fair bit about Chloe's life, including the fact that her daddy, although he was dead, had hair the same color as her. They had also baked six dozen cookies and frosted them with swirls of pink icing.

"I hope she hasn't talked your ear off," Rita said jokingly.

"Not at all," Claire answered. "She was a pleasure to have around."

Surprised at her own words, Claire meant what she said. Chloe had turned out to be a delight.

Rita began fishing in her handbag. "How much do I—"

"Not a cent."

Rita reached out and wrapped her arms around Claire. "Thank you so much. I just didn't know where else to turn, and you were truly a godsend." Rita said she would fire the unreliable babysitter just as soon as she could find a person more dependable.

Claire blurted out, "Chloe can stay here with me until you settle on someone permanent. After all, choosing someone to care for your child, that's not something to rush into."

Chloe's face brightened. "Say yes, Mommy, please, please!"

And so Chloe began to spend every day with Claire. Rita insisted she pay for babysitting, and after a bit of bantering they agreed on thirty dollars a week. On the day she received the first thirty dollars, Claire took Chloe into Union where the two of them had lunch at The Chinese Garden then went shopping. Chloe came home with a brown-haired Cabbage Patch doll and a new pair of patent leather shoes.

Weeks went by, and any number of times Claire asked Charlie if he'd heard anything about their missing grandchildren. Perhaps he should have told her the truth and allowed her to take part in deciding the best course of action, but he didn't. After the long months of watching her stumble through life like a dead woman, he enjoyed the newly-restored sound of her laughter. Finding Jeffrey was one thing, but convincing him to allow them to become part of the children's lives would be quite another. Charlie feared the ugliness of a possible reunion, a reunion likely to open old wounds and render them even more painful. As long as they had a tomorrow to look forward to, Claire could enjoy the small measure of happiness she'd found. Charlie felt reluctant to take that from her.

And Claire did enjoy her days with Chloe, even though she continually reminded herself that the child was a temporary part of her life, someone simply passing through, much the same as Adam and the other children in her Sunday school class. In time, all of these children would move on to relationships with permanent people—blood relatives.

That was how life was supposed to be. Claire would also move on, once the detective located Elizabeth's children. David, Kimberly, Christian—they were blood relatives, the permanent people destined to be part of her life forever. It was only a matter of time.

Frank Walsh's report remained inside the desk drawer for nearly three weeks. Each day Charlie took it out, reread every word, studied the photographs, and tried to decide the best thing to do. Obviously, Jeffrey did not want to be found or he would not be using another name. But there was always the chance he'd done that simply to avoid creditors, to hide from people trying to take the little he had from him.

Charlie reasoned he and Claire were not looking to take but to give, to help with the financial problems, maybe assist Jeffrey in finding a better job, and help him with the children. Each time Charlie thought he'd found the right answer, another thought came to him. Was Jeffrey too bitter to be reasonable? What about the woman living with him? What about the fourth child? Each time he remembered such things, he'd force himself to think through things again.

Two days before Saint Patrick's Day, Charlie finally reached a decision. While Claire taught Chloe how to make leprechaun-shaped ginger cookies, he took the report from his desk and turned to the last page with Jeffrey's address and telephone number. The picture of Jeffrey, Kelsey, and all four children slid from the envelope. Charlie looked at it one last time, then shoved it back into the envelope and began to dial.

After the Winter

The moment he said hello, Charlie recognized Jeffrey's voice. "This is Charlie McDermott," he began.

"McDermott!" Jeffrey screamed. "What the—"

"Please, just give me one minute. I'm not calling to make trouble, I only want to—"

"I don't give a crap what you want!" Jeffrey cut in. "What I want is to get as far away from you as possible, to never again set eyes on you or—"

"Claire and I would like to patch things up. We only want to help. You and the kids, you're family—"

"No, we're not!" he thundered. "To us, you're nothing! You're less than nothing! You're dog shit we're looking to scrape off our shoes!"

"I know you're angry, but maybe there's a way—"

"There's no way! I don't want you around me or my kids. Ever. You got that?"

"Look, all I'm asking for is a few minutes of your time. If we could talk—"

"You've got nothing I want to hear. Stay away from me and my kids!"

"Please, Jeffrey," Charlie begged, "Liz would want—"

"Liz's dead!" Jeffrey yelled before slamming down the receiver.

Charlie buried his face in his hands. *What now?* he asked himself. Sooner or later he had to tell Claire that Frank Walsh had found the kids, but what then? Would he kill the shred of hope she had by repeating what Jeffrey said? Was it better to lie and say Frank couldn't find the children? Was knowing better than not knowing? Or could he do something else?

These questions plagued Charlie in the days that followed. One week folded into the next, and still he felt uncertain about what he should do. At one point he nearly told Claire the truth. Then he overheard her explaining to Chloe about the Cabbage Patch doll in the closet.

"Kimberly is my granddaughter," Claire said, "and that doll is for her."

"Then why is it in the closet?" Chloe asked.

"Because Kimberly and her brothers are with their daddy, and he lives far away, so I haven't been able to give it to her yet." Claire turned back to stacking the dishes. "Hopefully I'll see them one day soon, and then I'll give her the doll."

Hopefully, she'd said. There had to be some other way, Charlie decided, some way that didn't dash her last bit of hope.

In April when buds began to appear on bare branches and crocuses sprouted along the walkway, Charlie announced he'd planned a business trip and would be gone for a few days. Such trips were not at all unusual, so Claire packed his bag, tucked in a package of freshly-baked cookies, and waved a cheerful goodbye.

When the plane landed in Minneapolis, Charlie rented a car and asked for a map of the area. Once in the car, he unfolded the map and traced his fingers along a series of highways until he located Plymouth. The town was northwest of Minneapolis, almost an hour drive. He slid the car into gear and began the journey.

As he pressed his foot down on the gas pedal Charlie tried to imagine what he would say once he stood face to face with Jeffrey. First off, he'd push himself through the doorway the moment it was open; then Jeffrey would have to listen. Although in his heart Charlie knew he'd done no wrong, he'd apologize as if he had. "I'm sorry," he planned to say, "sorry for any harm I've caused you and your family." He'd explain that Claire felt the same way, and then he'd offer financial help so Jeffrey could get back on his feet.

Charlie knew he had to make it perfectly clear that he was here to give, not take. He would ask for nothing, no favors, no concessions. He wouldn't even mention the possibility of moving back to New Jersey until they'd established a reasonably friendly dialogue.

But what if Jeffrey refused to listen? The possibility ripped through Charlie's thoughts, and his fingers tightened their grip on the steering wheel. There could be no "what if" he decided; he *had* to make Jeffrey listen. If he was thrown out of the house today, he'd come back tomorrow, and he'd keep coming back until he said what he'd come to say. Sooner or later Jeffrey had to realize that pulling the family back together was good for everyone, himself included.

Eventually Charlie left the highway and threaded his way through the streets of Plymouth until he came to Breezeway Gardens, a winding maze of single-family houses that looked much the same, except each house was painted a different color. 12571 Easy Way was the address he was looking for. After several wrong turns he found Easy Way; then he spotted the house. It was fourth from the corner, dark gray with burgundy trim.

He drove by once, then circled the block and passed by again. He had hoped to see some toys in the yard or a minivan in the driveway, but he found nothing. He circled the block again. This time he noticed that the blinds were closed, probably because Jeffrey was still hiding from his creditors. Charlie parked the car two doors down, walked back to the house, and rang the doorbell.

No one answered, but Charlie expected as much. Jeffrey seldom opened the door when he figured it might be trouble. Charlie continued to ring the bell for nearly fifteen minutes; then he began knocking with a heavy-fisted hand. After a good bit of that he took to calling out Jeffrey's name and pleading for him to open the door.

"I'm not leaving here until I speak with you!" Charlie said loudly over and over.

Around five o'clock a car pulled into the next driveway. A woman emerged with two small children and a bag of groceries. Charlie called out, "Excuse me" and asked if he was at the right house for the Thomas family.

"It's the right house," she answered, "but they moved last week."

"Jeffrey Thomas? He's got three—no, make that four kids?"

"Unh-huh," she nodded, shuffling the bag of groceries from one hip to the other. "His boy, David, went to school with my Chad."

"Oh." Charlie's shoulders slumped. "Got any idea where they went?"

"Afraid not. David's not in Chad's class anymore, so I'm assuming it's somewhere outside of this school district."

"Do you know of anybody else I might ask? Did they have friends in the neighborhood?"

"Friends?" she replied, raising an eyebrow. "I don't think they had any."

"Oh. Didn't socialize much?"

"Not at all. Probably because of the wife; she was always screaming about something. Even with the windows closed you could hear her. Most people in this neighborhood have kids and don't get involved in situations such as that."

Hearing his grandchildren belonged to a family of outcasts made Charlie's heart heavy. He wanted to say it wasn't always like that. When Liz was alive they were a family filled with love, a family people wanted as friends. Charlie could have said so much, but he didn't. What good would it do?

"Thanks anyway," he said, then walked away.

Charlie knocked on several doors asking the same question, but the answer was always the same—the noisy family in the gray house had moved, but no one knew where they had gone. One man claimed he didn't realize they'd moved.

"But," he said, "I have enjoyed the peace and quiet of the past week."

After he left Breezeway Gardens, Charlie went to Max and Martha's Waterfront Café. No, they said, Jeffrey wasn't there and he wasn't expected to come back. He had collected his pay and quit two weeks ago. One of the waiters seemed to think he might be moving to Wisconsin, but he wasn't sure.

"Thanks anyway," Charlie replied; then he paid for his dinner and left.

It was almost ten o'clock when he checked in at the airport motel. He felt defeated and wished he'd surprised Jeffrey with his visit instead of calling first. Now he knew his options had run out. The next morning he boarded a plane back to New Jersey.

Later that evening, after the dinner dishes had been cleared away and after he'd planned what to say, Charlie joined Claire on the sofa. He sat down and moved close enough to drape his arm across her shoulder so that it hampered her movements as she crocheted a sweater for Christian.

"Charlie," she said, laughing, "you can see I'm—"

"There's something I need to tell you."

Sensing the weight of the words he spoke, Claire set the sweater aside and turned to him. "Is it about the children?"

He gave an almost imperceptible nod, but Claire got her real answer from the sorrow in his eyes, in the lines etched across his forehead.

"I'm so sorry," he said, a tear already glistening in the corner of his right eye. "I tried, I swear to God I tried."

Claire listened as he told about Frank Walsh's report, about his telephone call to Jeffrey, and finally about his trip to Minnesota.

"I was prepared to go along with whatever Jeffrey wanted," he said in a trembling voice, "but they were gone when I got there."

Her heartbeat quickened into furious movements that thundered against her chest like the wings of a trapped bird. "But surely you can find them again. You found them once—"

"I'd hire an army of investigators if I thought that was the answer, but it's not. Even if we find them, Jeffrey is not going to allow us into his life. He's not going to let us see the children. He's made that perfectly clear."

"But how can he do such a thing?" Claire moaned. "They're our *grandchildren*. They're all we have left of Elizabeth."

"They're not all we have," Charlie replied solemnly. "We have our memories."

"Memories." Her tone held a mocking bitterness. "Can you take a memory to the park? Can you watch it laugh? Or play? Can a memory call you grandma and tell you it loves you?" A torrent of sorrowful sobs drowned her words, and she hid her face in her hands.

"We're not going to give up." Charlie eased Claire's hands from her face and pulled her into a protective embrace. "We'll just wait a while, give Jeffrey some time to cool down, lose some of the anger he's got, then perhaps—"

"If we wait Jeffrey will disappear completely, and we'll never find them."

"No," Charlie said softly. "I'll have Frank Walsh keep tabs on him. I promise you, we'll know every time Jeffrey makes a move. He won't realize it, but we'll always know where Liz's children are. Maybe in time we'll see them again."

After that they said little, but for a long time they remained on the sofa, their bodies fitted together like the two halves of a broken urn. The clock struck twelve when they rose to go to bed.

The next morning Charlie noticed that a lopsided ball of yarn had replaced the sweater Claire had worked on for Christian.

"Please, Lord," Charlie prayed. "Don't let her give up hope."

Over Time

As days turned into weeks, weeks into months, and months into years Claire continued teaching the Sunday school class. She also continued as Chloe's "temporary" babysitter. Halfway through the second year, Chloe was joined by Jack, a toddler whose mother had been incarcerated for stealing. Jack's father came to Claire pleading for help.

"I've got to work," he said with desperation, "and I've got no one to care for Jack."

"I suppose I could do it," she answered. "On a temporary basis."

Jack stayed for five years, and Chloe continued to spend her afternoons at the McDermott house long after she'd outgrown the need for a babysitter. But they were not the only ones. After Jack came a frail little girl afflicted with severe asthma, then an autistic boy prone to fits of screaming, and twins who clung to each other as a drowning man clings to a scrap of wood. Eventually Claire lost count of the number who came her way, but she never lost sight of their needs.

Many of the sad, broken children carried the burden of life on their tiny shoulders. Every one of them needed love. And thus it happened that Claire became a replacement for other people—a missing mother, a dead father, a sick grandma. The children who came into her life became whole and then moved on, leaving her to wait for the next knock on the door, the next child who would stand there wearing a mask of fear and sorrow.

Claire turned no child away. When the winter wind blew and ice crusted the trees, she made certain they all had warm coats and shoes. In the blistering heat of summer, she loaded them into the car and drove to the beach. She baked cookies, helped with homework, taught right from wrong, and gave them love.

She envisioned each child as a counterpart to one of her own grandchildren. Every little girl reminded her of fair-haired Kimberly, even those with dark skin or curls the color of a flame. She saw David in the eyes of boys who wore a pretense of toughness to cover their tender hearts. When their frustrations erupted in tantrums that sent toys flying across the room, she stepped aside and waited until it was time to hold them in her arms. She knew the least about Christian. Christian was always blurry, the child too difficult to recreate. He was Tommy locked inside his autism, he was Brigitte who seldom spoke, he was all those with hurts too deep to be repaired.

With each new child who came into her life Claire wondered about her grandchildren, and she'd pray that someone would take care of them. After a while she prayerfully struck a bargain with the Lord. She promised to care for and love all of His substitute children, if He in turn would send someone to do the same for Elizabeth's children.

After Adam moved up to the second-grade Sunday school class, Claire sadly figured he was gone from her life. But every Mother's Day he came back with a paper card he'd lettered himself, and every Christmas he came with a clumsily-wrapped present. At first it was a toy or candy bar but as he grew older it became a handkerchief, a book, or, in one instance, dime-store pearls.

One by one the children grew up and moved on, but Claire stayed. Year after year she taught children on Sunday mornings. Even after a decade had gone by, Claire insisted that she was merely a temporary replacement for the teacher.

"I never know when my grandchildren might need me," she'd say.

Charlie remained true to his promise, and for a good number of years Claire knew the whereabouts of her grandchildren even though Jeffrey had forbidden any contact. At Christmastime and on their birthdays Claire sent each of the children a card with a small amount of money folded inside, but all of the cards returned unopened with "Return to Sender" written across the face of the envelope with the harsh black strokes of a heavy hand. Jeffrey never sent an explanation or word of acknowledgement, and Claire knew her precious grandchildren had never received the cards.

Still she never gave up hope, and year after year when the unopened envelopes returned she tucked them into one of three cartons marked, "David," "Kimberly," and "Christian." The cartons contained a number of things: small toys she'd bought for them that first year, photographs of their mother, mementos Elizabeth wanted them to have. Alongside Kimberly's carton was the yellow-haired Cabbage Patch doll. Even after Claire knew they'd grown too old for such toys, she could not bring herself to give the things away. Emptying the cartons would mean she'd never again see her grandchildren.

Charlie kept Frank Walsh on retainer and received a report whenever a change occurred in Jeffrey's life. When a brown envelope from Parsippany Investigative Services arrived Charlie would close his office door and read through every word, sorrowfully shaking his head as he learned the details of yet another fiasco. It disturbed Charlie that this man, the man he'd once considered a son, should lead such a hapless life. Knowing the downward spiral of Jeffrey's circumstances weighed heavily upon his heart and Charlie believed it would trouble Claire all the more, so he filtered the reports when he relayed their contents to her.

Jeffrey married Kelsey Grigsby shortly after they moved to Wisconsin but Charlie told Claire nothing, nor did he mention it eight months later when they got divorced and the judge ordered Jeffrey to pay a sizeable alimony. After Jeffrey moved, Charlie simply told Claire that the kids were well and living in Brownsville, Texas, which he suggested was a rather pleasant town.

For the first three years it seemed Jeffrey moved every few months. He'd rent a house, accumulate a bunch of bills, and then run off without paying them. With his bouncing from state to state, it became increasingly difficult for Frank Walsh to find Jeffrey before he moved.

Within ten years, Jeffrey Caruthers, Jeffrey Thomas or, in two instances, Thomas Jeffrey had lived in at least six different states and married four different women. Each of those marriages had ended in divorce. The second wife rendered him deaf in his right ear when she hit him with a cast iron frying pan, and the last wife took his wages to collect her alimony.

Jeffrey's career, such as it was, fared no better. From waiter he became a bartender and then a short-order cook frying up greasy hamburgers. After he got fired from those jobs he began working the late shift in a twenty-four-hour gas station. When he was caught sleeping, that job went the way of the others. Eventually he became the custodian in an exercise gym and stuck with that for a while.

On three different occasions Charlie tried to offer assistance. The first time Jeffrey said, "Drop dead!" The second time he said he'd get a restraining order if Charlie didn't stop bothering him, and the third time he slammed the receiver down without a word.

When Charlie learned that Jeffrey had lost his job at the gymnasium, he sent a check with a note saying that Jeffrey need not respond. The check was returned to the bank with the envelope unopened and a scrawl of painfully familiar words: Return to sender.

In 1998 Frank Walsh retired from the investigation business. "I'm getting too old for this sort of thing," he told Charlie and offered the name of another investigator. By that time Charlie realized the futility of tracking a man who wanted nothing to do with them, so he declined and said nothing to Claire of Frank Walsh's retirement. He wanted to spare her the tears and sleepless nights she suffered at any mention of their grandchildren.

Eventually Claire stopped asking if there was any news, but Charlie knew she never stopped hoping.

In June of 2001, on a warm summer night when fragrant breezes drifted through the window and curtains fluttered softly, Charlie kissed Claire goodnight then rolled over on his side and closed his eyes forever.

They'd been married for forty-six years and they'd loved each other even longer. Together they'd endured so many hardships, but always Charlie had been beside her. He had held her in his arms and eased the pain. Now he too was gone. Claire cried aloud to the Lord asking how He could leave her alone in this world, but His silence deafened her.

On the day of Charlie's funeral Claire went to the church expecting to sit alone in the pew reserved for family, but instead of one pew the family area had been expanded to seven rows.

All the temporary children she'd cared for and loved filled the pews. Chloe with her husband and two babies. Adam, with his new wife on one side and his silver-haired dad on the other. Little thumb-sucking Brigitte who'd grown up and become a model. Jack, now an engineer. Frankie, Henry, Melanie. Row after row, the children she'd babysat and those who'd passed through her Sunday school class. Some now parents themselves, others who'd gone off to college and returned, some still in their teens, but all part of one family. Her family.

"Thank you, Lord Jesus," she whispered.

Claire McDermott

A fair bit of time has gone by since the day I lost Charlie, and I've become accustomed to spending my days alone. As the weeks and months turned into years, I came to understand that alone doesn't mean lonely. Only a person who's never known love can be truly lonely. I'm not. I've had more love than any one woman is entitled to. All those children I thought were just passing through have taken up residence in my heart. I can close my eyes and picture their faces, which is enough to make me feel warm all over.

I've also held on to my dream, the dream of a life filled with family. No matter how old a person gets, they can still dream. They can still believe in miracles.

I've carried this dream with me for the better part of a lifetime. Oh, there might have been times when I thought it had disappeared, but it was still there tucked behind my everyday worries.

The day I received the letter, my dream resurfaced. I could feel my heartbeat again, and I knew hope was stirring inside my soul. Hundreds of thousands of times I've prayed for just such a miracle, but I never expected it would appear in a dog-eared gray envelope.

"Dear Mr. and Mrs. McDermott," the letter began. "I don't know if you really remember me, because my family left New Jersey when I was only two years old."

The moment I saw those words, my heart began pounding. I grabbed onto the arm of Charlie's old recliner and lowered myself into the seat, collapsing under my own weight. After all the years of waiting I had no time to cry, so I continued reading through a waterfall of tears.

"Recently I came across some information that leads me to believe that Elizabeth Caruthers, my birth mother, was your daughter. My mother passed away in 1986, and her maiden name was McDermott. Other than this, I have very few details. I'm contacting you in the hope of finding my grandparents. I am anxious to learn more about my mother's life and the unclear details surrounding her death. If we are in fact related, would you be willing to meet with me?

"My name is Christian Caruthers," the letter went on. "I live in Doylestown, Pennsylvania. My older brother David is married, and we have a sister named Kimberly..."

He asked if I would be willing to see him. Imagine that—willing to see him! Why, for the past twenty years, I've wondered what he'd grown to look like. Two decades ago I spied a blue-eyed child at a playground in Westfield. I rushed over and asked the boy his name. Willing to see him? Why, I'd go to my grave a happy woman if I could have the chance to hug those children to my chest and tell them how much I love them.

Without a minute's hesitation, I sat down at Charlie's old desk and scratched out an answer to the boy's letter.

"Elizabeth most certainly was my daughter," I wrote, "and I was right there the day she gave birth to you." I went on to say nothing in the entire world would give me greater pleasure than a visit from him, David, and Kimberly. I wanted to say Kimmie, but since Christian had referred to her as Kimberly I was reluctant to say anything that might change his mind about coming for a visit. I signed the letter "Your loving grandma, Claire McDermott." I wrote my telephone number big and bold, the way people are inclined to do as they get on in years. Once that letter disappeared into the mailbox, I began waiting.

May 2006

Claire's heart fluttered as she peered from the window for the fourth time in less than an hour. It was too early and she knew it but she felt too restless to simply sit and wait, so she repeatedly searched the street as if doing so could somehow hurry them along. The trip from Doylestown would be two, maybe three hours according to Christian. He'd said they were coming for lunch. She glanced at the clock and wondered if they might come early and if after so many years she'd recognize them.

Claire stepped back from the window and lowered herself onto the sofa. She began leafing through the photo album she'd taken from the closet. The leather cover was worn away along the edges and many of the black and white snapshots yellowed with age, but in every photo she saw living color and could remember the time of its taking.

The first few pages showed Elizabeth as a bright-eyed teenager. Then came the pages where she was so obviously in love, picture after picture of her and Jeffrey clinging to each other as if no force on earth could pry them apart. After that was the photo of Liz standing sideways with her round belly and, on the following page, holding baby David in her arms.

The camera continued to click as David grew. There was his first tooth, several birthday parties, the day he started school. Kimberly was also there, a ball of bunting propped against a pillow, a toddler clomping around in Liz's shoes, her mouth smeared with lipstick. Of Christian there was still only the photo taken at the hospital.

How ironic, Claire thought, that the child who'd received the least attention should be the one to find his way back home. She felt the flutter in her chest a second time, so she closed the album and went back to the window. As she stood there stretching her neck to see to the end of the street, she thought about his telephone call. It came five days after she sent the letter.

"Hi," he'd said in a youthful, upbeat voice. "This is Christian Caruthers. I got your letter, and I'm looking forward to meeting you."

"Me too," Claire answered soulfully. Hungry for every morsel of the past twenty years, she asked question after question.

"Everyone is fine," Christian assured her. "Except Dad, he died last year. That's how I came across your name and address. It was on some court papers he had stored in the garage."

Christian didn't say anything else about Jeffrey. Instead he talked about his brother and sister.

"Dave, he's married and has a two-year-old daughter. Kim lives in New York now, works for an ad agency, Humphrey something and something."

"And you?" Claire asked.

"Well, I was hoping to be an elephant trainer."

"An elephant trainer?" she repeated.

Christian gave a mischievous chuckle. "Yeah, but nobody was hiring elephant trainers, so I settled for stockbroker."

"You rascal," Claire replied, then she swung into another string of questions.

They talked for nearly an hour, Christian telling of his family's life, Claire trying to erase the lost years.

"So, Grandma," he finally said, "what are you doing next weekend?"

A dark blue Ford turned the corner, distracting Claire from her thoughts, but once the car had passed she returned to thinking about her youngest grandson. He'd said he would bring his fiancée. How unbelievable. She'd last seen him crawling on the floor, and now here he planned to get married. Meredith; he'd said her name was Meredith.

314

A little red sports car turned onto the street and slowed, the driver alone. The car passed by the house, then turned and parked two houses down. Claire watched for a few seconds, but when she saw no other cars she turned back to the living room thinking she'd plump the sofa pillows one last time. Claire had barely lifted the second pillow when the doorbell chimed.

She flung open the door expecting to see Christian and Meredith, but instead a woman who she might have mistaken for Elizabeth stood alone.

"Kimberly?" Claire gasped.

The woman gave a smile and nodded. Suddenly Claire saw the little girl she once was. Through the years her hair had darkened to her mother's shade, a dark blond that at first glance looked brown.

Claire gasped, raising her hand to her heart, her knees collapsing.

"Grandma!" Kimberly's hand shot out and grabbed Claire. "Are you all right?" She led Claire inside and helped her to the sofa.

"Sorry," Claire said. "I suppose it was just the shock of seeing you after all these years, and I never expected—"

"I know. Chris wanted me to surprise you."

"Well, you certainly did."

"I'll get you a glass of water."

Claire began to tell her where to find the kitchen, but Kimberly obviously knew exactly where to go. When she returned, Claire asked, "Do you remember—"

"Yes," Kimberly said with a chuckle. "A good bit. It drives Dave crazy, because I can remember things he doesn't."

"Do you remember your mother?"

"Not everything. But I remember how pretty Mama was. Her hands were soft as velvet. And the sound of her voice, I remember that. I remember her reading to us and the way she would make those stories seem so magical. I had a brown bunny book that was my favorite."

Kimberly's face took on the glow of childhood as she paused to gather the sweetness of her memories. "I loved that book and held on to it for the longest time. I carried it with me every time we moved, but when we left the house in Baltimore it just seemed to disappear."

"Well if that isn't something," Claire said in amazement. "You remember all of that and you were just a tiny little thing, barely three years old, when Elizabeth bought you that book."

"I remember a lot of things, even you, Grandma." Kimberly smiled. "I remember you made cookies shaped like angels. Only back then you had brown hair."

"And less wrinkles." Before she could ask if Kimberly remembered the year they made paper Valentines, the doorbell chimed a second time.

"Stay there, I'll get it." Kimberly hurried to the door. "You were supposed to be here by eleven," she scolded in a whispered voice. "Grandma was expecting you, and when she saw me it almost scared her to death!"

"I'm glad to see you too." Christian grinned and gave his sister a hug.

He stood well over six feet tall and had the casual gait of a tennis player. Claire recognized the ocean blue of his eyes, the same color as Elizabeth's. Although Kimberly's hair had darkened over time, his was still the color of corn silk.

"Hi, Grandma," he said, then bent and kissed her cheek as casually as if they'd seen one another just days ago. "Meredith," he said, tugging the brown-eyed girl forward. "This is my grandma."

Suddenly they all began talking at once, about what used to be, who remembered what, where they'd lived, and what they'd done for the past twenty years. A tear came to her eye when Claire told them that Charlie had passed away five years ago. "He surely did miss you kids, especially David, because he's the one who used to follow your grandpa around all the time. Whatever Charlie was doing, David would tag along."

Claire paused a moment then said, "By the way, where is David? Is he supposed to be my next surprise?"

Kimberly shrugged.

"It's tough to say," Christian answered, "I asked him, but..." He hesitated briefly then said, "Dave's got issues."

"Issues?"

"Yeah, but let's not spoil today talking about him." Christian flashed a mischievous smile. "I'd rather talk about how I almost became an elephant trainer."

"You goof," Kimberly said playfully.

For a while they continued talking about the years they'd lost and their plans for the future. Almost nothing was said about Jeffrey, and Claire didn't ask. At two o'clock she caught sight of the time and recalled they'd come for lunch.

"Oh my goodness!" she said. "I've got to get some food on the table." She lifted herself from the sofa when the doorbell rang.

Kimberly arched an eyebrow and gave Christian a nod. He stood and turned toward the door, but Claire had opened it.

If Claire had recognized Kimberly by the likeness to her mother, she could just as easily know this caller by the likeness to his father. He had Jeffrey's square-cut chin, dark hair, and dark eyes in an emotionless face.

"Good afternoon," he said stiffly. "I'm David. This is my wife, Claudia, and our daughter Christine." He stood there waiting to be invited inside.

"Well, of course I know you're David!" Claire exclaimed joyfully. "Don't you recognize me? I'm your grandma."

When he didn't say anything for a few moments, her smile began to fade. Of all the children she and Charlie had known David, their first grandchild, the longest. Ideally he should have rushed in and thrown his arms around her. But Claire also remembered the way he'd begun to change just before Jeffrey had snatched David, Kimberly, and Christian from her. She remembered how David had become sullen and withdrawn during those last visits with Elizabeth. Claire held her breath and reached for him. He stood there, barely an arm's length away, but didn't respond to her gesture.

"It's nice to see you again," he said politely.

As they gathered around the table and ate, Christian and Kimberly talked non-stop. David said hardly a word. He barely touched the food on his plate, taking an occasional bite of one thing or another, then shoving the remainder to the side.

"If you don't care for turkey, I can fix you something else," Claire volunteered. Without even glancing in her direction, David shook his head and said there was no need.

Pushing past the awkwardness, Kimberly jumped into a colorful story about the school in Brownsville, Texas. "That teacher spoke with such a drawl I couldn't understand a word she said! And she kept sending notes home saying I had a language problem. You remember old Missus Cooper, don't you, Dave?"

He nodded, but his icy expression didn't change.

"You children have made me so happy," Claire said. "All those years I was without you, I kept praying and asking God to bring you back."

David smacked his napkin down atop the food on his plate. "Well, instead of all that praying," he said sarcastically, "why didn't you try sending a postcard?"

Kimberly smacked her hand against her forehead. "I knew he'd do it!" she grumbled. "He just couldn't keep his mouth—"

"A postcard?" Claire cut in. "I sent more than a postcard! I sent letters, birthday cards, Christmas cards! Every last one of them came back marked return to sender!"

"So you say," David countered.

"I can prove it!" Claire stood so quickly her chair toppled backward.

"Don't get upset, Grandma," Christian said, taking hold of her arm.

"Yeah." Kimberly shot an angry glare across the table. "Dave is just being Dave!"

"But it's true," Claire protested. "All those years, the cards, the gifts, I've saved them all. There's a box for each one of you." Claire went down the hall, Christian trailing behind her.

The three cartons sat on the top shelf of the closet in what had once been Charlie's study along with Kimberly's Cabbage Patch Doll. The time had finally come to take the doll from the shelf.

The Lost Years

Claire shuffled through the cartons, then handed each of her three grandchildren an envelope postmarked 1986.

"We sent these cards the year your mother died." A scrap of emotion got caught in Claire's throat. She paused for a moment and then continued. "Elizabeth was so sick that year, I'd be afraid to leave her long enough to go to the store. But taking care of your mom didn't mean we'd forgotten you. Your grandpa went to the drug store and bought those cards while I stayed with Elizabeth. Go ahead, open them."

One by one, they began to slit open the envelopes. David, whose birthday occurred in April, opened his first and as he slid the card from the yellowed envelope a ten-dollar bill fluttered into his lap.

"What's this?" he asked.

"It's what we could do for your birthday. I wasn't able to shop for a gift that year, so we decided to send money and let you get whatever you wanted." Claire gave a good-natured chuckle. "Of course, back then ten dollars was ten dollars."

"This is from you and Grandpa," David said, his voice registering a note of surprise. He began to read aloud. "Dearest David, we miss you so very much. There is not a day that goes by when we don't think of you and wonder if you are well and happy. This is a very difficult year and we can't be with you on your birthday, but we are certainly thinking of you and wishing you a wonderful day. Lots and lots of love, Grandma and Grandpa. P.S. When the Lord allows us to be together again I'm going to bake a big chocolate cake for your birthday! Grandma." When he stopped reading and looked up, a tear glistened in his eye.

"Dad never told us…"

Kimberly, with a May birthday, opened her card next. It also held a ten-dollar bill. She read aloud. "Dearest Kimberly, we're wishing you a birthday fit for a princess, because to us you truly are one. You are as sweet and beautiful as your mother. We miss you so very much, sweetheart, and wish we could be with you. Perhaps next year. Please be a good girl, and never forget how very much we both love you. Grandma and Grandpa. Hey," she said jokingly, "I didn't get a chocolate cake offer!"

Everyone laughed, their soft and gentle laughter woven with feelings of both tenderness and regret.

Christian, born in the same month his mother died, opened his envelope next. Inside there was another ten-dollar bill along with a letter. He read the card first. It was simply a wish for a wonderful birthday and much happiness. Then he unfolded the letter.

"Dearest Christian. We are thankful that you are far too young to read these words for they are truly the saddest we've ever written. Your dear sweet mother passed away just days ago, and although our hearts are too heavy to be thinking of celebrations, we want you to know that your birth was truly a blessing, not only to us, but to your mother. It is heartbreaking to realize that you will never know the joy and goodness of her, for she loved you dearly.

"Your mother did not have an abundance of time to spend with you, but she treasured every moment she did have. Please know, Christian, that although your mother has gone to be with our blessed Lord, you are loved. For we love you, your brother, and your sister, just as we loved your mother. Be well, sweet child, and we shall pray that better days are to come."

Christian's voice cracked with emotion as he finished. He took out a handkerchief and blew his nose.

Claire handed her grandchildren and cards from 1987, and each took their turn reading aloud. The cards all bore similar messages—we love you, we miss you, please write, please call, let us know where you are, how to get in touch with you. After 1987, they went through 1988, then 1989.

When David opened the envelope sent in 1990, a twenty-dollar bill dropped out.

"Inflation," Claire said, and they laughed.

David removed his glasses and began pinching the bridge of his nose.

"I'm sorry, Grandma," he said, pushing back the tears. "I've spent all these years being angry with you and Grandpa, because I thought after Mom died you wanted us out of your life."

"How could you think such a—"

"I know, I know, but I was a kid. A pretty miserable kid. And Dad—" David shook his head sorrowfully.

Claire crossed to him and wrapped her small arms around his broad shoulders. Without saying anything more, David laid his head against her bosom and cried.

"Don't cry, Daddy," Christine said in a tiny voice after a few minutes.

"Yeah, Daddy, don't cry," Christian echoed laughingly.

"I ain't your daddy," David said and playfully punched his brother.

When they began to chase one another around the room, Claire said, "You boys stop that!" and everyone broke into peals of laughter.

Stars sparkled across the black sky when they finally returned to the table.

"Oh dear," Claire said. "The turkey is cold and dry now. I'll just warm it a bit and make some fresh—"

"No, Grandma," David said, putting the weight of his hands on her shoulders. "Everything is fine just as it is. Besides, I'm famished!"

After dinner they returned to the living room and continued opening the cards and gifts saved for so many years. Little Christine grew weary and fell asleep on the sofa but no one else noticed when the clock struck twelve, nor did they notice when that day crossed over into the next.

When they finished opening all the cards and gifts, Claire took out one last box.

"This isn't from Grandpa and me," she said. "Your mother died before she could give it to you." She placed the box in her granddaughter's hands.

Tears cascaded down Kimberly's face. "Oh, Grandma, I can't believe Mama got me the yellow-haired Cabbage Patch Baby."

"You remember?"

Kimberly wiped her eyes and nodded. "More than remember. I can almost hear her voice saying it. I wanted this doll more than anything imaginable, but Dad wouldn't buy me one. He said they were too ugly. Back then every kid in the world had a Cabbage Patch doll except me."

"Your mother knew how much you wanted that doll," Claire said, "and when she was so sick she couldn't get out of bed, she called all the stores looking for one. She kept insisting that the doll had to have yellow hair, and eventually one of those stores got it for her."

"She was such a loving person," Kimberly said tearfully.

"Yes, she was."

Eventually Meredith fell asleep in her chair, and Claudia curled up alongside her daughter at the end of the sofa. But Claire herself did not tire until near dawn. When finally the conversation turned to sleep, Claire insisted that everyone stay over, and once again the McDermott house was full to overflowing. For the first time in many years, Claire's heart felt truly happy.

She ran from room to room turning down bed covers and plumping pillows. She put David and his family in the bedroom she had shared with Charlie. Christian and Meredith stretched out on the family room sofas, and Kimberly got her mother's old room.

Once Kimberly had slipped herself into one of her grandmother's night gowns, she came to say goodnight.

"It's been the most wonderful reunion ever, Grandma," she said. "I only wish Grandpa could have been here with us."

"He was," Claire replied tenderly. "He was."

Acknowledgements

A novel does not come together without the help of many people—readers, editors, designers and the technical geniuses who translate an author's words into readable electronic formats. I am fortunate to be working with some of those that I consider the best in the business, and I am eternally grateful to the following people:

Michael G. Visconte…Creative Director of FC Edge in Stuart, Florida… a design genius who finds the heart and soul of every story and transforms it into a breathtakingly beautiful cover. Thank you Michael.

Ekta Garg…Editor extraordinaire and a woman who catches all my mistakes without ever losing sight of my voice. No easy task, but she does it with grace and charm. I count Ekta among my many blessings.

Lucille Schiavone… Thank you for being an early reader and helping me to see beyond myself. Your suggestions are both wise and wonderful.

Geri Conway…I am blessed to have you as my sister and thankful for all the other roles you play—those of a listener, sounding board, advisor, early reader, and constant supporter.

Lastly, I am thankful beyond words for my husband, who puts up with my crazy hours, irrational thinking, and late or non-existent dinners. I could not be who I am without you, Dick, and I pray that neither of us ever lose sight of this awesome blessing God has given us.

Made in the USA
San Bernardino, CA
09 October 2013